END GAME

Allan Hendry graduated in Electronic Engineering at King's College, London.

He has run many high-technology projects worldwide, including secure communication systems, cryptography, covert diving systems, cryogenics, space breathing equipment, and aircraft instruments and fuel systems.

This career led him to becoming a main board member of a FTSE100 plc, and a Fellow of the Royal Aeronautical Society.

It also caused him to fly half-a-million miles, with time to create the book he would like to have taken on one of those flights.

Allan is the founder and owner of the hi-fi loudspeaker company MonoPulse.

END GAME

Allan Hendry

END GAME

Olympia Publishers
London

A CIP catalogue record for this title is
available from the British Library.

ISBN: 978-1-84897-243-8

First Published in 2011

Olympia Publishers
60 Cannon Street
London
EC4N 6NP

Printed in Great Britain

To Dad

Chapter 1

With their feet in the wishing well

South of Amman, Jordan

Peter had been enjoying this, maybe too much, until something like a slow-motion shiver went through him. Before he had time to understand that, it got a lot worse. He stopped the Land Rover.

"OK. Let me take a butcher's."

Peter Rossi almost fell out of his steeply downward-facing door, but he recovered his balance on the slippery dust and stones and, uncomfortable about standing below the tilted vehicle, went behind it. Looking back to where they'd driven from, immediately confirmed the reason for that involuntary shudder. It seemed there might be no way of turning back. To his right now was an impenetrable wall of rocks. The drivable bit close to those rocks, was itself now sharply sloping, and had become ever narrower, before falling away very steeply. Was it too narrow to turn round on without sliding down?

The angle of the track had made it real off-road stuff, driving tilted well over, both of them with their heads and bodies bent hard sideways. The wheels had occasionally scrabbled for grip, but each time just a touch on the accelerator and a bit of crabwise movement had brought the control back. Maybe too late, Peter realised he couldn't do that in reverse.

Just a brief glance all the way down the slope brought that shiver back. He instinctively pulled his head back as he saw the convex slope below him, quickly curving away out of sight, steeper and steeper with, somewhere just below them, a point of no return. It was the sort of profile which worries skiers and mountaineers, if they have their natural fears left.

But here it wasn't cold, or very high. This was the sweltering heat of a Jordanian midday, and only a thousand feet above normal sea level. That height though was more than two-thousand feet above the sunken surface of the Dead Sea, visible below, beyond that deadly curve. And way down there, even in the full sun, its blackness seemed to threaten them, as if it was waiting. Just looking down there gave him a moment of dizzy vertigo, so he turned to look back at the Land Rover, in which Bill Rawlings was still seated.

There was an odd contrast in the appearance of the two men. Peter was short, with dense black hair. Italian by background, he lived in England, but you'd not have guessed it from his slightly tanned and healthy-looking complexion. Rawlings, now a local in this desert climate, was pale, with a parchment-like skin which looked as if it'd never seen the sun.

From a few incidents, Peter knew that although Rawlings was a ruthless manipulator of people, in physical things he was a coward. And, right now, Peter knew he was being manipulated himself. Rawlings never did anything that wasn't planned and for his own good. You sensed he didn't even start a conversation unless he'd mentally rehearsed at least the first few exchanges. This little jaunt had a serious purpose for sure. It was just that Rawlings wouldn't tell him, and Peter couldn't work out, what the hell it might be. Still, he was curious. And it was that sense of adventure that Rawlings had played on yesterday to get him here.

He walked quickly below the Land Rover again to consider the new problem which had forced him to a halt. Ahead was the start of a steep-sided red-coloured valley cutting across their path, to go inland to their left. The wall of stones also turned away inland to follow it, and the slope below them became even steeper.

Ahead, far below, at the mouth of the valley was a wide beach area. Peter blinked a few times, at what had to be an optical illusion. The small river fanning out into the middle of that sand, looked like flowing blood. Probably just a reflection of the rocks at the edge of the valley he concluded, and carefully walked back to pull himself up into the driving seat of the Land Rover.

"OK," he announced to Rawlings. "We could try and turn. Very narrow and we might lose it. Or we go round to the left, following that valley inland. That surface is pretty hard, less than thirty degrees, and it looks like only about a hundred metres before it levels out a bit."

There was a frown on that pale face. "It looks steeper."

"This thing will drive across that angle." Peter's hand patting the crude dashboard of his hired Land Rover. "It's what they're for. It should be OK."

And it did seem OK – as long as you didn't look down for too long.

"Or do you want to go back? There are only two ways to go." He suppressed the thought of the third one.

"No." Rawlings replied, slowly shaking his head. "We have to go on."

Peter actually wanted to put Rawlings through this. Give him something real to be frightened about. So far the guy had been behaving like he was scared of every bend in the track, repeatedly making them stop and turn the engine off while he got out and looked ahead. And he was taking photographs of everything.

"OK. If that's what you want," Peter replied. "Let's do it." He pushed the gear stick forwards into first and looked across at Rawlings again. *Now he's scared shitless. And he still wants to do this. Why? And why the fuck choose me to go with him? He could have used a local.*

He turned the Land Rover to follow the track round to the left, and it tilted more alarmingly, but the wheels held as they moved slowly forwards. Peter knew these things could handle frightening angles, but he had to try to ignore that slope on his right.

Then suddenly, something was different. What he saw, and the motion he felt, were not the same anymore.

God. They were moving away from those rocks. And the surface they were on was coming with them.

The Land Rover started to roll from side to side as the ground underneath moved and buckled. Peter realised they shouldn't be sideways on the slope like this, or they'd soon tip over. His first instinct was to turn uphill. But, even as his head swung to look round and do that, he could see that some of the large rocks in that wall were now detaching themselves, and rolling and bouncing down towards them. Peter quickly swung the wheel the other way and away from that danger, to become part of the moving downward slide.

There was suddenly no feel in the steering, and the back started to swing sideways. Peter pulled the gear stick down into second and accelerated, terrified by what he was doing, but he'd straightened the car. In front, dust was now starting to burst up in plumes from the fracturing ground.

At this speed they were gaining on the moving surface, and Peter looked rapidly from side to side, desperately trying to find an edge to this deadly conveyor belt. Then those boulders started flying past. He instinctively lowered his head. One rock smashed its fifty pounds of momentum against the back door, blasting the inside of the cab with stinging shards of broken glass. The impact added another lunge to their speed. Peter lost his control again, so changed up another gear and accelerated even harder, sawing at the wheel.

"No!"

But Rawlings' scream of terror was hardy audible.

Suddenly they were airborne. The engine wailed as the wheels spun, out of contact with the ground. Peter clung on, floating in the weightless cab, and, for a moment, had a clear view of the small river again, now closer, and even more like a stream of blood. Then they were back into thick dust, and dropping with the debris around them.

There was a huge crash as the suspension smashed into the stops. Peter, from being up near the roof, slammed down into the thinly-padded seat, and a searing pain came from his back. His head also snapped back as the Land Rover shot forwards and up in the rebound. Twice more, desperately trying to sit with his back straight, Peter winced with the huge bounces. A third, lesser, impact was soon followed by the loud noise of the wheels kicking up stones. They were back in contact with the ground. Peter, thinking that half a mountain must be coming down after them, went flat out now, seeing nothing through the dust.

At last, this time a more gradual force pushed him down into the seat again, and Peter realised the slope was flattening out, and they were probably on that beach. Now worried about smashing into the rocks on the other side at this speed, Peter took his foot slightly off the throttle.

It was the wrong move. A wave of dry dust and small stones caught them from behind, picking the vehicle up and pitching it forwards in a somersault. The force as it first landed upside down almost pulled one of Peter's arms from the shoulder, but he managed to hold onto the wheel and turn the engine off as they slid along. Rawlings disappeared from alongside him, and must have landed in the back somewhere.

Peter, from being terrified of being crushed, now knew their real danger was suffocation as the dust poured in through the smashed rear window. He struggled to draw breath without getting more of the stuff in his lungs.

With another bone-jarring crunch, they were back upright. This time Peter was thrown against a windscreen he could see nothing through. They'd stopped, but the moving dust kept piling in. With a deafening impact, a single rock slammed into the middle of the roof, pushing it in about a foot. Smaller rocks struck them a few more times, one exploding a side window.

The noise became more of a clattering, as myriad loose stones found their way to the base of the mountain.

Then, finally, the sounds almost died away.

It was all over, and they were alive.

It seemed a long wait before the air cleared. But, with that, the sun came through and Peter felt the full stifling heat of this sunken place.

Once he was sure the stones had stopped falling, Peter warily pushed his door open and got out. Standing clear, and stretching himself slowly upright, he felt like his back would be OK, but it hurt. So did his left arm, but nothing seemed to be broken.

He surveyed the Land Rover. The heavy front bumper-bar was now pushed in and up. The roof was also pushed in, as was one front wing. Otherwise, it all seemed OK.

After taking this in, Peter looked back up at where they'd come from. Becoming visible in what was now a light-brown mist, was a steep two-thousand-foot fresh scar on the mountainside. Parts of it were still moving occasionally.

Rawlings, who had stayed as if frozen to his seat, called over. "It might start again. We have to get out of here."

"OK. Calm down mate. First we need this thing to work," he said, tapping the side of the Land Rover. "I'll check what state the mechanics are in." He lay down on the dust and pulled himself underneath to look.

A minute later he re-emerged, "The exhaust has all gone, but it looks like the wheels and transmission are all still OK. We can knock that wheel arch back with a stone. I'll give the engine a try."

A twist of the key produced an un-silenced staccato of explosions, breaking the quietness which had now settled around them. But Rawlings' reaction seemed more like fear than pleasure, as he looked nervously around. "We have to get out by nightfall."

"Why?"

"Never mind."

Peter knew there was no point questioning this, and his own elation now jammed any further awareness of Rawlings' reactions. "The dust has cleared, so let's get a sight inland."

It was an awkward, one-handed, clamber to get onto the Land Rover's crumpled roof for a better view. "This doesn't look too bad," he shouted down. "The centre of the valley's fairly shallow. It'll take us a good way in."

Rawlings at last now got out too, with his camera again.

Peter decided to take a few shots of his own. He slid back down, careful of his back this time. The camera was OK in his bag,

"We don't need to both do that," Rawlings hissed as it came out. "You're wasting time."

Peter took the photos anyway.

Rawlings got back into the Land Rover and was now looking straight ahead. Getting the message, Peter stepped up into the driver's seat and they set off over the newly-fallen dusty ground.

It was useless trying to talk above the noise of the exhaust, and Peter was left in his own thoughts. He'd never understood what went on in Rawlings' mind, even from when they'd first met at university. He'd been doing engineering and Rawlings had been reading theology. Normally, Peter would never have mixed with the 'theologs', except if they played football maybe. But in this case it had been Rawlings' sharp and beautiful sister, Angie. In the few months of Peter's relationship with her, he'd been to their small family bungalow in Blackpool a few times.

Back then, Peter had decided the Rawlings' had been 'better class' than his own Essex family. His own dad looked after the amusement machines on Southend sea front, whereas Bill's ran a small hotel. Not that the Rawlings' were much better off though.

But nothing about those parents explained how their son had turned into such a driven man. It was not for wealth and the pleasures of life, like himself. Rawlings just seemed to want power and influence. And somehow he knew how to get it. Not many people make it to president of the student's union in their second year.

Even after the affair with Angie had ended, Peter had always expected to hear about Rawlings again, probably in politics, on the fast track with whatever party gave him the quickest way to the top.

Peter, the bright one of the family, after university had started to design and make arcade machines like those his father looked after. That had taken him on to his simulator-based fairground shooting galleries. They had large projected screens, showing three-D moving targets to shoot at with electronic guns. All sorts of targets, big and small, fast and slow, day and night.

Then he'd made the big move, to developing those electronic shooting galleries for training people how to use real guns. And those, mainly military, customers made him much more profit than fairgrounds and arcades ever could.

It had been a surprise though when, about four years ago, he'd crossed paths with Rawlings again, not as a politician on the rise as Peter would have expected. Rawlings had walked up to him in the Holiday Inn in Dubai, and, apparently already knowing all about Peter's attempts to sell his gun training systems in the Middle East, had offered his help. Rawlings had become a man about as cold and impersonal as possible, but had influence around these places that Peter found difficult to believe. In just six months, with his contacts, the business in gun training systems almost overwhelmed Peter. But he'd never got to finding out just what jump Rawlings had taken to become such a fixer. He assumed it was something to do with the theological background. Peter also knew his own business was a tiny fraction of what Rawlings was involved with.

Reaching the edge of where the landslide had buried the sandy beach, Peter saw the red water again. That shiver came back. It was blood red. And soon it became more rocky on each side of the stream, forcing him to splash through it. This produced an unpleasant smell he couldn't quite identify.

Within a few miles the slope upwards became steeper and the driving harder, giving Peter a lot of pain in his back and arm from the jolting. The river was now cascading down over larger stones into deep swirling pools. These became dark scarlet with their depth. In the giant red landscape, the four-wheel-drive must have looked like a child's toy.

Making a climb round the side of a deep pool, maybe hurrying too much, Peter finally succumbed to his wrenched arm and lost his grip on the steering wheel. The Land Rover swung and pitched forwards. The engine died and the cab started to fill with the red water. It eventually got to his knee level, and Peter registered how hot it was, and the nasty smell became stronger.

The echoes from the high valley walls around seemed to take a long time to fade.

"We'll have to winch ourselves out."

Peter slid out of his door and waded round to the front, but the water there got suddenly deeper and his foot slipped. Going under the red surface, he banged his head against the steel bumper and the sharp pain made him take an involuntary huge gulp of the water. A horrible rotting vegetable taste made him want to throw up.

He struggled up, holding the cable end and pulled it. The hawser reeled out unexpectedly easily and he fell back, his free arm windmilling to keep his balance, and again splashed deep into the water, taking in a few more mouthfuls of the stuff.

He finally clambered out of the pool, spitting out a stream of the red liquid.

"If this is your local spring water," he concluded. "It tastes how rotten vegetables smell."

"There's no vegetation within five hundred miles," Rawlings said simply. "Not these days anyway."

"What do you mean, these days?"

Rawlings stared back without an expression on his face. "Ten-thousand years ago, this part of the world was fertile and green."

Peter looked up at the barren sand and rocks. "Difficult to believe. When did that change?"

"About six-thousand years ago, and quite suddenly. Before that, this area was the first place where man stopped being the hunter gatherer. The people stopped roaming, built settlements and cultivated the land."

"It was the start of modern civilisation. That's good."

"No it's not. It's more like the start of when we had to declare war on nature. From then on, we, the human race, decided what grows, where, and who eats it. We started running the environment, not living off it. Now we have to run it. No choice. Back then, the world's population was just six million. But now we're adding that many every month. What was once the total human population, added every single month."

"So now seven billion of us are ripping the biological fabric from the surface of the planet, and taking water from deeper and deeper. Around here, it's being pumped from two kilometres down. In just a few years, we've taken out all the rain which has fallen since Christ walked here."

"Bill, I know what's going on. I just get on with my life. And I thought you now did. You're an arms dealer."

Rawlings paused, as if measuring the wisdom of an answer.

"So we both use what we can."

Peter, turning to see whatever expression was on Rawlings' face as he'd said that, didn't even get eye contact, so he looked around for a suitable rock to loop the hawser round.

"Keep your head down," he said, getting back in. "If this breaks you might lose it."

Rawlings silently obeyed. Peter, also tucked down and, not watching, tightened the line an inch at a time. Between pulls, he let the battery rest a few seconds, but each time the sound from the motor was slower.

Finally, the stored energy in the cable almost took the two-ton vehicle out of the pool in one bound.

Peter was relieved when the engine re-started after a few turns, but again the noise made Rawlings look nervously around.

"Bill, do you know something about this place you're not telling me?"

Rawlings didn't even acknowledge the question.

Soon after they'd set off again, the river bed became wider and shallower again, and Peter went faster, now driving with one set of wheels in the river and the other on the red-coloured muddy gravel at the side. But Rawlings' reaction to what looked like their better fortune was to get ever more agitated beside him.

Peter sort of noticed this, but was being distracted by something else. A strange new noise had developed in the engine. Or was it? It didn't vary with their speed. He stopped and turned the engine off. The other noise was still there. Peter got out and tried to get its direction. It seemed to be coming from further up the valley. It was like some sort of machinery, maybe a pump, and loud. But that had to mean the place was accessible, and they could get out. He turned and punched his fists forward in triumph.

"Hear that? Know what it means?"

But the effect on Rawlings was the opposite of his own, and that face seemed even paler. Peter decided to ignore this and restarted the engine. Now driving faster and concentrating on the ground immediately in front of the wheels, he only realised that something had become visible further up ahead when Rawlings cried out.

"Oh shit!"

Peter had never heard him swear before. Then he looked up and saw the people in front, maybe a hundred figures, men, women, and a few children. After a day of seeing no one in this scenery, he couldn't quite believe it. But they were there, standing in an open flat area, and all motionless. The Land Rover's arrival seemed to have surprised them. Peter assumed it was the direction it had come from, and they hadn't heard it over the sound of that pump, or whatever it was, although he couldn't see what was making the noise.

Recovering from his own surprise, Peter took in more as they got closer. These people were all wearing identical sand-coloured, capes, some wet and clinging to their bodies, and all covered in a red mud. He guessed the source of that mud was the small red lake off to the left. Yes, some people were standing in it, almost up to their necks, enveloped in a slight mist of steam coming from its opaque red surface. That lake had to be the source of this hot little river. The whole place looked like some weird health spa.

Opposite the mud pool was a collection of unevenly-shaped tents in various blotchy colours, from sand to dull red. Like desert camouflage, Peter thought. Yes, this place would be difficult to spot from the air. Deliberate? And that noise? It was very loud now, deafening, and it seemed to be coming from the pond itself, as if high-pressure gas was coming from underneath it in a rapid series of loud bangs.

The people, motionless, were all staring at the now slow-moving Land Rover. And it wasn't friendly. Those eyes were cold and hostile. The exit to the valley had to be straight ahead beyond them, but it was blocked by all those mud-covered standing figures. Then Peter's attention was taken by a movement from Rawlings. He was sliding, as if to get out of sight, beneath the dash.

"Keep going. Get out of here!" he'd hissed through clenched teeth. "And don't look round! This place is not good to know about."

"Bill. I'd like to get out. But these people are – sort of all in the way."

He'd now been forced to slow to walking pace.

Then something moved in the human landscape in front. One person, looking different, wearing a dry, white, long robe and headdress, was walking quickly through the standing figures, making what looked like hand signals to them all as he came. He was alongside Peter's window as the Land Rover finally stopped.

"Turn the engine off," the man screamed, his face screwed up with aggression.

Almost out of sight, from down in the footwell, Rawlings had grabbed Peter's arm.

"I said get out of here!"

The man outside the window turned and made some more hand signals to the caped figures. Peter assumed this was rather than shout over the din which echoed round the place. At this signal, all of them started to walk slowly forwards. Peter felt the tingle from the hair on the back of his neck. It was those deliberate steps, all in unison. He sensed that whatever chance he had of getting away, was about to disappear.

"Peter!" Rawlings now screamed. "For God's sake. Get out!" There was no doubt about the fear which was making his voice break up.

Peter revved the engine and jolted forwards. This caused the man beside the window to jump away, signalling again as he stumbled backwards.

There was no gap in the moving line of people. Trying to force an opening, Peter made a bigger lurch forwards. But those steps, and the cold direct stares, never wavered. The nearest few were now only yards away.

Rawlings screamed again. "Go! Or we are dead."

The slow-stepping wall was coming forwards, the cold unblinking eyes getting closer. With every second, it was more of a solid human wall. Peter now drove at the advancing line and deliberately hit the first two people, who bounced off the front wings and to the sides. It made no difference to the terrifying slow steps of the others.

In an instant of unthinking decision, Peter pulled himself down below the dash, and accelerated hard, holding the wheel straight.

He felt the first full impacts, then the front wheels bounced high as people must have gone underneath. There were jarring crunches as their bodies were smashed against the chassis below him, but he kept blindly going. In the horror of what he was doing, amidst the noise and jolting, he didn't even know how many bodies they might have hit.

As the impacts underneath stopped, he dared to look again. They were through the line, and he accelerated to swing round an outcrop of rocks.

"My God Bill! What have we just done here?" He could hear the panic and confusion in his own voice.

There was no reply.

Peter got well away before easing off and turning again to Rawlings.

"We must've just killed six or seven people, at least. What the fuck made that necessary?"

Rawlings' reply was broken up by his own rapid breathing. "Just keep going."

"Stop saying that!"

Peter accelerated again, and covered another half-mile, before once more slowing to speak above the noise of the exhaust.

"You lied to me. That place was what you were looking for all along, wasn't it? And you knew from the start those people were dangerous?"

"It is best you don't ask these questions."

"Even though they'll all probably be looking to kill *me* now?"

"I'll get you out of the country. You just forget everything."

There was a familiar finality in Rawlings' statement. He didn't intend to say any more.

The route out was simple. They climbed another easy thousand-feet before emerging onto a flat plain, across which was the road they were headed back to.

Peter had only gone about three hundred yards before Rawlings beckoned for the Land Rover to be stopped. He jumped out with his camera and took another series of shots in different directions.

Peter looked back at the jagged but homogeneous line of boulders they'd come out of. From here it looked like an impenetrable wall. Peter had more on his mind than taking pictures. His breathing was only just getting back to normal, and he'd given up trying to work out what had been going on back there.

"Let's just stop sodding about and get away," he shouted.

Rawlings climbed back into the Land Rover.

When they got back to the hotel, at Rawlings' direction, Peter hid their battered vehicle round the back.

Rawlings led them to a side door. "There are some things I need to talk to you about. And I haven't much time."

"And I want to talk to you. But it'll have to wait till I've had a shower and changed. It feels like there's something I need to get rid of."

Rawlings looked annoyed at that, but agreed. "OK. I'll see you in the foyer in fifteen minutes."

As Peter left his hotel room again, he realised the shower hadn't worked. OK, it had got rid of the dust and the remains of that foul-smelling red liquid, but he couldn't get out of his mind what must still be on the underneath of the Land Rover.

Not really knowing why, he didn't want to get into the lift, so made his way down the two floors using the wide staircase. He felt a rising anger as he reached the foyer.

Right on time, Rawlings walked in and, with a wave of his arm, urgently directed Peter towards the empty dining room.

Peter tried to calm himself and collect his thoughts. "Hang on. I need to get myself a beer first. Then you've got some explaining to do."

When Peter returned from the bar, he'd only begun to get his questions together. And he didn't know whether to control his anger or let it fly. He'd been used in some way. Peter Rossi didn't *get* used.

He managed to sound calm. "OK. We just killed a load of people back there. I was driving. So their mates, any moment now, might just walk through the door over there and kill me. You very cleverly hid so they didn't see you. Well done. And you don't want to be seen with me now, do you? So I want to know what sort of fucking shit you've got me into." He stepped forwards.

Rawlings backed away and sat at the other side of a large table. "I will advise you on a few precautions."

"Oh fucking great. Like what?"

"Well. You'll need to leave Jordan tomorrow."

"I was going to anyway. Thank God."

"I'll fix a car to the airport. The driver will phone your room tomorrow morning. Make sure you don't appear until then. No dinner. No breakfast. Not even room service. Nothing. And you must never tell anyone what happened today, ever, anywhere, or you will regret it."

Peter tried to let his breathing settle as he sat. "You'd better just explain a bit more. When we set off this morning, you mentioned strange myths or something about what's out there."

"I don't remember that."

"Of course you bloody do. You were scared all along. Tell me what's going on. What am I running from? And how would I know them again?"

"Listen to me and you won't need to."

"Was that some sort of cult we found back there?"

"You saw nothing there. You'd better convince yourself of that."

"I know what I saw. And why are you messing around with cults anyway? I'd have thought since you got into arms dealing, you might have given up the funny beliefs thing?"

"You think so? People will always need to put pictures on an infinite nothing."

"So why did you have to drag me into it?"

Rawlings now looked directly back. "That wasn't meant to be. The person who should have come with me was sick. Throat cancer. Suddenly decided to fly back to London for an operation. Knows it'll leave him a complete mess, maybe no voice. But something that's happening around here seems to have convinced him he has to stay alive."

"So who is this bloke?"

"He runs a conservation research institute in Costa Rica."

"So what's he doing with a fixer like you?"

Rawlings now seemed to be withdrawing into his own thoughts, and he spoke in no more than a whisper. "Maybe he wants to save the world? He needs me though."

Peter had been forced to lean forwards to hear, but somehow misjudged it, and now slipped off his chair onto all fours on the floor. "Christ! What the hell's going on? I've only had one drink."

"Dehydration," Rawlings replied coldly. "It can do funny things. Stick to water for a while,"

Peter pulled himself up again. "You still haven't told me who those people were."

Rawlings had stood up and leant forward, as if to make very sure his quiet words were heard.

"More knowledge would be dangerous. Just don't come back to Jordan, even near it, ever. That might keep you alive for a bit longer. I'll fix the Land Rover disposal, and all the bills here. Go back to your room now."

Then he walked quickly out of the room.

Peter tried to follow, but his head spun with the sudden movement, so he slumped back onto his chair again.

That night, the crunch of breaking bones under Peter's bed, each time he nearly drifted to sleep, seemed to repeat itself for hours. So did the images of what must have happened to those bodies as they rolled and broke between the rocks and the chassis.

Suddenly he was wide awake. He felt frightened, but didn't know why. Perhaps something had happened in the room? Tensed, listening for any sounds, he could only hear faint street noises over the background hum of the air conditioning. He could feel the pounding of his pulse, but didn't understand the fear.

Risking the slight rustle as he moved his head, Peter looked all around. The room was almost dark. Just a dim light filtered through the curtains from somewhere outside, but not enough for him to see anything clearly. Away from that light by the window, he could see nothing at all. He felt a cold shiver. Something might be there in the unlit corners. Something he was even frightened to imagine. This fear just wasn't rational, and Peter fought it. But the grip of terror got stronger and stronger.

He lay absolutely still, afraid to move again, and for several minutes heard or saw nothing, but the panic didn't go away. He wanted to reach for the light switch, except for what it might reveal. So he lay like this, motionless, until he became aware of a new sensation, the desperate need for a piss.

Even so, it took a few more minutes before he tensed himself enough to get out of the bed, very slowly, so not to disturb what was in the corners. He then started to worry about what might be hiding in the bathroom. Standing back outside the doorway, he flicked on the light switch. The fluorescent lights flashed a couple of times, before they came full on.

The sight of his own outstretched arm, made Peter jolt in reaction. It was green. He looked down at the rest of his body. Every part of him was blotchy, dark, almost reptilian, green. What had been irrational fear now had a cause, and became absolute and convulsing.

Peter heard himself cry out as he ran back for the cover of his bed – and wet himself. But all that mattered was that he could hide under the covers. Tucked in there, he was now a child again, and all those long-gone fears were with him. Was he turning into something else? And something was in the room with him. There was no use crying. The noise would only make it angry. He had to do what it wanted. That way it wouldn't hurt him.

It seemed a long time before the terror subsided a bit, and his reason started to resurface. Curiosity was taking over. He felt his skin. It seemed normal. Then he lifted his head out of the sheets. Some light from the bathroom now illuminated the room. He pulled his arm up to look at it again. It was still dark green. He wanted to see it better, so, holding his breath, he reached out and turned the bedside light on.

It made him jump when the arm immediately seemed to turn to light brown. He turned the light off again and the greenness came back. Weird, Peter thought, and did it twice more before he realised. It was the two types of light, a normal bulb by his bed and fluorescent in the bathroom, which were making his skin look different colours.

Then Peter noticed something else. The wall by the bed, which had been pale green last night, was now covered in purple blotches, and the white of the paintwork looked red. He understood. His body hadn't changed colour. He just wasn't seeing right. It was something to do with his eyes.

But why? And why the fear of everything? It was a bit less now, but still there.

He switched the light off and pulled himself under the blanket again, but away from the wet bit. *Lie here*, he thought, *and it will all go away.*

Peter woke with his normal vision almost restored, but with what felt like the worst hangover of his life.

At exactly eight, the call came. No one saw him get in the lift. On the ground floor, he walked quickly, head bowed, to the hotel door. Yes, a car was there, and the driver immediately got out, as if he'd been given Peter's description.

Walking through the airport, he felt that even looking around would give him away.

It wasn't until he was on the Royal Jordanian flight back to London that he tried to relax a bit. He couldn't. Yesterday was still too vivid. One memory kept returning – those crunching bones.

To distract himself, Peter watched the details of the dry Jordanian landscape descend from his view. Soon, once they were above thin high clouds, its features became almost invisible. The slight glimpses of things out of the corner of his eye, vanished when he turned to look.

Peter noticed just how dark the sky was, almost black, and he could see some stars. He was used to the sky looking darker at altitude, but this was strange, almost like night. Almost instinctively, he looked at his watch.

At least this confirmed it had to be nearly midday on the ground now far below, so it was time to have a large drink and try to deaden a haunting unease, and maybe shift that hangover. Something had gone very wrong. And somehow he knew this was not the end of it.

Chapter 2

Help me make it through the night

Ten years later

New Mexico, USA

Why do multi billionaires find exotic ways of risking their own lives? Like flying a single-engined nineteen-thirties plane you'd only just bought, across the Rockies in one day?

As Brad slid once more into the cockpit after his refuelling stop, the Ryan PT17 seemed very small, old, and fragile. The sky ahead had faded to a pale cold blue, and a weakening sun had moved round to behind him. Early this morning it had been in front, and he'd felt its warmth in a deep blue sky as he'd first risen above the LA smog. Now, from here in Farmington, up in the top left-hand corner of New Mexico, this next leg was always going to be the most dangerous.

Settling down after the take off, Brad noticed the headwind had increased. And the land below now looked as nasty as possible. Long-since-vanished rivers had carved the red and orange surfaces below into sharp angles. Good for dramatic photographs, but not for landing on.

Brad tried to relax and ignore that ground. He'd never taken a plane as old as this over the fourteen-thousand feet crossing of the east ridge of the Rockies, the continental divide. He just wanted to be on the other side, to above the source of the Arkansas river, with its water destined for the Mississippi and New Orleans, the other side of America from where he'd started this morning. He set the plane into a long and slow climb, to rise as the fuel load lightened. There was no temperature gauge, but it felt bitterly cold.

Since the end of his disastrous celebrity marriage, two years ago, Bradley O'Connor, the Third, born into millions of old railroad money, had almost turned into a recluse. All his time was now devoted to his three passions; his computer business, the educational charity started by his grandfather, and the family collection of old aeroplanes, out east of Denver. That was where he was trying to get this thing to, and now wished he'd thought more about just how unsuitable it was for the journey.

The old plane made the climb. Why shouldn't it? But Brad still felt a wave of relief as the ground started to fall away below, and at last he could rotate the nose downwards and back off the throttle.

The relaxation didn't last long. From living in Denver, Brad knew all about the contrasts of weather at each side of the divide. Sometimes it was like they were in two different seasons. Even so, it wasn't supposed to be anything like this. The forecast had been wrong. Feeble low sunshine was still behind him, but in his path was an intense black cloud-bank, reaching up, with no way to go over it. No one would dare go into it without instruments, not in these mountains. Thinking of turning back, Brad did a quick fuel calculation, and got the wrong answer. There was no landing place he could get to back on the other side of that ridge. He had no choice but fly on, down close to the ground, and hope there was some gap of visibility below the cloud-base there.

Soon, the little aircraft was only just missing the alternate jagged-black of rocks and the whiteness of new-lying snow below, as Brad skimmed it down near to the steep slopes. Straining to see, in an instant he realised his problem. Under that thick cloud, he could be running out of daylight, still in the mountains, and with no night-navigation.

He quickly called up Canon City, now the closest airport.

"Snowing here heavy, sir," the reply came. "Sure caught us. Everything we've got's out there clearing it. I'll get them off if it's an emergency. But it would be very dangerous. Advise your status."

Real serious panic, Brad wanted to say. Below, he could see that the rocks, trees and the snow-covered ground, once contrasting, were quickly shading together to an even dull grey.

"What in hell's it doin' down at that altitude this early? OK. Thanks. I'll call when I'm closer and have to make a decision," he radioed back.

With a few fleeting visual clues, and a lot from memory, Brad guided the lonely plane round the unlit blackness of Curl Peak, and headed it down the valley of the Arkansas River. Ahead below, the lights of the town of Florence and the moving stream of headlights on US50 made him realise it was almost full darkness down there.

He radioed Canon City again.

"'Fraid I've no choice. Permission to land please."

"I'll clear the vehicles. Lights are all on. Snow's still thick on the runway though. And some in ridges. Emergency's on standby."

That snow was now starting to stick solidly onto his windscreen. Very soon, he wouldn't be able to see anything, and a shiver of that most total fear went through him. A realisation that you could be trapped in the air is a feeling that only pilots can know. He had to go down now, anywhere, whatever the risk, while he still had something to see.

Land on 50? No. Just too dangerous with that traffic. And he knew there were lots of overhead lines near it. It would be certain suicide in this visibility.

He had just one other chance.

"Thank God, I know this place," he whispered, and then called up Canon City again.

"No visibility. I am making an immediate forced landing on the track to the Teller reservoir," he yelled into the radio. "I'll call you when I'm on the ground. No more than five minutes."

"OK. You just take care. I'll keep emergency on standby. They'll be out there real fast if I don't hear from you. And good luck."

Brad could only just make out the forest track below, and he sideslipped the aircraft rapidly towards its straight but narrow outline. He was willing himself to stay calm, but the next problem now emerged in his mind: *How deep is that snow?*

He'd read during his training, although that seemed a long time ago now, that landing a tail-dragger like the PT17 on snow was difficult. You pitch over if the main wheels catch – no nose wheel to stop you.

He tried to remember that textbook. *Land with plenty of power on to keep the tail down. Hold direction when the billowing snow covers the screen. Remember your line and stop slowly.*

Moments later, the wheels skimmed into the snow and threw it up ahead. Suddenly he could see nothing. Gritting his teeth, he only slowly shut down the engine, desperately trying to keep that invisible straight line of the track in his mind.

There was a final judder as snow packed under the wheels – and the plane stopped with just a slight rock forwards. Brad collapsed back in his seat, drained.

Eventually more mundane realities, like reporting back to Canon City control, returned to his mind.

"I'm safely down," he radioed.

"We were worried about you. Well done. Can we send someone out to pick you up?"

"What's the forecast?"

"Seems like this lot's about to go through. Quick thaw after that. Should be fine by morning."

Brad saw the snow was already falling more lightly. "Then I'll stay here to make sure the plane's OK. Get off early tomorrow. Come in there for fuel."

Brad checked his mobile. "No phone signal way out here," he continued, "If you could contact my base and tell a guy called Karl Matuik I'm OK, that would be great." He gave the details.

"Sure then, sir. If you're happy with that. Sleep well if you can."

"I'll report again in the morning before I take off."

Then he hauled himself out of the cramped cockpit to have a pee and stretch his legs and to get some blood flowing, for what was going to be a long cold night.

After a few minutes stamping in the snow, he was surprised to see a pair of headlights coming towards him, downhill from the north. That was unusual so late in the day on the normally deserted track. Someone coming to check on me anyway? No, he thought. It's a bit too soon, and from the wrong direction. He reached into the cockpit and flicked on the plane's lights.

As the vehicle slowed and eventually stopped, it turned out to be an old pickup. When the driver got out, Brad could see by his stocky build, wide face, and straight black hair that he was a local American native. The man, not showing any surprise at the situation, walked over to the track edge, appearing to work out whether his truck could get past. He was ignoring Brad, and behaving like the plane was no more than a fallen tree.

Brad forced the introduction.

"Hi. I'm Brad O'Connor. Sure sorry about this being in the way."

"It's late. I need to get through."

"If you helped me turn it through a one-eighty, then your truck could pass the front as it goes round," Brad suggested, moving an arm in a half circle to show what he meant. "Also, that way, tomorrow I can take off downhill – much better."

The man seemed to think about that a while.

"Why are you here?"

"Forced down. No light."

"And you're going to stay here tonight?" Even though he didn't know the guy, Brad sensed real concern in the voice.

"Yeah," Brad responded. "I'm sure not leaving this thing unprotected. Or when it gets light, some dumb hunter will be taking pot shots at it."

For the first time, the man looked Brad straight in the eye. "I'm Charlie. I know this ground well. Not many hunters come. And never at night. They think this place is bad. Strange things happen. You should come with me."

"Thanks. But I need to be with the plane. Let's get it turned round?" He walked to the tail.

Together they swung the aircraft round, pulling the tail-wheel, two feet at a time, through the snow at the other side of one ditch and, after each move, edged the pickup round the front a bit.

When that was finished, Charlie had his truck on the correct side to drive on south, and climbed back in it. Then he seemed to have an afterthought, got out again and walked back to Brad, who, nicely warmed up by the unplanned exertion, was squeezing into the plane for his night's sojourn.

"You'll get very cold here. Let me take you to Canon City. I'll bring you back at first light, before anyone could start shooting."

Brad waved a flat palm. "Sure good of you. But no thanks. I'll be OK."

Charlie didn't react, but continued to stare up at the cockpit. Even in near darkness, Brad could now read something intense.

"If you have to stay here, just listen to me carefully. If anyone comes to talk to you, remember two things. First, don't get curious and start asking too many questions. They won't like it."

Brad tried to speak, but Charlie hushed him with a just-visible wave of an arm.

"Second," he continued, "whatever you do, from now on, don't get out of that plane. Not even for a moment."

That confirmed Brad's instinctive refusal of the cab service. The guy was obviously deranged. Then Charlie surprised him even more.

"Are you armed?"

"No."

"Borrow this, then."

Brad hadn't been taking all this too seriously. But that changed as he made out the black shape of a large handgun in the outstretched arm below him.

He forced himself to reply calmly. "No, thanks. I try and avoid those things. And I don't like them waved in front of me."

Charlie put it slowly back in his jacket. "Maybe it doesn't matter. They'll think you have something. And if you ever used it, you'd be dead for sure."

"Partly my thoughts. But who in hell would be doing that?"

Suddenly, Charlie looked apprehensively around. Then, without saying anything more, he walked back to the truck and set off.

Brad tried to dismiss this as a crazy guy, who might even have been dangerous. But, as the taillights continued to move away, he wasn't sure. Whatever, his feelings weren't good. He lowered himself in the cockpit and tried to make himself comfortable. This was a different ending to the day than he'd wanted, but he shut his eyes and tried to forget what had just happened.

Marriage to Liz could never have worked. He could see that now. OK, he had the money and she had the looks. But it took him into a lifestyle he just didn't fit into. He didn't even look right. Untidy, lanky light-brown hair, with an unfashionable touch of red, topped his tall, skinny, but somehow clumsy frame. And the introvert scientist only felt awkward conversing with her celebrity world. Most times, he hadn't even formed answers, before those people saw the next person they absolutely *had* to talk to.

First, you are aware, then realise, before that you'd been asleep. Brad immediately wished he still was. It felt like only a couple of hours had passed, and the air now had a sharp cold sting, something familiar to those who know high-altitude night time.

He didn't know what had woken him. And he couldn't see anything. A few more flicks of his eyelids, and a look round, confirmed the blackness around was total. He couldn't even make out the difference between the mountains and the sky. Shutting his eyes again, he tried to relax himself back to sleep.

What happened next brought him fully awake, and raised his heart rate by a hundred beats. But it was only a normal, quietly spoken, Midwestern voice.

"What brings you here, pal?" it had said. But Brad had no idea where it came from. He could see nothing. It was like he'd imagined it. But it had to be what had first woken him.

"Strange place to be?" This was another, different, voice.

There were two people near him, in the blackness.

Then he heard the shuffling feet. There were people round the plane.

"What's the problem?" the first voice said. "Run out of fuel or got an engine go dead?"

Brad prickled all over. It was the middle of the night, on a lonely track, miles from anywhere, he couldn't see a thing, and these invisible guys were talking to him as if everything was normal. Like his car wouldn't start in the tennis club car park.

He wanted to reach out and try to touch one of them, but began to remember what Charlie had said. Charlie must know who these people were, and was frightened of them. Maybe he wasn't crazy?

The voices continued. "You must be cold. Want to jump out and warm yourself up?"

For the first time Brad replied, and what came out was high pitched and quavering. "Don't worry. I've got a good flying-jacket on. I'm quite warm enough."

"What would you use this sort of aircraft for?" Asked another voice.

Brad couldn't think of anything better to do than explain.

"It's called a Ryan PT17. PT stands for pilot trainer. It's what it once was. Now just a few are left in collections." His voice had come back to something like normal pitch.

"Why are you here then?" the invisible question came.

"I was taking it to Denver, and ran out of light."

"Yes, that would be a problem for you."

Gradually, Brad began to sense what was around him in the darkness. This must be what it's like to be really blind, he thought. He could just about make out the pattern of noises coming from their footsteps. Twenty or more people? Yes. And all round the plane. Maybe they're blind, and don't know it's dark? And he'd noticed something else. They never spoke to each other, just some of them to him.

The interrogation went on. And with each reply, Brad was revealing more details of himself. He felt he shouldn't be.

"It's too cold to spend the rest of the night there," the first voice said, now with a harder intonation than before.

It's happening, Brad thought. Just as Charlie said.

"Thanks. But I really don't want'a leave the plane. And I need some sleep if you don't mind. I've still a way to fly in the morning."

"We can get you somewhere more comfortable," the voice said.

Brad definitely sensed a touch of determination in that. He flicked on his radio switch. "Canon City control."

There was a quick rustle of movement around the plane.

But there was no reply. Brad repeated the call. Still no response. He knew they must have shut down for the night.

Go to emergency frequency? Not with a plane safely on the ground. There was still no signal on his mobile. Brad reluctantly switched off the radio, and heard another sound. Like someone was patting and touching the plane.

"Jus' leave this thing alone," he called out.

"We need to see what equipment you are carrying."

"Such as what?"

"For your spying."

Brad didn't answer that. The tapping noises continued for a few more minutes, systematically, the length of the fuselage and under the wings.

"OK. We can't find anything. But you have to get out and come with us now."

Brad looked around. To the left he could now just see the difference between land and sky. What would they do to force him? Their shapes were now beginning to be discernible in front, but Brad couldn't quite see the faces yet.

Then the shadowy figures all moved slightly away into a group, like something different was going on, but it was all in silence.

Just one person came back to him a few minutes later. "Listen carefully, Mr O'Connor."

Again, just the simple statement stunned him. Brad knew he hadn't mentioned his own name.

The man continued. "Now we realise who you are. It seems you are of use to us. But you will not mention to anyone that we met here. The consequences would be serious. We watch people carefully."

This person was talking to him from just a few feet away but, even though he strained, Brad still couldn't quite make out a face. Then the man turned away and walked out of Brad's sight, to follow the rest of the group back up the track behind the plane.

Brad left it a few moments, then stretched himself up to look backwards. He could now see the nearest figures more clearly, outlines against the snow, not looking behind. It was all silent. They weren't talking to each other, but making odd-looking hand gestures.

He watched those strange movements until the group went out of sight, then tried radioing Canon City again.

It was a different operator from last night. "Hi. Good to hear from you. Frank left a message. What sort of night did you have?"

"Very cold – but uneventful. What would you expect in the middle of nowhere?"

"Suppose so. Depends on who you listen to maybe? You goin' to try a take off?"

"Yes, but I'll confirm that in about an hour."

"OK sir, call me then."

Moving in slow motion, Brad turned the radio off.

Why didn't I say anything? This must be what it's like to see a flying saucer. Who do you tell? He wished he'd just imagined it all.

There was still what would be a long and cold hour before there would be enough light for takeoff. Brad tried to make himself think about anything else but last night – like that interesting project in Oxford, England. He was about to go there and get more involved in it. It was one of several he'd got into because of his computers.

From his wealthy start in life, after his post-grad in computer science at UCSF, Berkeley, San Francisco, Brad had then made his millions into billions, almost without trying to. The machines Brad had created were huge in processing power, and self-learning. They were computers to see patterns, tools to use where, at the beginning, you weren't quite certain of what you were looking for, or might find. They could be set to recognise some form of order, in sounds, images, stock movements, or in sequences of anything. He was amazed by how many he'd sold, and what they were being used for.

He'd followed some of the projects. Like, a few years back, there had been that one of Peter Rossi's from England. At first, Brad didn't like what the guy wanted to do – military target recognition. But he'd had to admit it was challenging. Taking the image of any sort of terrain and, with no knowledge of what should be there, identifying what was likely to be out of its natural place, like something in camouflage. Brad couldn't say he liked Peter. From Brad's old-money perspective the guy seemed too pushy and brash. Funny an American thinking that about a Brit, he'd thought.

If Peter Rossi wasn't Brad's favourite person with a UK project, there was someone else who was. She'd been special. Dr Kiri Williams, once from New Zealand, now based in Oxford University, England. He loved that name, Kiri, and still remembered those slim hips, long legs and the copious dark hair.

She'd wanted to use one of his computers to analyse lifestyle and health records from all over the world and way back in time. Her idea was to unearth the secrets of which environments, foods and natural treatments caused or prevented the world's diseases. But Kiri had only slowly realised just how unconventional and difficult his computers were to use. You had to sort of cajole them to focus on the patterns you were interested in, and then to look at the right things. It had been a problem with the mixed-up type of data Kiri had as input. But, eventually, she seemed to have got through it, and she'd now invited him over to England for the big announcement of the results.

Brad smiled at the thought. He wanted to see Kiri again, and he'd enjoy a trip to Oxford. He'd never been there, and also wanted to make a few contacts at the university for the O'Connor educational charity.

The weather forecast had been right this time and, as it got properly light, Brad could see that the remaining snow on the track was already thin enough not to worry him. With that light, he also felt safe to get out of the plane at last, get his circulation going, and check if there were any rocks or clumps of snow down the track.

He kicked a few loose stones clear, before going back to examine the outside of the plane and the external controls. All OK. Whoever they were, they didn't seem to have damaged anything. He got back in for the rest of the pre-flight checks, and radioed back to Cannon City.

It was a perfect, slightly downhill, takeoff.

Once the PT17 was a couple of hundred feet up, Brad banked it to the left. The track came into view again through the side window. Coming uphill towards him was a pickup truck. Even though it had been nearly dark last night, he recognised it. Charlie's. The guy sure had known about something. Brad didn't want to think what would have happened without his warning. Too late to thank the fella though.

Then, further away, he saw another, bigger, pickup. It was his own. Karl must have come out to check everything was OK. Brad knew he should've realised that would happen.

Karl Matuik was his part-time aircraft mechanic. His day job was with United Airlines at Denver International. The deal Brad gave him was extra money and a good apartment, in return for doing some maintenance on the old planes. Plus, Karl also got to fly them and take them to shows. That had been the clincher. German born, and still with the accent, Karl was the most reliable person Brad had ever met. If your life depended on an envelope being put through a particular letterbox in Pittsburgh, on the stroke of midday, in a week's time, you'd choose Karl to do it. That also made him a good guy to look after your old planes.

He swung round to fly over the two trucks, wiggling his wings before turning back to his course for the refuelling at Canon City.

Back home in Denver, Brad woke from two hours of catch-up sleep and walked over to the hangar.

Karl had now got back as well. He was examining the Ryan. "Great plane," he announced in that thick German accent. "But I think you were lucky back there. What happened to bring you down?"

Brad explained the flight, and the failing light. But he didn't say anything about what had happened on that track.

"So you didn't get much sleep?"

"Why do you say that?" Brad replied in an involuntarily sharp tone.

"Well, I mean, stuck there in the cold."

"Oh I see. It was OK." He tried to change the subject. "Did I do any damage to the plane?"

"No. Doesn't look like it. But, like I said, you could've had a bad one. I looked at what was left of your wheel tracks up there. On your landing you got inches from dropping off the side of that road."

There was an odd mechanical slowness in the way Karl had said that, looking straight at him. And Brad realised that if Karl had studied any tyre marks in the snow, then he must have seen all the footprints as well. He'd have worked out they were on top of the landing tracks, but not the take-off tracks. That would have seemed weird enough. Brad knew that if he said nothing, it would make it all seem stranger still. But he wanted to check on something else.

"There was another pickup on the track ahead of you. Did you talk to him?" he asked.

"Yes. He'd stopped to look at your tracks as well."

"What did he say?"

"Was on about something." Karl had now changed to sounding artificially flippant. "I couldn't make any sense of it."

Brad didn't quite believe that. "Well, at least I got away safely," he said quickly. "Now, I wonder if I've got the time to fly this thing down to Florida next week and show it off?" The intonation was rhetorical, and it allowed Brad to turn away and walk back to the house.

I've done it again. Why do I say nothing?

Still disturbed, he tried to settle down and respond to his e-mail messages.

If Brad's normal computers were massive, they were nothing to the power now hidden away in the basement underneath this huge house. Tron was the most computing power ever put together in one place. The name went back to when Brad, as a computer studies student, back in Berkeley in 1982 had gone with a few friends to see the film. He'd thought it was the first where the computer became a character, what he'd once hoped for in his own Tron.

The project had started with Brad's fascination. What is consciousness? Suppose you make a huge collection of semi-autonomous processors, each deciding for itself how many other processors it communicates with, and when, and about what? Like neurons in the brain? Make a computer like a newborn baby? Then give it millions of inputs. The brain of a two-year-old child is making about a million new connections a second.

Brad's machine was its billionaire creator's attempt to replicate the brain of that newborn child. OK, he knew a child is born with so much pre-wired: speech and grammar structure, how to organise shape and colour inputs, a wish to copy behaviour, even a preconditioning for what it will perceive as truth. But, Brad thought, a computer with so much power, with enough data input, and left for long enough, there had to be a chance. Maybe even the ultimate, self-awareness?

It had taken many years to build Tron, and for ten years it had been connected to the whole world, using giga-stream internet connections to hal-a.com, his personal web site. This was a name that, unlike Tron, he'd never explained to anyone.

A sequel to the original film had been made, but it seemed like Brad was no nearer to his ambition.

Tron was certainly doing something. It would go into spells of having huge amounts of incomprehensible traffic in and out. Brad couldn't make any sense of the code, but it was reason to keep on hoping. Although it still left him with a fundamental conundrum. Just how would he tell if Tron did become self-aware?

That night, for the first time since he was a child, Bradley O'Connor the Third, wanted to leave the lights on as he slept. He felt invaded, as though something had latched onto him. They knew who he was. He had to even things up. For that, he needed to know who those people were.

Chapter 3

Twenty-four hours from nothing

Oxford University, England

Dr Kiri Williams faced her boss across a magnificent three-hundred-year-old mahogany desk.

She knew where he was coming from. He just wanted some results, any results, from this over-time and over-budget project. He didn't care about what Kiri had gone through in putting so many of those old medical and health records into the O'Connor computer. The thousands of old files from the University archives had been difficult enough, but the others from around the world had been in different forms and languages, some little better than myths, legends and superstitions.

But now, years of hard work later, Brad O'Connor's machine seemed to have found patterns, and shown how some foods, lifestyles and treatments, caused or cured the world's diseases. Or had it? Now Kiri couldn't suppress her suspicions about the results. Some of the conclusions looked just too good.

"No. We can't say anything yet," she pleaded in her quick Kiwi accent.

Across that desk, her one-man audience was Professor Ivan Gothard, Head of Community Medicine at Oxford. He seemed puzzled – or pretended to be.

"But you've discovered natural cures for several diseases. It will be a triumph for the university. A landmark in medicine. And we will announce it with the famous Bradley O'Connor present. The creator of the ultimate computer, will see its most humanitarian application. That will get some real publicity."

Kiri clenched her fists, but then pushed them onto the tops of her thighs, out of sight. "But it isn't why I asked him over."

"Yes. Getting him here was your idea. Brilliant."

"I wanted him to check the results!" Kiri's long dark hair swung with the movement of her head as she spoke. "You know the problem with those computers of his. They're almost human. They see a pattern, then they favour data that agrees with it. Those things are machines which form opinions. Almost human in fact eh?"

Kiri knew she wasn't being honest about Brad's computer being the only issue. Another was that she'd put in so much data from closed communities like religious orders. She'd once thought their fixed diets and living patterns would give purer inputs. But, as the project had gone on, she'd wondered if these people, maybe motivated by their own beliefs, might have fed her the facts as they wanted them to be. She'd been even more suspicious when these amazing results appeared.

"All right," Gothard said. "I know about the characteristics of that computer. I agree some final checks should be done before we announce. So which are the crucial areas?"

Christ. He's agreed. "Well. I suppose the results that look very conclusive. Like there's one little community in Australia, which shows this incredible link between their diet and cancer of the pancreas. And some data from Cyprus says we've almost found a natural cure for arthritis. For things like that, before we say anything, we should go right back and check the source data."

That frown was on Gothard's face again. "But I thought you said it was the computer?"

Kiri was ready for the question. "There's no way all the data can be perfect. If the wrong stuff gets in early on, it could have steered the computer off course."

"OK. Then it's just those two inputs? Australia and Cyprus?"

Kiri didn't dare say how many other sources she now had doubts about. "Well. They are the most extreme. So, I suppose if they are OK, I'll be more happy with the others."

"Only more happy? And if they're not?"

"Well. I suppose we'd need to check on some others."

Gothard now put on a practised look of stunned amazement. "No. You mean the whole project would be suspect? Maybe I should be getting a proper computer expert looking at this?"

After all Kiri's desperate efforts, that hurt. "No. Let me do what I need to. It will be OK."

There was a long wait. "I agree then," Gothard eventually conceded. "We will do the checks."

"OK. I've got my timetable all planned."

"I didn't say you could go. I have plenty of medical contacts in these places."

"No. I have to talk to the people in those communes. I know what's important and what isn't."

Gothard leant back, as if suddenly understanding something. "Oh, I see. If my memory is right, these are about the only two places in the world you haven't already managed to visit so far on the back of this project. And this is your last chance?"

"That's nonsense. This is for the project."

"There is no need for you to go to these places yourself," Gothard pronounced with finality.

"Look, I've put ten years of my life into this, so if I don't go and believe it myself, there's no big presentation of the results."

"That is not an option," Gothard announced. "If needed, I will take over."

Kiri drew breath. "How about the option that all the sodding data gets mysteriously screwed. I know more than anyone here about that computer – and what's in it."

"You wouldn't."

"Try me!"

In the silence which followed, Kiri thought she could hear her own heart beating. Then, to her surprise, Gothard's confidence wavered first.

"OK," he conceded. "But no more than two weeks. I don't want any more delays. Let me have a travel request."

"I've made one out." She handed over the form, supporting her outstretched arm at the wrist to stop it shaking.

In one way, Gothard's remark about her various travels had been too near the mark. The visits to arrange data sources had been one of the few compensations in the long and tedious project.

Kiri had once had a sort of life plan in her mind. That was back when she'd first left New Zealand. And nothing in it had involved being fixed here for ten years. Quarter Maori, the rest Celt, she'd left that distant home with a medical degree in her pocket, with an idea to experience the world, and do some good as she passed through.

And to start with that's what she'd done, and realised the injustice of medical treatment around the planet. She'd seen some spend thousands on cosmetic treatment, and watched others die for the sake of a few dollars.

It was here in Oxford she'd had had the idea. How about all the natural treatments around? These went without research. And she understood why. Who's going to spend money investigating something that you can't then patent and exploit?

The then Dr Kiri Kirkwell, had realised that Oxford University held the largest archive of medical records in the world. They were from well back in time and from all over the planet, covering the lifestyles and medicines of so many different cultures. Buried in there had to be the answers to a lot of questions. But how do you analyse those millions of confused records when you don't really know what questions you're asking? It needed a computer that wasn't told what to find. It had to see the patterns in the muddle for itself.

That was all ten years and so much work ago. Was it now all about to fall apart?

****

Not far away in the same hospital, the man who was now Kiri's husband, Dr Tony Williams, was also having to face a difficult issue in his project, but so far was not sharing it with anyone. Right now, those thoughts were strong enough to distract him into pausing before picking up the next case-folder.

His project, also started ten years before, was originally into mob behaviour, such as in riots or violent crowds. With some illegal and risky experiments, Tony's team had recorded the brain activity of people in the middle of crowds going out of control. Whatever was being triggered, mainly in the frontal lobe, seemed to take control, overriding conscience, inhibition and fear. The team had also detected certain chemical changes as this happened. Evolutionary scientists had explained it all as a Darwinian advantage for a species that once had to face animals much larger than themselves. For a group to win the fight, some individuals had to take unjustified risks with their own lives, but the whole group then benefited.

Those early experiments had arisen from Tony's long history in protest movements. Since childhood, he'd gone though CND, Greenpeace, Friends of the Earth, and a few other phases. About ten years ago, it was as if he'd deliberately wanted to infuriate his medical research colleagues by supporting animal rights. That one had been the most violent. But it had given him the chance to find volunteers to take the dangerous step of going into a crowd they knew might turn violent, but with their brains wired up with probes, and a small pump taking blood samples. It was dangerous, but had to be done that way if you wanted to know the brain activity of someone about to throw a brick at a policeman.

Despite his methods, Tony got away with it. Maybe it helped that he didn't look or sound like a lawbreaker. From about twenty, he'd had this rather pink complexion, been slightly overweight, and had large white-grey streaks in his hair above the ears. In his protest days, this super-respectable look, and his slow and measured speech, made him just so plausible in court. But, under that appearance laid a mischievous humour, and contempt for establishment and its authority. That was the bit which had so appealed to the woman who was now Dr Kiri Williams.

But then, mystifyingly to those around him, Tony had suddenly dropped all the protest activity. His research had continued, with the same techniques as those in that illegal start, but much more secretively. Mostly even his research assistants didn't know where the inputs had come from. Volunteers had gone out, heads all wired up under hats or balaclavas, but only Tony and those few subjects knew where they'd been. At least, the lab assistants noticed, they weren't these days coming back with detached probes and other minor injuries. In fact, now never. With this change, Tony's once populist research papers had become as if deliberately obscure. Despite that, they were still regarded as world leading.

A phone call took Tony's mind off his deliberations.

"Are you in a position to talk?" the voice at the other end asked mysteriously.

"Yes," Tony replied. He said even the simplest things slowly. It had the effect of making them sound more considered.

"Excellent. My name is Giles Owen-Winter. I am, as you might have guessed already, what is referred to as a head hunter. Would you like me to continue?"

The pomposity of the plummy accent just amused Tony, but he decided he would listen. He didn't get many of these calls. He was too non-establishment maybe.

"Yes."

"I have been asked to approach about a significant opportunity. It concerns a large laboratory based in Switzerland. We are seeking someone to take over a major research programme there. This work is very related to what you are already doing. But the difference would be that you could have whatever resources you required. Money is no obstacle."

Nice words to the ears of a British research scientist. But puzzling. "For which laboratory is this, could I ask?"

"I'm very sorry," Owen-Winter continued in his smooth voice. "I am not able to tell you that until we have met. I need to establish certain things first. Could I propose a meeting? Say, for a week on Tuesday, in London?"

Nodding slowly to himself, Tony agreed and took the details. "One question," he said at the end. "How big is this laboratory?"

"About a thousand people," Owen-Winter answered.

"Thank you."

Tony sat back. Some of his reaction was from flattery, but it was also confusion. An outfit that huge, doing work in his specialist area, with so much money to spend, and he didn't even know it existed?

Anyway, it all meant he couldn't settle to any more work for the day, so he packed his briefcase for an early return home. He wondered how Kiri had got on in her meeting with Ivan Gothard. If she'd got her way, she'd be off travelling again. He'd never liked that.

****

Kiri had decided to investigate the commune in Australia first. Then she was going to return via Cyprus.

After the long flight to Perth, then an internal connection, she'd managed to get a jet-lagged half night's sleep in a hotel near Alice Springs. It was now sixty hours since she'd left Oxford, and early morning again, although it didn't feel like it to her.

After three hours driving, Kiri finally thought she'd sighted what had to be her destination through the hire-car windscreen. It was still about ten miles in front, but the only visible thing in the endless sandy scrub.

She'd been told the isolated Rumera Community was a breakaway religious sect formed by early Eastern European settlers here. But, even at this distance, it didn't look like she'd expected. The light from the sharp morning sun seemed to be flashing off new metal, and the whole place glowed in a fierce red-colour.

It was a further twenty-minutes before she got up close and confirmed she'd made some sort of mistake. Fronted by imposing new security gates, the place looked more like a military base, not a commune where some religious group had chosen to hide away from the world. There were no signs or notices anywhere. Two huge black-windowed trucks were parked behind the fence, in front of the low building there. They were also unmarked.

Confused, she grabbed the map and got out of the car anyway to stretch her legs. Once out of the air con, she was hit by the already-rising heat as she unfolded the map on the roof.

Suddenly, behind her, there was a mechanical clank. "Dr Williams," someone called as she spun round.

Those gates were now opening slowly and with a slight rumbling. The voice had been from a solitary man who had now appeared behind them.

"Hello. I am Dr Isaacs. I got your message. I hope you found us easily."

"It wasn't too difficult to see," Kiri said, still surprised. A sharp movement of her head indicated the fifteen-foot-high fence and gates.

"Have you seen how high a 'roo jumps when it wants to?"

By then turning and pointing to a parking space inside the gates, Isaacs made it clear he wasn't expecting an answer.

Kiri got back in the car, waited for the gates to fully open, and parked it where Dr Isaacs had shown. After getting out, she walked towards Isaacs, briefcase in left hand, right hand slightly outstretched, but he offered no welcoming handshake.

She dropped her hand again. "What is that red stuff all over the ground?"

"Plastic sheeting. It's part of what we do here. This isn't just a sleepy commune. We have a big business selling the vegetables we grow. It is a special technique which recycles our water. That red plastic stops it escaping."

Puzzled, Kiri nodded. This wasn't the image of the place she'd had from ten thousand miles away. "Why is it that red colour though? Doesn't look very agricultural?"

"It keeps out some of the heat which we don't need, reflects it you see, but lets in the ultraviolet for the plants. Apparently it has to be red to do that."

Then, as if to end that conversation, he again turned away.

Kiri followed him to a long single-storey building. Inside, it was dark and cool, with only a few small windows to let in the light. But it was welcome after the brightness and heat outside.

The two of them sat at opposite sides of a large and long table, which Kiri put her briefcase on. Dr Isaacs looked straight at her, but said nothing.

"Tell me more about the way you grow plants," Kiri asked. "It sounds interesting."

He seemed to think briefly before replying. "All the water vapour given off by the plants is held, and then re-condensed when it cools at night. After that, we mix it with organic nutrients and feed it back again. So most of the water we use is what actually goes out in the vegetables we deliver. It makes very efficient use of the limited water supplies we have."

Then he stopped, as if that was the end of the matter.

Kiri opened her briefcase. "OK. Thank you for meeting me. And we have a lot to do. I need to review the data you have given to your government about your diet and health records here. I included a checklist attached to that e-mail I sent."

"Yes. I remember that," Dr Isaacs said vaguely. "Let me look at it again." He pointed to the copy she'd pulled out of her briefcase.

Kiri passed it across. Dr Isaacs turned the pages slowly, scanning the document as if it was completely new to him. "There's a lot here."

"Yes. That's why I got it to you well in advance."

"That is irrelevant. The question of revealing medical records is a matter of personal privacy."

Kiri was beginning to feel a slight irritation at his continuing distant manner. "I don't need to see the individual names, of course. Just confirmation that these records have been accurately kept for the people in your community."

"How would you like me discussing personal details of your life with complete strangers? Our doctors here send all the required medical reports to Canberra. It is up to them what they release to you. So maybe that's where you should be?" Isaacs was now almost dismissive.

Kiri forced herself to pause, so as not to over react.

"No. As I explained in my letter, I want to do some checks to make sure nothing has been distorted, maybe even by those civil servants in Canberra. Suppose they'd sent the diets from here and the medical records from somewhere else? That would really mess me up. It's why I am talking directly to you."

"All that, is maybe what you'd like to do. But don't assume everything happens just the way you want it."

The patronising tone was infuriating, but Kiri deferred.

"I'm sorry. Suppose we leave the question of medical records for the moment, and start with what you can discuss?"

Dr Isaacs nodded at this, but said nothing.

"OK. Let's look at your agriculture," Kiri continued. "Is it possible for me to look at your soil and water analyses?"

Dr Isaacs tilted his head and frowned, like he was thinking of how to explain something to a child.

"From what I have already said, you must realise that the growing conditions here are rather special. But, once again, the statutory returns go to the Agricultural Commission. Those are the people who have the information."

"What about the details of the plants you grow?" Kiri persisted. "Can we check those?"

"We grow these crops to make a living. This information is in our production statistics. We give them to Canberra."

"You just don't seem to understand," Kiri said slowly. "I know all that. But I have come here to make sure there hasn't been a mistake anywhere along the line. My whole project depends on information like this."

"We are very careful with filling in all those forms."

Kiri changed tack. "Can I try something else? The dietary information you have given is also vital to our study. Can we check those records?"

A different look came over Dr Isaacs' face. It was as if he was savouring something – and then he delivered the words very slowly.

"You seem to be confusing things. We have to submit information about the crops we grow, but not anything about our own diets. In fact, our people here eat very little of what we produce. So any conclusions you have come to about that will be – in error."

She was beginning to hate the self-satisfied smile on that face.

"I'm sorry," she said. "I must have made a mistake there."

"Then that is your problem. We are forced by law to give information to Canberra. So, once again, I suggest that you talk to them. Now, I think we have finished this conversation."

Kiri began to feel unreal, and the lack of sleep wasn't helping. But she had to go on. This difficult sod seemed to be her only link. She'd seen no one else around.

"Well. Could I give you time to consider what you might discuss, then come back to see you tomorrow? I had hoped to spend about three days here."

Dr Isaacs smiled briefly. "I am pleased that you visited us and explained the status of your project. It had caused us some concern." Then the smile faded. "But I cannot see the point in any further discussions. Nor should your spies try to get any more information about us."

He abruptly stood.

Outside the gates again, Kiri started the car's engine and air con, but stayed outside it with the door open to let the accumulated heat escape. She looked back towards the commune buildings and the red plastic-sheeted ground, then hammered on the car's roof.

"Shit. Shit. Shit!"

The heat made the jet lag, irritation, tiredness and confusion worse. She just wanted cool sleep, but knew she now had to get to Canberra.

By eight-thirty the next morning, following a few phone calls, Kiri had found the head-of-department she needed in the Canberra government offices. Ian Massey was the chief of the group assigned to collate the Asia-Pacific regional information for her project. He didn't seem to welcome her phone call.

"Yes, of course I know who you are," he said. "But this is not the proper way to arrange a meeting with me."

"There's a problem. I've come a long way, and I need to talk to you."

"In which case I will pass you over to my secretary," he said in a slightly admonishing tone.

The line went quiet.

"Mr Massey is prepared to see you at twelve o'clock, but can give you no more than half an hour."

"Oh. Can't he?" Kiri said, and slammed the phone down.

At five-past midday, Kiri was seated awkwardly on a hard-backed chair, drinking tea out of a small China cup. Ian Massey, a small grey-haired man in his fifties, was sitting a metre back from the other side of his desk, hands gripping the arms of his chair, and addressing her. "And perhaps you will tell me your real objective?" he said tersely.

"I am here to do a final validation on the key inputs to my health-data project. Those inputs which have given rise to our most extreme conclusions."

"And what is your problem?"

As Kiri described what had happened in Alice Springs, Massey's mood got visibly worse. His fists on the arms of the chair became patched in white.

"So why did you pick on the Rumera Community to check?" he snapped.

"I've just told you why. Its data was one of the most influential single inputs."

"There must be other areas which are almost as significant."

"Yes, I suppose so," Kiri replied. "Between fifty and sixty of them around the world."

"So I say again. Why Rumera?"

"It was the most pure. What seemed to be the cleanest data, and giving the strongest conclusions."

"And the furthest away from England no doubt? Fancied the trip did you?"

Not again, Kiri thought, but didn't respond.

"You should have involved me in this much earlier," Massey had continued. "That is what has gone wrong. The consequences are your responsibility." He looked at his watch. "Our business is finished. I have to go to lunch. My secretary will escort you out." He stood up.

Kiri was dazed and, as she was led down the corridor, had no idea of what to do next. They went back to the ground floor in the lift and then towards the main door.

"Dr Williams?" was shouted from somewhere behind, and Kiri spun round.

Her caller was ginger haired, wearing shorts, trainers, and an open-necked shirt.

"Hi, I'm Des Hinkley. It is Dr Kiri Williams isn't it? I heard you were here."

Surprised, she replied, "Yes."

"Well, I'm the poor bloke who's done all the real work on your project." He faced Massey's secretary. "Can I take over?"

She frowned momentarily, then nodded and left them.

Kiri turned to Des. "So you're the Des name that kept appearing on my data screens. Great to meet you. Now I know what you look like at last."

"Not good eh? But how did your session with our boss go?"

"It went nowhere."

"I can imagine. But follow me."

Des led her into a room full of filing cabinets, microfiche readers, and CD ROM units.

"Welcome to where it all goes on," he turned and announced. "These are my guys, and we're here to provide you with information."

Kiri clutched at the helpfulness. "I certainly need that."

"And you've got real problems with that Rumera stuff, I would think?"

She nodded. "Well, with getting them to confirm it all."

"Tell me then."

Almost as soon as she started to talk, Des cut her short. "OK. You've said enough already. I get the drift. It's kinda what I expected. You picked a right place there, didn't you?"

"I didn't pick anything. You sent the information and the computer found it."

Des held his hand up and conceded. "Well, however it was, that's just what the boss was also frightened of. Up there, you met a man who doesn't want to do anything, just make sure he can never be blamed, whatever happens. The condom on the prick of progress we call him. Now you come along, from thousands of miles away, and look like you're gonna empty the dunny on him.

"What do you mean?"

"Well. The Rumera data. We've learnt a bit more about the place since we sent that info to you, and now it all looks like a big balls-up."

"What's wrong with it then?"

"Well, as you saw, nothing's normal there is it?"

"That doesn't mean the information is invalid?"

"Well. It was way. Digging that data out and sending it to you, made me really think about it for the first time, and look at it better myself."

"And?" Kiri asked warily.

"In their defence," Des continued, not answering directly but almost musing to himself. "With how they grow their crops, our agricultural type questions just don't make sense. Can't be answered sensibly."

"It doesn't make them wrong."

Des shrugged his shoulders. "Look. Even if they wanted to obey the rules, if the questions are wrong, the answers must be."

"So why didn't you tell me when you first realised the information was suspect?"

Des's flow stopped, and he paused and looked down slightly, before giving the next answer.

"I wanted to." Then his head came back up again. "But our glorious master up there wasn't prepared to admit the mistake." Now his eyes looked up at the ceiling. "Anyway, I bet he's somewhere messing his shorts right now. And I'll be in trouble if Linda says I spoke to you. But she might not. Sometimes difficult for her, but she's OK really."

Kiri tried to salvage something. "I think I understand. Now, OK. That's the agricultural stuff, then what about the rest of it?"

"That was mainly medical, wasn't it?" Des responded. "On that stuff, I just don't trust the buggers, although I can't quite get a hold on it. They are so secretive. It must be they're trying to hide something. It's the only explanation. But I couldn't begin to say what."

"Look. I don't know how much you've looked at their records. But what about the high rate of cancer of the pancreas they report?"

"Hey, I tell you, we were curious about that as well." Then Des thought on for a second. "We've looked at it all now. And it is odd, I agree. Since the place started, those doctors of theirs have only ever given a few causes of death. Like they've only got a short list of things which are fatal. And they just pick one of those to explain how anyone pops it."

"Can't you go in and check what's going on?"

"Some of us have suggested that. We are suspicious. But, each time, the request gets mysteriously blocked, somewhere up there." Again, he tilted his head upwards. "Maybe not even by him. I just don't know who by."

Kiri hardly heard that. She'd just been hit by something else.

"Hang on? I've just realised what you said. You said 'since that place started'. It's supposed to have been there a couple of hundred years!"

"Yeah. Funny that," Des responded in a matter-of-fact way. "It's like they try to convince themselves, or maybe their new members, that the whole thing is as old as time. They've even created a 'history', I hear. They've made up this story that it all started with the appearance there of some holy disciple or something."

Kiri slumped back, trying to believe that a huge hole wasn't about to be blown in her project.

"OK. So you're saying the place itself is all new. But maybe the people themselves were somewhere else before?"

"No. As far as I can tell, nothing like that was in Australia before nine years ago. And I think the big development there has really been in the last five. Also, it's not a fixed population in there, like they pretend it is. They take in people, keep them a while, then they seem to come back out, and more go in."

"What do they do after they're out?"

"Another odd thing. They say nothing about it. So you don't know who's been there. Certainly no one seems to admit it."

Kiri began to feel that everything was falling apart. She knew the Rumera data was a write-off. She could only hope it was a single freak.

"Anyway," Des had gone on cheerfully. "If I can be of any more help to you, let me know."

"Thanks," she replied slowly. "But you've already told me almost everything I didn't want to hear."

Kiri just wanted to get out of Canberra, in the desperate hope she'd get better news in Cyprus.

That evening she collapsed onto a bed in a Sydney hotel room, thinking maybe she'd just wasted ten years of her life.

Two days later, Kiri could feel her tension building. She suspected that whatever she now found at the Cypriot commune, could make or break her project.

Using the map which her local contact had faxed, the Telaka Community was easy to find. In the hilly landscape Kiri came across it quite suddenly, but then stood in disbelief in front of another military-looking high fence and set of large gates.

She didn't want to believe it. The place in front of her was exactly the same as in Australia, even to the red plastic on the ground inside, although here there was only one black truck with those deeply-blackened windows. Kiri wondered what excuse they had here for the height of the boundary fence, presumably not 'roos jumping.

Her meeting this time was shorter, but equally fruitless. And the man who met her seemed to know she'd been to Australia. Whoever these people were, they were in communication – and didn't want to give anything away.

She tried desperately to think of an explanation for what she'd seen. Other than that her O'Connor computer had just latched onto these artificial communes, and created a nonsensical set of results from the false data they'd submitted. Because, if that was true, her project was worthless.

Kiri got back home mid afternoon. Then the full jet-lag, so far masked by the distress about her project, hit her. She fell asleep, half undressed, on top of the bed, without even getting into it.

Some time later, she realised Tony was beside her with a mug of tea.

"Hi there sleeper. I think you'd better wake up soon, or you'll never sleep tonight."

There was a brief moment when that journey to Australia hadn't happened – it was all just a nasty dream. Then it came back. She felt the tears coming and couldn't stop them.

Tony knew it was serious. He'd never seen her like this before.

"I thought there might be a problem with you being back so early. Tell me about it when you're ready."

"I'm not sure I understand it myself. I need to do some work on the computer to see what the hell it all means. There's nothing you can do to help. Just don't tell anyone at the university that I'm back."

Then, despite his protests, she spent most of the next week, without much sleep, at her terminal. But everything she did just made the whole project look like more of a mess. All the main conclusions seemed to be based on about sixty small communes. They were all over the world, but their information was oddly similar. Brad O'Connor's computer confirmed that. In desperation, she finally called its creator in Denver.

She noticed the delay as the call was diverted, but immediately it did ring, Brad answered. "Hi Kiri," he shouted.

But she only just heard the words against the background noise.

"Hang on a second," he continued. "I'm over in the hangar, and Karl's just checking out an engine."

She heard the noise for a few more seconds, then it spluttered to a halt.

"That'll wait. Hi again. All's OK over there I sure hope," Brad continued casually.

"Well, no," Kiri said slowly. "That's why I'm calling. Things are looking bad. The health project data looks like it's all wrong. I've had this instinct for some time, but now I seem to have proved it."

"Hey, how does that happen then?"

Kiri briefly explained her disastrous visits to Australia and Cyprus.

"That's real terrible for you. I feel it. Can't you get anything sane out of it?"

The sympathy in his voice suddenly brought her close to tears again. She tried to control herself. "No. I don't think so."

"Take the false data out maybe?"

"There are fifty or more lots of it. I've been sitting here, most hours of the day, for nearly a week. The computer tells me I can't just pull out the incorrect data. It's one of your sodding machines remember, and as far as it's concerned, that stuff isn't data anymore. It's become the truth. That's the way they work. You should know."

"Yeah. I'm sorry. But look, as it happens, even if you're not going to do the announcement just yet, I've already fixed up a few other things over there, so I'm flying to the UK anyway. Get there on the fifth. I'll come in late morning to see if I can help."

"You're about my last hope. I'll keep the people at the university stalled till then. And you'll get to meet Tony. That morning he's got some weird interview for a Swiss medical research outfit he doesn't believe even exists, but he should be back for lunch."

"OK. That's great."

Kiri noticed a change of voice, and suspected Brad wasn't keen to be reminded of Tony.

"I'll call from the airport when the flight gets in," he continued after a pause. "But, from what you've told me already, don't get too hopeful on the project."

"So how should I be?"

"How about, say, curious. Like you seem to have dug up two little communities, nine thousand miles apart, just so similar, and maybe with others the same? What are they then?"

"I couldn't give a shit what they are. They've screwed up my project."

"Real strange though," he replied. "And is all that data you collected still in the computer? You haven't messed it up too much?"

"No. Not at all."

"Well keep it in there, please. I think the whole thing's weird. But I'll talk to you when I get over."

"Great. And it'll be good to see you again."

"Same here."

Kiri wanted to stop herself thinking any more about the project until he arrived. "Enough about my problems for now," she said. "How are you getting on?"

"Fine. But I had the spookiest night about two weeks back. Makes a good story to tell you next week. Get some rest till then. I wanna see you looking great."

Chapter 4

I can see clearly now the light has gone

To San Jose, Costa Rica

The lingering fear of an avenging assassin sent from that cult by the red pool had only gradually receded. Even up to a couple of years afterwards, Peter Rossi had remained wary of any stranger who suddenly approached him. Now, ten years later, although that fear had gone, the memory of those crunching bones still occasionally disturbed his sleep.

But Peter had his life to get on with, so just what that strange group had been doing back there, or why he'd woken that night into a discoloured and terrifying room, had by now all slipped into being little more than a background puzzle. Nothing like that night's experience had ever happened again.

It had though, all remained just worrying enough for Peter to have obeyed Bill Rawlings' instructions not go back to the Middle East. And Rawlings, although never mentioning that red-pool episode again, had kept ordering the gun-training simulators.

A thing Peter had noticed was that Rawlings' customers seemed to have gradually changed since then. In the early days, they'd all been government military people in the Middle East. Starting about a year after that incident, the simulators were being shipped all over the world, to organisations that weren't identified. And, perhaps to hide who these customers were, the paperwork always came through Switzerland. Despite this, all the documentation was good enough to make those deals look legitimate enough to get export clearance.

'Secretive buggers, the Swiss' was Peter's simple explanation to himself.

Even these orders, though, had tailed off in the last five years. So, he had started some other projects. He'd used the Brad O'Connor computers for automatic target-recognition. That had worked well, although he'd got zero interest from Rawlings, which he couldn't quite understand.

The O'Connor computers were difficult to use, and he'd had to go on a course over in Denver to be trained in programming by the man himself. After that, Peter's only contact with Brad had been strictly business.

But he'd stayed in closer contact with the only woman who'd been on that course, a Dr Kiri Williams. Since then, she'd really struggled with the way Brad's computers worked, and he'd helped her a few times.

The trilling tones of the phone disturbed his thoughts. He paused the TV and pulled himself to the end of the sofa to pick up the cordless handset, noting from the base display that the call was a diversion from his office line.

"Mr Peter Rossi?"

"Yes."

The voice sounded Spanish, Peter thought.

"We have a number of your systems."

He frowned. He knew those armies who had several of his weapons trainers, and somehow this didn't sound like one of them.

"I can't comment," he blandly stonewalled. "Who are you?"

"I am not able to say."

"Then I don't do business," Peter snapped. He'd been enjoying that match. West Ham playing well for a change.

The calm voice was unchanged by the outburst. "Think a bit more then. You certainly have done business."

The comment made Peter check for a second before responding again, and realise what this might be. It had to be about Rawlings, and all those anonymous orders via Switzerland.

"I'm sorry," he went into guard mode. "There are government regulations and export restrictions I must comply with."

"We need to discuss things directly," the man went on, ignoring Peter's comment. "The details are complicated, and I do not have any time to waste in misunderstandings."

"If you want another system, then just order it the way you did before."

"Listen to me, will you." There was a harder edge in the caller's voice. "We do not want another system. We need changes to the systems we have. And, as you will soon find out, this isn't a sensible conversation to be having on the telephone. So you will be given the necessary information when you come out here and meet us."

The statement took Peter aback. "Out where?"

"Costa Rica. You will receive the airline ticket and instructions, and will be travelling next Wednesday. A room has been booked at the Hotel Palasio, in downtown San Jose."

"You're making some bloody big assumptions there. Who the hell do you think you are?"

"A customer with a large and urgent potential order, Mr Rossi."

Peter calmed himself a bit. "OK. But I don't like people telling me what to do. Anyone."

"If you do not comply, then we will immediately get other people to do the more advanced development on your equipment."

Peter definitely didn't want that happening. Also, if they were so keen, there could be good money in this. He decided to go along with them. Apart from anything else, he hadn't been to Costa Rica before.

"Suppose I were to agree, then?"

"That would be very sensible of you. And you would need to understand one more thing. This must be done in total secrecy. No other person must ever know of your destination, or the reason for your journey."

The line went dead before he could react.

Slowly, Peter replaced the phone, in a mixture of curiosity and disquiet. And it left him a problem – with someone he'd met about a year ago.

Iona Duncan had started with as ordinary a Scottish background, as his own Essex childhood. But she matched Peter's drive for excitement, and his financial ability to go anywhere for it. For work, she travelled the globe dealing in exotic and tropical plants. With this, and Peter's international work in arms, the two of them had cherry-picked the world's experiences. They'd lain in bed watching dawn mists roll under the Golden Gate Bridge, got drunk on yachts in Sydney Harbour, lunched in the frantic buzz of Manhattan, and had long dreamy dinners in Paris cafés.

But they weren't completely compatible. She liked the travel, the fast cars, Peter's wisecracking humour, and the way he made things happen; but hated his football and everything about it, which included most of his friends.

Also, Iona was not prepared, any more than Peter was, to give up her ultimate freedom. So she'd kept her little cottage, near Henley, west of London, with its frilly decor and neatly-ordered exotically planted garden. Peter just used a rented, luxury furnished-apartment in Windsor, to which he'd only added a monster-screen 3D TV and a five-hundred-watt sound system.

Peter's problem now was that a flight next Wednesday would mess up a night he'd fixed with Iona. She didn't often ask him to stay over at her cottage, but it had been a while since they'd been on any trips together, so he'd had a special invite. It wouldn't be easy to call it off without explaining why.

He picked up the phone again, and dialled her number.

"I've just come to bed," she said softly. "I was thinking about you."

"Wish I was there."

"You will be soon."

Peter decided to get this over with. "I called because I've got some bad news. I can't make it next Wednesday."

"What's the problem?"

"Some urgent business."

"What? Something more interesting than me?"

It felt stupid as he said it. "I can't tell you."

"What the hell are you up to? You've never *not told me* anything before."

He gave up. "OK. Sorry. It looks like I've got a mystery customer in Costa Rica. But he's told me to keep it absolutely confidential. And he sounded pretty serious about it."

There was a pause, as if Iona was changing gear. "Costa Rica?" she said in a different voice now. "That just does not make any sense."

"I think they want me to modify something there."

"Peter. Don't be so stupid. Are you lying to me?"

"No. Of course not."

"Listen. That little model of a democracy abolished the death sentence in 1882, and disbanded its army more than sixty years ago!"

"Look. I'm telling you what's been said to me. I promise you."

"I've been to the place a few times, remember. I get a lot of plants from there. So, with no army, you say they've bought military training kit from you?"

"I'm just telling you what the guy said to me. But, like I said, he did make a big thing of it being confidential. That might explain something?"

"I don't see how. But what the hell. As it happens, I wanted to go there soon anyway. Something seems to be wrong with my plant suppliers, Philippe and Maria. I haven't been able to contact them for a couple of months, and was wondering what to do next. So I'll join you."

"You can't."

"I can do anything I want. And, anyway, someone's pulling your plonker about the whole thing. How about we go the day before and stop over Tuesday night in Florida? You could make up for ducking out on me."

Peter thought about it. That did sound like a good idea.

"OK. But, until I'm sure there's nothing in this, we first make it look as if I'm alone when we get to Costa Rica."

"We'll soon be together."

Amongst all the junk in the post the next day, there was a simple little white envelope, the sort you normally open first. Yes. Inside were an airline ticket, a hotel name and booking reference, and just one other small piece of paper. On it was a one-line instruction. *Meeting. Marriott, San Jose. 9 a.m. Thursday.* He checked the ticket – top left corner, no restrictions – centre column, fare basis J. This was a fully-flexible business-class IATA ticket. That suited his plan, so he walked over to his computer to fix their flights.

He called Iona with the details, restarted the West Ham game, and settled back feeling pleased. But that was only to last five minutes, before the next phone call.

"Mr Rossi," that Spanish voice said sharply. "You have altered both the airline and day of your first leg to America."

Peter's reply did not sound defensive. "Yes. Of course I have. You told me to do this in complete secrecy."

"So why the changes?"

"Look. I know what I'm doing. I'm in the business. The first rule of secrecy is not to make anyone suspicious in the first place. What if I just told my people I was going off out to Central America, and refused to tell them anything else about it? So, I've organised some legitimate business in Tampa for the day before. From then on, no one misses me for an extra day. I'm off enjoying myself. I do that sometimes. Now do you understand?" Peter ended almost patronizingly.

His caller paused before responding.

"I see, Mr Rossi. But just be very careful you don't get too clever for your own health."

A chill came over Peter, and he found it hard to shift.

Peter and Iona checked in separately and sat well away from each other on the short flight between Tampa and Costa Rica.

Crossing the coast, Peter gazed down at the spectacular air approach to Costa Rica's capital, San Jose. He could see it spread out in the central valley, with mountain peaks forming a giant bowl round it. As he looked, those peaks were soon level with the descending aircraft.

On the ground, the two new arrivals walked into the terminal separately, Iona first. Peter watched her blond hair and compact figure. She was small, but then Peter felt difficult with women who were taller than his five-foot eight. And the good bit was that her shortness had made her develop an erotic throw of the hips as she walked.

They exchanged slight glances from ten places apart in the immigration queue. Then, outside, they gave different drivers directions to separate hotels. Peter's taxi had started just behind hers, but then went more slowly so he started to lose sight of Iona's in front.

Suddenly Peter changed his mind about going to his own hotel first. It had been from watching that hip-swinging walk. He leant forwards, holding some money in his fist, and pointed to Iona's taxi in the distance.

Some of the moves the driver made to catch up worried even Peter but, ten minutes later, the two taxis pulled up almost together at her hotel. He followed her in and got into the same lift.

"I hope you're going to let me put my stuff away before you distract me," Iona said, smiling.

"OK. I'll freshen up while you do that."

Ten minutes later, he came out of her bathroom with only a towel round his shoulders. "Why don't you join me?"

She was already holding an opened bottle of champagne and a glass for him. "Room service works fine. So see, I told you everything would be all right here."

He took the glass and led her into the shower.

Early the next morning Peter took the short walk back to his own hotel. He was vaguely aware of some disturbance in the foyer as he checked in, but ignored it.

It seemed sensible to get some food before going to what might just be a serious meeting. So Peter asked a porter to take his bag to his room while he nipped across to grab some breakfast.

After some strong coffee, a bowl of fruit and an omelette, he took the lift up to his room.

Even hurriedly unpacking his bag, he realised something was wrong. Someone had been at it, although it had been refilled with care, so he hadn't been meant to notice. He went through his money and documents, and they were all intact.

With all this, time was now tight for the taxi which was to run him the eight-miles out to the Marriott Hotel for his mystery meeting, and he didn't have time for a shower.

A hazy morning sun had now risen and brought an oppressive humidity which hadn't been there the day before. The taxi had no air-con, and the heat made him aware of his missed shower.

Happy to get out of the taxi, Peter paid the driver through the window and walked quickly into the hotel's small and low-ceilinged lobby. He was still sweating, and couldn't have felt less prepared for whatever was to happen next – information missing on that brief instruction.

He soon found out.

"Walk forwards at once."

The command had come from behind him. He wiped some sweat from his face and at first obediently went ahead. In front were the stainless-steel doors of a lift. Just before he got there, he tried to turn, as if casually. The instant response was an unseen tight grip on his arm, just below the shoulder. It stopped his swivel.

"Press the call button, to go up," the voice commanded. Peter did what he was told. Soon, a ping sounded and the lift doors opened. Obeying the slight push, he stepped forwards, and the lift doors started to close again.

"I am going to put something over your eyes," the voice said. "Don't struggle."

Whoever was behind pulled a large paper bag down over his head. In a moment of panic, Peter wondered whether this was an attempt to kidnap him. Wary of something like handcuffs he tensed himself, holding his hands forward and apart, and was ready to kick backwards.

The lift went up a few floors. He couldn't tell how many. The doors opened again and he was turned by a hand on each shoulder and pushed out, but the bag stayed on and was now sticking to his forehead in the heat. It also messed up his hearing a bit. Enough to kill any acoustic sense of the space he was in. Clever.

Peter counted his paces out of the lift. After twenty, he was stopped, heard a door click open, and again was guided forwards. The door clicked again and, to his relief, the hot and claustrophobic bag was then pulled off.

He was in a small, plainly-furnished, room. In front of him were two men. One, strikingly tall, was standing by the closed curtains. Perhaps the dark glasses were meant to hide his appearance. They didn't. That face was distinctly angular, but with strangely soft-looking skin, flabby even.

In the centre of the room, a second man, this one balding and also darkly bespectacled, was sitting at a small modern desk. That and the vacant seat, across the desk nearer to Peter, were the only bits of furniture there.

"I am sorry about the precautions," the seated man said, and Peter immediately recognised the Spanish accent from the original phone call he'd answered in Windsor.

"I am Vincenzo Armanino. We spoke on the telephone," he confirmed. "Sit down, please." His hand waved towards the empty chair. He did not introduce the man by the window, or the one still out of sight behind Peter.

Peter didn't sit. "Someone has been into my hotel room and searched my luggage. I would like an explanation."

Armanino turned slightly to look over to the man by the curtains, who nodded slowly.

"It seems that something did happen." There was a fractional roll of his head backwards at the large man standing by the window. "Nothing would have been taken, and there will be no repetition of it."

"Also," Peter then said more softly and coldly. "I have been in the weapons business twenty years and can keep a confidence without these games." He swept his arm to indicate the man behind."

"The precautions, are in case you become curious about who we are."

"Why should I? I just stick to what I need to know. Rule one of the game."

Armanino seemed to briefly frown at the use of that word, and then took some time to continue. "At some stage," he said slowly, "the things we will be asking for might strike your interest too much. Then less knowledge would be better for you."

"OK. So let's just discuss what you want," Peter replied. "Nothing more." He finally sat and pulled the chair forward to the desk.

"Good. Then I will explain our requirements," Armanino continued, now leaning slightly back. "We need improvements to some systems you have made in the past."

Peter chose not to confront Armanino by asking the obvious question. He just nodded.

"First, we would like a change in the target characteristics of your systems. We need the kill area on each human image reduced to about a third of what it is now."

Peter again nodded, knowing this would sharpen up the accuracy of the trainees.

Armanino continued. "And the area which simulates injury should be eliminated."

This idea left Peter puzzled. In armed conflict, an injured enemy is better in the short term than a dead one. Someone else has to get involved helping the guy. "So you're taking no prisoners, eh?" he quipped.

Armanino's response was again unamused. "I have already said that it would be best for you not to be curious. Just say whether you can do this."

"Yes. That is the sort of thing I can program in," Peter confirmed. His mind was already working on the numbers.

"Good. And we would also like more variety of targets. We need to assume anyone could be the enemy, such as civilians, even women and children."

Peter knew this was the nature of too many wars now. Again, he just nodded in response and continued to listen.

"We also want better simulation of urban conditions. We require scenes like normal houses, gardens, railway stations and restaurants. There needs to be much more of that sort of background." He pushed over a few pictures.

Peter knew that was also modern war. He examined the computer-created drawings. "You know all this is going to be quite expensive," he said.

"So tell me how much," Armanino simply replied.

"Let me have a minute to think."

Peter cupped his chin in his fingers, and wondered what he could get away with.

"At first assessment, about fifty-thousand sterling for the non-recurring development costs," he threw in, watching for any sign of surprise. There was none. "And about twenty-thousand for each modification kit and software issue," he went on, knowing this was high. "But of course that part is more difficult to estimate until we've done some initial design, so I'll need to confirm it once we've done that," he added, to give himself an escape route.

At this, there were some unreadable looks between Armanino and the soft-faced man.

"We would like you to make that a firm price now," Armanino stated. "We will transfer the money at once for the development costs, and also half the payment for the system kits. The final payment will be on the day of delivery. Do you agree?"

It didn't need much thought, but Peter left it a few seconds before responding.

"Yes. I can agree."

"Good. But for that amount of money, *which I know is high*," Armanino said with hard emphasis, "we would also like a change in the target illumination and emitted spectrum. To be in accordance with this."

He pushed another piece of paper across the small table. "Is that achievable?"

"A different light-level and electromagnetic spectrum? No problem."

"So you are sure that you understand everything?"

Peter briefly checked the figures again. "Yes, I've got it. This spectrum goes well into the infra red. We already do night-time stuff. I assume that's what you want to do?"

"I told you not to be curious," Armanino snapped. "You start work at once. And in one month, you will deliver seventeen conversion kits. We will let you know where and how."

Peter couldn't believe the quantity. "Seventeen!" he involuntarily reacted, his voice going to a higher pitch. "I can't possibly do the design, and then deliver that many in one month."

"I told you we are aware of your high charges," Armanino continued, as if to threaten Peter with the fact. "Some of our plans have been advanced. So delivery will be when I said. The money will be transferred into your usual business account."

Peter didn't bother asking how they knew its number. His expression just signalled acceptance. "OK, but I will need the serial number and present mod status of each system you are going to upgrade."

"We are not idiots. You will be informed about these things, as you said, when you need to know them."

Then Armanino's voice went much colder.

"You protested about our methods, so let me now warn you. We have given you information which is of extreme consequence to us. Yesterday, you chose to outrun the car following your taxi, and then evade us for over twelve hours. So you will have no communication or contact with anyone before you leave the country. And if we suspect any further compromise of our project, you will not be leaving at all."

There was such a hard edge to that statement that Peter felt the reaction in his stomach. He realised that, thank God, they must have lost him after his last-minute decision to go to Iona's hotel. So they didn't know where he'd been. Now, the slight commotion as he'd checked in this morning made some sense. The problem was that, at seven tonight, she was due to come round to his hotel. He had to warn her somehow.

The large soft-faced man had beckoned to whoever was still standing unseen behind Peter. There was a rustling from what he hoped was a new paper-bag. He turned quickly towards the sound, trying to get a look at the man, and just managed it as the bag came down. He memorised the thin features.

Perhaps soft-face had noticed that move, or maybe his parting remark was coming anyway.

"Don't get clever. You will now be watched all the time, even after you return to England."

This time, after the lift had descended, Peter was pushed out firmly as its doors opened, making him stumble and half-fall across the lobby as he pulled the bag off. The doors had closed before he'd managed to look round.

The taxi which pulled up so conveniently, just as he walked back out into the heat, had to be something they'd fixed. So he asked for it to go straight back to his hotel and didn't try to use his mobile.

Shutting the door of his hotel room, Peter had several problems on his mind. The most urgent was to stop Iona from coming round for the night. If she did, she'd walk straight into the people who would now be guarding him. He checked his mobile phone. It displayed some words in Spanish he hadn't seen on it before, and didn't respond to the numbers he pressed. The room phone was silent when he lifted it. Like Armanino had threatened, they'd cut him off.

He opened his door again and looked each way. Along the corridor, a cleaner was busying himself with his supplies trolley. The man didn't look up or give the usual friendly greeting of the locals. After pretending to check that his key was working properly in the lock, Peter gently closed the door.

But he had to get to Iona and warn her.

Chapter 5

Where have all the flowers gone

To Puntarenas, Costa Rica

Iona's sixty-mile journey northwest, to the nursery gardens of her out-of-contact plant suppliers, started as it had each time before.

After picking up the hire car, she'd started by driving up into the forested rim of mountains which surround the high central valley of Costa Rica. Then, after crossing the ridge, her route was downhill a long way, towards the city of Puntarenas, on the Pacific Ocean coast of the country. She enjoyed swooping the car round the curves in the twisting and dipping road, through the changes of scenery, as it took the ten-thousand-foot descent towards the river Tarcole.

She drew up two hours later at the base of a hillside which had long-since been cleared of trees and terraced for cultivation. The heat and thick humidity told her she was now nearly at equatorial sea level.

Looking around, she immediately sensed that things were different from her previous visits. The small excavation in the steep slope, which formed a parking area, was almost as she remembered but, further up, things all seemed overgrown.

Walking up that slope, she saw that the once-tidy pathways, and those terraces, all looked neglected and covered in blown leaves. There was no sign that anyone had been here recently.

Iona walked around the deserted plantation for five minutes. Everywhere was in the same state, with weeds now mingling into overgrown cultivated plants. Lank parched plants in dried-out pots were still waiting to be planted. It was like all work had suddenly stopped a few months ago, and Philippe and Maria had not come back since. Something about it all was making her feel uneasy, and Iona walked quickly down the steps back to her car.

She decided to drive to the village bar, half a mile away. It was where she'd often gone for a drink after doing her deals. She'd know someone there, perhaps one of the locals who'd liked to practise their English on her.

Ten minutes later the sight of the closed bar, looking as if it was no longer even in business, deepened the mystery. She didn't bother stopping. There was another possibility. One of the regulars of that closed-down bar was Anna. She might be at the small grocery store she worked with her mother.

After parking her car, Iona almost involuntarily scanned up and down the road before walking on. Down the almost deserted street was a car she was certain had been behind her on that last short drive. The two men in it were looking away, but it seemed at nothing. She decided to test whether they'd been following her, and immediately got back into her hire car, turned it to point back up at the dark-green mountain slopes, and set off at speed.

She kept watching through the mirror. Almost immediately, the other car started and swung rapidly round in pursuit.

Iona enjoyed driving quickly. Fast cars were one of the good things about knowing Peter. Right now, she had a slight start on the driver behind, but not the proper car to do a getaway in.

"I wish this was downhill, you bastards," she muttered as she struggled with the compact Chevrolet's column change and underpowered engine. "Then I'd really show you."

But soon she grinned. The larger car behind had fish-tailed coming out of the first couple of corners. Iona's adrenaline flowed, and she tried to calm herself.

Her pursuers progressively dropped back. With each corner they were further away, and soon out of sight except on the occasional longer straights.

She had just taken a sharp bend, and in front was a side road. "Now take your time," she whispered to herself.

She checked her speed, and so left no curving black tyre-marks to give away her right-angled turn off the main road. Once round, she tucked the car in to the left and, fifteen seconds later, the chasing car went straight past on the road now behind her.

Still with her heart thumping, Iona immediately turned her car round, and again took that corner without leaving a mark.

Going downhill, she judged her breaking points and apexes to the inch. She didn't look in the mirror. Even if those guys had turned round at once, they wouldn't have kept up with this.

Back down in the village she wanted to make the Chevrolet inconspicuous, but able to make a quick exit. She chose the village car park, putting the car between two vans, and pointing outwards. Then she made a fast walk with her head bowed, aware that her whole body was still shaking.

She almost bumped into Anna's mother outside their small grocers. The woman dragged her into the shop doorway. "Don't worry, I know who you are," she said. "I expected you to turn up eventually. But you shouldn't have. It is dangerous."

"I just came to ask where Philippe and Maria are."

"They have gone, and so has Anna." There was something combining anguish and panic in the woman's voice.

"Gone? Where to?"

"First they were at Canas, north from here. Learning about special herbs, they said."

"And?"

"They were different when they came back."

"How do you mean?"

"Come here."

Anna's mother took Iona back into the light nearer the window, then moved her own face up to just two inches away and stared intently, eye to eye. Suddenly the woman's hand whipped round hard. Iona moved her head back just in time, so only the fingers clipped her chin.

"Why did you do that?"

"I used to know my daughter. When she was young and did something wrong, I would sometimes pretend to hit her. Like I did with you. But Anna knew what was coming, and always dodged it. But when she came back from that place in Canas, she couldn't. Nor could the others. But you did. It's my test now. It was like someone had drugged them. They were different people – cold people. Another thing. They kept making secret signs to each other. Trying to keep me out of things."

The woman went to look out onto the street again. "You must leave now."

"OK, but where have they gone to?"

"I don't know. After all the years, Anna left without even talking to me."

"Have you contacted the police or anything?"

"They do nothing. And you must leave." The woman's voice made it clear she was frightened, and desperate to get rid of her visitor.

Iona looked both ways before she stepped onto the street. No one was around.

Just before she got back to her car, over the quietness of the little place, she heard a vehicle approaching fast. She slipped down by her car, looking through the gap towards the road. Her pursuers had returned, and drove on by. As soon as they were out of sight, she set off back on the road to San Jose, leaving inconspicuously, but then speeding up.

****

Perhaps it was the realisation that it was now well into lunch time and he was hungry gave Peter the idea. He had to do something other than stay incommunicado in this room. Otherwise, in just a few hours, Iona would walk into a trap that would be dangerous for both of them.

This time he didn't pretend he was checking his key, but walked straight out as if all was normal. The 'cleaner' was still in the same place. And when Peter reached the lift he was joined, it seemed out of nowhere, by a man in brown workers' overalls, carrying a toolbox. Again, there was no greeting, and those overalls and his fingernails were far too clean. This guy had never seen the inside of a lift shaft.

In the foyer, Peter could see a couple of phones. Could he call Iona on one of those perhaps? But that 'maintenance man' immediately came close as if to intercept him, making almost no pretence now. Peter realised he had to go on with his half-formed plan.

First, it needed a large newspaper, so he picked one up from a table in the foyer. Then he walked, again as if without a problem on his mind, into the hotel café – a spacious place of faded grandeur. Now he needed a corner table

"A bottle of some decent dry French white, please," he said quietly to the waiter, as if trying to convey some sort of secrecy between them.

The brown overall was less attentive now that Peter was clearly visible at the closed end of the large room. It gave him the chance to practice what he had to do next. This was to hold the paper up as a screen, and carefully tip the first glass of that wine onto the floor.

Soon the bottle was empty, but with only one glass drunk. The four tipped under the bench seat didn't show on the dark carpet.

"And lots of chilli sauce on it," Peter said, more loudly at the waiter's next visit, ordering one of the bland Mexican-style dishes of Costa Rica. "And another one of these, please." He tapped the bottle.

When the meal was on the table, Peter went into a display of clumsily waving and folding the pages of his paper, in the process knocking over his glass of water.

Peter waved away the man who came to sponge the carpet. "I'll be finished soon," he snapped. "Do it then."

Even less than one glass from the second bottle of wine went down his throat. The rest went on top of the spreading water.

"A large brandy," also went onto the carpet.

As Peter got up, he stumbled, knocking over a nearby table, then walked unsteadily towards the main entrance. This time it was someone different who approached him.

"Good afternoon. It is Mr Rossi, isn't it?"

"Yes," Peter replied, turning to look waveringly at the person.

"I am Anton Vargas. Mr Rossi, you have been warned to avoid any further contacts whilst in the country. You can't leave the hotel. You need to return to your room."

"No. I tell you what. Let's enjoy ourselves." Peter leant closer, and Vargas flinched away from the arm round his shoulder. "I need anosher drink." Peter slurred. "Thersh the bar."

"It would be better if you went straight to you room." Vargas said in a terse whisper, so that a group of people, now looking towards them, didn't hear.

Being unnoticed wasn't part of Peter's plan, though.

"What? You are telling me where to drink," he shouted. A pointed finger of accusation waved unsteadily, and annoyingly, near Vargas' face.

After seeming to nearly lose his balance a couple of times, Peter reached the bar. "Two large scotches!" he called out loudly. "We'll start with a toast from you, and then a toasht from me." He now had the attention of a gathering audience.

Once he'd got the drinks, Peter exaggeratedly downed his in one, and pushed the other glass into Vargas' hand.

"I don't drink," was the response.

Peter turned to the people now hovering carefully on that margin between watching and getting involved. "Here is a man who won't drink with me!" he shouted. "Then sod him."

He grabbed Vargas' glass, spilling most of it in the process, but then drinking the small remainder with a flourish.

"And I'll hash another one," he called out to the barman, with his apparent state now advancing fast.

A spluttering cough spat most of that whisky out, to make a large dark patch on Vargas' shirt.

"I'm sho shorry," he said. "I'm not normally like this, but I've been working too hard, you see. Maybe I will go back to my room. I don't feel very well."

"Let me help you," The relief was apparent in Vargas' voice.

Upstairs, after fumbling incapably with his room key, Peter eventually opened the door, and received a hard shove from Vargas, which sent him stumbling into the room's small desk. He gave a cry, then finally landed on the bed, the impact moving it sideways. His arm was across his face but, through almost closed eyes, he could just see the door. It was some time before Vargas finally clicked it shut.

Even so, Peter waited a while before he slowly sat up, but continued making loud grunting and guttural noises.

Fifteen minutes later, Peter lurched out into the corridor, with flies open and penis in hand. There was nobody there, so he didn't have to pee against the wall opposite.

His best chance had worked. Assuming he was drunk, they'd relaxed. The exit to the emergency stairs was only ten yards away. Clothing readjusted, he went quickly down and out of the small back entrance of the hotel. The road was quiet and no one seemed to take any notice of him.

He looked round for a payphone. Nothing in sight. He'd hesitated long enough, and now decided a fast walk the two blocks up the street to Iona's hotel was the best idea. But, unlike last night, he then needed to get back in here without them realising he'd ever gone.

Out of breath after the final scurry up the hotel staircase, Peter had flopped into the only armchair in Iona's room. She had perched herself in the middle of the bed, with her legs tucked under her, listening to his panted words. He'd only got as far as telling her about the searched luggage, when he was stopped mid-word by the sound of a key in her door-lock.

Peter looked towards the bathroom. It was too far away. The room doorknob was already turning. He slid out of his chair and rolled fast towards the old-fashioned high bed, hoping it didn't have six legs. It didn't, and seconds later he was hidden by a bedspread which came to within an inch of the floor. It was still waving slightly as the room door was slammed open so hard that Peter could hear the clattering of falling bits of plaster, knocked out of the wall where the doorknob hit.

Iona screamed. "Take what you want. Then get out!"

Peter tensed himself, about to move if they went for her.

"Quiet!" a voice had said. "We are just here to ask you some questions."

There were the sounds of some people moving in quickly, and the door slamming shut again.

"What were you looking for today?" the same voice continued.

Peter held still.

"Who are you?" she said.

"You just give the answers. What were you doing today?"

"Trying to buy plants for my business in Europe."

"And behaving like James Bond?"

"No," she replied. "And what is this about? Show me your authority."

Under the bed, Peter's thoughts spun in confusion. He'd thought these people would be after him.

"I said no questions. Who did you speak to?" the man had continued.

"No one. There was nobody there."

"Who made you come out here?"

"I came on my own."

"You lie," a new voice said slowly and coldly. But, from those two words, Peter knew who it was – Anton Vargas. What in hell did that mean? And if they'd realised he was with her, why wasn't Vargas asking about that?

"I'm telling you the truth," Iona had replied.

"No. You are going to tell us the real reason you are here," Vargas continued.

Iona's feet were just visible to Peter, near the side of the bed. From where his voice was coming from, Peter reckoned those were Vargas' feet, beyond the bottom of the bed. There were two other pairs of feet behind him.

"I have told you the truth," Iona was saying, now more calmly. "And you have no right to be in this room."

"You British seem to think you can carry your *rights* around with you," Vargas replied.

"I'm going to call the embassy," she snapped, now sounding more confident.

Peter saw her move towards the phone on the bedside table. Then Vargas walked round, as if to intercept her. Peter tensed, but Vargas stopped just short and there seemed to be a silent stand-off.

"When are you leaving the country?" he eventually asked.

"Tomorrow afternoon."

"Let me look at your ticket and passport."

He heard a click as Iona opened her briefcase, then half a minute slight rustling of paper. It seemed to satisfy Vargas.

"OK. But don't move out of this hotel until then," he eventually said. "We will be watching you."

There were some whispers in another language, then the three sets of feet turned away to leave the room. Peter decided to risk taking a better look, and slowly lifted one edge of the hanging bedspread. Even in rear view, he recognised the other two. They were the two other men from this morning at the Marriott. He slowly lowered the bedspread and drew back, his mind racing.

Peter waited for a minute after the men had left, then carefully rolled out from under the bed, as Iona finally managed to close and lock the damaged door. He could see she was shaking.

"Are you OK?"

"Yes. I am now."

"Then what the fuck is going on?" Peter whispered. "I didn't finish telling you what happened to me, but the same people are following us both around. So what have you done to get them all stirred up?"

She gave a wry smile. "I saw someone trying to chase me, and deliberately got away from them. Like James Bond, it seems. But I can't believe that trying to buy plants here gets me shadowed. It must be something to do with you."

"I don't see how. But I hope to God they don't work out we're anything to do with each other. They've told me if I break their security then I don't leave the country. Probably because I'd be dead. And I'm sure they'd now do the same to you."

"How could they?"

"Quite easy. The way you drive. A little traffic accident maybe?"

"I don't believe it!"

"I do. Although right now, they probably believe your story. And when they check, it will stack up."

"So buying flowers is OK?"

"It has to be. But you shouldn't be seen with me, even on the planes back. They seem to know every schedule change I make, and probably even the seat allocations. We'll talk when we're back in the UK."

Iona nodded. "OK. I'll get them away from the room by going downstairs, and you can get back to your hotel. Good luck."

"We've both still got the same bookings with separated seats," Peter said, "so I'll see you in the queue at the airport again. But be careful not to know me. And you'll have to catch a taxi at the other end."

"I won't leave if you're not in that queue."

Soon Peter was on the street. It was more crowded now. He matched his pace with some others walking in the same direction, staying behind them, head low. At the last moment, he stepped sideways into the back entrance of his hotel, and then made it three-a-time up the stairs.

As Peter steered his BMW out of the airport car park, there was a squeal from behind of a car accelerating. It had come, from being parked opposite, into the traffic behind him. The small red car, clean except for its muddy front-plate, stayed in obvious sight. Armanino had not been bluffing. Peter felt that in his car he could drop the guy, but decided not to. He was heading for the office and they obviously knew where that was anyway.

Chancing that these people couldn't eavesdrop his mobile calls in the UK, Peter called Iona. She'd caught her taxi.

"Iona. I am being followed. They said they would. We mustn't let them make a connection to you. I'll contact you when I've finished this order of theirs. That night at your place will have to wait I suppose. Pity."

At the office, Peter found that a package had been delivered for him. He took out the wad of papers. They were the full details of seventeen of his training units, with two things which linked them all; Bill Rawlings and Switzerland. They'd been delivered between five and ten years ago, all around the world, but never more than one kit to each unknown customer. So who would now be doing a mass upgrade?

A phone call interrupted him.

"Is the data sufficient?"

"Yes it is. Very comprehensive."

"Good. Our first payment has been made, and delivery will be on Tuesday the fifteenth of August. I will call with instructions on the Monday. And there must be no lapse in security."

Peter felt himself teeter on the edge of reacting, but just held himself back.

Then the phone was dead.

"I'll make you one of the fucking civilian targets," Peter shouted at it. "I know what you look like."

He switched on his computer and checked his business account. Two hundred and twenty thousand pounds had been transferred in, from an account in Switzerland. "What a surprise," he whispered.

He then called in Mike Howell, his chief engineer, to discuss how they were going to design and make the kits so quickly.

They had completed three weeks of intense work, when Mike Howell raised the problem.

"I think we've got a wrong figure in the specs."

Peter looked at the paper Mike was holding. It was the one Armanino had given him with the details of the background illumination level and the target infra-red emission.

"Mike, don't worry. Not that one. They were very specific about those figures."

"We can't measure it then. It seems to be about one-hundredth of the lowest calibration on our best meter."

"Look, leave them here," Peter said, slightly exasperated, pointing at the meter and the paperwork. "I'll sort it." He had been concentrating on the software, and knew they were already running late. This was something he could have done without.

Much later that night, when all the others had long gone home, Peter finally leant back from poring over an old physics book, a relic from his university days. That, and their 'best' meter, had confirmed that his written number for illumination was, in fact, near to total darkness. Peter remembered the words, *"A change in the target illumination level."*

"Armanino you shit," he whispered to himself. "You could have sodding told me what the numbers really meant."

It took another frantic day of phone calls to find an instrument which would read to that level, then achieving it needed a few more modifications to the kit. Peter drew on favours past and yet to come as his team worked all weekend, night and day. But they were ready when the next instructions came.

"Be in the car park of The Portsmouth Holiday Inn, tomorrow midday," was the brusquely telephoned message.

Peter made the delivery on his own, using a hired large Transit van. Circulating the hotel car park, he soon recognised the men from Costa Rica, the ones he could only refer to as 'soft face' and 'paper bag'. They were both stupidly wearing their dark glasses in the rain. He was directed to a far corner, where another anonymous-looking van was parked. It had its number plate covered.

"Disappear for half an hour," Soft face commanded, almost without acknowledging Peter's presence. "You can use the time to check that payment has been made."

A phone call to his bank confirmed it had been, again from Switzerland.

Half an hour later, the other van had gone.

Peter drove away slowly. An old feeling came over him. Back in school, Rossi, P, had been small and slight, and a bit of a bright sod. It made him a target. But he'd developed a defence, the warning from some sixth sense when something was being planned against him. Right now, the much older Rossi, P, felt that intuition very strongly.

Chapter 6

All in a dream, the loading had begun

Denver, USA

Brad was busy making final preparations for his visit to the UK. He'd just decided he needed to do a bit of shopping, when the call from his technical support people came through.

"Normally wouldn't think to bother you boss, but we've this guy who's come on our line says he has to talk to you personally. Says its life or death."

"Tell him we do computers and software – not life and death."

"Insists I tell you it's Charlie."

"What outfit's he with then?"

"Didn't say anything about being a customer, but went on about the track to the Teller reservoir?"

Brad had to pause a moment, if only to make his reply sound relaxed. "Look, you don't need him taking up your time. Put him on. If it's nothing I can get shot of him."

The transfer was immediate.

"Mr Brad O'Connor? It's Charlie. You remember who I am?"

"Sure. You helped me swing my plane round that night."

"Yes. And I need to talk to you about it. Something has happened to me. You are the person who can understand."

Brad checked himself. "It'd better not be a bad-luck story. I don't fall for those."

"No. It's those people up there. No one else knows what they're like," Charlie continued.

That held Brad's attention. He'd thought about that incident many times. How had they found out who he was? And how was he going to be *of use* to them? Despite that curiosity, he still wanted to play safe with Charlie.

"I guess we'll meet up then," he replied. "I was about to head for Cinderella City Mall. Got some shopping to do. Guess it might take an hour. So how's about you meet me here? Like, that'll make it midday?"

"There's a coffee place in the central plaza," came a quick reply, as if frightened that Brad might change his mind. "Some sort of French name."

"Yea, I'm fine with that. Know it. I'll wander along about twelve then. Gotta go now."

The café was still quiet before the lunchtime rush, but Brad had to walk well into it before he recognised the face. Charlie was sitting at the counter, up against the end wall, and jumped slightly as he realised someone was approaching him. Seeing who it was, he sat back again and swivelled the seat next to him for Brad to sit on. Then he looked round the café, eyes darting to look everywhere.

To Brad, no place could have looked less suspicious. It was open, well lit, and sparsely occupied. "So how's business up in the hills?" he asked as he sat.

"Gone," replied Charlie. "All gone."

Brad remembered Kiri's problems from her desperate phone call yesterday. "Seems it's disasters for everyone then. What's yours?"

"They're all dead. And someone's tried to kill me."

"What are you talking about?"

"They all poisoned themselves."

Now Brad wished he hadn't come here, and started to think about a quick exit. He tried to sound light and cynical. "No shit. What, a whole group?"

Charlie nodded. "Yes. Hundreds of them."

Brad now had a hand on his seat-back and one on the counter. He leant forwards and took his weight on them to stand up. "So then. Why's it not in the newscasts?"

"No one knows about it."

The only thing that stopped Brad from finally getting to his feet was Charlie's obvious terror. "OK then," he asked slowly, slightly relaxing back. "Why would they poison themselves?"

"They were told to."

"This is bullshit." This time Brad's movement was only stopped by Charlie's vice-like grip on his right hand.

"Don't go."

"Leave my hand alone."

The grip fell away. But again, something about the genuine fear in the man beside him, and his own experience that night, made Brad stay where he was.

"Look," he said. "How about you just explain yourself real careful and slow. I've got the time. Tell me just what you know about these guys. Do you understand?"

"Yes."

"Great." Brad pointed to the empty cup in front of Charlie. "Another one?"

There was a nod. "Thanks."

Then, as Charlie seemed to be putting his thoughts together, Brad sat back again and signalled to the waiter.

"I did buying for them," Charlie eventually started. "It made good money for me."

"So why didn't they do it themselves?"

"Didn't like it in town, they said."

"You bought everything? For hundreds? With that little truck?"

"No, just small, local, general hardware sort of stuff. Their main supplies came in from somewhere else. Not local."

"OK. Go on."

"Well, two days ago, I made a delivery. They always made me go in just before sunset. Like, I was on my way back when I first saw you. But, two days ago, the man I always saw told me there were no more orders. Then he cries. Says his two sons will die. They were all to take poison."

"Come on. Why?"

"To be punished. He said their faith hadn't been good."

Brad wanted to make it a joke, but somehow could only manage an imitation laugh. "Bet he'd been reading about these suicide cults. Like at Jonestown and Waco."

"No!" This time Charlie annoyingly clutched at both of Brad's hands. Brad shook them loose.

"Please let me go on."

"OK. But don't do that again."

"So – I'm talking to my regular guy. And then another person walks towards us. Younger, never seen him before. Before he gets to us, my guy whispers to me, *'Go away. A long way. Never come back. Tell no one'*. Then my guy went."

"Had you cheated them?"

"No. I did well for them."

"So, they just wanted to get the stuff a different way? You said you only bought a few things. How did the rest actually get in then?"

"A big black truck with black windows. And there was a bus. It had dark windows too. Could never see who was in it."

"So they were going to use one of those instead. Your man didn't have the balls to tell you. He invents a dumb story instead. Reckon they're all up there joking about it right now."

"No. There is more. I went back yesterday evening to take a look at them. I took my truck, no lights on, to a rise in the road, a mile from the camp, up that slope you were on. I turned it round in case I needed to get away quick. I was going to walk from there. Then I leant over to get my jacket, otherwise I'd be dead."

"Why?"

"They shot at me. From a long way."

"Just to scare you?"

"It nearly killed me. The shot came through the back window, just where my head had been."

"So they didn't sus how far shots drop at that range?"

Charlie got agitated. "No. I drove off at once, with my head still down, holding the door open to see the side of the track to steer, and three more slugs came through. Like this." He held his thumbs and forefingers in a small circle to show the accuracy – inches from each other.

"The guy shooting was close to you then?"

"No! I told you. And I've been shot at, lots, in Afghan. You get to know the distance by the sound. Yesterday, up there, it was more than a mile."

"Good shooting, then?"

"Even the Taliban didn't shoot straight in the dark."

Dark. That last word did it for Brad. He remained silent. His own memories almost made him believe what he was being told.

"Those people are not good," Charlie continued.

"I was there, remember?"

"Yes. They found you. I saw those footprints, all round where your plane had been."

Brad felt caught off-balance.

"So? And why are you talking to me?"

"The man was my friend. So were his children sort of. And I was a boy in that area once. Played there, like they did. I need to know what happened to them."

"Then, like, what do you want me to do about it?"

"I need help to find out what is going on there. But then no one would believe me. They would you. And you are a pilot. We could fly there and look?"

Brad realised he was about to be dragged in. But, this was the chance that in some way he wanted himself.

He nodded. "OK. But you'll need to come with me. Guide me to the right spot. You're not the only one who wants to know who they are. Let's go."

He was talking, but it was like listening to someone else's voice.

It was mid afternoon when Brad walked into his workshops with Charlie in tow. Karl spotted them and broke from working on a huge engine.

"Karl. Do you remember a guy called Charlie?"

"Yes I do. Hello again."

The two men nodded to each other.

"Could you get the Wright Robin ready for me?" Brad continued. "I want to run down that way again today with Charlie to take a look at something."

"Didn't you have enough excitement last time?"

Brad remembered how Karl must have seen the trodden snow round the plane, like Charlie had.

He tried to sound casual. "How do you mean?"

"That difficult landing," Karl replied, realising his mistake. It didn't sound convincing.

"That's the plane we're going in." Brad said to Charlie, changing the subject. He pointed over to the nineteen-thirties single-engined plane.

"My truck is bigger."

"It's this or nothing," Brad responded. "So while it's being gotten ready, I'll make a phone call. To an English guy called Peter Rossi. He's a real expert on shooting."

The phone call to Peter's apartment in Windsor was answered quickly.

"Rossi."

"Hi, Peter. It's Brad O'Connor. Glad you're there. Mind if I run something by you? About your sort of business."

"That? From you? Matey, I'm curious."

"I guess you will be. It's about some super-accurate shooting. And like, at a friend of mine."

"OK. I can tell you about accurate shooting."

"Well then. Jus' suppose someone can put four rifle bullets in a six-inch circle?"

"Easy peasy."

"At a mile range?"

"Maybe just possible, but bloody difficult."

"In the dark?"

This time there was no snap reply from Peter.

Brad tried to prompt him. "Well? What does that sound like to you?"

The silence was so long, Brad almost thought the line had gone dead.

"I know exactly what it sounds like," Peter eventually said. "That or fucking lies. Are you certain this friend of yours is telling you the truth?"

"Pretty well. He's sure scared enough. And from the sound of you, you're saying it just could happen?"

"Yes, maybe it just could," Peter said slowly.

"How come?"

"Mate, I've had some seriously heavy warnings about keeping this thing secret. I think we need to talk face to face – and alone."

"As it happens, I'm over the pond in a couple of days. Kiri's had some real bad problems with that project of hers, and I said I'd drop into her place and help."

"Yes. I know she's been struggling for a while. And I'd like to see her again. I'll ask her if we can meet there."

Brad felt irritation. He almost wished he hadn't mentioned Kiri. He sort of wanted the meeting with her to himself.

Peter had continued. "Can you find out any more about exactly who these people are before you make it over here?"

"Well, it may be a real stupid thing, but I guess I'm about to do just that. Seems like they know about me. And I don't know about them. That ain't good. So I'm gonna change it."

"Brad, in a sort of way, I'm in the same position. And I don't like it either. But be careful. Just in case they're the same people. They've followed me, and my girlfriend Iona. Really threatened us both."

"Well, I s'pose with this guy Charlie here they shot at, I have the perfect guide."

"Maybe. Just don't you assume those shots at him were some fluke. And keep quiet about it all. Careful who you trust."

By mid-afternoon, the small plane was flying over the track where Brad had made the emergency landing. This time there was no snow.

"Which way?" Brad spun a finger round in the air. He knew this was old silver-mining country, but wasn't sure what they were looking for now. It would be some sort of settlement he assumed. Because of the engine noise, he'd instructed Charlie, who was now sitting beside him in the two-seater, on some basic signals. Charlie, who was clutching a black plastic bag he'd collected from his truck, duly pointed up the track. A few minutes later, he pointed left – then suddenly backwards.

Brad, realising that Charlie was being confused with the view from the air, decided to start a more systematic search. He flew the small plane back about half the distance they'd come, then swung left and made increasing circles.

Those circuits had got to about five-miles radius, when Brad spotted something. Charlie had also leant forward with a raised thumb, so Brad banked over to take a look.

What soon lay below reminded him of Hollywood's version of a small wild-west town. In the middle of open scrub, was a half-mile 'street' with building frontages. The buildings had no depth, and the side streets went nowhere. One end of 'Main Street' ended in the parched grass, and the other end petered down to an access track.

Around it, there were no signs of people or vehicles. Brad checked the building heights, and for any cable poles, then he went in low, straight down the middle. Closer to, he realised this wasn't Hollywood Wild West. Those fronts were new in style, brick and concrete, shop fronts, modern-looking office fronts and a small apartment block. Maybe it was an abandoned film-set? But, there was a tidiness which wasn't right for a derelict place. And he hadn't heard of anything like that, not way out here. No one made films here. Wrong climate. He pulled up again. Charlie tapped his shoulder and pointed in another direction, towards dense trees. Brad couldn't see anything there, but did as Charlie seemed to want.

Just before they had to turn to miss a ridge, Charlie pointed down. Brad made the steep turn and looked out of the side window. Something was down in there, under the thick tree-cover. But he couldn't make out quite what it was. A large truck perhaps?

At the edge of the trees, he levelled out again and skimmed over a wide area of open ground. It had been marked out in some way, in evenly-spaced parallel lines, about ten yards apart.

Then they were over bare earth beyond that. Here, below them was a ridged pattern of recent cultivation. But there were still no people coming out to look, or animals running. He noticed that for about the last fifty yards, before more trees, the ground was covered in bright red. It seemed completely wrong for up here in the mountains. He turned the plane round to look at it all again.

After several passes in the next fifteen minutes, there seemed to be nothing more to see. What was in the trees was almost certainly a dark-coloured truck, but Brad had solved nothing in his mind. Annoyed, he turned to head for Canon City. He had another idea.

About an hour after they'd hired a four-wheel-drive at the airport, Brad and Charlie turned into the start of that uphill track towards the Teller reservoir. By then, although there was still another hour to go before true sunset, the darkening mountain slopes to the west had already hidden the day's sun, and the light was fading fast. Brad began to have doubts.

"Just how well do you know the ground here?"

"Every tree and rock. Around this place, I could escape from anyone, now I know how they shoot."

"OK. Take care of us then."

At Charlie's instruction, they turned off the track before they reached the stretch where Brad had landed the plane, and Charlie's truck had been shot at. Then, driving through thick woods, just obeying instructions, Brad soon lost all sense of direction.

Eventually Charlie asked him to stop. Here, the cover of the trees had become thinner. Ahead, the ground rose more steeply, and was bare apart from occasional rocks sticking out.

Charlie got out, still holding that black plastic bag, which Brad was beginning to be curious about. With a wave of his hand indicating the direction to go, Charlie set off, walking uphill. Brad was soon struggling to keep up. He was grateful when, after about half an hour, Charlie's own progress became more careful. By then, the two of them were making their way through an outcrop of larger rocks at the top of a ridge.

"Dangerous now. They are over that bank," Charlie said in a whisper.

In the growing darkness, they moved into the cover of a small dip. With a rustling noise in the silence, Charlie at last opened his bag. It revealed two balaclava helmets and a large flashgun.

"Put this on," Charlie announced, handing over one of the balaclavas. "Wear it before you look over there. Some of my old tribe still move in these hills. They think these guys see human flesh in the dark."

"What's the flashgun for then?"

"They hate bright light as well."

Charlie slid his balaclava on and started to move up the slope. Brad copied him and soon they were both peering cautiously at what lay down a hundred-metre slope. The light was fading, but Brad could see they were on the ridge he had earlier banked the plane to avoid. Then, before Brad had the chance to register anything, Charlie pulled him down again.

"That big truck. It's the one I said came here."

"OK. Just give me a chance to see it myself," Brad whispered tersely and crawled back up again. The semi, well tucked into those trees, had clean shiny black paint with no markings. It looked oddly out of place here in the dirt of the mountains. There was no activity around it, or anywhere else.

After a quarter of an hour, during which their eyes adjusted faster than the enveloping darkness fell, nothing changed. Brad wanted to get a closer look while they still had some light, but when he went to move, Charlie fiercely gestured for him to stay still.

Then, it was as if a switch had been flipped. In the gloom down in front of them, something was happening. Brad made out about thirty people emerging from the darkness of the trees. No one said anything. Instead, they seemed to be making signs to each other – a bit like the people who'd surrounded his plane, Brad thought.

After a few minutes of this silent movement, a driver had jumped into the semi and an engine started. The truck's tailgate wound up and some small handcarts were pulled forward as if to load the trailer. Two things hit Brad. The noise wasn't the truck's main engine, but probably a refrigeration unit. That almost confirmed the other, much worse, thing. Those oddly-shaped dark things about to be loaded, were body bags. The air around him seemed suddenly ten-degrees colder.

He hauled Charlie down sharply. "Those look like they've human corpses in them."

"Believe me now?"

Brad gave himself a few seconds to get calmer, and then raised his head again. The light was fading fast now and the darkness frustrated him. Wanting to get a better look, he scurried sideways along the shallow trench. It put him a bit closer, but in the failing light he couldn't see much more from there. He strained forward and guessed there were about eighty bodies in the queue of trolleys.

Suddenly, the pattern of movement froze. Next, the vague figures seemed to be running in different directions. With every second, the barely-visible scene looked more confused.

Charlie nearly wrenched his head off. "They've seen us. Follow me. And run!" He set off over the back of the ridge, and was soon running fast, downhill, between barely-visible rocks. To avoid hitting the boulders they were running between, Brad desperately tried to follow tight in Charlie's footsteps. But he soon started to fall behind, and a couple of times bounced hard off rough stone.

Soon he'd completely lost sight of Charlie in the darkness. Then he smashed almost head-on into a rock and fell sideways, arms windmilling.

"I can't do it," he croaked as he got up again, not knowing if Charlie could even hear.

A gunshot rang out, and Brad heard that unmistakable *thwuck,* of a bullet parting the air a few inches away from his head. The shock forced him to drag out one more impossible effort, and he stumbled on, blind. They'd been running through the bottom of gullies – but suddenly the echo of surrounding rocks was gone. They were in exposed ground. Those guys had guns. Why was Charlie leading him out into an open turkey shoot? Here, he had to keep going, but couldn't. In another thirty seconds, Brad, more used to sitting in front of a computer, was at his final limit, lungs seared with pain and his legs about to collapse under him. He stopped, standing as if frozen in a nightmare.

Out of nowhere, Charlie ran into him, knocking him into the dirt, then holding him there.

There was a blinding flash of light beside him. It instantly turned the blackness into a brilliant high-resolution scene. Captured in that picture were about thirty running figures. For a few seconds the image stayed imprinted on Brad's retina, and he saw their pursuers were male, although some seemed to be little older than boys.

"Face down!" Charlie growled in his ear.

Brad saw every grain of dirt as Charlie fired the enormous flashgun once more, and then a third time.

"Up you get."

Brad struggled to obey, but somebody knocked into him.

"They'll get us," he shouted.

"No. They can't see for a while."

Whoever had run into Brad, didn't attack.

"How long does it last?"

"A few minutes."

"Then I can't make it back to the truck."

"I know that. They don't."

Taking Brad's arm, Charlie started walking, quickly and quietly, in the direction they'd come from. Soon, sensing again the slight change in sounds, Brad could tell they were back between the walls of rock.

Charlie stopped. Then, a hard push to Brad's back started him climbing a sloping rock-face, his soft fingernails breaking on its hard surface as he dragged himself up, seeing nothing. His next grab for a handhold only found air. Brad plunged forward, falling in the darkness, hands stretched forward in instinctive fear. Then he was sliding, headfirst down a rock slope, banging his nose and forehead.

There was a crunching split-second of impact – then nothing more.

Brad didn't know how long it was before he was next aware – first of how much his head hurt. The memory of that fall began to form. He brought his hands up to feel the wounds. His nose, forehead and the back of his head were too painful to touch. The balaclava was still on, and felt damp.

"Charlie?"

"Good," was in a quick whisper. "You are OK then. But stay quiet. And don't move."

The throbbing pain got worse. It didn't help that Brad was lying, head down, wedged into a steep narrow gap in the rock.

It seemed a long time later when Brad was aware of light somewhere above him, up beyond his feet. Charlie had noticed him turning to look at it. "OK. You can talk now."

"My head hurts. You pushed me over the top of a rock."

"No. Into a hiding place for us. I meant to do that. But not for you to hit yourself."

Brad could now make out that they were in a sloping and narrow fissure in the rock.

"Are those people still around?"

"Not here. I've listened hard. Good time to be going."

With that, Charlie started to worm his way upwards. Brad painfully wriggled to turn himself round, then followed.

When they reached the top of the opening in the rock, Brad saw why it had been such a good hiding place. It was a crevice at the back of a narrow ledge, above head-height, its entrance invisible from anywhere at ground level.

Charlie looked all round, then nodded. "Now let's go. No noise."

They slid down off the ledge, Brad with his feet first this time. Then they set off to find the Chevy. Charlie moved in a series of noiseless and quick short runs, using the cover of each large rock to stop and look ahead. Brad tried to copy. But, when they were in the trees again, he couldn't help making noises in the undergrowth, and each time he did, Charlie turned sharply. He'd seemed cool last night, but was now acting nervously.

Closer to the truck, he made Brad hide in some bushes.

"Wait here," he said. "In case they've found the truck and staked it." He slid silently away.

The blood all over Brad's face seemed to attract ants, and a few other things. He tried to take off the balaclava, but only managed to roll it up as far as his eyebrows. It felt too painful to tear away the bits which had now welded themselves with dried blood to the gashes in his forehead and the back of his skull.

Charlie's check took half an hour, but eventually he appeared again, surprising Brad who'd not heard him approach.

"Some tracks are around, but none at the truck," he whispered.

They still approached the Chevy carefully. Brad checked it for any signs that it had been booby-trapped or disabled.

"Once you start it, move quickly," Charlie said. "They will hear it."

Despite this warning, Brad beckoned for Charlie not to get in, and he carefully turned the ignition key at arms' length from outside the door. The engine fired, and there was no explosion. After they'd both leapt in, Charlie started screaming directions as Brad crashed through the undergrowth.

They only slowed when they were back on the track and several miles down it without any sign of pursuit. It had given Brad a bit of time to think about what had happened.

"We have to report this to the police. They could look for the truck. It had bodies in it."

Charlie shook his head. "It's sure to be too far away already. And it will look different now. All the goons can do is come up here. They will just see a community, like a load of places in America, people living by their own rules. The only way to find out what's going on is at night."

Suddenly something made sense to Brad. Yes. When those people had been round his plane in the dark, they'd accused him of spying. Not on foot, but from the air, maybe with an infra red camera? They'd searched the plane for something like that. So they didn't want that done.

"You're right. And I know what to do next," he said.

"Nothing with me", Charlie replied. "Now I'm sure my friend is dead. There is no more I can do. And they know who I am, and that I've come back here, twice."

"They know who I am too."

"Then you watch out for the signs. Always."

Brad had stopped the pickup at some lights.

"What do you mean?" he asked.

"I have to leave you here," Charlie said.

"I want you to explain more."

"No. We shouldn't be together."

Then the door was open, and Charlie was walking away.

"Look," yelled Brad, leaning over. "You can hide at my place in Denver if you need to. I'll be away for a week, but I'll tell Karl to expect you."

Charlie hadn't turned round. "Thanks," came the reply, drifting above his shoulder.

A horn sounded. The lights were green. Brad pulled away, heading back to the plane.

What the hell had Charlie meant by 'the signs'?

Five hours later, Brad was sitting, still agitated, in seat 1A of the Continental Airlines connection to Newark, on his way to see Kiri in England. He felt he was running from something, and wanted to hear that reassuring thud of the outside door being closed.

After taking off on the transatlantic leg, the gashes in his head started to throb and it took a few glasses of wine before he put his seat fully back and began to relax in the flying cocoon, almost soothed by the gentle bumping movements of the plane, and the hissing noise as its fuselage parted the air in front. His mind turned to Kiri's data from the strange communes. He wondered whether he would be able to get anything out of that computer of hers.

And what sort of power do you need to order a mass suicide?

Those thoughts mixed, and kept repeating themselves in an uneasy floating dream he couldn't break out of.

Chapter 7

It riles us to believe that we perceive the web they weave

Oxford, England

Tony Williams hoped he'd understand at least a couple of things better by the end of the day.

The first was just what had happened to his wife Kiri's health project. He knew it had some big problem, but when she'd first got back from Australia and Cyprus she'd been too frantically working on that computer to explain. That, irritable, or asleep. Now she'd gone all quiet about it. It was like she wasn't going to accept anything until the computer guy Brad O'Connor had confirmed it. Anyway, Brad was due here today so he might find out something at last. It would be the first time Tony had met the guy.

The second thing Tony hoped he was soon to know more about was that Swiss research job. This morning he was going to the interview.

Since the phone call from the head-hunter, Tony had tried all ways to find out about any laboratory in Switzerland doing anything like his now-secretive neural studies. He'd come up with absolutely nothing. It didn't make sense. Any neural research was pretty specialist, and Tony knew almost everyone who was doing it. OK, he'd kept some of his own recent work very low profile, but most academia is about self-publicity, not secrecy. He'd also checked for French or German-language stuff published from Switzerland. Again, nothing.

At least he'd confirmed the head-hunters existed, and that there was a Giles Owen-Winter working there. So, on the pretext of asking what information he should bring to the interview, Tony had called him.

That plummy voice had first sounded relaxed and friendly. "You know, just the usual formal CV stuff. We already know a lot about you of course. My clients are very thorough and have read all your research papers."

That caused a frown on Tony's face, although he knew the university had to make these available if asked. But it was also the opening he'd wanted.

"Well, that's exactly the point. I would also like to do some mugging up on the work they've done so far. Is it on their web site maybe? I can't find one though."

There was a silence, as if someone at the other end had clamped their hand over Owen-Winter's mouth.

"That sort of thing can wait I'm sure," was all he'd eventually said.

"Then I'm not sure I should be taking this seriously. And maybe you don't know anything about it yourself? So I don't see the point of coming to an interview with you."

Another long pause.

"Let me assure you I make myself fully familiar with each commission. Also be assured that our thinking is well advanced. So, if things go well at your first interview, in all probability we will fly you out to Switzerland to visit the laboratory for more detailed discussions."

"So you are certain yourself that the research they are doing is similar to my work on neural interceptors?"

"Exactly old boy. Discussed it in detail with them. But I must go. Keeping someone waiting." The line had gone dead.

Tony had put his phone down slowly. There was no such thing as a neural interceptor.

That had been two days back, but he'd decided to go along anyway, out of curiosity if nothing else. Now it was eight in the morning and getting close for making the London train. He called out to Kiri.

"This mystery interview. Don't know quite how long it will take, not long I think, so try not to start lunch without me. I'll phone as soon as I get out," he finished, hurrying out to catch the eight-thirty. "See you later."

"Hope you get the job!"

Kiri had already been up for about three hours doing a last check of her project data on the computer before Brad arrived. As far as the university knew, she was still sick from something she'd picked up in Cyprus. Brad was going to use her terminal in the house.

It was the first time Tony had ever asked a taxi driver to take him to 'St. James's Square'. It made him feel a bit important.

Then, when he arrived, the huge and sumptuous entrance hall, combined with the dismissively-cold receptionist, had the opposite effect. Tony sat awkwardly on the low chair he'd been directed to, and sipped at the offered cup of coffee. The day's Financial Times lay on the large, even-lower, expensive-looking, pale-coloured wooden table in front of him. Picking the paper up, he pretended to be interested in it.

About five minutes later, a man walked up and, in that plummy voice, Owen-Winter effusively introduced himself. He then led Tony to a lift, asking him how the journey had gone. Mid height, grey suit, grey hair, but tanned, Tony noticed.

The corridor on the fourth floor was much less grand than downstairs, and the interview room he was shown into was small. Its only window looked out at a blank brick-wall about ten feet away.

"Please sit down," Owen-Winter waved his hand towards one of the two chairs in front of the desk, then he sat himself in the larger chair behind it.

After the openings, Tony had then expected at least a bit of information about the Swiss laboratory. Instead, Owen-Winter started with a rambling series of questions about Tony's politics and his involvement with CND, Greenpeace, and a few others. And all several times over. It seemed like the man was unsure himself what he was trying to find out. The result was a mess.

Tony guessed that all this protest-movement stuff would be counting against him. He'd been fairly active in all of them. That was the reason for the questions. But he didn't avoid the answers. All this time, although Owen-Winter had a pad in front of him, not much was being written on it. He didn't even seem to be listening to Tony most of the time.

After about half an hour of this, Owen-Winter looked at his watch.

"Would you like another coffee?"

Tony just wanted a break. "Yes, please."

"Well, let's stretch our legs."

Owen-Winter led Tony to a small kitchen area and took two cups from a cupboard by the coffee machine.

Standing up made Tony realise that the first cup he'd had in reception was already having an effect. "But first," he asked, "where's the toilet please?"

"Turn left out of here. Just beside the staircase." There was a wave in the general direction.

By the time he came back along the corridor, Tony, puzzled by the whole thing so far, had decided to try something. He caught Owen-Winter about to pick up the two cups of fresh coffee.

"While it's on my mind," he announced, in his usual slow and deliberate diction, as if weighing each word. "I've been thinking about what's being said about carbon dioxide as a greenhouse gas."

"Great. We can cover that back in the interview room."

"No, wait, I've started here so I'll finish," Tony said, now as if joking. "I think it's all nonsense. Just the Greens cashing in on public ignorance."

Owen-Winter just turned his head and looked blank, after this apparently out-of-character remark.

"You see," Tony continued." The absorption spectrum of carbon dioxide is narrow and, with just its naturally occurring levels, it is already electromagnetically opaque across that specific bandwidth. So any more concentration adds nothing to the total greenhouse effect, you see?" Owen-Winter just nodded, finally picking up the cups and heading back to the interview room.

Then it was back to repeated questions, this time latching onto the animal-rights stuff, Tony's most violent episode. Although he'd now dropped that, he again decided not to be apologetic about it all, now sure he was failing the interview anyway.

Then came what Tony had half-expected. A comment from Owen-Winter, trying to sound casual. "Oh yes. Back in the kitchen, you were telling me something about carbon dioxide."

"Yes."

"Well, could you explain a bit more?"

You mean repeat it. "Certainly. What I've worked out is that over a narrow valency-spectrum, and with short-wavelength electromagnetic radiation, it can be absorbed by other compounds, bringing them to acidic saturation."

There was a look of suspicion from Owen-Winter. "So that's what you were saying before?"

Tony nodded vigorously.

And it was as if this had somehow ended the interview. "Please wait here," Owen-Winter suddenly said, and walked out.

Tony knew the guy wasn't stupid enough to have completely fallen for that – more like he just couldn't be bothered asking any more. But this was now a complete waste of his own time. He paced around the small room. Kiri's visitors would be arriving.

He was still standing when Owen-Winter walked in again, sat behind the desk, and slowly put a few sheets of paper in front of him. Obeying a motioned hand, Tony sat again.

Owen-Winter looked down, obviously reading now. "The initial interview has been almost all satisfactory," Tony was amazed to hear. This had to be a joke. But the man continued. "The natural environment of this planet, its plants and animals, is of overriding concern to my clients. You have shown a long history of those beliefs."

Tony realised the interview maybe hadn't been quite what he'd thought, and tried to adjust. "Yes. And I still have the beliefs, although I'm not as active now. Which I'm sure you know."

Owen-Winter ignored the comment and continued, still from his script. "Now I can tell you more. My clients' project is to predict what will happen to this earth if humanity carries on destroying and polluting it."

"That is good." Tony said slowly. "We need something to frighten some sense into politicians who don't see any further than the continuance of their own salaries and power. Or use the issue just as a way of self publicising – and raising taxes."

"Yes. And how my clients are making these predictions, is with a series of experiments, and some powerful computers, to model the planet as if it were a living thing."

Tony nodded. "I know about that concept. Gaia, after the Greek goddess of the earth. It was conceived by James Lovelock. It sees the earth as a stable, self-regulating, organism. But the question still is, can it survive what we are doing to it?"

Owen-Winter again carried on as if Tony had said nothing. "My clients are analysing all the chemical and biological forces acting on the earth, and the ways to manage their consequences in the next thousand, or even ten-thousand, years."

Now Tony was perplexed about something else. "OK. That's all great and fine. But I'm a neuroscientist. How does that fit in?"

Owen-Winter looked down, and obviously found something in his papers about that. "Much of your work has been in investigating the parts of the brain which influence peoples' reactions when they are under stress?"

"Yes, in a way," Tony replied guardedly. "But I would see it as way off beam for what you say your people are doing. So why are they interested in me?"

"No, it is not, 'off beam', as you say. You see, my clients need to know how humans might react to increasing social pressures as the planet becomes overpopulated."

Tony just nodded. *That was just about credible? No, not really.*

Owen-Winter had continued. "They have reviewed your recent interesting paper suggesting biological control of extreme behaviour? You also mentioned possible agents which could act the opposite way, to stimulate people into violence."

They dug deep to find that. And where is he going? "Theoretically, yes," was all he said.

"For all that work, this would be an opportunity for you to take your research much further forwards. You would have unlimited finance and the use of the best computers. Surely this would interest you? My clients have many of the O'Connor super-computers."

What a coincidence then. "Yes. Interesting. Put like that," Tony replied slowly. "But how long has this project been running? And why haven't I heard anything about it?"

"I am not able to give any further details at this stage."

"What a pity. How can we possibly go any further then?"

"As I had indicated, my clients will now wish you to visit the laboratory in Switzerland for a day. There is much urgency in this programme. We will fly out next Wednesday. I will meet you at nine o'clock in the morning at Southampton Airport."

"Oh. It's like I don't have a choice?"

Owen-Winter's expression just showed irritation.

"OK," Tony continued. "Let me think on it and I'll let you know tomorrow."

"I will convey that message."

Tony followed Owen-Winter out of the small room. They took the lift back down to the foyer, this time in silence.

Tony got back home at one o'clock. Kiri immediately came through to the hall. Her face was pale and her eyes slightly reddened.

He guessed the reason. "The news on your project? It's not good?"

"No. Brad's been on the computer for a few hours. I think he's confirmed the results are all wrong. He's still back there in the study."

"Leave him there then." He held her closer and kissed her. "Do you still want to do this lunch?"

"Yes. I'll be fine. I sort of knew as much anyway. And it gives us a chance to explain to you what's happened."

"About time." Then his face changed. "And remind me why that man Rossi is coming. I don't really take to him."

"Brad needs to talk to Peter about something that's happened in America. I know how you feel, but he has tried to help me with the project a few times, so I said he could come along." And, before Tony could comment on that, as he was about to, she continued, "Anyway, how did your interview go?"

"That was the strangest meeting in my life."

The doorbell rang. "But I'll tell you about it later."

Tony only gave a half-hearted greeting as Peter Rossi walked in. "Hello again. Good timing. We can do all the introductions at once. Ah, but of course, you've met Brad O'Connor before?"

"Hello. And yes. A few times."

Kiri had now brought Brad in from the study. Tony turned, inadvertently pausing in surprise at what he saw. Then he extended his hand. "Tony Williams. And you are the famous Brad O'Connor. Welcome to Oxford."

"Thanks. But I ain't so sure I feel too famous right now. And hello again Peter."

The two other men stood and looked at Brad. With the scars all over his forehead, he looked in a terrible state. He was rotating his shoulders and gently rubbing his eyes, obviously weary from an overnight flight and a few hours at the computer terminal.

"Good God mate," Peter eventually exclaimed. "Is that the result of the little exploration you told me about?"

"Fraid so." Brad lightly touched swollen red weals. "I ducked out on explaining these to Kiri so far. I wanted to get on with her project. But I'll take a break now, and tell y'all about it."

"So how's the bloke you went with?" Peter asked.

"Charlie. He's OK. And I'd be dead meat if it wasn't for that guy."

"Talking of dead meat," Tony quipped. "We've got some cold lunch and a spot of wine in the fridge. I'll get them."

Once Tony had returned and sat at the table, Brad started to explain the gashes in his head, touching them carefully again, "This was a bad encounter with a crazy sect. Or at least their successors. The first lot I met seemed to have all killed themselves."

Peter Rossi held his hands up. "Woah. Too fast. This is what I wanted to hear about remember. And please can you go right back to the first things that happened to Charlie?"

It then took Brad a good half-hour, interrupted by a few questions from Peter, to explain what had happened, first to Charlie on his own, then to the two of them.

At the end, they all looked to Peter to react first. He seemed reluctant to speak, but eventually did. "I've heard more than I expected. You've added something new there Brad. Show me those hand signals again, like the people by your plane did."

Brad's slowly-moved arms and swivelled hands looked a bit like Thai dancing movements. But it seemed to make Peter's mind up about something. "Look you lot. This is not for repeating. I was told never to tell anyone. But it was ten years ago now, so maybe it's OK."

By the end of Peter's recounting of what had happened in Jordan, and his repetition of those silent hand-signals he'd seen by the red lake, Tony seemed to be getting agitated.

"Can I just get a grip on where we're going?" he said. "I thought this meeting was to explain what's happened on Kiri's project."

"Yes. Sorry about the diversion, mate," Peter replied. "What went on in Jordan's been on my mind a long time. Never made any sense. Then suddenly there's this weird connection with what Brad just said. With those hand signals."

Tony nodded. "OK then. Interesting. But can we get to Kiri's project now? Let her and Brad tell us exactly what has happened to it." He turned to Kiri. "Are you OK to do that?"

She nodded. Then, with the interruptions and questions, Kiri also took about half-an-hour in explanation, and in the end turned with a despairing look to Brad.

"Nope. It's not good," he confirmed. "I think I pretty well proved this morning that the project's dead. Sure for the moment anyway. But it's like there's these strange things I don't understand. Sort of connections. Like, what's with those two places? Just the same, so far apart, and with more of them too, at least according to her computer. Then the black trucks and the red sheeting on the ground were the same as I saw in the Rockies. Now this Peter's thing. It just gets weirder."

Tony was beginning to feel detached. This was too unreal. "Just a minute. Can I do a bit of the devil's advocate bit? Brad, for example, you don't really know they were loading bodies into that truck. It just looked like it. And this hand-sign thing Brad and Peter saw?" He turned to Peter. "Ten years is a long time to remember something like that."

"Wait a tick, sunshine. It may be. But I'd never bloody forget it. We *killed* people on the way out remember. And I was told never to tell anyone. So think yourself lucky. "

"OK. Calm down. I'm just confused about just what we think's going on here." Tony turned to Kiri. "You say the black trucks Brad saw in the mountains were like the ones you saw in Australia and Cyprus? One black truck looks like another. And the same with the cultivation under red sheeting. Maybe it's a new technique used in lots of places? It's just that we don't know about it." He shrugged his shoulders and held his palms out.

"There is more," Peter said quietly. "But I'm not sure I'm sure I should be telling you in particular about it." He looked directly at Tony.

"And why not?"

"I don't talk much to anyone about my job. Armaments are a serious business, and secrecy is everything. And I know about your green, pacifist, anti-nuclear, animal rights, and God knows what else, leanings."

"I'm also a doctor. I know all about confidentiality. And I have this feeling that something about all this is getting to you. You need to talk about it. Am I right?"

"OK. Well done – doctor." Then Peter seemed to relax. "Yes. It was those gunshots at Charlie. Dead accurate, and in the dark. Maybe I know a connection. A while back, I got a very strange upgrade order for some of my training systems. The customer was very secretive. No. That's usual. This lot were fucking paranoid. Anyway, all my systems have simulated targets for the trainees to aim at. Well, this customer in Costa Rica – and shit – I didn't mean to mention the place. Anyway, they asked me to make up only civilian scenes. Like ordinary streets with people walking around. *And* they ordered an incredible spec. The light level they wanted was very, very, low. With the target areas very small."

"So," Tony summarised in his usual slow voice, "you supplied systems to these people, to train them to shoot civilians, accurately, and in the dark?"

There was silence around the table.

Peter looked around them, almost defensively now. "No. I'm not too chuffed either. And sorry, it gets worse. I haven't told you how many upgrades I delivered. Whoever it is bought them, now have enough systems to train whole armies. And they were in a hell of a hurry."

"So it's gotta be all thanks to you that I was shot at?" Brad remarked.

"I know you don't really like my business either, Brad. But this order wasn't normal. I was seriously threatened. I didn't think I had a choice."

"So where did all this kit go to?" Brad asked.

"All over the world, as far as I can tell. The original equipment orders were all organised by this guy Rawlings. Lives in Jordan. Dealt with him for years. But it's been nearly all secretive stuff more recently. So secret, my records are only as far as the local handling agents. Then the stuff vanishes. And the payments were from obscure companies in Switzerland. All different."

"It's all happening there then," Tony joked. "Amazingly, I passed a weird interview this morning. And they want me to go off to visit some secret place – in Switzerland," he added, raising his eyebrows. "Funny that."

"So what was weird?" Peter asked.

"Well, this pompous head hunter was like a ventriloquist's dummy. I'm certain he was reading the questions, and someone else was listening in to the answers via a mike. It was all about this huge research lab, so this headhunter says, doing work which includes my neural stuff. And I've never heard of anything like it. They won't tell me either."

He turned to Brad. "And another strange thing. If I'm to believe it all, this place in Switzerland has lots of your computers."

Brad looked as if he'd tried to frown, but actually winced slightly. "Heh, don't assume that's wrong. I just did get some funny orders from there a while back. A bunch of them each time. But sure secretive. The *only* times we haven't been involved in helping a customer with the application. Confident guys to use them without our help."

"Right, you lot," Peter interrupted, picking up his briefcase and pulling out a laptop. "That's enough talking. There's now something we can do to see if there is a connection." He sorted through a few CD ROMs and held one up. "I've got my sales records on this. At least it has details of what was ordered, when, and how they were paid for. Have you got the same Brad?"

"Sure. I can get all the info on the Swiss orders from my computer, Tron." He stood, then went into the study to the terminal he'd worked on during the morning, and was soon rattling at the keys.

Tony and Kiri seemed as if all this had left them behind. They settled for clearing the remains of the lunch.

"We've found something," Peter announced about twenty minutes later, shouting through to the kitchen.

"OK," Tony said as they both returned. "Can we hear it then?"

"We can't get any company names to match. Not surprising. Every one of my trainer orders pretends to be from a different outfit anyway. Brad's two orders are also from different names. But it looks like the bastards made a couple of slip-ups with their banking arrangements. We both know where our Swiss payments came from. All mine have bank and account details which are different from each other. But, with Brad's two payment transfers, *each* corresponds with *one* of mine. Twice an identical bank and account reference. There's a crossover they missed. Didn't expect us to compare details like this, did they?"

Brad nodded. "Sure didn't."

"Pity then," Tony said slowly. "You two seem to be pleased. But, if that's all, there's no way we can investigate it. Check on Swiss banks?"

"Why do you carry on being so bloody negative?" was Peter's response. Then he held his hands up. "No. Sorry about that. But we can at least try and find out more. Anyway, I'm going to do that, whatever you lot do. As it happens, I'm going out to Singapore next week. What I'll do is stop off in Jordan and take another look at that red river and the funny lot by the mud pool. These buggers took on the wrong bloke. I don't like being threatened. And it's long enough for them to have forgotten me. I hope."

Brad was nodding approvingly at that. "And I don't like people taking shots at me. So I'm about to find out more as well. What those guys who came all round my plane seemed to be really worried about, was being spied on from the air – at night. In the day, it's like they do nothing anyway. And they can defend themselves on the ground at night. Like sure scared the shit out of us. But they can't hide from a plane with an infra red camera. So I'm on my way back to the US, first thing tomorrow, and I'm gonna to do exactly that to them. My other stuff will have to wait."

Tony looked back at the two of them. "I suppose I was going to do something anyway. Like go to this Swiss interview. Apart from anything, if something like my extreme behaviour work is going on there, I ought to know about it."

"That's all fun then," Kiri announced. "All of you off doing your things?"

Tony looked back at her. Had she deliberately sounded like she'd been talking to three small boys? His tone changed. "Look. I'm sorry. Christ, we're getting all exited, and you've just lost ten years' work."

Kiri looked sullenly back.

"But if some group has done that to you, don't you want to know more?"

"Yes. I suppose I do," she eventually said.

"And then we meet up again?" Tony asked around.

He got nods.

"How about a week's time then? You've got to come the furthest Brad. Could you make it back here then?"

"Yeh. I need to anyway. So that would be fine."

"Slow down lads," Peter interrupted. "As a bloke in this sort of business, could I put in a bit of professional caution here. Let's just think on this. We might be about to stick our little noses into the business of a dangerous bunch, who definitely don't like publicity. What if they find out, and have a bit of an opinion about that?"

"How would they know we're even connected or doing anything?"

"Obviously they know about Kiri, and that she lives right here," Peter said. "Now Brad's here. That's a connection. And somehow, they watch. When I was making those mod kits for them, they were always around, like a bad smell. Believe me, if they think you're a problem to them, they'll be watching you. And Kiri, you might be a problem. You've found a couple of their places with that computer."

"OK. Maybe I did get that warning in Australia. That arsehole Isaacs in Alice Springs said not to spy anymore. But, probably all I did out there was tell them that they've screwed my project with all that nonsense data. They should feel safe about me now. So why bother watching?"

"Maybe. But what about you Brad?"

"Well, I've sure seriously spied on them, and Charlie did tell me to watch out. For the signs, he said. But I caught the plane over here to the UK so soon after. They couldn't possibly have had time to latch on and trace me here. But I'll be damn careful when I go back though."

Peter looked for Tony's response. "I suppose I'm OK," he replied. "If they really want me to join them, they won't think I'm a threat will they?"

"Not quite so. Whoever's in charge over there is obsessed about security. Frightened of being known. That's why they got a dummy to do the interview with you, and the main man listened to the answers, probably from Switzerland. So you might just be taking the biggest risk of all. Looks like they may be about to let you in on something? For sure they'll keep tabs on you after that – or worse if you don't cooperate."

"Maybe I shouldn't go then? I don't really believe the job exists anyway."

Kiri looked over. "I thought you were doing it for me?"

"Look, from what's happened to me," Peter came in, "you may already be in too far. If it's the same people, they get what they want. Maybe best to find out more. But watch your back. All the time. And the connection to you will make this place here dangerous." He paused. "Too dangerous. We need somewhere else to meet next week. Kiri, can I use your phone privately in the kitchen? I need to make a call which could be a bit sensitive."

He returned a few minutes later, smiling slightly. "My girlfriend Iona agrees we can meet next time at her place. It must be the safest. But everyone must be careful going there. Don't get followed."

"So how would we know if we *are* being?" Tony asked.

Peter pulled a quizzical face. "Well. That's a peculiar sodding thing. They use so many people, so they're doing it seriously. But then, if you do a bit of looking around, they are so bleedin' obvious. Also, once you've clocked them, they aren't that difficult to lose. In fact, I even used to drive deliberately slowly so as not to annoy them. Mostly I didn't see the point of getting their knickers all twisted up. So watch carefully, and, if you really need to, run or drive fast. Incidentally, their being so obvious is why I'm sure they're not following me anymore since I made that delivery."

Then, even while Peter was giving the directions to Iona's cottage, Brad succumbed to his night in the mountains and an overnight flight, and was slumped forward onto the table.

Kiri looked over at the inert figure. "We'll look after him and tell him where we're meeting up."

"Mind if I take a look through that computer data of yours?" Peter asked.

"Help yourself."

Chapter 8

Wash me clean

To South of Amman, Jordan

It was late evening before Peter left the Williams' house. He'd got nothing new from that nonsensical information in her computer.

He looked carefully around, but tried not to make that too obvious. There was a car up the road with someone in it. A small Peugeot. It wouldn't have been able to stay with him anyway. He wasn't about to play the easy to follow game right now. But, as he pulled away, it didn't move, so he assumed it was innocent enough.

His route, cutting down from the M40 to the M4, would take him within a hundred yards of Iona's place in Bisham. But, after today's discoveries, he didn't want to risk it. He called her, without saying how close he was. She promised he could stay the night next week, after he'd met up again with the Williams' and Brad there. Even if they were all wasting their time with this stuff, that would make it worthwhile.

As he slowed for the roundabout where he could almost see Iona's small cottage, it was so tempting to swing right. Almost in determination not to, he pulled the steering-wheel hard right to take the first exit and, with a squeal of tyres, accelerated the BMW hard up the steep dual-carriageway. With no traffic at this time of night, and knowing where all the cameras were, his apartment was now only twenty minutes away.

The road ahead was straight but undulating, and the headlights' almost-solid beams swung up and down, cutting through the blackness, sometimes catching trees half a mile away. The engine hummed louder as Peter knocked the gear stick to the left to engage sport mode, then forwards to force a downshift, giving a jolt of acceleration down into a sharp dip. He felt himself forced down into the seat as the car swooped through the bottom and accelerated on out.

Soon near to home, Peter turned the car off the main road and slowed it almost to a crawl. A few minutes later it rolled, almost silently, to the private parking spot outside his Windsor apartment. The remote-lock briefly flashed the indicator lights as he walked up the front steps. Then everything was silent as Peter stopped in front of his door. In that second, he heard the faint but distinctive beeps of a mobile phone being used. Involuntarily he spun round.

Thinking fast now, he realised that if someone was watching, it would be better if they didn't know their quarry had realised it. To pretend he hadn't noticed anything, he justified the sudden turn by immediately going back down the steps, two at a time, and striding back to the car, muttering to himself, then taking out a couple of maps. He locked it again and returned, walking casually, without looking round, back up to his front door.

But why was someone out there? Shit, yes. After they'd told Tony about the job in Switzerland, those people must have already started to keep watch on his house, and of course seen all of them there. If that guy in the car outside Tony's place had recognised him, or phoned his photo to someone who did, no one would've needed to follow, just put someone here.

As soon as he got inside, Peter decided he had to warn Tony, and pulled his own mobile phone out. He was surprised when the call was answered at the first ring, and more so when he realised it was Brad's voice.

"Christ. I didn't think you'd be conscious for a long time yet."

"Wish I wasn't. Tony & Kiri have gone to bed. But I suddenly woke up. Realised there was something else that puzzled me."

"Like?"

"Well. You know Kiri went to those places in Australia and Cyprus because the data she'd collected on the computer showed they were unusual. But they weren't the only ones, she said. So I took a look at some of the others, and found one was near Canon City, back home. It's just gotta be the place Charlie and I went to. Real strange. And there's one in Switzerland. Haven't heard of the place though. Anyway, why're you calling?"

"Because I've just had a nasty surprise mate. Got back home – and to a welcome. Someone watching for me here. It must be they first spotted me back there with you lot. That's bad news. Have you noticed anything suspicious?"

"Kiri thought a couple of cars coming past looked a bit slow."

"What sort of phone line is that you're on now?"

"Kiri's broadband through the local cable."

"That's pretty secure then. OK. We now have to assume we were all seen there. So, when they eyeballed me and worked out who I was, they didn't bother chasing me, just put someone to stake out my apartment. All a bloody nuisance. They know we've been talking to each other. I suppose they could think you and I were helping Kiri with her project – just about."

"What do we do then?" Brad asked. "I'm on an early-morning flight out."

"OK, when you leave, it's maybe best to pretend you're not suspicious about anything. Don't even look round. That way, they don't know that you know, and you have that advantage, OK? But, if some day you really need to lose them, like I said, driving fast or running through a crowd seems to do it. I want to test that a bit more myself though."

"What about Tony and Kiri?"

"Well, tell them. Then I suppose they'll just have to put up with it. They're not about to do anything these people don't already know about."

"OK. Sure will do. I'll get some more sleep now. See you at Iona's place when I get back over next week. I'll get directions from Tony and Kiri in the morning."

"Good. And for Christ's sake, make sure you're all careful when you go to Iona's."

"Don't y'all worry. We will."

Peter turned the phone off. "Right. I'll show the bastards who they're up against," he whispered.

In the next two days, Peter made complex preparations for his trip to Singapore, now to be via Jordan.

He took a few trial car-journeys, and discovered that he was always followed. By doing a few tests, he reconfirmed it wasn't too difficult to shed these tails, and without doing any completely mad driving. So he took to making some journeys with this company, and at other times making an impatient burst through traffic and dropping them. The fact that it all seemed so optional, puzzled him. What actually disturbed him though, was that there were several cars and, either a lot of disguises or about twenty people. How could he be that important?

Using his mobile, Peter modified the airline booking for his Singapore trip, to divert through Amman. He paid the difference with a credit card he hadn't used for a while. Then he arranged the cover for his departure.

In the ten years since his last visit to Jordan, Peter's football had turned more to coaching. He was getting too old to enjoy being kicked around. And he'd taken up golf, also to Iona's disgust, but it was about to be useful.

Almost hoping that his fixed-line apartment phone was bugged, Peter used it to call some Scottish golf clubs. He asked each of them about green fees, the chances of getting a game if he turned up on spec', and what the conditions were like. By the end, he almost fancied doing that instead.

It was only on the final evening in his apartment, Peter remembered those photos he'd taken in Jordan on his last visit ten years ago. And it took most of the evening going though old disks before he traced them. He was relieved when, after the intervening three computers and different operating systems, they printed out OK.

The next morning, dressed in those light-coloured clothes golfers seem to like, he made a slow and obvious job of loading his clubs and a suitcase into the boot of the BMW. In the same manner, he then dawdled the car along the road for about fifteen miles, before he pulled a sudden move on his pursuer. This lost the small Ford with an ease which was beginning to almost worry Peter. Still suspicious about it being this simple, he drove a directionless route for another half hour, making absolutely sure that no other car, or several of them, had taken up the chase. After bursts of alternately going extremely fast and then very slowly, he was satisfied, and finally headed for the airport.

Ten hours later, the Jordanian customs man was looking through Peter's luggage, and suddenly seemed to pay more attention when he came across the photos of that red valley. There were a few seconds of silence as he scanned through them.

"I hope you take better ones this time."

Peter relaxed again, pleased with his decision to tuck the pictures into a ten-year old tourist book on Petra and Jerash, which he'd found near those old disks.

Once cleared of this dawn check, Peter hired a light-brown Toyota truck at the airport and set off towards the Jordanian desert to the south of Amman. He guessed he didn't have much time here to do what he wanted. Rawlings had contacts everywhere and it wouldn't be long before he found out.

He was very unsure of his chances of success. His first target was a distantly-remembered opening in fifty miles of closely-packed large rocks, the one they'd emerged from after the encounter at the red mud pool. Unfortunately, in those few photographs he had taken that day, all to Rawlings' annoyance he now remembered, a vital one he'd missed was a photo of that gap in the rocks.

After seven hours of stopping and looking at miles of huge rocks, Peter had seen nothing which he recognised, or even looked promising. He was now suffering badly from the overnight plane journey, with his six bottles of water almost gone, and so tired that he was on the point of giving up. Ten years after the incident, he now really hadn't a clue what rock shapes he was looking for.

Then, stopping again for what seemed like the thousandth time, he realised that the setting sun was exactly as it had been when he and Rawlings had driven out. And, in this light, he seemed to see a contour in the line of rocks which jogged a memory. He turned the Toyota to drive towards what looked like a slight opening there.

During his hours of searching, he'd seen no one and now wasn't even being careful anymore. Something brought him suddenly back to awareness. Becoming distinct against the rocks, he saw two men in sand-coloured tunics, and was already close enough to see they were holding guns. Gently, and keeping the same speed, he swung the Toyota slowly round so as not to head straight for them, hoping they hadn't spotted his original course. One of the men made a slight movement, and Peter crouched to make a smaller target for the shots he thought might come. He desperately resisted speeding up. That would probably have made it certain.

Eventually the distance increased and he relaxed, but it was a couple of minutes before he allowed himself to ponder his luck, apart from the fact that he wasn't dead. Why do you guard a gap in a pile of rocks? It had to mean he'd found what he was looking for. He noted the coordinates on the built-in sat nav. Also, it meant they didn't know yet that he was loose in Jordan, or they'd have had him for sure. But those guys would report that they'd seen something and, he reckoned by tomorrow, someone would've worked out who'd hired the truck. But anything he did would have to wait till morning. From what Brad had said, being in those rocks at night would be very dangerous.

Peter checked into an airport hotel, managing to register under a false name and give an American address. To go with this he spoke to the man at the check-in desk, in what he thought would pass here for a Southern States drawl.

"Just make sure you avoid any real Americans," he whispered to himself as he turned away from the counter.

From the small shop in the foyer, he bought a few newer guides and maps of the Dead Sea, Jerash and Petra areas. Planning to visit a few tourist places would look OK, he thought. It was time for something to eat. Taking the maps to the restaurant, he ate keeping his head low, as if studying them.

After the overnight journey and long day, he was glad to get an early night.

The next sign of trouble came early the next morning when Peter was about to leave the breakfast room. Two men had taken up positions by the door, and were now obviously scanning everyone who came past them, in and out, and occasionally stopping people.

Peter pushed himself into the middle of a group of surprised Germans who were just about to leave. *"Vans istra durgun archen Petra,"* he announced to them in music-hall German. It was nonsense, but made him seem momentarily part of the group as they went through the door. *"Vernschlachen vor pluchen?"* he added, getting confused shaken heads from the real Germans, as he stayed with them a bit longer.

Two hours later, the German-tourist act seemed to have worked. He'd driven slowly so as not to raise clouds of dust, and watched behind carefully. He was certain no one had followed.

It was mid morning and the sun was rising fast in a cloudless sky as he stopped again by the line of rocks, this time about a mile west from where those gunmen had been. He hid the truck as well as he could in the closely-packed wall of boulders.

After quickly eating a couple of sandwiches, he set off walking south to intercept the red river at a point somewhere below the noisy mud-pool. In his bag, he now had some water, a small compass, and his old-fashioned Olympus camera. Peter had wondered whether to take the digital one, but decided the old one had a better lens, and it was somehow the one he trusted more. It was a decision he was to regret.

Keeping out of sight in here wasn't a big problem. Making progress round the bases of the enormous boulders, was. He realised that to make each mile forwards, he'd have to walk two or three, and all of it in the baking airless heat reflected from the rock surfaces. Also, he could never see more than fifty yards in a straight line, and had taken so many blind alleys that he'd started to disbelieve even what his compass was showing. The sun, now straight overhead, was no use.

By mid-afternoon, Peter had no idea how much distance he'd made. He wouldn't dare spend a night here, and was worried about running out of time. He risked a climb to the top of one of the rocks. To the south was a definite valley. It had to be the course of the river.

After another half hour of increasingly desperate scrambling, the rocks around him at last became smaller. Now he was able to move faster, and almost scurried down the final slope to the bed of the valley.

It was dry. There was no red river there – in fact no red at all.

Was this the wrong place? In other ways it looked so right, exactly the sort of terrain he and Rawlings had driven the Land Rover through.

Now, forgetting how exposed he was, Peter moved around, kicking at the stones. They were oddly clean all over, almost as if they had been washed. He crouched against a two-foot-diameter boulder and, with a heave, rolled it over an inch. Swinging one arm down, Peter wedged a stone underneath it, and, forgetting about the things that live under rocks in deserts, his hand went into the small gap.

He stared at his emerging finger nails in triumphant disbelief. That red was exactly the shade he remembered. Peter moved his dirty fingers to beneath his nose, and sniffed. From that unpleasant and distinctive rotting-vegetation aroma, there was now no doubt. This was the place he'd been looking for. But why would a river vanish – and then someone scrub every stone to eliminate all traces of it? And still guard the place?

That thought made Peter aware of his open position. He pulled out his pen and scraped enough of the dried red muck from under the propped-up stone to half-fill the plastic top. Then he jammed it tightly back onto the end of the pen and scrambled back into the cover of the larger rocks.

Peter now wanted more than ever to see what was going on at that red pool. He had to do it now. The search could already be on for him, and he might not get a chance to come back. There was still just time. So he overrode the urge to run out of this place before the fast-falling night of these latitudes. Breaking into a run, and not using the cover of the rocks, he moved fast up the steep valley. Thank God, he thought, he still turned up at the football-club training sessions. He only slowed when the ground started to level out. It would be close to where that muddy lake was.

Now Peter stayed amongst the larger rocks, giving himself cover as he made his way up the final part of the old river-valley. The land around was almost flat here, just like he remembered from ten years ago.

Coming between two larger rocks, he gasped, dropped to the ground, and scrambled sideways into deeper cover. In front, he'd had a brief view of something which he couldn't begin to explain. After two days of the same scenery, Peter took some time to absorb the new image. It also meant there might be people there guarding it. He didn't move again immediately, but lay in the dust, thinking through what he had to do next.

Then, only lifting himself to his hands and knees this time, Peter crawled forward though the bottom of the channels. That thing came into view again, clear, even in the fading light. He was looking at the formidable frontage of a huge temple, although it wasn't in any style he recognised.

He sank down again. "I just don't believe that," he muttered, and then shuffled backwards into the cover of the larger rocks, where he sat and looked again at the maps and his few photos. They were telling him that, ten years ago, this was where the noisy red mud-pool had been. Everything else was right.

"So let's just get a few pictures, and then I'm out of this hell hole," he whispered to himself.

Holding the camera, he climbed up on one of the larger rocks to get the whole view. There were no other buildings there, just this huge ornate stone construction with four tall towers and a large statue above the main doorway. Around it was what looked like a construction site. It was as if the whole thing wasn't quite finished. Then he saw the guard.

He slid down again and banged his knees hard.

"Shit!" came out inadvertently, and too loudly. He froze – listening.

The man had been wearing the same sand-coloured camouflage as the two who'd been guarding the entrance. He was also carrying a gun, and was probably not alone. Peter knew that if they ever got just one sniff that he was in these rocks, he would be dead for sure. In this place, they were the masters.

But he was now running out of time to get those pictures. He crawled back up in slow motion. Looking more carefully for them, he now counted eight guards. Remembering what Brad had said, Peter realised their vision would be getting better by the minute in the quickening dusk.

He slid the camera out of its case, twice checked he'd suppressed the flash, and raised it.

After the first press of the shutter-button, the whir of the auto-wind-on seemed to echo all around the stones. Peter froze, staring forwards, but the guards didn't move. He wanted this over with, and rapidly took more shots in different directions and a couple, with full zoom, of that statue.

Peter inadvertently jerked when the auto-rewind started. He'd forgotten about that – and it went on and on. Forgetting the need to stay still, he dropped down and bent to hold the camera to his stomach, trying to smother the sound. It continued for what seemed like another age, then finally ended with a loud click. Peter stayed frozen, desperately listening, heart thumping. Why hadn't he counted the photos? He wanted to see if the guards had reacted, but realised that would be the worst thing to do. If they'd heard something, and were now looking this way, they would see the movement for sure.

After about ten minutes, he'd heard nothing. Now he just wanted to get out while he still had any daylight. He started running round the bases of the rocks, having to trust a compass he could only just see, and expecting one of those sandy-clothed gunmen round each new turn.

Suddenly he emerged from the rocks and turned left, back towards the Toyota. Then, in almost full darkness, he nearly went past it.

He made himself only sip at the spare water he'd left here, while he thought what to do next. Headlights, in the black of a moonless desert, would be visible over the horizon to those people. But he couldn't drive without them. He had to spend the night here, and then head off to the airport only when the sun was well up.

The next day, after driving across open desert for a time, Peter eventually found a dirt road which he saw from the sat nav headed towards the airport, running parallel to the main road. Perfect. He turned onto it.

After a few miles, he was seeing occasional low concrete buildings, and, half-an-hour later, the very welcome sight in the long distance of the airport's high control-tower. Peter knew he had to dump the Toyota soon. He'd hired it in his own name and they would be looking out for it by now, he was sure. Noticing the occasional crashed or half-cannibalised abandoned vehicle, Peter thought there was now enough dust on the Toyota for it not to look immediately out of place with them. He deliberately dropped it at forty-five degrees into a ditch before jumping out. That control tower was now shimmering in the heat, and he had an hour or so to walk.

He'd been going about half that time when there was a noise from behind. Glancing nervously round he saw a battered bus and, on an impulse, held his thumb out. Still, he was surprised when it stopped beside him. He climbed on, acknowledging the driver with a slow nod of thanks. This was good, he'd been beginning to feel conspicuous as he got closer to the airport. The bus was full of locals who, from their dress, looked like cleaning staff. Optimistically, Peter now thought this might be the perfect way in.

But, when they got nearer, his confidence sank again. He could see uniformed and armed soldiers checking all the vehicles. Jumping off now would be obvious. They were already too close. He lowered his head, as if in disinterest, and stayed where he was. He was lucky again. The soldiers, who were turning out the occupants of the cars and taxis, didn't seem to worry about a load of local cleaners.

When the bus stopped, Peter detached himself from the rest of its occupants and went round to the front doors of the terminal building. His fears were confirmed. Inside it was infested with security men, and worst of all was the Royal Jordanian check in. He was booked on their non-stop to Singapore. There were two policemen at every counter.

He turned and walked away. A quick check of the departures screen told him that the first alternative way out was on Gulf Air via Bahrain. He walked, trying to look as casual as he could, over to their ticket sales. Some seats were available, and he bought a one-way economy.

Thinking that if one thing in his luggage would draw attention it would be the camera, Peter removed the film he'd shot. He replaced it with a new roll and then took out the battery. Finally, to conceal the film, he used a trick which had so far worked every time for hiding photos, documents and memory sticks. He went into a toilet and found a half-used toilet roll, and pushed the film into the centre of, holding it there with some sheets of the paper. Then it went into his toilet bag. He'd found that very few casual searchers were keen to pick up a half-used bog roll in someone else's toiletries. And the film-roll's x-ray image wouldn't look too out of place in the various small containers and bubble packs also in the bag.

The camera did attract some attention but, with a few gesticulations, he showed how disgusted he'd been that the thing hadn't worked, and not taken any pictures.

He was through there just in time. As he left the departure hall, every airline's check-in desks came under full security. They must have realised he wasn't going to check in for the flight he was supposed to be on.

Peter had promised himself a special meal when he finally got to Singapore, and went straight to what he thought was one of the best Indian restaurants in the world, The Rang Mahal, under the Imperial Hotel. A meal here was something they always looked forward to when he came to Singapore with Iona. But he got little pleasure from it this time. Whatever was going on, was dragging him ever further in. They'd known he'd been into the country, tried to spy on them, and got out somehow. He had to make himself realise that something had now changed his life. He couldn't run the clock back, or decide not to play any more.

So, after a hurried end to the meal, he didn't go to the hotel he'd originally booked, but to one he hadn't used for years. It seemed tired and run-down now, but that was good. He relaxed a bit.

He still had to make the run back to England, but decided to leave it as late as possible, to get back just in time for the meeting they'd all arranged at Iona's place.

Peter only broke cover once, to risk doing a bit of shopping in one of the malls off Orchard Road. He needed a few clothes and personal things if he couldn't go back to his apartment. Passing by one of the fast film-processing shops, he noticed how they worked. It was ideal. He could stand and watch the film going through the machine, making sure there were no copies made. And he could see if anyone else was taking an interest.

Maybe an expert on religious architecture would have been mightily baffled, but the Chinese guy in the photo shop couldn't have looked more bored.

When the time finally came, he took the overnight to Frankfurt, less chance of anyone checking for him on that route. He also repeated the bog-roll trick, this time with the photos and negatives.

Once the plane was in the air, Peter's thoughts were forced to turn to the problems that now lay about eleven hours ahead. His attempts to find out more had solved nothing, just made it all even stranger and more dangerous. The enormity of not being able to go back to his own apartment, or office, began to settle in.

Chapter 9

Where the shadows run to themselves

Denver, USA

Brad was awakened by the soft Texan tones of the Houston-based flight attendant. "Sir. I'm afraid you'll have to de-plane now."

He opened his eyes and realised that all the seats around him were empty.

"I'm sorry."

She smiled. "Don't worry. You're the best passenger we had this flight. I wish I got a few more like you."

Collecting his carry-on bag, Brad only dimly remembered the early morning departure from Kiri and Tony's house. Before leaving, he'd ended up doing most of another night's work on that computer of hers. He'd realised that these people, whoever they were, might by now be aware of just how much data, pointing to them, had been collected by her project. He'd found a lot during the night. So, in the morning, he'd asked Kiri to go to the university, erase all the backups there, and withdraw all other access to her computer.

He'd noted that he hadn't been followed from their Oxford house. That all seemed a long time ago now. It had been a long journey via Houston, and he realised he must have fallen asleep immediately he got on the plane for the final leg. His seat back wasn't even reclined.

Brad emerged from the jet-way door, minutes after everyone else. Looking around he saw that Karl Matuik, his part-time aircraft mechanic, who was due to meet him, had started walking the other way, like he was about to abandon his wait in the concourse.

"I'm here, Karl."

"Brad. Where'd you come from? Thought I'd missed you someway."

"Sure sorry about that. Thanks for meeting me anyway."

"It's about all I can do though. I'd run you back to the house myself, but they've put me on a long shift at United tonight. I've fixed a limo for you. Let me take your bag." He grabbed the carry-on and set off towards the taxi pull-up. "All OK on your trip over there?"

"Yes. Just a few surprises. How about here?"

"That guy Charlie's at the house. Said it would be fine with you."

"Yeah," Brad replied, not really taking it in. "Told him he could. No problems with him being there?"

Karl shrugged. "Suppose not. I put him in one of the spare rooms over by the workshop. Only thing is, every time he spots anyone approaching, he's off like a jackrabbit that's seen a wolf. It's spooky to see anyone that frightened."

Brad's half-awake mind didn't really want to work on that. "Something must have happened then. I'll talk to him. But in the morning."

He slid into the back of the large white limo, reclined the seat the small distance it would go, and tried to sleep again.

Karl handed the bag to the driver, shut the door and gave a perfunctory wave to the inert Brad, before walking back into the terminal.

When the car started, Brad was only dimly aware of the turns and stops as they exited the multi-storey, and then soon succumbed to sleep again as the limo's engine became a steady drone. The next thing he knew was when the partition behind the driver slid down. "Which entrance, boss?"

Brad pointed up the road to the gate nearest the main house.

Once they'd stopped and the driver was unloading the bag from the trunk, Brad looked around. He was puzzled that the guard hadn't come over to greet them. He had to be here and on duty, otherwise the automatic gate should have been deactivated. Those were the rules. But Brad was too tired to investigate, and headed straight for bed.

"Police! Open up!"

In a stupor, Brad pushed his cover aside, quickly put on his trousers, just a fleece jacket on top, and some sneakers. He stumbled down the stairs and reached the front door as the rising level of the shouted warnings announced that whoever was outside was about to knock it down. He quickly flicked the catch and stepped back.

The uniformed man who strode through was short, with a red and pockmarked face.

"Deputy Sheriff Jock Posner," he announced. "Are you Bradley O'Connor?"

"Yes."

A second officer followed in, looking around the room.

Brad tried to wake himself. "Hold on. What are you doing in my house in the middle of the night?"

Posner looked at him accusingly. "So we got here a bit too early for you then?"

"What do you mean?"

"Eleven is the middle of the night is it? Or maybe it is for someone who's planning to make a real early start?"

Brad now just-about remembered coming back from the airport. "Just tell me why you're here."

"Look, O'Connor. We had a tip-off about this place. Could be it was some sort of accident, and you wanted to cover it up?"

Brad realised he must've only been asleep for a couple or three hours. So Karl wasn't back yet. But where the hell was the guard? How had these guys got in?

"Please just stop talking in riddles. What is this about?"

The second policeman moved forward. "OK. I'm Lieutenant Dave Shoffner. Bit earlier, we got a call from a guy who said he thought he could see a body on your land. Couldn't be sure in the light, he said. Well. We are sure. Just found someone, very dead, and right close to here."

Brad couldn't quite take this in, and looked blankly back.

Posner butted in again. "And I think we've seen how you and your sidekick were going to get rid of the body."

"Sidekick?"

"We have your buddy, Mr Matuik, in custody."

Despite knowing his own innocence, Brad began to worry. "So where is this body?" he asked.

"Just inside the entrance to one of your buildings."

"Then I've no idea how it could've got there. Did someone just dump a body here?"

"Dump it you said? Then why was it neatly lying beside a bunch of fencing-posts and wire? There's even a spade there, all next to your little truck, ready for the burial in the morning maybe? Bet you jus' thought that was a neat little idea, didn't you? When it gets first light, so easy for you to drive the ol' truck out to somewhere round the boundary. Then you take as long as you want, and even if anyone sees you, people fixing fences gotta dig holes, eh? The perfect cover – in both ways." Posner grinned slightly at his own humour.

"I'm sorry, Mr O'Connor," Shoffner stepped in. "But that all seems to be true. You do have a problem."

This was the last sort of complication Brad wanted. He had other things to do.

"OK. I'll help for sure. Can you let me take a look where this body is?"

"OK. Follow us," Shoffner said calmly.

A silent five minutes later and they had walked, via the footpath on the inner side of the fence, over to the goods entrance, which was also unlocked Brad was surprised to see.

He was led to the open door of what he called 'the trash shed'. It usually wasn't locked. Stan the guard's pickup truck was sitting there, backed into the doorway. Two men in light-coloured overalls were beside it. So were a neat stack of fencing posts and, nearby on the floor, something covered by a sheet.

"These guys are from forensic," Shoffner explained.

"Maybe someone took the truck, and used it to bring the body here?" Brad suggested, indicating the open gate.

"The engine was dead cold," one of the men pointed out to Posner.

"We do check these little things you know," Posner added.

"Body's pretty cold as well," the forensic guy added. "My guess is he died sometimes about this afternoon. Single shot to the heart."

Brad realised he must have been on a plane when it happened. So he was definitely in the clear. It would be on the airline computer, and one flight attendant, probably now back in the warmth of Texas, would remember him well enough. But he had an instinct to talk to Karl before saying anything more to these two. "Can I take a look at the body?" he asked.

The forensic guy moved one end of the cloth down. A man's figure was lying face up. Brad knew who it was.

"Shit! That's Charlie!"

"So you know him then?" Posner asked.

Brad hardly heard the words as he stared down and took in a new reality. This wasn't someone taking a few shots up in the mountains, defending their territory. It was his house. These people would get him anywhere. Then, returning to his immediate problem, he realised he might just have made a mistake by saying he recognised Charlie. It had to make him more of a suspect.

"Yeah. I know him. But not too well," he replied.

"And how might you 'not too well' know him?"

"Oh, he comes around. Offering to do jobs. That kinda thing."

"You sure seemed to recognise him a bit fast for that. So, I think you should come with us and give some better answers at headquarters."

Brad had planned to tell someone in the police what he thought was happening at that place up in the mountains, but not these two-bit policemen from Denver. It needed to be his high-level contacts in Washington. And if they were going to believe him, he needed to get a few more facts himself – and an update from the others. Now, despite his alibi, it might be days before this mess with Charlie got sorted. He decided to risk getting away from these two. He could fix the problems later.

"Sure I'll come along," Brad said, as he stood looking at the small bloodstained area, almost in the middle of Charlie's chest. He turned again to the forensic guy. "Say. What d'ya make of that wound?"

"Looks like it was a small-calibre handgun. Low power."

"So there's no exit wound?"

"No. But we'll know more when we recover the slug."

"Let me be helpful," Brad said. "When you do get that thing out, I think you'll find that a small handgun is exactly what it didn't come from. And I bet you didn't find a cartridge case."

"No. We didn't find anything yet. And we'll take a good look at the slug."

Brad turned to Shoffner. "If I'm coming along with you, can I get back to the house and put on some decent clothes please?" He opened his fleece to show a bare chest, and immediately shivered. The thin mile-high air was cooling fast under a clear night sky.

Shoffner nodded, and they all turned to walk back to the house. Brad deliberately slowed the pace. He needed to get in some thinking. The slow walk meant the three of them took some time to cover the two hundred yards. His best chance of escape was in his Chevy Corvette. It was parked well away from the main house, over at the back of the hangar. From there it was straight down the south drive and out at the opposite side of the airfield. But first, he had to get across the field to it. For that, he hoped his cooperative attitude was about to relax the two policemen.

"I'll just change," Brad said when they reached the house. "Will I need an armed guard doing it?"

"Stay with him," Posner ordered. "I'll check to see if there's any evidence around down here."

Shoffner followed Brad up the stairs and stood in the middle of the bedroom. Brad went into the recessed dressing area, and kept up a stream of casual comments. He hoped it was distracting attention from just how long it was taking him to put a few clothes on.

"What in hell are you guys doin' up there?" Posner's muffled bellow came from downstairs. It was what Brad was waiting for.

He immediately walked back into the bedroom, pulling on the jacket again, this time over a few other clothes. "Must take a shit. OK?" he said, pointing at the toilet door beyond the dressing room.

"OK. But keep talking, and don't lock it."

"It hasn't got one," Brad said.

Shoffner walked to the landing outside the bedroom door to yell back down at Posner.

Seconds later Brad was out of the small toilet window and sliding down the kitchen roof. He hit the ground hard, stumbled briefly to his knees, then ran on. He'd reached the main flood-gully, which ran across the field between his house and the hanger, before he heard the shouting.

The gully was deep enough to hide him as he moved at a crouch, and it was thirty seconds more before he saw the light-beams from the high-powered torches. But at night, with a torch you can't spot a trench in the middle of a grassy field.

As he reached the car, Brad switched his phone off, so that from here on it couldn't signal his location. Starting down the exit drive, he didn't even know which way he intended to turn at the end of it.

OK. He swung right, waited till half a mile away on National 36, then opened the Corvette Z1 up. The steady growl of the big engine took over. Brad loved that noise, and it almost relaxed him.

The next part of this instantaneously formed plan was to drop his car out at the International Airport – and quickly. Peña Boulevard, the main route in was too dangerous, its last eight miles were across a raised open flat plain, with almost no exits. The back way in took Brad into the half-mile-long row of car-rental compounds. He swung into the first gate, and no one seemed to notice as he parked in the employee spaces. After locking the Corvette, his fingers stroked its roof. "I hope they look after you baby."

Then he walked over and caught a courtesy bus going to the terminals.

"United. And drop me off first please," he yelled, trying to be conspicuous. Then, confidence in his plan suddenly wavered when several police cars, with sirens and full Christmas-tree lights overtook the bus at high speed.

It got worse in the terminal. There were uniformed police everywhere. His plan had been to use his cash card to its limit, which they could trace, and think he'd used the money to get a flight out. Or why else go the airport? A question he was now asking himself. Maybe Posner had outguessed him? But he'd needed to divert them to the wrong track while he returned to do something back at his place. At least the ATMs were close to the entrance, and he could stand facing them. But then he had to get out of the airport.

Head still low, he slipped out of the automatic door and towards the courtesy-bus stop area again. But police were now moving everywhere and they were checking all the buses. He looked over to the cab pick-up point – also covered. Coming here had been walking into a trap.

It felt safer staying outside the buildings and, head bowed and shoulders rounded to disguise his height, Brad walked slowly along. In the busy comings and goings of the buses and cabs, he didn't look out of place, but it was getting him nowhere.

In one gap in the traffic, a white vehicle with a light on its roof pulled sharply up beside him and a man jumped out. Brad ducked his head further and turned around as if he'd just realised he'd forgotten something, but he heard the footsteps coming after him.

"Get in the truck." The order was in a thick German accent.

"Karl! Talk about the cavalry turning up."

With a look around to see no one had noticed, Brad jumped into the United Airlines pickup. "But I thought the police had you?"

"If you work here, you've got smart-card security. They know every door I go through, and when, every computer file I access, and when, and from which console. Seems it all proves I was here and working all around when Charlie died. They want to talk to me again, but I'm not a suspect. Came back on duty again. Lucky I saw you."

"Sure is."

Karl looked across, "So what's going on then? I could sense from the way Charlie was so scared that something was up, and you hadn't told me about it." There was a slight rebuke in his voice.

"Where is Stan the guard?" Brad asked.

"He's vanished."

"Oh shit. Then he'll be dead too – somewhere."

"You have to tell me what is going on?"

"When I get the chance. First, we need outta here."

Karl stopped the pickup. "Even I can't get you on a flight. The police are everywhere."

"I don't want that. I'm only here because I was trying to be too clever. Fool them into thinking I'd flown out. Give me some time to do other things. Can you get us back to the house? I need to take a look at something with one of the planes, urgently, and it needs to be at night."

"With people being killed, you want to go messing around? Also, nothing that's instrumented for night flying is anything like airworthy."

"We can get something else prepared. I don't need instruments."

"There are no lights on the runway. How will you take off?"

"Use the reflectors there."

Karl looked back in disbelief at what that meant. "That is mad. And what about landing? That's completely impossible without lights."

"Good point," Brad conceded. "But if I take off about four in the morning, it will be light enough to land by the time I get back."

Karl pushed Brad to the floor as the airport security men waved the familiar company-truck past the barrier.

An hour later they slowed by the south gate Brad had come out of. The hangar block was a hundred metres away. The house, now hidden by the hangar, was half a mile beyond. Karl killed the lights and drove up to the back of the hanger.

"Which plane is nearest ready to fly?" Brad asked as they went into the small rear door.

"I've thought about that. The 'Lectra, I suppose."

Brad's 1935 Lockheed Electra was probably his favourite. With its two huge rotary piston engines, it was also his largest.

"OK. And I'll need the high-definition camera strapped on – with the fastest IR enhancing film we've got."

Brad went over to look out through one of the hangar's few small front windows. He could see there was a car by the main house. So the police were still around, and most of the inside lights were on over there. That bit was good. They wouldn't see much outside. Brad and Karl covered the hanger windows with dust sheets before they put on the minimum lights just near the plane.

Karl had spent a while checking the engines, before he finally broke a long silence. "If this is so important, then you should let me fly it for you. I know it a lot better than you do."

Brad knew what Karl really meant – that he was a better pilot.

"Yes. But I'm not going to. I'm not putting you in any more danger."

"You can't possibly fly it, dead-reckon navigate at night, with almost no instruments, and operate the camera, all at the same time."

Brad thought about that. Karl was too right. "OK. Maybe I do need you to navigate. We're going back to where I did that forced landing. And nothing down there will be lit. So we'll have no landmarks. I know that."

By three a.m., everything had gone well, and they were ready. Brad turned off all the lights and thought he might get an hour's sleep before it was time for take off. He settled in a chair and quickly went into a deep slumber.

That hour was nearly up when Karl started to open one of the main hangar doors in preparation for getting the plane out, leaning well over to get his weight behind it as he pushed. Maybe it was that unusual stance, or the moving background of the door, but the shot just missed, ripping across the back of Karl's jacket.

"Fick!" Karl swore in his own language as he rolled forward and landed inside the door.

"What the hell?" Brad shouted in alarm as he woke. Then saw Karl. "Are you OK?"

"Yes. Just. But who's damn shooting?"

"Ain't got time to explain now," Brad said. "But looks like we've got dangerous company somewhere out there. Not just the police. Let's work out where that shot came from. But don't show yourself again."

Standing back, just into cover, Brad tried to estimate a sight-line, from the bullet mark on the far wall, and out past the edge of the hangar door at the height of Karl's shoulders. It seemed to point at what he knew was a small rise about a mile beyond the main house, well outside his boundary, and on the only bit of high ground near.

"Ah shit," he concluded. "If that shot's from where I think, they can see everything we're up to. And I reckon that, for whoever it is over there, the range is easy. We try to walk or drive out, we're dead."

"They might try to move in closer."

"Not while the police are still here. But they can pin us down and wait their time. Which I don't have."

"Maybe it was a lucky shot?"

"Listen Karl. I've found out a few things about those spooks over there. If you put the palm of your hand round that door, they'll put a bullet through it for you."

A doubting look was the only response.

"I'm serious," Brad continued. "So don't hope for another mistake."

"In the dark?"

"Yes. That's what they've been trained for."

"So where did you find out all this?"

"In England, two days ago. And I met the man who made the training gear. Now don't ask any more questions. I may not know the answers."

"But whoever it is up there, hasn't worked out what we're up to then," Karl remarked.

Brad thought about that. He could see that with the hangar door now slightly open, part of the plane's wing and an engine would be in view from that hill. A few bullets would've been enough to wreck the engine.

He nodded. "No. Seems not. But it won't take him long to realise it once we start the thing up. That takes three minutes before we can even move. Enough time for him to pump it full of bullets."

"Then just in case it occurs to him to do it anyway, I'll shut the door."

Karl did that slowly, keeping himself out of view this time, and returned. "Shall I try and get round the back to where that guy is?" he asked.

"Good of you to volunteer. But killing at night is exactly what those people have been very well trained to do."

"So what now?"

"Whatever. It'll sure have to be something good. Are both those trucks over there working and fuelled up?" Brad had pointed at two of the old Toyota flatbeds they used around the estate. They were standing in the hanger, behind a small, roll-up door.

"Yeah."

"Great. Then let's go mannequin making."

Brad led Karl into the rear workshop and, ten minutes later, they'd made two crude dummy torsos out of stuffed sacking. Each had a head but no arms or legs.

Karl had worked silently to Brad's instructions but, by the time they'd walked back to the hangar and put a dummy in the driving seat of each Toyota, his expression was of absolute disbelief.

Then Brad filled the electric kettle and switched it on. "This may not work, but unless we do something we've had it anyway. So I'm gonna arrange a distraction. Help me with some cargo," he said cryptically.

Again at Brad's direction, they hauled two drums of aviation fuel up into the back of one Toyota, and Brad then unscrewed the caps.

"Right. I'll explain," he said. "I am going to drive out of here as if I'm making a run for it."

"But you say he'll shoot you?"

"Not me." Brad motioned towards the crude dummy in the driving seat. "But this. I'll drive the thing from under the dash."

"If these people are so good, this won't fool them."

"Well, our theory back in England was that they are using some sort of infrared vision-assistance. So, if I pour hot water on the dummy's head, it'll make it look like a warm body to those guys over there. They'll probably shoot before looking too closely. At that moment I do a little swerve to tip up the drums."

"You're crazy. Gas will be running out all over the place."

"The truck will be going slow. I'll put it into a slow turn for fifty yards or so, then throw a match and jump out. After that, there'll be so much infrared about, it'll completely mess up his sights."

Karl thought for a moment. "It'll shield you maybe. But it won't be enough to hide the plane."

"No. That's your bit. We need to load the other truck too."

Brad explained what he wanted Karl to do.

"Hell. That'll do thousands of dollars' damage."

"I can afford it." Brad looked towards the plane. "Turn those props back to clear the oil from the bottom cylinders so we're ready. I'll open the doors in front of the trucks."

Brad set off in the first Toyota. His guess was right, and it took just five seconds for a single shot to smash the windscreen, and exit via the centre of the dummy's head. At that, Brad swerved sharply, tipping the drums, then coasted in a wide arc. He was almost pointing back at the hangar before finally stopping. Behind, was the curved trail of fuel which had spilled out. Brad held a lighter at the soaked flatbed. An explosion of flame raced back in a long, curving, red wall.

Behind this cover, Brad ran back to the hangar and watched while Karl sent the second truck on its way. This one had a tool-bag weighing down its throttle, and its steering wheel tied at straight ahead. It was loaded with open drums of the high-octane gas, and was pointing straight at the site's main fuel store. As it went through the wall of fire Brad had laid, it became a rolling fireball.

The truck's final crash into the fuel store sent all the drums flying and a bigger explosion of orange heat thumped up into the darkness. Brad held up his clenched fists. Everything had worked perfectly.

They quickly opened the main hangar doors and leapt into the aircraft's cockpit. Brad worked the wobble pumps to prime both carbs at once, counting, it seemed painfully slowly, to forty – then he hit the left-hand starter motor. The huge engine started rotating. He counted to ten this time, then switched in the magneto. There was a deafening staccato of explosions and smoke as the engine fired.

Brad nursed the one coughing motor, and hit the other starter. The ten seconds of cranking-up seemed longer this time but, when he cut in its magneto, the second engine also fired.

The noise would have been heard by their attackers, but they had to be blinded by the wall of flames. Still, Brad needed to get the plane out quickly. That main fuel store was now enveloped by the fire, and he wanted to be well away when it all went up.

Desperately trying to rev up the half-cold engines, he sent the plane lunging forward out of the hangar and onto the airfield. They were soon moving out of the cover of the flames and the rapidly-heating exhaust manifolds would be perfect infrared targets.

There was a huge explosion behind, and a fierce glow lit up the whole field. Even a quarter of a mile out on the runway, they felt the wave of heat.

"Yeah!" Brad yelled in triumph. But he still had the tricky job of using the plane's small nose-light to pick up the single line of runway-reflectors in the darkness.

"You've got them!" Karl shouted.

The reflectors then started to accelerate rapidly under the plane. With a loud crack, a bullet hit the canopy near Brad's head, but he concentrated on the elusive flashes of light.

Another bullet hit somewhere. But distance and speed were beginning to be on their side.

"Nearly ready. Airspeed sixty," Karl called out.

"OK then, I'm going for it."

The front of the aircraft lifted, and the roar of the engines changed as the ground's echo fell away. But moments later, the noise of rushing air seemed to stop.

"It's stalling," Karl screamed. "Get the nose down!"

The controls went slack in Brad's hands as he slammed the stick forward again, engines on maximum. It seemed an endless five seconds before the airspeed got to sixty-five again.

"Now take her back up again," Karl called out. "You're too low!"

A silver shape flashed past to their left.

"Shit!"

Brad, realising he'd just missed a huge grain silo, banked sharply, lost any sense of what angle he was at, and looked down at the gyro horizon for help.

"It's not up to speed yet. Don't believe it!" Karl shouted.

"OK! I understand!" Brad, now with all his body shaking, lifted his eyes to see the few isolated lights dotted around on the flat farmland below. He tried to calm himself and work out where the horizon was. He knew Karl should be flying the plane.

Just in time, he straightened it. Then, still breathing heavily, put it into a slow climb.

"Time for a check on everything?" suggested Karl calmly, as if it had all been routine so far.

Brad tried to be just as controlled as he scanned the dials. "OK. It all reads normal. Those bullets don't seem to have done any damage."

He levelled out and increased speed to one-hundred-and-thirty mph. The Electra was tracking parallel and to the east of Interstate 85. In the daytime it was busy, but now only well-spaced truck lights marked it out.

"OK. I'll take the navigation and do the camera," Karl said above the noise. "We're going well. It's about eighty miles down to Pueblo."

Despite being up here at night, almost without instruments, Brad was now relaxing. He knew every landmark between here and the New Mexican border. The snow-covered fourteen-thousand-foot Pikes Peak, well above him to the east, looked ghostly in the faint moonlight.

About half an hour later, they crossed over the city of Colorado Springs, and were soon above the floodlit ordnance depot, which Karl was using as the marker for their turn westwards. From here on, it would get more difficult.

"OK," Karl called. "Make due west. Go down to six thousand feet, and speed one-hundred all the way. It makes my math easier."

Karl knew whatever he was to photograph was five-and-a-half-thousand feet up – and just beyond it was a ridge a thousand-foot-higher.

"Got you."

Brad turned the plane to head straight for the highest Rockies. As they gently descended towards the invisible ground, the controls were heavy and unresponsive. Ahead was an enormous patch of black, fourteen-thousand-feet, nothingness, blotting out the stars in front. Flying towards it in the darkness, and dropping height, was against all his instincts.

"OK, that's twelve minutes," Karl called out. "Ready to turn due north, and don't lose any more altitude as you go round. Now!"

Brad levelled the plane at six thousand feet on its new heading, and lifted the revs again.

Another five minutes later, Karl called out, "Camera started." Then he loudly counted out thirty seconds. "Now! Go back on the same course."

Brad made forty-five-degrees right, then a tight two-seventy left, to go back and repeat their pass – but with a difference he didn't want. Concentrating on the compass, he'd lost three hundred feet in the turns.

"Watch your height!" shouted Karl.

"Shit! How accurate is that altimeter?"

"It's good. But don't drop any more. And I've started the camera again."

Brad felt four small jolts in quick succession. The exhaust note suddenly changed.

"Full throttle! Climb out!" Karl snapped.

"Starboard engine! I've no oil pressure."

"Stay on the throttle. It might seize. So get yourself ready for that. Remember, dead engine – dead foot, so when it goes, immediately take your right foot off the rudder to compensate. Then just use left rudder – hard down."

Brad tensed, waiting for the lurch to the right as the engine stopped. There was a loud bang and the plane lurched violently – but to the left. Brad did what he'd been tensed and waiting for. He slammed the left rudder down. It changed what would have been a sharp turn, into an altitude-dropping near-spin. But he stayed momentarily frozen, left foot hard down – till a fist hit his head.

"NO!" Karl screamed. "Other foot. It's the port-engine that's gone!"

Brad finally reacted. But the old plane was already falling fast. Karl continued to shout instructions.

"Feather port-prop! Full throttle starboard-engine! Right foot hard down! Bring it straight!"

Brad was hardly aware of his own actions as he fought with the controls. But eventually he saw the altimeter needle had stopped rotating.

"It's holding," he said. He was shaking, even on the heavy controls.

"Take it to heading seventy then," Karl responded. "What's the height?"

"Five four. But it's going up. Fuck. That must've been close."

"Very."

"Karl. Do you understand?" Brad said after a tense minute. "I had no oil-pressure on the other engine. Not the one that stopped."

"Yes. And then you reacted to what you thought would happen. Not to what did happen."

"OK. What was it anyway?"

"Those jolts must have been bullets hitting us. And they got both engines."

"At the same time?" Brad asked.

"They're your friends. Which you still haven't told me about."

"Right now, let's just worry about the other engine."

"Maybe they just hit the pressure sensor," Karl said, but with some doubt in his voice. "But let's take a shortcut back anyway. For that we'll need another two thousand feet to clear the Palmer Divide. Does it feel right enough for that?"

"It's running a bit hot, but yes."

"OK. Richen the mixture a bit then to cool it. We've plenty of fuel, and time. So easy does it."

They settled into silence again.

An hour later, they were in a sky beginning to be washed with a faint grey, but below them, the ground was still a dark mass. Brad was worried by that. He'd been watching the engine temperature-gauge steadily rising.

"What if the other engine goes?" he asked. "Do you know what's down there?"

"It's some farmland alongside I70," Karl replied. "I used it once when I had problems. So it's OK. But it's not nearly light enough to go in there yet. How about you circle – and hope we stay in the air long enough."

Brad's right foot was numbed from the effort of holding the rudder against the one-sided pull of the working engine. "Great idea," he replied, easing off and letting the plane go into a natural one-engined turn.

"Time's near up," Karl called ten minutes later. "That engine's about to break. I can hear it. You'll have to go down now."

"But I can't see."

"I know. And it could be anything from eight-foot corn to grazing cattle. But we can't stay up here."

Brad pushed his right foot down again to straighten the plane again, and then throttled back to descend. That produced a lurch back to the right.

"You need to slacken off that foot when you reduce throttle," Karl said. "And I'll remind you again when we land and you throttle right back."

"OK."

As they got closer, the ground turned from black to a featureless dull grey, but still gave no clues about what was on it.

Karl started to call out instructions. "Go in a tad fast, say half-throttle, in case we need to get out again. Then, when you commit and throttle back, take your foot completely off that rudder for an instant. After that start again with both feet – back to normal. Or we'll spin and smash this thing to bits."

"Got you."

The ground came near now, and they seemed to suddenly be going much faster. Brad mentally rehearsed what he had to do. Then, when he heard the sizzling sound of grass whipping against the wheels, he simultaneously feathered the engine and pulled back his right foot. They lost speed quickly and thumped down.

Instantly, he thought the dim horizon looked strange, and realised there was an earth bank in front. But he'd slowed too much to take off again.

Acting instinctively now, he put the one engine into reverse-pitch. There was a roar as it bit on the air, pulling them sharply sideways. It was followed by a sharp lurch as the undercarriage collapsed. The starboard wing dug in. That swung the plane the other way and briefly straight again. Brad ducked his head away from the clattering and flying bits of wood, dirt and metal, as the propeller blades swashed themselves into pieces on the hard ground.

Then they were side-on the other way, but still sliding fast, with the floor under Brad's feet beginning to buckle.

The extended wing softened the impact as they crunched into the bank but, even so, Brad banged his head hard. He didn't feel the pain as they scrabbled out. The wing tank had split and he could smell the fuel as he desperately unloaded the film from the camera. Then they ran fifty yards clear.

"I don't know where that bank came from," Karl said in an almost mechanical voice. "But well done. A perfect landing in the circumstances."

Brad wasn't listening. He needed to make some decisions.

"Karl. I don't see how anyone can connect you to this. Why don't you go back to the house in a couple of hours and just act dumb? The police can find out what time you left the airport, but you spent the night with a woman maybe?"

Karl nodded slowly. "OK. I know someone who'd say I did. What about you though?"

"Yeah. Pity I can't do that. It's all gone too far now. But I can sort myself for the moment. When you're out of the way," he ended sharply.

As if reluctantly, Karl set off over that bank, towards the nearest road to Denver.

Brad looked back at the wrecked plane. It hadn't caught fire, and the earth bank was hiding it from the road pretty well. But he knew it wouldn't be long into the morning before one of the pilots going into DIA reported it.

He put a hand into his jacket and felt the thick wads of notes he'd taken from the airport cash machines. At least that was good. He found a breakfast diner half a mile up the road, and phoned a cab. It was the first of several he took. The last one dropped him by a run-down used-car lot off East Colefax, Denver's main east-west street. The owner got an early-morning cash sale and didn't ask any questions.

Brad took the old Buick back out to the freeway and headed west, towards the mountains, on I70. The first twenty miles, round the north of Denver, were four-lanes deep in slow moving commuter traffic and Brad felt safe in the middle of it all.

That secure feeling went as the road cleared on the long, slow and steep climb towards the eleven-thousand foot Loveland Pass, the continental divide over the Rockies. Brad was tense, but none of the police cars he so carefully ignored seemed to take any notice.

By the time he was running down the other side of the divide, past the ski resorts, and towards the Colorado River canyons, Brad at last relaxed a bit.

About three hours after starting his journey, and now beginning to think ahead, he decided to stop off in the small Rockies resort town of Glenwood Springs. He needed to get those photos developed and buy some provisions.

He was not to know that about ten thousand miles away, in a different time zone at the other side of the Pacific, Peter Rossi had done very much the same – nor did Brad know just how unhelpful both sets of photos would at first appear to be.

And Brad still had a long way to go to his hiding place.

Chapter 10

Welcome to my nightmare

To Lac Neuchatel, Switzerland

Aware of Peter's warning that the house was almost certainly being watched, Tony had looked up and down the road as Brad left for the airport. There had been a stationary Mondeo thing with someone in it, but it hadn't moved as Brad drove past.

Nor did it when Kiri went to the university an hour later, to follow Brad's instructions to erase her computer data there.

Now on his own, Tony took a swig at his half-cold cup of coffee. Was all that stuff about cult suicides and sign languages just too bizarre? Maybe Peter and Brad had got themselves too worked up with it all, and just imagined some Swiss-based conspiracy?

But Tony couldn't duck the puzzle of his own strange interview. How could he not even *know* about a research outfit that size? He had to follow it up anyway. So, as he'd agreed with the others, he'd at least tell Owen-Winter that he'd take the flight out to Switzerland.

Two mornings later, it was exactly nine o'clock when Owen-Winter, with a uniformed man close behind him, walked quickly up to Tony at Southampton Airport.

"Hello there again. I am most pleased that you have decided to pursue this opportunity further. May I introduce you to Frank, our pilot. "

That plummy accent was already annoying him. And, surprised to be introduced to *our* pilot, Tony, aware that he must have had a startled look on his face, just acknowledged the other man.

"So we can leave at once," Owen-Winter continued, then turned and waved his hand for Tony to follow.

Led by the pilot, the three of them walked through a small side-door, along a corridor, and, after nothing more than a wave at the security guy by the exit, emerged out into the noise and wind of the open airfield. Tony was increasingly amazed when their walk took them towards what he took to be something like a Lear Jet. He hadn't been on any private plane before, never mind an executive jet.

Then, by the time Tony had wedged his large frame into a seat in the cramped interior, and sorted out his belt, the engines were already making a noise which precluded any further conversation with Owen-Winter. That didn't upset him.

The noise built to a crescendo as they took off. Absorbing it all, Tony had to wonder what the hell was an organisation, supposed to be green, doing flying a twin-engine jet plane to Switzerland, with just two passengers in it?

As they came down through the clouds, Tony looked out of the small window. Certainly, there were mountains around, but no landmarks he could identify. It could have been any number of countries.

At the small airstrip where they landed, theirs was the only aircraft in front of the single shed of a terminal. As soon as Tony had angled himself through the plane's doorway and down the flimsy aluminium steps, Owen-Winter seemed to be in a hurry to get him into the back of the waiting stretched-limo. The huge shiny-black car, with its blackened windows, also looked all wrong for an 'earth saving' outfit.

After being hastened in, Tony realised that, with the dark windows, and the back compartment's interior-lights turned bright, he couldn't see much outside.

Owen-Winter explained this. "My clients will be keeping the location of their laboratory confidential for the moment. Also, I will be taking no further part in these proceedings, so there is no point in you asking me any questions."

That didn't surprise Tony.

Despite the reprimanding looks from Owen-Winter, Tony occasionally cupped his hands round his head to keep out the interior light, and pushed his face to the window. Like this, he could dimly see what they were driving past. Mostly it was neat but otherwise featureless countryside. Except, near the end of their half-hour journey, he got just one short glimpse of a huge glass-fronted building, before they drove round to behind it. It had no signs he could see. He'd probably recognise it if he saw it again – but as for working out where it was?

Soon after that, the limo doors were reopened. They were inside a large garage, and the sense of haste then continued as he was led in silence, along a wide but dimly-lit corridor. Owen-Winter eventually stopped by an opened door, beckoned for Tony to go on in, but did not follow himself. The door shut.

The room was also only dimly lit. In front was a large man with a grey clay-like face, sitting behind a plain desk, also grey. Immediately, a piercing look from deep-set black eyes seemed to go straight into Tony's mind.

"Welcome. My name is Carlos Simou. You may have heard of me. Please take a seat." His arm motioned towards a chair. The voice had been deep, and also horribly broken and hoarse. It made Tony want to clear his own throat. He thought he'd heard of Simou, and sort of recognised him. Something to do with conservation?

That slow painful-sounding voice continued. "Dr Williams, I have been following your progress for some time."

Tony just nodded. He wanted to ask this man exactly who he was, but the way he'd said *may have heard of me*, sounded more like it actually meant, *will of course have heard of me,* so he didn't know how to put the question. And why was this person who was so famous, 'following' him?

It was to be half explained. "Our concern," Simou had continued, "is about the way humanity continues to destroy so much on this planet. Animals, plants, even the environment we ourselves depend on. I have seen your earlier writings, pointing out that in just in our lifetimes, almost a third of the earth's other land-based life will be eliminated by humanity. You still believe in the same causes I hope?"

"Yes. Even more. I assume you listened in to my London interview?"

Simou didn't react, just leant back slightly. Tony could now see scars on his throat, as that grating voice continued. "So, we are together in that. But most people don't really seem to care about other life forms do they? It's only when we realise that our impact on the planet might actually affect us humans, that we suddenly panic about global warming. Although, even then, we do little that will have any real impact. So, buying some 'ecological' products and recycling a few things makes some people feel good, while two billion others are really the ones saving the planet by living on less than a dollar a day."

He looked at Tony questioningly. "Is that not true?"

"You could look at it like that."

"That's an inconvenient one to face though. If maybe you can't believe in conserving the planet and ending poverty at the same time?"

Simou didn't seem to be expecting an answer, as he just briefly looked Tony hard in the eyes, before lifting himself slowly from his chair, using his arms for support.

"Let me show you some things. Oh, but first I need to take your mobile phone. There are measurements being taken here which would be ruined, even if you just accidentally switched it on."

He put it in a drawer of the desk.

"I will return it as you leave. Come."

As he followed out through the office door, although large himself, Tony felt quite short behind Simou's very tall figure, now striding ahead, saying nothing.

They eventually stopped by a pair of heavy, rubber-sealed doors. Simou pressed a button, and a few moments later a green light came on. They entered what Tony saw was the anteroom of a two-stage environmental-control airlock. After a minute, the pressures balanced and the green light above the inner doors showed. Through them was a changing room. Simou scanned Tony as though to work out his size, and handed him a white one-piece tunic from a cupboard. It was complete with integral boots and head cover. It took Tony a while to get this on and zip it up.

Still without speaking, Simou led him through the next door. The sight of a molecular biology lab was familiar to Tony: the clean-chambers and flow hoods, the freezers and centrifuges. But what most struck him here was the size of the place. He'd never seen so much kit. What this lot must have cost, he couldn't imagine. There were banks of electron microscopes, spectrometers and magnetic resonance imagers – millions of dollars worth.

At Simou's invitation, he wandered around, looking in admiration, and beginning to take in more detail. He noticed the number of red emergency-shut-down buttons. It seemed you could hit one from anywhere without moving. Tony had only once seen a safety system like this, in a visit to the category-four laboratories at Porton Down, where they handled the most dangerous nerve agents and organisms known.

"In these laboratories, we are looking for a complete understanding of how living human cells might react to contaminated micro environments," Simou was saying in the background.

That hardly explains all this, Tony thought. "But there aren't any people working," he actually remarked.

"No. A shift has just finished."

"It looks incredibly expensive. How is it all funded?"

"Through donations from people interested in the future of the planet."

"But that would be me, and I didn't even know anything about it."

"We are particularly well supported by a number of agricultural cooperatives around the world. We don't need to make appeals outside that."

"I see. And this is sponsored by the United Nations or some such, and you are responsible to them?"

"I report to no one." Simou had raised his voice at that, and it grated horribly. "This laboratory is my creation. I have one partner, but he concerns himself with other matters. Now, you have probably seen enough here. Next, perhaps you would like to look at our computer facility?"

Tony just nodded.

Back in the airlock, Simou discarded his tunic in a large bin, and Tony copied him. The bin had been empty, he noticed.

On what turned out to be a longer walk this time, Tony started looking into side-windows where he could. There were more labs, but still no people. Seeing what he was doing, Simou waved an arm to speed him up.

The computer area was also protected by an airlock, but a single stage type, and he didn't have to wear any special clothing this time.

"As you can see," Simou said once they were inside. "This looks like any other large computer department, except that these are all O'Connor machines. We use them in a different way to most people. Almost like conventional computers, but they give us a very high level of security."

"How do you mean?"

"With the way these computers work, it would be impossible for anyone to hack into them and find out what was going on, or disrupt a network of them."

"Why do you need so many?" Tony asked. "My wife's project is only using one, and it's got plenty of data to handle."

"We know about her work. It has been a failure I understand."

"Yes. Completely. And all the data has now been erased. The university wouldn't keep up the funding."

That seemed to make Simou nod slightly. "There is more to show you, but you had an early start," he'd then continued. "Shall we have some lunch now?"

"That would be good."

The food in the large and basically-furnished canteen was simple, just cheese and a few raw vegetables. For the first time Tony saw other people around, but even now not many of them. The standard dress seemed to be baggy, off-white jackets and trousers. Everyone but Simou was wearing them. Nothing about all this was making sense so far. He had to break it open somehow.

"Owen-Winter said what you are doing is now very urgent. Why is that exactly?" he asked.

Simou looked surprised. "Do you know how many additional people live on this planet – every month – every day?"

Tony knew he'd have got to somewhere near the answer, by dividing down from near to a billion a decade, but he wasn't given the chance.

"I'll tell you then. Six million more a month, that's about two-hundred-thousand a day. That many more mouths to feed, every single day." Simou almost growled the words. "And how many new fields are needed extra, to feed, clothe, house, heat, provide roads, water supplies, places to be buried, I could go on, for two-hundred-thousand people?"

Tony shook his head.

"I'll tell you then. The world average is about five of your acres, two hectares, to provide support for each person. So, we are ripping four thousand square-kilometres a day out of the natural environment, by destroying rain forest, wilderness, tundra, wetlands. This much, each day. And, if it were to provide for your privileged European living standards, multiply that by three."

"I didn't know that in particular, but I appreciate most of what's going on."

"No. You don't appreciate nearly enough my friend. The behaviour which has brought us our civilisations is too deeply established. Those religions have driven our beliefs and given control: of discipline, diet, cleanliness, sexual behaviour, all often in great detail. Many with good reason, certainly in past circumstances. And they have created the stability to control and preserve those beliefs. But is that about to destroy us? Doesn't every system contain the seeds of its own destruction?"

That penetrating stare went straight into Tony.

"Just say it straight," he responded. "We are heading for overpopulated catastrophe unless most religions radically change their behaviour – which they won't. Therefore, we only reach stability when we also manage to kill six million a month with conflict, starvation or disease? Or maybe some sort of total disaster, probably caused by us, completely tips it the other way. But, before then, there is no point blaming anyone or anything for what is inevitable."

"See," Carlos growled. "Again, you are only thinking of the human population. We will completely destroy most other life in the process. But there is a solution."

He stopped and stared, more darkly this time.

But Tony seemed to miss that. "Oh yes. I know about solutions. Get a population graph, then draw a dotted line of forward prediction, and make it turn down. Problem solved. Been done. Even if it doesn't begin to pass a credibility check. We agreed nothing on global warming in Copenhagen or Cancun. The real issue wasn't even on their agendas. Anyway, I've had loads of these conversations. Why have you dragged me over here for another one?"

"There is a very good reason you are here. I have read all your research papers, especially the most recent ones, in detail, and between your so carefully written lines. And I have had some spies out. Let me guess what sort of places some of your 'subjects' are secretly going to, all wired up."

"OK. Go on."

"Something like Alpha Courses, or Scientology gatherings, perhaps even BNP meetings?"

"So, what if?"

"Those messages would be so very different. But let me guess what you have found. The pattern of neural responses you see are almost identical?"

This time Tony didn't answer.

"And if those volunteers, just suppose, had gone to a meeting of the Hitler youth, I think your own guess, is that it would be the same again? Yes? There are a lot of messages which will work? If you use the right methods?"

"That's not in any paper, or between any lines."

"But it would explain why you are being so cautious about who might draw the real conclusions from your research? And having done your unusual experiments, you now know more about this than anyone on earth?"

Tony stayed silent.

"No, don't bother trying not to react. You have already shown me enough to confirm that we need you."

"For what?"

"I have said enough. Our task is urgent. It must be done now." Then he calmed slightly. "But you have not yet seen everything here. When you have done that, and thought about it all, then you must look to your conscience."

Simou threw his napkin down on the table, stood, and set off at his previous rapid pace. This time he led the way to a lift. Getting in he pressed the only down-button, but the descent took a long time, to what had to be well below ground level.

The opening doors brought them out into another long corridor. Simou started moving quickly again, this time talking over his shoulder. "Owen-Winter probably mentioned our combined physical and computer simulations."

"Well. He mentioned a series of experiments."

"Yes. While most of our computer's input data comes from what occurs naturally around the world. Our lands and oceans are the greatest experiment ever. We also want to study what might happen in conditions we have not yet seen on earth. The answers to that come from our environmental simulators – our most expensive creations. Let me show you."

A minute's walk took the two of them to an enormous wall, where Simou opened the external shutter of a window. What lay beyond, looked like the view into another world. It was the size of three or four football-pitches, with rich mixed hues of green vegetation around a lake. Above that, a high dome formed a blue sky with what seemed to be its own sharply-bright sun.

"This particular room is simulating possible stages in the destruction of the ozone layer," Simou said. "It also has higher levels of carbon dioxide and certain pollutants. We are about two actual years into the test, but have accelerated it to represent about two hundred. That could be well towards the doomsday we are all heading for unless something is done."

"Amazing," Tony said, still peering through the glass.

"We have ten of these laboratories," Simou explained. "They are simulating different possible outcomes for the planet. Two are marine, one of them desert, the rest more like this."

"So with these," Tony asked, "you think you can predict the future?"

"Or maybe plan it?" Simou growled.

"How do you mean?"

Simou looked hard back at him. This time the words were more measured. "If we can show the outcome of certain types of behaviour, and get people to change, then we have altered the future."

Tony's slight confusion must have shown.

"Not really very much more to see here," Simou said. "Let's move on. We can talk more detail later." He closed the shutter and set off quickly again.

Although struggling to keep up, Tony was beginning to look around. Down here, there were no windows in the blank walls. Then he noticed someone ahead, walking towards them.

Only half turning, Simou held a palm out, signalling for Tony to stay, presumably outside listening range, as he strode forward to the other man. The two of them went into terse conversation, inaudible to Tony, although he could sense it was the sort of exchange which signals a problem.

Tony noticed he was next to a short side-corridor, which had a single small window at the end. Moving as quickly and silently as he could, he scurried towards it and looked in.

The interior was almost completely dark. At first, he saw just a line of small lights, stretching back to where he could hardly make them out individually. It took a few seconds, and then Tony saw that each light was actually on the side of a huge vertical cylinder.

"No," came as a drawn-out slow whisper, as he tried to see more detail. But there was no other explanation. And so many? What would even one of them be doing here?

There was a deep shout, and heavy noises of someone running. In a scamper, Tony made as much distance as he could from that window. Then Simou was there and facing him. Tony stopped on one foot, and tried to look aimlessly about him.

There was no doubt about the anger in Simou's cracked voice. "You have gone the wrong way." He looked towards the end of the corridor, then hard back at Tony. "There is more we need to talk about. But I have some urgent business now, so our conversations will have to wait until tomorrow."

"But I'm due back tonight. I've got appointments tomorrow at the hospital."

"In which case, we will try to get you back by mid morning. Go in front this time. And keep to this corridor."

Tony thought of running, but doubted whether he'd get away from the taller man, or out from the bowels of this building. Also, all pretence of innocence would then have gone. At the end of the corridor, they entered another lift, and the long ascent in tense silence took them back up to where Tony could see daylight through some windows. He was then guided on by one-word instructions, through several sets of double doors, all the time hearing Simou's heavy footfalls just behind.

"Stop," Simou commanded, then beckoned Tony through a side door.

Going through, he found himself in a small and sparsely furnished room. In it, there were just two chairs, a bed, and a cabinet with drawers.

Simou's rasping voice came from the doorway. "Tomorrow, I will find out your real reason for being here Dr Williams."

"You know my support for ecological action."

"I had hoped for it. And it would have been better for you to leave it at that. But I don't think you have, Dr Williams. Which is a pity, because you have no idea what you are up against."

"I want to help you."

"Maybe Dr Williams. But it seems you've had some interesting visitors recently. Such as a Mr Bradley O'Connor?"

Tony guessed that's what the other man must have been telling Simou. "Yes," he replied. "He was helping my wife with her project."

"I thought you said that was dead."

"Yes. That's what O'Connor finally confirmed."

"Then why is he now attempting to spy on us out in America? Do you know about this?"

"No. He's nothing to do with me."

"Well, your actions may have also confirmed my suspicions about another of your guests – a Mr Rossi?"

"Yes. He was helping with the project too." Tony immediately wished he hadn't reused, 'helping'.

"It's strange that this *helping* a dead project then leads to such strange behaviour. Mr Rossi was one person I thought would stick to looking after just his own interests. However, as I say, I'm sure tomorrow will be very productive. Until then, I hope this is suitable for your night's stay."

Simou left the small room, not locking the door. But, a few moments later, there was the clunk of a large lock from a door in the corridor outside.

Tony immediately reached for his phone.

"Shit."

He slowly absorbed his position. A prisoner. He looked round the place. In the bedroom, there was a single small window, too high up in the wall to see out of. It didn't appear to be openable. Off to one side was a basic bathroom with a toilet. Tony walked in there. On the back of the sink was a small bar of soap, and shampoo and something else in two little bottles. Next to the sink was a white towel on a rail.

He walked back through the bedroom and pushed on the door to the corridor. As it opened, he noticed that at head-height was a wired-glass panel. So this wasn't any sort of hotel room, more like a hospital room. In a research lab? For tests on human subjects?

Out in the corridor, the lights were now a dim glow. He confirmed that the nearby set of double-doors were what he'd heard Simou lock. They were very solid. Through the full-length wired-glass panels, he could see the first bit of the corridor beyond. Further away was now in complete darkness. At this side of the doors, there seemed to be a number of other bedrooms like his. He tried a couple of the doors. They were locked, and he could see nothing but blackness through their glass panels.

One door was different, without a glass panel. It did open, but was just a small cleaner's cupboard, containing a vacuum cleaner, a broom, a floor polisher and a set of overalls.

Further back, just before another set of locked double doors, he spotted two narrower passages leading sideways. At the ends were emergency exit doors with release bars across them. They would open out to either side of the building Tony assumed. Maybe he should just throw his large bulk against one of those bars and run. But they were sure to be alarmed, and he knew he wasn't fit enough to get very far. He also began to remember about these people and the darkness. With night approaching, now would not be the time to try an escape, even if he dared. He walked slowly back towards his little room. They would have to let him go in the morning anyway, or Kiri would report it.

Standing on the bed, he took a look out of that one high window. In the dusk, all he could see were trees about fifty yards away.

Suddenly aware that he was feeling very tired from that early start, Tony sat on the bed, and then lay back for a moment.

Even the most vigilant person, could not have noticed, or resisted, the soporific effect of the odourless and invisible gas, carbon monoxide. After half an hour, with its strength just one part in a thousand of the air around him, Tony was in a rapidly-deepening sleep. Beyond that point would have been quiet death, had his captors

145

not shut off the supply and come in to give a less-dangerous sedative to prepare their victim for what they were going to do next.

Tony's first conscious awareness was intense fear, like he was surrounded by horrible danger. So horrible he didn't dare open his eyes to look at what it might be. Then he was swamped by the feeling that he just wanted to stay this way – hidden, buried, and safe.

It was a feeling like Tony had never experienced before. Sometimes he drifted up, more aware, but this then seemed threatening, and he wanted to retreat again. The clinical portion of his brain told him something had to be very wrong.

It took a while, but he began to get a grip on these strange swings of consciousness and fear. On one high, and with an effort which brought stomach acid to his throat, Tony finally managed to overrule the terror, and force his eyelids to open. The scene was a confusion of dark and threatening colours. He clenched his eyes shut again and lay very still.

Thinking again, he remembered what Peter had said about his nightmare in Jordan. Maybe this was something like it, and it was his vision that was being effected? But, even in those distorted colours, he'd registered one thing which was very familiar, and standing right beside him. A drip! Someone was putting something into his blood. Trying to ignore the fear, he looked again, and, apart from that false colouring, it all looked normal. The walls stayed fixed. Nothing turned to hands and claws. So why was he so frightened?

Taking a better look around, Tony realised there was no one in the room with him. But for how long? Despite the fear, he had to do something quickly. He raised his other arm to pull that tube out, having a moment of real terror when he saw that green hand. Then, gritting his teeth till he felt they would break, he pulled the intravenous connection, slowly and shakily, away from the bandage which had held it in place.

He sat up, swung his legs sideways, noticing they'd taken his shoes off but otherwise he was still fully dressed. How long did he have?

He looked up at that high window. It was daylight again and the window was big enough for him to get through, but would have to be broken.

The plan he was now forming wasn't quite that simple though.

Trying to stand, Tony immediately lost his balance and hit the floor hard. It was as if his normal reactions just hadn't worked properly. He could only respond in slow-motion. It was something else to add to his problems.

Reduced to crawling, so that gravity wouldn't catch him out again, Tony pushed one of the chairs under that window. With the care of someone on a thousand-foot cliff, he slowly stood on it, balancing himself with both hands against the wall, stretching up till he could see out. The grass outside was at the same level as the floor inside, and OK to jump to. That was good, although not what he intended to do. The window didn't seem to be alarmed, which was also good, because he was going to break it and didn't want attention too soon.

Cautiously, Tony lowered himself again. He crawled over to check the corridor immediately outside. No one was around. Whatever they were putting in him, they must have trusted it to keep him quiet. He crawled back to the bed, found his shoes underneath it and pulled them on. Thinking that if he ever got away, a sample of that drip would tell him a lot, he carefully washed out one of the small shampoo bottles in the bathroom. After filling it with the drip, he cleaned out the drip-bag and filled it with water.

After putting these on the bed, he then dragged the heavy infusion stand over to that chair. Slowly, he stood on it again, this time lifting the stand with him.

The weight and momentum with which Tony swung the heavy metal base, comprehensively smashed the window, but also propelled him backwards. Letting the stand drop, he grasped for support. It kept him on the chair, but he felt the sharp pain as his hand clenched hold of the spikes of glass remaining attached to the window frame. He immediately let go and looked at the wound.

Tony had almost got used to his skin being a strange colour, but still winced at the dark-green blood. The cut wasn't deep. He held the hand outside the broken window, like a cup, until it half-filled with blood, then he splashed it onto the grass outside, as far away as he could. Repeating this, he managed to get his second throw even further. Then, clamping the wound with his other hand, he slowly stepped back off the chair, careful not to leave any blood drips on the floor inside the room.

Tony realised, if he ever got away, a sample of his blood with that stuff in it could also tell him a lot. Hurrying now, he washed out the other small bottle and let some blood run into it. Then he stopped the flow by wrapping the pillowcase tightly round his hand.

Carrying his two samples and the supply of water, Tony moved out into the corridor, taking a look to each side. Still no one there. He was now getting more used to this slowness, realising he could still do things, and accurately, just not quickly. He went over to that small cleaner's room, and closed the door behind him. With the broom, he pushed up a false-ceiling panel, then, after switching off the light, used the massive, industrial-style floor polisher as a support to lever himself upwards through the opening. After rolling over onto an electrical conduit tray, he replaced the ceiling panel.

Now he had to lie still in the near darkness, and the fears returned. He was trapped in hallucinations, with imagined demons in the blackness up here. The tray which supported him wasn't very wide. In the sudden spasms of fear, it would have been easy to roll off and crash back through the flimsy false-ceiling.

That broken window must have eventually attracted attention, and noises started below. This perch, Tony realised, was a good place to listen to what was going on in those rooms and corridors.

"There's blood out there," someone called out. "He'd have caught the glass as he went through."

"So he cleaned that infusion bag out, used it to hold water, and made a run for it."

"I told you we should have weighed him properly. He was far heavier than you thought. You got the dosage wrong."

"Doesn't matter. Even with what we gave him, and injured, he won't get far."

Tony relaxed just slightly. He seemed to have fooled them.

It only required a first painful-sounding clearance of the throat for Tony to realise Simou had arrived in the room below.

"He got out through there," one of the other voices said.

"Then issue weapons and put a full-area search on," Simou growled. "But don't kill him. He's needed."

People moved around down there for a while, and there were some banging noises, but no one said much more, then eventually it all went silent.

Tony guessed it was now the middle of the next day. There'd been no sounds for a long time. He had calmed, and the terror of what lay in the distant corners had subsided. But his small water-supply was finished, so it was time to escape whatever. He just hoped that the armed search had been abandoned, or maybe moved to further away.

Returning carefully to his room, Tony saw that the window he'd smashed was now boarded over. Through the cracks, he was pleased to see bright light. He'd learnt enough from Brad to know it would be best to make his escape in sunlight.

The double-doors in the corridor had been re-locked. He then went to re-examine one of the fire doors on the side corridors. He looked carefully but, against his expectations, it didn't seem to have any security contacts wired to it. That made a weak plan look a lot better.

He pushed the bar down firmly and opened the door enough to get out. In front was a gentle slope of mown grass, leading up to trees. Walk fast, don't run.

In the bright sun, a figure in rather tight-fitting cleaner's overalls walked out, as if to attend to something by the edge of the trees, and soon vanished into them.

Once in cover, Tony pulled the overalls off and set off under the canopy of leaves to find a road.

It took a mile of panting uphill-walking before he stood at the wood's edge and looked out at a road. Then he waited behind the hedge for a few minutes, and took a look at the first car along. By the red cross on its rear number plate, Tony at least knew this was probably Switzerland.

He was now on higher ground, and could look back over the top of the building he'd escaped from. Beyond it was a wide lake. Seeing this open vista, he realised something looked wrong. The sun was still quite high over the water to his left, but the sky was almost black. Strange, but Tony concentrated on trying to work out where he was, frustrated by his limited geography. To the right on the far shore was a city. He took a guess.

"This must be Lake Geneva," he said to himself. "That is Lausanne over the other side, and Geneva itself will be at the end where the sun is. That's where they'll think I'm heading."

Tony decided he'd walk the other way till nightfall, then look for some shelter. In the morning, he'd have to risk getting a lift or a taxi to Geneva, but he'd go round the other side of the lake to get there.

To start with it went well. The road was downhill again now, and he made good distance, only a few times hearing approaching cars and having to take cover in the hedges and shrubs around.

Half an hour later, a blue sign announced the edge of St. Aubin. The village didn't look big, but there was no obvious way round it. To his left was a river, and on the right a hill, steeper than Tony could make his way up. But he didn't want to waste the remaining daylight. He had no choice but to walk on in.

Before they saw him, he'd spotted the small group of people standing together in conversation. Tony steeled himself to continue. Going to the other side of the road, he tried to look preoccupied. As he passed, the group fell silent and he was sure they were looking at him. He must have seemed all wrong in his crumpled grey suit and with two days' growth of beard. Tony walked on without looking across, self-consciously, almost finding it difficult to put one foot in front of the other.

There was slight laughter at the drunk, and the conversation came back. Tony started breathing again.

He saw a few other people, but they were further away down side streets.

Tony felt he hadn't got nearly far enough away when dusk came, but knew he'd have to stop. He was also dog-tired, cold, and desperately thirsty and hungry.

He was looking for a sensible place to spend the night, maybe an outhouse, when he noticed all the signs around were now in German. Up the road, the sign of 'Gasthof Sternen' faced him. The change of language somehow made him feel safer. It was a barrier of some sort. The place up in front looked like a little hotel and bar, and it could give him food and a warm bed. Tony walked in.

They had a vacancy, but he couldn't get the German-speaking owner to understand 'room service' and had to risk attracting curiosity in the inn's half-full, informal little restaurant. He ordered by randomly pointing at the menu, ate as quickly as possible, and then went upstairs to hide in his room.

The security latch on his door was old-fashioned but reassuringly solid. He didn't turn the light on, and made sure the window was unlatched and there was a route out that way. Dropping onto the bed fully clothed, although desperate for sleep, the fear of what had happened last time kept him awake for a long time. Occasionally he heard footsteps on the stairs and stopped breathing, lying there, tense, until another bedroom door clicked shut.

He didn't understand what had been going on in that place – or really want to take in what he'd seen in that dark basement.

At least he'd got out, and with his samples. They would explain those weird fears and colours. He would do some analysis when he got back to Oxford. And tell people about all those vessels.

But then for the first time he realised. Even if he got back, whoever these people were, they would be waiting for him, at his house, and at the hospital. Everything had changed.

Where could he go? First, it would have to be where Peter suggested, his girlfriend Iona's place. But he didn't have the address or phone number with him.

Tony had never felt so lost and alone.

Chapter 11

Working on the night moves

To Quasado, Costa Rica

Iona relaxed and leant back, rolling her head of blond hair, and letting the warmth of the evening sun wash through it. From the bar inside, sporadic waves of laughter reached her, and any thoughts of danger were far away.

She knew Peter would be annoyed about her coming out to Costa Rica again. But it was her business, and he'd annoyed her. She'd hardly seen him since their weird last visit here. But one call from Kiri Williams, and he was straight round there. Then he'd wanted them to have some sort of meeting at her place, because Kiri would be in danger if it were in her own house.

So she didn't see why she should've told him about being here. She needed to get a supplier of orchids, and didn't see why just doing that should be a problem. What happened last time here were due to Peter's funny deals.

But she wouldn't go searching for Maria and Philippe again. There were plenty of other growers. And this time she hadn't bothered with a flash hotel in San Jose, but taken her hire car straight up north to the small town of Quesado.

Everything had gone just fine. She'd watched for any reaction at passport control, and again when she gave her name to the hotel receptionist. There had been nothing. After unpacking her case, she'd left the hotel to walk to a restaurant just round the corner. She'd noticed it from the car, and decided a quick dinner before an early night would be great. Back home it was already past midnight.

It was a perfect choice. Separated from the busy sidewalk by huge and overgrown, late-summer flower tubs, the outside tables really caught the evening sun.

After just a one-course meal, and not bothering with a coffee, she set off back to the hotel, and decided a nightcap in the lobby bar would work just fine. She'd be ready for sleep then.

She'd half finished the whisky and lemonade when her relaxation was interrupted.

"Iona Duncan?"

It had been a just-loud-enough whisper. Almost as if she'd only imagined it. But she knew she hadn't. It had come from the man on the high stool next to hers. He wasn't looking towards her, but straight ahead. Iona felt unsure, and didn't answer.

"Never mind," the man continued quietly, still looking away. "I already found out that's who you are. Thought I recognised you, and asked at reception. The guy there just assumed I'd come to meet you, and told me."

She felt off-guard, but turned her head slightly. "OK. What if I am?"

His whisper this time was through clenched teeth. "Just don't look towards me. And what the fuck are you doing here?"

The shock ran through Iona. Suddenly, her calmness had been shattered by this man, and she didn't know how to react.

"Does Pete know?" the man had continued.

This was bringing back memories of that last visit here – nasty ones. Iona went to move away.

The man saw this, and now turned slightly to make brief eye contact for the first time. "If you want to live, you'll stay right there and listen."

She slowly slid back onto the bar stool. "Pete?"

"Your boyfriend, dummy."

"Peter. It's nothing to do with him why I'm here."

The man didn't seem to hear that, but went on. "Maybe he doesn't know how crazy these people have got. Something big and bad is about. If they suss out who you are, and that you know Pete, you both just got your life-expectancy changed."

Suddenly he looked the other way and went quiet. At the other side of the bar, the waiter had walked past.

"Get to your room," he then continued, swivelling slightly back. "And out of here tomorrow."

"Why should I listen to you?"

His whisper was now sharp and angry. "Check with Pete then. I've done enough."

"I might. What's your name?"

There was a wait. Then he threw a ten-dollar note on the bar top and muttered almost inaudibly as he slid off his stool. "Garcia. Joe Garcia."

After he'd gone, Iona waited a minute, recovering, then got her drink topped up with a double, and signed the tab. She carried the glass with a shaking hand, which was wet and sticky by the time she'd got to her room and closed the door behind her.

Her mobile, which she turned on for the first time here, quickly registered locally, but calling Peter's home and mobile just got his messaging services. She didn't bother leaving any. Of course, he'd gone out to Jordan and Singapore. She had to find out about that Joe tonight. Mike Howell, Peter's number two at the factory, was her only chance. Ignoring the time difference, she called him.

It was two in the morning for him, so Iona understood why he sounded immediately concerned. "Iona. What's up? Is everything OK with Peter?"

"Yes, I suppose so. And sorry about disturbing you, but I need you to answer a question for me. Do you know a man called Joe Garcia?"

Mike spoke slowly. "Yes. I know of him. Peter deals with him."

"Go on."

The guarded voice remained. "OK. You know Peter does the weapons training kit. Well that guy Garcia gets things for the real shooting, things that actually go bang, and he's not fussy who for. Deals in Central and South America. So guess what that means? Dangerous company."

"You've told me enough. Thanks. Sorry to wake you."

She turned her phone off, and then used what was left in her whisky glass to wash down a couple of sleeping tablets. Tomorrow, she'd decide what to do.

Iona wanted to wake, but seemed to be losing the struggle. There were too many layers to fight through – sleep itself, now two hours in and at its strongest, the jet lag, wine with the meal, the drinks at the hotel bar, and finally those Temazepams.

Through this blanket of unconsciousness, a noise was coming from somewhere, bursts of sound which were strangely extending, like time was slowing, and soon would stop.

She made a convulsion of effort, and was at last awake. The dying fire-alarm bell gave its few last clangs, and went silent, its batteries drained.

Iona could see nothing – and it took a few seconds to remember where she was. This was her hotel room. In the blackness, she reached for the bedside light and, after a few fumbles, found it. But pushing its little switch back and forth did nothing.

She tried to remember the room layout. She needed to get to her clothes, which were hanging in the room's small entrance hall, and fast. If that was a fire and they evacuated the hotel, she at least wanted to be dressed in something. Right now she wasn't.

Stumbling off the bed, her foot caught and she lunged forward. Outstretched hands, intended to break her fall, missed the top of the heavy central table, and she felt stabs of pain as the edge of it rammed into her rib cage and her face hit the hard surface.

"Shit!"

She slid sideways, rolling on the floor, now disorientated. Staggering up again, only just managing to balance, her arms flailed at the blackness, trying to find something in it.

Her hands found a wall, and then swiped great arcs against it. After a few feet along like this, at last she found a light switch and toggled it furiously. Again, nothing happened. Another switch was near, but it did nothing either.

Suddenly, a flash from outside lit up everything, even through the heavy curtains, and left an image in her eyes of the room. The flash was instantly followed by a heavy, sharp-edged thump, which echoed briefly.

"Got it. A thunderstorm, and right on top of us." In relief, she'd said it aloud. "It's taken out the power and set the alarms off."

Iona liked thunderstorms, and walked over to pull the curtains aside and see more. There were no lights anywhere out there. It looked like a power-cut all over town.

The brilliance of another flash dispatched its shockwave. This one was much louder, and drew crackling sounds from the window's fixings as they took the impact of the air-pulse. That instant of light had left a memorised image, which Iona had a few moments more to consider in disbelief. It was like a picture of the buildings she'd remembered from last night, but as silhouettes. The flash seemed to have been at street level behind those buildings. That wasn't lightning.

Then there was a new noise, lighter and more distant. Iona tried to hear it as something else, but couldn't for long. She knew it had to be automatic gunfire.

She pulled the curtains back together again, as if isolating herself from what was happening on the other side of them, and then retreated back into the darkness. Feeling her way to the bedside table, she turned her mobile back on. This time it didn't register a local network.

"OK. Where's the normal telephone?" she said in a controlled voice, as if trying to reassure herself that she was taking charge. From outside, another sharp edge of a shockwave crackled the window.

The phone was dead.

Iona now realised that the next explosion might just come right through the window, and she was standing naked behind it. She moved back into the small hallway and grasped in the darkness for those clothes.

She'd managed to find and put on trousers, a shirt, and some shoes, when she was startled by a hard knock on the door out to the corridor. They are evacuating? Someone come to get her? Her hand had reached the lock to open it, when a second, much harder, impact smashed through the centre of the door, throwing splinters into her. In instinctive panic, she ran into the bathroom. Trying to hide behind its door in the darkness, she ended up falling into the bath.

The third impact on the outer door was so hard she heard it crash open. Then the sound was like three or four people had bundled into the small hallway behind her. They were shouting, in Spanish she thought, and a torch beam was flashing around out there. Iona squeezed herself right up to the end of the bath, behind the door and just out of their sight. No one came into the bathroom, but they seemed to move on through into the bedroom.

That burst of gunfire was deafening. It was followed by the clattering of falling glass, as the bedroom's double-glazed window disintegrated.

Without that window, the noises outside were now much sharper. Iona could clearly hear the rattle of small arms, and the occasional crash of something much heavier. Soon there was also the stench of smoke pouring in through the smashed window.

Terrified, she remained hunched up and motionless. Whoever was in the room must have ripped the curtains down as well, and now the room was being sporadically illuminated by the flickering light of warfare.

Iona noticed the huge mirror in the wall at the other end of the bath. In it, she could see the reflection of the hallway and broken-open door, and realised that made her visible from the hall. There was nothing she could do about it, but huddle herself into a smaller ball.

The people in her room were now firing intensively, several guns at once. In the bath seemed like the best place to be.

For about the next hour she stayed there, and in that time the battle, or whatever it was, seemed to reduce. The people in her room were firing less, and the flashes of light from outside were replaced by a modulating background of red light. Fires must have started burning out there.

If her immediate panic had subsided, a deeper concern, that she was in the middle of something very serious, grew. To Iona it made no sense, certainly given anything she knew about this country.

It was in one of the longer spells without an explosion that Iona became aware of a slight new noise, and saw something reflected in that large mirror on the far wall of the bathroom. She concentrated, looking hard to see what was in that hallway. Yes, an almost invisible figure had come through that open door from the corridor outside, and was now standing just outside the bathroom.

Suddenly, an ear-splitting noise filled the small room and, in the darkness, she saw the stabs of white heat from a gun muzzle. The person in the hallway was firing, and the sound resonated from the tiles and earthenware around her.

She knew what was happening, and something rose to block her throat. He was shooting at whoever was already over by the window – into their backs. It lasted a long ten seconds, then there was silence again.

Iona, now frozen in terror, tried not to make any noise that might reveal her presence so close. Through the mirror, she kept watching the person's vague outline, just visible in the light of those distant fires. Nothing moved for about another fifteen seconds, then the figure slowly turned. It was now facing directly into the bathroom, and must have been her reflection in that mirror. It seemed like an age, and Iona didn't dare breathe or move.

Then whoever it was had gone.

The hallway was empty, but Iona was shaking in terror. It took another half-hour, remaining tightly pulled up to the end of the bath, before her reactions subsided.

Even after the immediate fear had gone, she felt safer staying where she was. None of her explanations of this added up. Was it connected to what had happened last time with Peter? But who was fighting who?

A realisation stopped this thinking. It had all gone completely quiet outside. For some reason it made her tense up again. In the silence, every element in her consciousness was connected to her ears, straining to hear anything. No one seemed to be around anymore, in the hotel, or outside it.

It slowly got light, but there was an unreal silence for morning in a city. Then she heard that new sound. Slight slow footsteps were out in the hotel corridor, getting nearer, stopping, and starting again, but always approaching. They were searching. Iona didn't have the cover of darkness now. She thought how a gun would rip her to pieces in the bath, but she stayed, as if paralysed.

The sound got to outside her doorway, and stopped for longer.

She held her breath.

"Iona. Are you there? It's me. Joe."

She collapsed forwards in the bath, taking in great gulps of air.

"Christ! Why did you do that?"

"Are you OK then?"

She almost wept. "Yes. But I don't know how. Someone had the chance to kill me. Looked at me for long enough, but didn't shoot."

"Sure glad he didn't."

"What happened to you?"

"I just kept quiet in the wardrobe of my room until it all seemed to be over. There's nobody around now. We should get out. I got a rental car in the parking lot behind this place."

"You knew something would happen. You're involved in some way aren't you? And that's why you're still alive."

"Lady. You don't know. Keep it that way," Joe said quietly. "I don't owe Pete no particular favour. But he's a fair guy, so I'll try and get you out of this."

Iona started to pull herself out of the bath, and the pain in her joints let her know how long she'd sat, rigid and tense, in there. Finally standing, she stretched herself and walked, a bit stiffly, into the bedroom.

She'd forgotten and, with a small cry, backed away, her face covered by her hands. It was now nearly daylight, and the briefest look at the just-recognisable lumps in the corner made her retch.

Joe moved in behind her, and was even less ready for the sight.

"Oh God!" he cried out.

The human shapes were surrounded by blood and bits of flesh, splattered all over the end of the room and halfway up the walls.

As Joe pulled her out of the room, she grabbed her jacket and handbag. "Joe, what's happened?"

"Let's just get away."

"But you know something don't you?" Iona persisted. "Those guys in my room. Who were they? And who were they shot by?"

"Crazy people."

They went down the main staircase and out into the foyer, too quickly, again not ready for what lay beyond.

Over by reception, were about thirty bodies, men and women, mostly in dressing gowns or pyjamas, but now covered in so much blood they must be dead. Iona guessed they must have come down here dressed like that when the fire alarm started – for safety. In her room, the men's clothes had hidden something of the impact of the bullets, but here the guns' destruction of human flesh was all too clear.

Joe pulled her back to the staircase.

Iona couldn't take it in. "Do you realise? Those people weren't caught in crossfire or anything. They were deliberately shot where they were.

"So, like how many times do I have to say it? Let's just get out of here." Joe started moving, then stopped. "But let's do a check outside first. I need a window overlooking the goddamn parking lot."

Iona followed as he went up the wide stairs, three at a time, and they soon stood at either edge of a second-floor window, staring at what lay outside. A spiralling tower of smoke was coming from a building still burning in the next block. The broken windows and the destruction were repeated everywhere, and a sky of black hung above it all. There were no signs of any activity. It was as if they were the only two people alive in the wreckage.

Iona spoke first. "Who would do this? It's not just the hotel. It's the whole town. And it's daylight now. So why has no one come to help?"

Joe turned back from the window. "For God's sake, will you stop trying to work things out. Let's look after ourselves." He walked back to the stairs.

At a rear door out onto the parking lot, there was still no hint of any movement around, so they ran the short distance to Joe's car. It had one broken window, but otherwise looked undamaged. He opened the back door and a waved hand directed Iona to lie on the seat, then he did the same in the front.

After five minutes, there'd been no reaction to their appearance. Joe hit the power button on the car's radio, and a booming voice leapt out.

"Christ! Turn it down!" Iona yelled.

But Joe did so only slowly, as if in a daze.

"I don't understand. I was listening to this channel yesterday evening, and it wasn't a strong signal. Now it sounds real local."

"Do you understand what it's saying?"

"Yes. This guy's announcing that the enemies of the land have been removed."

He listened on, and half relayed the broadcast monologue, with amazement obvious in his voice.

"... those committing themselves to the proper future of Costa Rica have nothing to fear..."

Iona did a whispered addition to that. "Some people didn't have much chance to commit."

"He's gone on," Joe interrupted. *"... there will be a return to the land. All cities will be depopulated ..."*

Then the voice stopped, and a few seconds later the radio broke into a hiss.

"The carrier's gone," Joe announced. "Station's off the air. Maybe we should try to get some real news."

He turned the knob. Another man was talking in Spanish, but this time the signal was much weaker. Joe listened intently.

"So what's he saying?" Iona asked impatiently.

"Sounds like they don't really know what's happened. He's talking about some local earthquake cutting communications, and causing gas-explosions and fires."

"Why believe this guy then?"

"I recognise the voice." Joe explained. "News guy called Eduardo Vincent. Been around since I was a kid. At least something here still exists."

"Is this where you're from?" Iona asked.

"Sure a bit late for polite introductions," he replied, lifting his head and suddenly smiling back at her for the first time. "But yes. I'm half Costa Rican, born here, left young – and the other half's Irish, that's the Joe bit. I've never been there, but my dad still sounds like he comes from what he calls the old country. But me? S'pose I'm all American now."

"I'd wondered about that mixed-up accent of yours."

The sudden loud sound of an aircraft, low overhead, surprised them.

She sat up. "Joe. That must be on reconnaissance. Signal to it."

"No." His voice was sharp. "Keep still, and look out for any more."

"Why?"

"It's about to get very busy and complicated around here. And I don't want to be part of it."

Iona leant forwards to look him in the eyes. "But you are, aren't you?"

"Not directly, I promise you. OK. I was warned something might happen. Some religious sect has gone out of control. The authorities have been secretly and seriously re-arming the police for some time. Almost an army. That's as much as I'm going to say. And Pete isn't that innocent either."

Joe started the engine and drove quickly out of the car park, too quickly, nearly hitting a body lying in the road. It was the first of many more corpses he had to drive past. Most were fallen where they'd been shot, with their blood spread over the road surface. Although Iona tried not to look, she couldn't keep out the hiss each time the tyres went through those half-congealed pools.

"Why is nobody just injured?" she asked. "This has been absolute slaughter."

Joe didn't reply, but continued listening to the radio, giving an occasional commentary to Iona. "They're beginning to fudge it. I think they're finding out how bad this has been, and don't want to say any more."

They were well out of the town when Joe slowed and started looking around, as if uncertain. Soon after that, he turned through a gate in a long hedge and drove under some trees, out of sight from the air. Two men were standing there. They looked relieved as Joe got out, but their expressions changed again when they saw Iona.

Joe quickly moved over to them, and started whispering something that she couldn't hear. Not far away, she noticed a small, twin-turbo-propped aircraft. It was an odd-looking machine, with a high wing, but an enormous belly of a fuselage coming to within about six-inches of the ground.

Joe returned after a few minutes.

"They've agreed to take you on the plane," he announced.

Iona dreaded confirming what 'you' meant.

"You're not coming?"

"No. I've some business to finish. They'll get you out. It's all I can do. But you'd better act dumb, and don't ask again about what happened here. That'll get you killed – instantly. Probably me as well. Now I must go. Wait here until they call you over."

He beckoned her out of the car, and she obeyed reluctantly, then watched it drive away. Should she have stayed with him whatever? Right now, it felt as if she'd lost her only protection.

The two men went back to sitting cross-legged on the ground, smoking and talking. She could tell from the occasional looks across that she was sometimes the subject of their animated conversation, as if they were arguing about her. Now Joe was gone, they could've killed her without worrying. It would just look like she'd died with all the rest here. She sat, leaning back against the tree, trying not to draw their attention.

It was only when dusk was well set in, and Iona could see the glow of those cigarettes, that the two men stood, and one of them whistled and beckoned her over. He pointed to the rear two seats in the six-seater aircraft, then ripped her handbag away, throwing it into the grass. Iona instinctively moved to retrieve it. Without its contents, it would take a long time to identify her body. She just got an arm wrapped hard round her neck from behind, and was thrown back towards the plane.

"Do what we want or you will be killed," was almost reassuring.

They forced her into the small cabin, pushed her head onto her lap, and threw a heavy plastic sheet over her. The tin-box of a fuselage was still baking hot from the day's heat, and the stench of paraffin made her retch.

A few moments later, something large was put on the two seats in front of her. Then she heard the men get in. After that, the sound of the engines drowned everything.

They had been noisily airborne for about two hours, when Iona felt the plane losing height quickly. Assuming that making a landing would distract the two in front, she lifted the plastic sheet slightly and got a glimpse of the compass – heading 30 degrees. She tensed up for an impact on the runway, but it didn't come.

It was another two hours later when the landing then caught Iona completely by surprise. There was a sudden roar from the engines and the air-grabbing sound of propellers on reverse pitch. At the first bump, while the pilots had to be busy, she quickly moved the plastic again and took another look. Through the bottom of the windscreen, she couldn't see any runway-lights, but just what looked like the headlights of a car directly in front of them.

The aircraft stopped quickly, and she felt it spin round, engines still revving hard. A door was opened and the noise became incredible, drowning the two men's shouting. Whatever had been loaded in front of her was being pulled out.

Thirty seconds later, they grabbed her and dropped her on the ground.

"Say anything about us, and your friend Joe is dead." It was shouted from about two inches away but, in the noise, was only just intelligible. "Now keep your face down!"

The plane roared to full-throttle. Iona, lying just behind the propellers, was blasted with dirt and stones, but didn't even hear her own screams of pain.

When the blast and noise had gone, she slowly opened her eyes. And it didn't make much difference. She sat up. It was pitch-black, silent, and hot.

Even after several minutes to get her eyes accustomed, she still couldn't see anything. "I could walk into anything," she said to herself, and decided not to move till it got light.

When dawn came, it then moved in fast on what was a flat grassy plain, but its light revealed little else. Iona walked around, aimlessly. From the direction of the about to be visible sun, she had a compass bearing, but how did that help?

Then she had a bit of luck, noticing a couple of marks where a car had spun its wheels on the grass. She guessed that the direction they pointed in was probably the shortest way to a road.

After about an hour's walk, she was amongst the fifteen-foot-high trees of an orange grove. They gave her some shade, and fresh food for a breakfast. Also, for the first time, there was a definite track here.

Twenty minutes later, she emerged onto a narrow, surfaced road.

She was contemplating which way to go, when her lonely walk suddenly changed. With a roar and cloud of dust, a red car swung out from a side turning up ahead, and drove fast towards her. She leapt onto the verge as it went past. With the sun's reflection on its glass, she hadn't made out anything of the occupants. She was about to. It skidded almost to a halt twenty feet further on. A man in light brown leapt out. Then the car accelerated on away down the road. The man came towards her – head low and a gun pointing.

"Deputy Sheriff Shaefer, Polk County," he announced. "You stay right where you are."

The American accent surprised Iona. She tried to wrench her thoughts round to this sudden new scene.

For a few moments, the man seemed to concentrate on the departing red car, but then turned towards Iona again.

"OK. So, jus' what you doin' here?"

"Please excuse me. Where is Polk County?" Iona said.

Judging by his expression, this was neither the accent nor the response that Shaefer had expected.

"You tryin' to be funny?" he asked.

"No. I was dropped in here by plane last night, and I don't know where I am."

"Dropped? Where from?"

"Costa Rica."

"Now that's sure a different one. Take your jacket off and put your hands on your head."

He checked through the pockets of the discarded jacket, and looked over Iona carefully, but didn't touch her.

"Where's your ID?"

"My passport's gone."

"This jus' gets better."

The car returned, and its only occupant, another policeman, got out.

"No one around," he announced. "They send her walking up the road first. We break cover. Then the rest vanish."

"This one seems different," Shaefer said. He went back to the car, and then was in radio contact with someone. Iona couldn't hear the words.

He got out again and faced her. "It seems like if you really have come from Costa Rica, some people want to talk to you real bad."

"I still don't know where I am."

"Polk County, Florida. Now keep quiet! We're taking you to DEA headquarters in Tampa, and no one's to talk to you till then."

Route 60 between Bartow and Tampa is not scenic, passing a collection of fertiliser processing plants, then mile after mile of sporadically-placed trailer parks and shacks. As instructed, Iona remained silent as the unlovely vista went by. She needed to collect her thoughts anyway. There were just an occasional few words exchanged between Shaefer and the driver.

Nearer to Tampa, the view became a long ribbon of big gaudy signs as they continued to head downtown. The car eventually stopped in front of an unattractive building. *'700 Twigs. Drug Enforcement Administration'* it said over the door. They went into the dowdy front entrance. It smelt strongly of disinfectant.

After they'd taken the lift to the fourth floor, Shaefer led Iona into a small and cluttered office. A man was sitting at the only desk. He moved fractionally off his seat, introducing himself as John Doble, Resident Agent. As directed by the wave of his arm, she sat on the only other chair, while Shaefer remained standing behind her.

The only other person in the room, stood in the corner behind Doble, was dressed in suit, tie, and white shirt, which made him look like the senior person here.

But it was Doble who immediately went on the attack, his eyes narrow with suspicion. "So you just happen to be wandering around in drug-running territory, with no ID huh?"

"I've been flown from Costa Rica," she announced.

Both Doble and the man behind him looked at her intensely. "So who brought you in?" Doble asked.

"I don't know."

He leant forward. "You'd best do some more explaining than that – and about all of it."

Iona remembered the pilot's warning. But she started on her recollection, of the black awakening in her room, the gunfire and explosions out of the window, and the men breaking down the door.

At this point, the man behind Doble asked Shaefer if he could leave, and forget all about this. "That bit will also apply to you," he added to Doble. "Continue please," was directed at Iona.

She then recounted the civilian's bodies in the hotel, the total destruction, and her drive out of the city. Everything she said was about as it had been, except there was no Joe in this version. It was the best she could do for him, and probably Peter, she thought.

"My car was stopped by these guys. As they questioned me, I noticed they had a plane hidden away," she continued. "I got one of them aside and tried to do a deal with him."

"What sort of deal?" Doble asked.

"I think I know," the man by the back wall said slowly, his eyes wandering obviously off Iona's neat face and blond hair, and down to the rest of her body. Then he nodded for Doble to carry on.

"And did he agree?" Doble duly continued.

"Yes. But the other guy didn't want anything to do with it. They argued before we set off, and on the way over. I couldn't understand what they were saying. It was in Spanish, I think."

"And then?"

"I ended up getting thrown out in the middle of a field somewhere here."

"And did anything else come out of the plane?" Doble asked.

"They said they would kill me if I said anything."

"Was anything else taken out?" Doble repeated.

Iona paused – for a second only. "Yes, but I didn't see what. Big container or something. They held me down."

"Did the plane look like this?"

Doble slid a postcard-sized photograph to the edge of his desk. Iona leant forward to look at it.

"Yes. Exactly."

Doble turned to the man behind him, as if to explain how local operations worked.

"That plane's an Aero Commander 680. Stick an extra tank inside, and it'll fly you from Colombia all the way to here. Then you just drop in on a dirt strip, using car headlights."

Iona broke in. "Yes, I saw that."

Doble continued. "In fact, we even tracked that plane in on the radar until he dropped height over the sea. So we knew the son of a bitch was coming in, but we didn't know where. Around here, unless we're real lucky, a stakeout doesn't work. There are thirty-two illicit strips over in Polk County alone. And those are just the ones we know of. So, after chucking out the drugs and the extra fuel tank, you land somewhere else looking perfectly legal."

"Could you describe the men?"

"Not very well. They were both about the same. Short, dark, and wearing green overalls. They had very strong accents – to me anyway."

There was a knock on the office door, and a fax was brought in for the man in the corner. He silenced Doble while he took a minute to read it.

"Well. It could be you are who you claim," he then said to Iona. "We know an Iona Duncan came in to the country two days ago, with your British Airways," he emphasised, as if proud of their research. "And then caught a flight on to Costa Rica the next day. Yes?"

"Yes," Iona nodded. "That's me."

"OK. So I might accept that. If you now cooperate. Do you know we could now make life sure difficult for you?"

Iona frowned and looked up at him.

"Illegal entry by someone who can't prove their identity, and is involved with known drug trafficking? It could be a long, complicated and very expensive time before you get back home. You understand?"

This time Iona nodded.

"But I am prepared to do a deal. I don't want you talking to anyone about what happened in Costa Rica."

"Can you tell me what did happen?"

"We don't know for sure. That's why it's gonna be kept quiet for the moment. So, if you wanna be sensible and say nothing about it, there are some other arrangements I could make."

It didn't take much thinking about. "If it gets me home, I agree."

"That's good. But understand. You say anything about it before you go, then you don't leave in quite some while. And once you're in the UK, still keep quiet, if you ever want to visit the US again."

Half an hour later Iona was back in the dull entrance-hall again, but this time with two female, plain-clothes, minders. They took her to the Sheraton Hotel near the airport. .

"We've got a bit of a wait here before we get a flight up to New York," one of them said.

"What then?"

"You meet up with some paperwork, then you're on a transatlantic flight. But we stay with you till then."

Iona was the first passenger to be put on the American Airlines daytime flight to London. She'd been looked after well, given new clothes and other essentials, plus a sealed envelope to be given to UK immigration.

"I will remind you again. Do not talk to anyone on the plane," was the parting remark from one of her guards.

Iona was too confused to want to do that anyway and, when a man sat next to her, she continued to look intently out of the window at the baggage loaders.

After takeoff, Iona started watching the news channel on her backrest video screen. In quarter of an hour, it became obvious that

CNN had reached its point of recycling the main stories, and they hadn't mentioned anything about Costa Rica.

The man in the next seat was also watching his screen. "Are you checking for the stuff about Costa Rica?" he asked casually. Iona pretended not to hear.

"The news has broken about something major happening there you know," he persisted.

Iona briefly glanced at him, showing irritation.

"Apparently it was a total bloodbath," he went on. "Amazing in such a peace-loving country, isn't it? Do you know the place?"

Ignoring the stream of comments became easier when she heard the ping of the seat-belt light going off, and was able to recline her seat sharply back and close her eyes. But any sleep was impossible.

It must have been two hours later, when something touched her shoulder. Iona instantly pushed an arm away.

"Steve Withers, CIA," the man next to her said this time. There was an identity card in his hand. "I need you to tell me if you know anything about Costa Rica."

"Well I don't. Never been there. And you do anything more with that hand, and I'll call the flight attendant – for your protection."

Iona shut her eyes again, now even further from that refuge of sleep she wanted.

It seemed like a day later this time, when the announcement of the plane's imminent landing, forced Iona to raise her seat back. She was still tight with awareness of the man beside her.

He immediately spoke again. "Guess I'm sorry about touching you. And well done. You didn't fall for it."

"Fall for what?"

"Talking about what happened in Costa Rica. And you'd still be back in Tampa now if some of us had been listened to. I don't know why he wanted to get you out so fast."

She looked blankly back as he continued.

"Listen lady. I think you're much more involved than you're saying. If so, it's important you tell me."

Iona busied herself collecting her belongings from around the seat.

"Have it your way then," he said. "But there's a story about to break which suits some people at the moment. It's the sort of thing the media will latch onto. But it's not true. I need to know what is the truth. So, if you change your mind, contact me. Otherwise, you jus' keep ever so quiet. You're messing with something very dangerous."

He handed over a card.

Whatever was in that envelope certainly worked with immigration, and going into their offices probably helped to lose the CIA guy.

Half an hour later, released back into the main airport after surprisingly few question, Iona bought the first newspaper she saw. It had nothing about Costa Rica. Then she had to catch a taxi back to her place in Bisham, and ask it to go straight back to the airport again after she'd picked up her spare car keys.

Finally back in the cottage, she turned on the TV to look at the news, and wondered what had happened to Peter and the rest of them.

Chapter 12

Never, ever, go home again

To Bisham, Buckinghamshire, England

Peter's clandestine route back from Singapore via Frankfurt meant that, with waiting for the connection, it was Saturday afternoon before he arrived back for the meeting they'd all arranged at Iona's place.

He'd seen no one suspicious on the flights, and wasn't followed as he came out of the long-stay car park at Heathrow. So they probably hadn't found his car there and watched it? But that didn't stop Peter worrying. Going round the M25, he did several dummy exits, moving fast from the outer lane to the inner as if he was going off, but not doing it. Anyone following the manoeuvres would have been obvious. Still, he was super-aware when he swung off the large dual-carriageway roundabout, and into Bisham village's narrow street of old red-brick cottages. They had no front gardens, and were crowded up against the pavements. The first one on the other side was Iona's, with the access road just this side of it.

With a final look in the mirror, Peter checked that no one else had come off the roundabout, flicked the car sharply right, then left to swing round into her walled-in parking space. Nothing had followed or passed the end of the road. He was now hidden.

Turning the engine off, he suddenly relaxed. Here, in this little protected place, everything would be normal again. He was back to welcoming shelter and safety.

But his reception jarred that feeling out of him. She must have heard the car, and, almost the moment he knocked, she unlatched the door, and hauled him inside.

"You've got some answering to do."

Surprised, he almost backed through the door again, but she grabbed it, slammed it shut and did up all the locks.

"About what?"

"What's just happened to me in Costa Rica."

"Christ! You didn't go there again? After last time?"

"Why shouldn't I? I've got a business to run. "So what the hell is going on out there? You know, don't you?"

Peter held his hands towards her. "I told you before. I have no idea."

"You bloody do. A guy out there even knew you."

"Believe me. I don't. So tell me, who is this bloke?"

"I intend to." But she turned and walked into the lounge.

He followed. A TV news programme was on.

"It's being hushed up somehow," she announced angrily. "It wasn't in any of the papers at the airport, and it's not on the TV."

The news item seemed to be about a flood in Africa. He was about to ask what she was expecting, when the phone rang. At first Iona hovered, as if reluctant to leave the TV, but then walked back into the kitchen to answer it.

Through the doorway, Peter could hear the concerned whispers of what was mainly a one-way exchange. "That's incredible. --- Yes, he's back. --- No, not Brad. --- Just be careful you're not followed."

"And what was that about?" he asked as she returned.

Iona's face was total confusion. "I don't believe it. That was Kiri on her mobile. Seems Tony's contacted her. Lucky to have escaped. He's in a hell of a state, and daren't go back to the house or the hospital. I said they could both come over."

Peter looked back and shook his head slowly. "Him as well? I was nearly killed."

"What!" She held her hands to her face. "Hell. Then I'm sorry. This is stupid. What the hell is going on?"

"OK then. Let's just reset. You tell me what happened to you."

"I will. But I want to watch this. So maybe let's wait till Tony gets here?"

Peter shrugged his shoulders. "Then I know what I need right now. Can I get us both a drink?"

"Yea, good idea. And sorry again." Iona picked up the remote control, switched the TV over to another news-channel, and sat down, straight-backed, on the sofa.

Peter poured two gin and tonics, like always before, one weak, one strong, and slid in beside her. She leant into him, and he moved them both into a more comfortable position, but she still concentrated on the television. Peter finally succumbed to the tiredness of the long flights, and, in the next half hour, almost nodded off to the background drone of the alternating CNN, Sky News and BBC news coverage.

He was roused by the doorbell, and by Iona leaping up at the sound. He half turned as she ran to the kitchen door.

Again, she almost pulled Kiri and Tony in, and locked the door again.

Seeing him, Peter stood up. "Good God! What's happened to you? You look bloody dreadful."

Tony walked unsteadily forward. "Oh, thanks for that. But I'll be all right. And glad to see you're OK, Peter. Someone at that place in Switzerland knows about you and Brad. And I might have given you both away."

"Well, seems everybody knows me then. And they did nearly get me," Peter said. "But I don't think it was down to you. Maybe we should contact Brad though?"

"I know the numbers," Kiri said.

Iona picked up the phone and handed it over.

"Use a 141," Peter suggested.

Kiri made two calls, but said nothing during either of them. Putting the handset down, she turned to the others. "That was Brad's house in America and his mobile. But I only got his answering services."

"He should be on his way here anyway," Peter commented. "It's what we agreed. He might even be on a plane. And we can check if he left an e-mail."

The rest of them followed in silence as Iona went into her small office, turned the computer on, and checked her mailbox. Peter looked over her shoulder. The e-mails all seemed routine – except one. It was from *brad@hal-a.com*. She clicked on it.

Iona,

Hope you're all OK and have met up. Fraid I can't make it. Things have gone real bad here. Worse still, now the law are after me as well. I'm going to tell someone high up, but I think I could get a lot more out of that computer of Kiri's. When she gets there, can she give me its address and security codes?

Brad.

Iona beckoned Kiri to the computer, and she immediately hit the keys.

Brad,

Address is kiri-health@oxon.org. But don't try yet. To make sure I'd protected the data like you asked, I physically isolated the external line. I'll go to the house to reconnect it and contact you again. And yes, we've all met up, but things are bad here too. The others will send updates while I'm fixing the comms.

Kiri.

Peter looked on as she typed. "Is your house safe to go to?" he asked.

She stood up. "Well, I've led a normal life there so far this week, so what's different now? And while I'm away, Tony can also get some rest."

Iona turned to Tony. "There's a spare room upstairs. You can lie down there."

He looked as he was about to fall down anyway, and just nodded.

As Kiri left the house through the kitchen door, the TV news from the other room suddenly drew Iona's attention.

An estimated four thousand people have perished in an unprecedented civilian massacre in Costa Rica.

She ran through, grabbed the remote control and turned the sound up.

At night, over a period of eight hours, mercenaries rampaged through a small town, killing everyone in sight. Was this a drugs war? And maybe with a whole town caught in the crossfire? We're just getting some pictures through.

It seemed the first cameramen with satellite links had got there, and found the mutilated bodies in the hotel. The difference was that they had been laid in a line across the lobby floor – and covered up. Then the pictures went to scans of the wrecked town, now full of frantic-looking emergency workers in face-masks.

Peter had sat down again to be beside Iona, and they both watched in silence while the item ran on for a further five minutes.

"You weren't in the middle of that?" he asked at the end.

She nodded. "I was."

"On your own? How the hell did you get out?"

Iona shook her head. "No. Not on my own. There were two of us. He helped me. Your mate."

Ignoring Peter's puzzled face, she began hitting the programme button to get the other news channels. Now they all carried the story, and with similar pictures, but there were no different facts.

An hour later, Iona and Peter had swapped most of their experiences from Costa Rica and Jordan, and then sent a long e-mail to Brad, updating him as well. The two of them had moved into the kitchen to get some supper when Tony came down the stairs. He looked a bit better, but seemed agitated.

"Kiri should be back by now," he said, worry in his voice.

"Probably still working on the computer. How about calling her?" Iona pointed at the phone.

Tony nodded and moved towards it.

"No," Peter said urgently. "Use my mobile, just in case. More difficult to trace to here." He handed over his own phone.

Tony punched rapidly at the buttons, then seemed to exhale with relief as the call must have been answered. But seconds later his face froze – and stayed that way while he listened to whoever was on the other end. Then he suddenly switched off the call and the phone dropped to the carpet.

"They've got Kiri," he said through clenched teeth. "Kidnapped her. To make me do what they want."

He started pacing round the room, quickly and in huge steps. His fists were clenched, and it looked like he wanted to attack someone. Tony's weight normally made him look soft. Now he seemed tensed and dangerous. Peter felt the hair on his neck rise as he moved out of the way. He didn't dare say anything.

"Why didn't I realise?" Tony shouted at the air. "The bastards! They've gone for her instead. And it was my fault. I should have realised that's what they'd do and ...." He stopped again.

"How could you know?" Peter asked gently.

"Because those people want me – badly. Though I don't know why."

"What exactly did they tell you on the phone?"

Tony drew breath, as if about to say something difficult. "She's being taken to Switzerland and I will only see her again if I cooperate. I report this to anyone and she dies."

"Couldn't be worse then," Peter whispered. "Normally you'd say, go to the police. But unless they believe all the rest of the stuff, how do they take you seriously?"

Tony seemed to consider that. "So they start by just making 'routine enquiries', contact the Swiss authorities, and it all gets to whoever's doing this. It means I've got no choice. I have to try and get her out myself. And, if they need me somehow, then I can use that to get back at the bastards."

Peter shook his head. "Please Tony. This is all now just so dangerous. We have to think before we do anything. Our lives mean nothing to these people. You don't know what's happened to me and Iona, and Brad by the sound of it."

Tony scowled. "Yes. It was Brad who wanted her to do something at the house. Perhaps you'd better tell him what's happened."

Peter couldn't quite read the sharp intonation and, not wanting to ask, he just moved over to the computer terminal and sent a short message telling Brad what had happened.

Soon the reply came.

Peter,
It's real terrible news. But I just checked Kiri's computer. She didn't contact me, but must have got to it first. It's on line now. This was all my fault.
Brad.

Tony took one look, pushed Peter aside, and immediately started hitting the keys himself.

Brad, it's not your fault. I should have seen it. So use Kiri's computer to do everything to find out who these sods are. And fast. Can you get in though? Only she knew the passwords. And how secure are these e-mails?
Tony.

Again, the response was instant.

Tony,
Remember, I created Kiri's machine. All of us designers leave a back door. About your other question. E-mail ain't so secure, but I'm using Tron as a link. Its traffic is massive, terabytes, finding anything in it would be v difficult. At your end it would be easy, if they knew it was Iona's e-box they needed to look at. If they don't, I think we're OK. It's morning here. I'll work on Kiri's computer and have something ready for your morning over there.
Brad.

Tony remained staring at the screen.

Peter put a hand on one of his shoulders. "Well, it looks like we're taking them on. And there's plenty we can do here as well. Let's go through what we know. The important bits, and fast. I know from those urgent gun-trainer orders I got, that those people are in a hurry and we may not have much time. But that may mean they've got a weakness too."

This seemed to bring Tony back to life. "Yes. And I've got some stuff here which will definitely tell us something."

From the back of a chair he grabbed the dishevelled jacket he'd arrived in, and took out the small shampoo and shower-gel bottles.

"They were giving me some sort of treatment, and these will tell us what. One of them is what they were giving me, intravenously would you believe. The other is my blood after they'd done it. It was like being on some weird and strong drug. I felt terrified and saw colours all wrongly." He looked over at Peter. "You remember when we first met at my place, you told us about that nightmare you had in – was it Jordan? Could it have been something you ate or drank? Does that make sense?"

"Well," Peter said slowly. "I'd drunk the water from the red river. Fucking weird taste it was."

"Then I think," Tony explained. "Whatever was in that river, was given to me in Switzerland."

"Sounds pretty unlikely," Peter replied. "But if that's right, we might've got a bit lucky. I've just been back there and got a sample of that stuff." He reached into his briefcase, took out his pen-top of red mud, now wrapped in a small poly-bag, and held it triumphantly up.

Tony took it. "I'm going to do a laboratory analysis on my stuff. And I'll include this."

Peter was doubtful about that. "It won't be safe for you to go to the hospital."

"I know. So that's not where I'm going." He turned to Iona. "There's another path lab about twenty miles from here. Don't see how anyone would be watching that. They'd do it for me, and they work twenty-four hours. Could you run me across?"

"But you're completely knackered."

"Doesn't matter. We don't have much time."

She slowly nodded. "OK."

"As you leave here, lie in the back," Peter suggested. "You shouldn't be seen near this place."

Through a window he watched them drive off. No one followed.

Two hours later they were back, with Tony carrying a large white envelope containing the lab analyses. He immediately settled at the desk and started looking through them.

Peter joined Iona by the TV, where she continued to watch the news broadcasts. He turned it low and pulled up close to her again.

Those lab results seemed to be taking a long time for Tony to understand, and gradually Peter noticed his heavy sighs and shifts of position. Whatever he was looking at, seemed to be giving him some sort of trouble, but Peter decided not to interfere.

In the next half hour, nothing new came on the TV, but Tony's mutterings and sighs got worse. Finally it came.

"Peter. Help me please. I'm going mad."

He stood and walked over. "What's wrong then, mate?"

"This stuff makes no sense."

"Go through it with me. Don't know much about it, but two minds and all that."

Tony started slowly. "Those samples I got. I was so certain they'd show what that bunch were trying to do to me." He drew a deep breath. "But nothing here looks suspicious. I've been through it again and again. My blood shows as perfectly normal. Can't see anything funny. Anything. So I took a look at the stuff they were putting in to me. According to this, it was just vitamin A. Doing that doesn't make sense either. And it certainly doesn't explain what was happening to me."

"Some mistake in the analysis?" Peter asked.

"It was done on the most sophisticated kit made," Tony now snapped back. "And with me standing over it."

"OK. It is strange then," Peter said, trying to calm him. "What about the red mud I brought back from Jordan? What was that?"

"That's just about as odd. No. Even odder. And I can't understand anything now," Tony replied, almost as if giving up. "That's mainly vitamin A as well. In a river?"

"An ex river. But at least that sort of ties in with what happened when I drank from it. Like it had the same shitty effect as what they put into you."

Tony's voice now sounded as if he could soon cry. "It may 'tie in' as you say, but it doesn't begin to explain anything to me. There's something about this I'm just not getting."

Peter touched his shoulder. "Christ, mate, maybe because it's now two in the morning, and you're buggered and distraught anyway. It might make all more sense tomorrow?"

"Maybe you're right." Tony slowly stood up. "Night Iona," he added softly, then in slow steps, like a much older person, he went upstairs.

Peter woke first the next morning, left Iona asleep, and came down to put the kettle on. Then he went to the computer and opened her mailbox. There were three in from Brad. One of them was labelled *'Photos for Peter'*.

He felt a tinge of excitement. Soon the printer was spewing out strange-looking images. They all looked the same, mainly black, but with small white blobs. Some text followed.

Peter,

These are IR shots I took at night, from the air, of the cult here. I can't make sense of them.

I've realised the vague whitish blobs are people on the ground. A heap of them around for the middle of the night!

From the flight nav and timings, I've also worked out where they are. The first fifty pictures are in that film-set street. They're using it someway? The second fifty shots are in the open ground. The bit that I told you was marked out with lines.

Other than that, I can't work out what the hell's going on. Can you? Don't get confused by the really small bright marks. I reckon those are fault spots on my film — otherwise why are they different on each frame? The film a bit old, but there are none on the second pass we made. The film near the center of the reel must've been better preserved.

And something else, which you know a thing-or-two about. We got hit. Both engines with rifle shots. We were five-hundred feet above them, and doing a hundred-and-fifty knots. Nearly killed us. Is that your kit again?

Brad

Peter spread the pictures out.

Fifteen minutes later, although he'd re-read Brad's short message a few times, those images still tell him very much about what might have been going on.

With his brain almost in neutral, Peter was pondering the bright-dot 'faults'. Why hadn't Brad used decent film? Then it struck him that those dots weren't quite random, like spots on duff film would be. It took him a long time to check it on all the pictures. But he was right. There was something about all of them. Every single one, on every frame, was right next to one of the larger white blobs, the images of the people.

He re-scanned all the pictures to check again – and then noticed something even stranger. On the pictures Brad said were of the open ground, the dots were always on the same side of the people blobs. Suddenly his mind was racing again.

It took a few more minutes before he whispered to himself. *"No Brad. Those aren't faults. Those are infrared pulses. The hot gas at the muzzle of a gun – just as it's fired."*

Peter knew each pulse would last only a moment, so they would be different on each frame – why Brad would think they were random faults. He also began to realise what it all meant.

Peter's next discovery was just by chance. He was stacking the photos away to clear the keyboard, when he noticed one of them with just a single bright dot. But it was on one of Brad's photos of the second pass, the ones he'd said were without the 'faults'.

Peter carefully checked all the others from the second pass, and saw it wasn't quite like Brad had said. There were 'faults' there, but only four of them. Then he realised what it meant – and it made the whole thing even more amazing.

"Shit," he whispered. *"That's impossible – almost."*

He reached for the keyboard.

Brad,

Those pictures are incredible. I can't quite believe it, but I think I know what's going on.

The little bright marks aren't faults, they're from guns firing – small ones – rifles – or handguns. Two different patterns though. On the open ground, all the shots are in the same direction. What would explain that? They must be all shooting at things in the same direction, like at targets on a rifle range.

That 'film set' is a bit different. The dots are in all directions, as if the targets are all around in the buildings. Knowing what I've been asked for, that place is a shooting range with a difference. Like it's for practise in urban shooting – not a simulator – but with real buildings all around.

And I don't need to tell you the crazy thing about it all – that it's happening at night, with no lights. No wonder they didn't want you looking.

Now, even stranger. On your second pass, you thought there were no dots. There are though, but just four of them. So they'd stopped the other firing, probably because they heard you go over first time. But, when you came back, they fired just four times at you, and hit both your engines!!!

Those people must be using my kit for training. Maybe this place is the final outdoor proving range. Just before they graduate maybe? But to what?

Peter.

Peter then opened the second e-mail Brad had sent overnight – titled *'locations'*.

Peter,

I did the data searches in Kiri's computer. A group of places came up. Fifty-eight of them. I guess they'll all be like the ones Kiri went to in Australia and Cyprus. Looks like we've found the suckers!

They are all over the world. In America there are two – Marion in Ohio, and Canon City in Colorado. That last one's just gotta be what I got those pictures of.

Also, there's one in Russia. Japan has two, Britain one – in Scotland. There's an interesting one in Canada, where that huge mass-suicide took place. The Mounties, or whatever, are still crawling all over it. Also, there are the ones Kiri went to, AND one in Switzerland. I've put a complete list as locations 2.

So it looks like what's happened to us, is that we all stumbled onto these places. That's the real connection between us – and why we weren't too welcome.

I'm still working on a follow-up idea I've got. I'll send the results when I finish.

Brad.

Peter, concentrating on the computer, hadn't noticed that both Iona and Tony had come downstairs.

"Morning." She announced, and scanned the screen. "Well? Let's open that list."

Tony looked much better, but did nothing more than acknowledge Peter's greeting with a nod.

Peter opened the attachment, hit print, and the sheets started rolling out.

Iona grabbed one. "Look! Costa Rica. Canas. That's near where that massacre has just been. It's also where my disappeared flower suppliers were supposed to have gone, to learn about magical new herbs or something."

"OK," Peter continued. "Let's put some things together. Five of these places we know about: Australia, Cyprus, Colorado, Switzerland and Costa Rica. That leaves fifty-three others around the world. But now we know where they all are."

Tony broke his silence, and from the cynical laugh it was obvious that, even if he looked better, his mood hadn't improved. "And they will all turn out to be strange, but perfectly law abiding. Just like the ones Kiri went to. We keep finding out these things. And it just doesn't get us anywhere, does it!"

Iona turned to him. "Brad's still working on something. Let's wait for that. I'll get some breakfast."

"And there might be something more," Peter added, picking up his briefcase. "I took a camera out to Jordan." He pulled out the twenty-five photographs he'd taken, and put them down on the table as Iona started setting the breakfast around them. "Does anyone know anything about temples or whatever?"

Iona looked briefly at the photos. "No way I do," was her only comment before she passed them on to Tony, and went back into the kitchen. At first, he looked dismissive, almost about to throw them on the floor, but then seemed to spot something, thumbed through them again, and finally selected four, which he put down on the table and frowned at.

"So do you recognise it?" Peter asked.

"No. It's not that," he replied distantly. "Something else. It's strong, but I can't quite get it."

He was then silent through the meal, eating only slowly, as if transfixed by those pictures.

Suddenly he held one of them up. "I know who this is!"

Peter looked over at the photo. "Who? What do you mean?"

Tony seemed to have to calm himself before he could go on. "You see that statue in front of the cathedral? Well, I know who it is!"

"You know which Saint or whoever it is?" Iona asked.

"No. It's the bastard who's got Kiri. Carlos Simou. The person who showed me round the laboratory in Switzerland."

"Tony," Iona said quietly. "A lot's happened to you. Why would someone running a Swiss laboratory, have his statue on a temple in Jordan? It has to be someone who just looks the same?"

"No!" Tony snapped. "Believe me. This guy is very distinctive, and very memorable." Then he seemed less certain. "But you're right. Why he'd be there, I don't know."

"Hang on a minute, matey," Peter said. "Don't drop it quite so fast. Tell us a bit more about Simou. Something bloody strange has to be going on anyway. Why else does a new temple suddenly appear in the middle of the fucking desert? So who is this guy?"

"Well. He says he's in charge of that laboratory, with some mystery partner. He is obsessed with ecology, and preventing the destruction of the planet's wildlife by human overpopulation. And he's a very big guy, with really creepy black eyes."

At that, Peter grabbed one of the pictures. "But, as Iona said, why put his statue on the front of a cathedral, or whatever it is?"

Tony sharply came back. "I don't know. And, see what I mean? Again. You've nearly got yourself killed finding out something, and what does it get us? Nothing!" Then he immediately held up his hands in an apology.

There was a ping from the computer. Peter had left it on line and a new e-mail had come through.

Peter,

Something Kiri said was bugging me. She said the cult in Australia recruited people – lots of them. I assume the one back here in the Rockies would have been doing the same. But, no one I've ever spoken to hereabouts has even mentioned a center like that. And it was just a few miles away. How do they attract people then?

I got Tron working on the net. Thought it would be no-brainer for it. It went searching for 'cult' sort of keywords. Started with sort of religious ones: Scientology, Moonie, Wee Free, Seventh Day, Wicca, Charismatic, Gnostic, Pure Land. You name it. There are hundreds of them. It got loads of hits. There's a whole bunch of that stuff out there. But NOTHING that came back was from any of the fifty-eight sites. How come? It would be real odd these days not to use the net if you were after people to convert – or whatever they are doing.

So I tried other sorts of mysticism: astrology, magic stones, paganism, dianetics, occult, alternative medicine, homeopathy, herbs, even dietary stuff – you could go on forever. Again it turned up nothing on the cult sites. Those places give out no information to the web, nor do any local publicity. So how do they recruit people? Sure makes no sense to me. Will keep at it.

Brad.

Tony had been looking over Peter's shoulder at this, and now shook his head. "See. We still haven't an idea what's really happening. So time's up. I go to Switzerland anyway."

"No. Please," Peter said. "Not yet. We haven't finished working out what we know." He turned to Iona. "And this is a strange one. When I was in your bathroom this morning, I thought about your hotel in Costa Rica. Can we go up there, so you can explain something to me?"

Tony gave him a look of disbelief, but Peter stood and they all went up the stairs, Tony last.

After wiping some water from the bottom of the bath, Peter sat in it – fully clothed.

"Now," he asked Iona. "You were looking this way?"

In the bath, Peter was facing away from the entrance, with most of his body behind the opened door beside the bath, and his feet towards the wall at the end. She nodded to him. Tony had stayed outside the door, his impatience showing in his body language.

"And that lone gunman was behind you," Peter continued. "Near the other side of the open door?" He leant forwards and turned his head round the end of the door to nod towards where Tony was now standing.

"Uh huh," Iona agreed.

"But he couldn't see you directly? You'd tucked yourself behind the door?" He slid back to be behind it, and pulled his legs in.

"That's right. Trying to hide."

"But you said he seemed to look straight at you?"

"Well, not straight. That bathroom had a big mirror." Iona pointed at where she had a radiator and a towel rail on the end wall. "There."

"So. That is, he looked straight at your reflection in the mirror? But he didn't react?"

"No. And it seemed ages he was standing there."

"And I think," Peter mused. "He didn't see you, because it was through that mirror."

Tony stepped forward and looked down at him. "You're not going to start saying she's a vampire now, are you? Invisible in mirrors – and not leaving a shadow maybe? Christ." He turned away.

"No. But just please think about it," Peter pleaded. "I've been puzzled all along about something. How do these people seem to see in the dark so well? Now I think I realise."

"Which is?" Iona asked, arm out to beckon Tony back.

"They can somehow see things differently. And it wouldn't need to be a big change." He got out of the bath and turned to Tony. "And not seeing in the mirror is the key."

There was no response, so Peter went on. "Normal glass only lets through a small bit of the electromagnetic spectrum. The bit we see as visible light. Maybe that guy mostly sees a different bit. One that doesn't go through glass?"

Tony shrugged his shoulders. "You'll have to explain more."

"Suppose these people have found something which changes their eyesight. Maybe they've taken some sort of chemical? It would be the optical equivalent of breathing helium to make your voice go all squeaky. Just a change in frequency. Nothing magic."

"I don't know of any such thing."

"But think about what's happened to the two of us? Amongst other things, our vision went weird? Don't you think that's odd?"

Peter was staring straight at Tony, as if waiting for some realisation from him. It didn't take too much longer.

"Christ, you're right! Something in those samples we've got, is a substance to change vision. It's just that we haven't worked out what it is. The analysis programmes only look for things they know about."

Iona looked at him in surprise. Peter nodded, smiling slightly.

Tony had now gone on full flow. "What we need is the full works. Gas chromatography, mass spectroscopy, x-ray crystallography – the lot. And we can do it all at The Rutherford Lab, up the road near Oxford, and it's about the best in the world."

"Excellent," Peter said. "But perhaps Oxford's a problem for you. They'll have some sort of watch out. I'd better go instead. The lookout for me will be somewhere else."

"OK. I'll do you a chitty for it."

An hour later Peter was looking, with another man, at a high-definition computer screen. It showed a massively enlarged molecule, with every atomic detail showing, but at a size which made it seem like some child's construction-kit.

The Rutherford Lab's, Dr Philip Wong, knew enough to be baffled.

"The only trouble with that thing," he finally said, "is that it doesn't exist." He pushed aside yet another thick reference book. "It is retinol. But then it isn't."

"What's wrong with it then?" Peter asked.

Dr Wong turned to face him. "What do you know about vitamin A?"

"Not much I suppose. It's in carrots and a few things, and we need it for our eyes in some way? And, at least up to now, I knew the bit about making you see in the dark wasn't true."

Wong looked puzzled at the last comment, but didn't pick up on it. "That's about a normal understanding I suppose. Not wrong, but a bit short on detail. So let's add some for you." He gathered his thoughts. "Vitamin-A, or retinol, or beta carotene, is indeed involved in sight. In fact it's fundamental, and an amazing substance."

He hit a few keys on the computer and the picture on the screen changed slightly.

"That's better. The proper stuff. As you see, it's a column of atoms. Carbon in fact. It also has these little side-chains added on."

Peter just nodded as he looked at the complex image.

"But it has an incredible property," Dr Wong continued. "When certain wavelengths, or frequencies, of electromagnetic radiation fall on one end." He pointed at the top of the screen in front of them. "Then this thing changes shape slightly – sort of twitches. And our eyes have nerves which sense that movement – to tell our brains that something's happened. In fact, that we're receiving what we call, light."

Peter nodded again. He liked things he didn't know being explained.

"Even more convenient," Dr Wong went on, "is that, over a limited range, different wavelengths cause slightly different movements, and send different messages through the nerves. That range is the visible spectrum, and we call those differences, colour. We interpret the shorter waves as blue, the longer ones as red, because this molecule reacts differently to them."

"So this vitamin A is all very fortunate for us," Peter said.

"But it gets better," Dr Wong continued. "In terms of being fortunate that is. Our bodies can't make it, but it comes conveniently packaged in carrots like you say, and many other vegetables. They all make it the same way, and exactly as we need it. But this ...?"

He called up the first image on the screen. "I've never seen it before. It's almost the same as vitamin A, but the main column is made up differently. The structure is coiled, more like a spring."

"If you took some, what might it do?" Peter asked.

"What? Ate it?"

Peter nodded.

"It would depend whether it fooled your body into thinking it was normal vitamin A."

"If it did?"

"And got incorporated into your retina?" Dr Wong thought a moment. "Well. This stuff, with its extra bounciness, would probably respond to lower frequencies – longer wavelengths."

"Infra red in other words?"

"Yes."

"Some of which doesn't go through glass," Peter said, leaving Dr Wong looking puzzled again. "But other than that, being able to sense IR would make you see much better in the dark? And maybe lose your blue vision?"

Dr Wong just gave a confused nod.

Peter stood. "Thank you. I think I've found what I was looking for."

"Where is this stuff from then?" Dr Wong asked.

Peter looked back. "I'd like to tell you that. But it wouldn't make any sense till I've got a few more facts. But don't scrub that stuff from the computer memory. I may need you to help us explain a few things to people. Until then though, please forget I ever came here today."

"A bit difficult," Dr Wong said, but then saw it wasn't a joke.

"I mean it," Peter had added coldly. "Don't talk to people."

He got back to the Bisham cottage in the afternoon.

"I think we're on to something new," he announced. "The 'vitamin A' they were putting onto you Tony, and was in my red river, is not what it seems to be."

He briefly explained it. "Good enough to tell Brad?" he asked. "Something real he can pass on?"

"Hang on," Tony said. "Literally a small problem. Like we've only got a few milligrams of the stuff. Too little to do many tests on. And also, we've got it, not Brad."

Peter's enthusiasm subsided. "See what you mean. He tries to explain things, but all his proof depends on a few milligrams of some unbelievably weird stuff, which is on the other side of the Atlantic."

"Not good then," Tony said. "But Brad's sent another e-mail. Looks interesting."

Peter walked over to the computer.

Peter,

So we didn't find any mystic stuff put out by our cult sites. But Tron has huge comms – a few gigastream data-pipes. It can download from thousands of domains simultaneously.

I did a different sort of search. The whole nine yards this time. I got Tron to get ALL the pages out there, on ALL those mystic subjects, ANYWHERE in the world, WHOEVER sent it. It read close on a billion pages.

Then Tron went through all the text, pulling out every word that was a place name. It's so powerful even I don't know what it can do. And success. It's found something, a geographical correlation, so strong there's no doubt. For these topics, places which are near to these cult sites pop up FAR more often than they should on a random basis.

The picture I get's like this. The communes are hiding themselves, but they put out a bunch of cosy little web pages on mystical stuff. These will seem to come from what looks like, maybe just a local person or two. This bait gets people to go along, not to the main cult sites but always to somewhere near, to get their holistic, ayurvedic, treatment or whatever. Then they maybe get persuaded to go into the main center? And, after that, something happens.

BUT. Only fifty-seven of the sites are doing that, not fifty-eight. The odd one out is Switzerland. It doesn't show up at all. Is it the headquarters? The dark heart of the dark hearts?

Do you like it? So what about some gen from you guys? What've y'all been doing there? I need to take a few actual facts to someone.

Brad.

"OK," Peter said, turning to the other two. "I'll explain to Brad what we know about the funny vitamin A, even if we've hardly got any of the stuff. At least he'll have some good contacts to pass the info to."

When he finished and went back into the lounge, he found Tony morosely staring at a blank TV screen, as Iona walked in with some coffee.

"I'm going to Switzerland to get Kiri out." Tony suddenly announced, almost to himself. "They seem to need me, and badly, although I've no idea why. What makes the neurology of persuasion and indoctrination so important to them? Anyway, they won't get quite the help they expect."

Peter looked down at him. "Then I'll come along too. You said Simou had a partner. And I think I know who it is. Although I can't work out what's in it for him. But he's bloody dangerous."

"Peter." Iona pleaded. "Then you'll both get yourselves killed."

Tony stood and faced them. "Peter, thanks for the offer. But there's something I haven't told you about that Swiss place. It's much worse than you think."

"Like how?"

"There is a Russian bacteriological weapons production plant at Stepnogorsk. Shut down now. I went there as part of a UN monitoring team.

"And?"

"I saw exactly the same thing again in that Swiss place. But even larger. There must have been a hundred fermentation vessels."

"But germ warfare isn't practical," Peter said.

"Oh I forgot. You like your guns don't you. Most people don't realise just how easy it is to make biological weapons. Or how devastating they would be against a modern society."

"Easy to make?" Peter asked.

"Ebola – not difficult to get hold of. Anthrax – I could dig it out of the ground of a Scottish island. Bubonic plague – can be found in several countries. Even smallpox. It's supposed to be held in just two places, one in the US and one in Russia. Russia? With enough money, you could probably go there and buy it. Then you genetically modify a cross with Ebola, easy with today's techniques, and you have the fastest acting, most deadly, organism ever seen."

"But delivery though?" Peter asked. "That's the problem isn't it? Keeping the bugs alive while you get them to the target?"

"That's why you'd probably go for smallpox as a base. That virus can survive about two and a half years outside the human body. It beats everything else by a mile. Flu viruses for example, only survive about fourteen days.

And also, it doesn't matter if the delivery is inefficient, because, after that, every victim is another weapon. You need to read about how people actually behaved in the great plagues of history. There is total fear of any human contact. Our advanced societies would just break down – with no water supplies, no power, no food, no medical care."

"OK. OK," Peter said, trying to calm him. "But if that's going on in Switzerland maybe we should tell someone?"

"Useless. I've seen the place. They'll have a watertight cover story. It would probably take weeks to break that down. Whatever you accused them of."

Peter raised his hands. "I see the picture. And in the meantime, we'd mysteriously stop a few stray long-range bullets. So the best form of defence is attack. We go in ourselves."

Tony looked back. "And Simou isn't going to get what he thinks from me. Also, there might be a way of resisting the funny-vitamin-A treatment."

Peter raised his head. "How?"

"Take huge doses of normal vitamin A first, and probably afterwards. From what Kiri said about that place in Australia, they seem to be obsessed about controlling diet, and I think that could be why."

"OK, we go, and let's hope you're right," Peter replied. "Also, Iona, maybe you should contact that Steve Withers CIA guy you met on the plane?"

She moved slowly to pick up the card from her desk and looked at it. "OK. He's got UK and US numbers here. So let's tell Brad about him as well.

Tony and Peter went to the computer.

Iona looked over at their backs. "But I wish you weren't doing this."

Chapter 13

While the living outnumber the dead

San Francisco, USA

In his e-mails, Brad hadn't told the others exactly where he was hiding – just in case. He'd had too many surprises already.

In fact, he'd holed up in his old apartment in Berkeley, San Francisco. This place was a throwback to his days at the university here, to fifteen years ago when the family trust had bought it. Even after he'd left Berkeley, and built Tron back in Denver, he still used to come to SF for research meetings. It had been good to have his own private place to stay.

But eventually, as his hope of Tron ever becoming self-aware had faded, and keeping up with the latest research seemed less relevant, these trips had become occasional, then hardly at all. Now though, this place was just what he needed, and about as secure as he could've managed. Records of its purchase were buried somewhere in the vaults of the New York lawyers who were the family trustees. Even the utility accounts went to those guys.

The journey from Denver had been bad. Two days, an uncomfortable night's sleep, and a thousand miles in a beaten-up old Buick. Brad wasn't used to all that, or to rigidly obeying all the speed limits. The relief of finally turning into the apartment block's secluded and private basement car-park had been unbelievable. Down there it had been, as in the old days, quiet, and he'd slipped unseen into the lift.

Since locking himself in, Brad had relaxed a bit. Using the old, and huge, PC he'd once left here, he'd fixed up some e-mail data encryption on the broadband back to Tron in Denver. That way he'd felt safer contacting Iona's place. OK, so Tron was sending them on from Denver to her mailbox un-encrypted but, mixed with all the rest of its traffic, that would have taken some finding.

He read the latest e-mail from Peter and Tony, about their gen on the strange vitamin A. But – it still wasn't enough. To anyone else, the whole thing would sound like just a crazy set of incidents and suspicions. Exactly what was he going to warn his Washington contacts about? Germ warfare being launched from Switzerland? And being connected to rampaging gunmen in Costa Rica? Who was going to take all that seriously? So, if this was all he was going to get, there were probably only two old friends who would listen. Even then, it would have to be face to face. That might get him believed, or enough so at least they'd do some more investigation.

He'd need to phone them to fix any meeting, and that couldn't be encrypted. The first call would be to the Pentagon, and then possibly one to the CIA. But had this strange organisation penetrated even those places? If so, how far? Were they waiting for him to make contact, and immediately set up a trace? His mobile would be safest, and he knew how to disable the GPS it came with, but even so, they could locate his local cell, and it would narrow them down to a small area. He had no choice though, so turned the phone on, turned off caller ID, and keyed the number of an old family-friend.

Thomas O'Leary had been the person who'd first interested a young Bradley in the O'Connor collection of old aeroplanes, telling stories about how each one had played its part in American history. Brad knew he could trust that guy with his life, and maybe he was about to.

O'Leary was now a five-star air force general, who these days usually sat behind a desk in the Pentagon, responsible for the welfare of all overseas US Air Force support personnel – and Brad no longer called him uncle.

But today was to be one of those when Tom wasn't behind that desk. His personal direct line was diverted to his answering service. *"I am out of the office today,"* the recording said. *"Returning from a weekend fishing trip to Alaska. I will be back here on Tuesday the eleventh."*

Brad was uncertain. Did he call the secretary? Even if she knew where Tom was, it would probably need another call or two to make contact, to his plane or hotel. He could leave his number for Tom to call back on? No. Brad decided not to even leave a message, and pressed the end button.

His only other contact, although it wasn't so personal, was Helmut Swanson. Helmut was in charge of computer security for the CIA, and Brad had helped him many times. He called the number, and Mary, his secretary, came immediately on the line.

"Hi Brad. Good to hear from you. But if you're after Helmut, he's out of contact."

"Mary. I need to talk to him a bit urgently. And it's serious."

"'Fraid he's over in China this week. But as it's you, you could call him there. Do you want a number?"

But Brad needed that face-to-face meeting, and a week was too long. Then he remembered one of the e-mails from Peter – about the CIA guy Iona had met on the plane. Maybe he should talk to him? It was against his instincts to talk to a stranger about this, but he felt desperate now.

"I won't bother Helmut over there. Sure he's busy enough already," he replied. "But do you know of a fella called Steve Withers who works with you?"

"Yeah," Mary immediately replied, then paused. "Perhaps I shouldn't tell you this. But it's odd you should mention him. He's gone out of contact somewhere in Europe. We're worried. But you could talk to the guy who's acting for him right now."

Without waiting for Brad's reaction, she went off the line.

He hung on, unsure.

"This is Mark Baker. Is that Brad O'Connor?"

"Yes."

"Hi then Brad. Understand you've got a problem. How about I try and help?"

There was something wrong in that instantly friendly but direct question.

"It's difficult."

"Best thing we could do is meet up then. Where are you?"

"On the move."

There was a pause. "OK then, how about you come to meet me somewhere?" Despite the casual words, Baker had sounded irritated. "Like, could you get over to Marion, Ohio?"

Brad thought fast. "Yeah. That would be neat. Just a short flight from here. How about tomorrow morning? Give me a direct line to call you on when I get to the airport. Then we'll meet up for lunch. I got a lot to tell you."

"Great." Baker recited a phone number.

Brad didn't even listen to it. "See you tomorrow then," he said quickly, then shut the phone completely off.

He wasn't going to Marion. Apart from the voice and manner he didn't trust, that place had been one of the US cult sites Iona's computer had found. He hoped Baker believed the meeting was on though, and not do an all-out trace on him before then.

After a check on the door to the apartment's external fire escape, in case he needed to get out in a hurry, Brad then settled uneasily, watching the TV news. It was turned down low so he could hear any noises. In theory, the lift wouldn't stop at his floor without his personal key, but even its occasional movements made him run to the door by the fire escape. He knew the block's owners held a master key which could make the lift stop at any floor. Once again, he was in for a difficult night's sleep.

****

Peter and Tony had been suspicious of everyone about them on the Geneva-bound plane. Then, as they disembarked into one of the round concrete annexe-blocks at the airport, they felt everyone in the country could be the enemy.

Half an hour later, they were in a hire car and, as soon as they left the airport, turned it onto the northeast bound RN1.

Peter, driving, turned to Tony. "Are you sure you know the way to this place?"

Another look at the map convinced Tony. "Yes. I got confused when I escaped last time. Thought then I was on Lake Geneva. But I've worked it out. The place has to be on the southern shore of Lake Neuchatel. One up. Didn't even know there was such a lake."

Less than a hundred kilometres later, the two of them, with the car now rolling slowly, were looking across a manicured lawn and a wide courtyard, to a building fronted by a ten-storey wall of dark-blue glass. It stood alone in the otherwise quiet rural surroundings.

"Is this it?" Peter asked.

"Yes. I'm sure it is. I saw this frontage out of the limo window as we arrived, and the room I was in is on the other side."

"It's pretty fucking amazing," Peter breathed out. "Like one of those corporate palaces off the turnpike in New Jersey, except I notice this one doesn't want to say who it belongs to. But, before we announce ourselves, let's go round the back and take a look at where you got out from. The hospital wing, or whatever you said it was."

"Nearly was that."

Peter sped up the car again, already feeling conspicuous to whatever invisible eyes were behind the dark glass walls of that huge place. "But first let's drop this," he added. "And I want it safe. It's our getaway."

Tony directed him to St. Aubin, the village he'd walked through in his escape. They put the Audi in a small car park. The locals would probably notice its arrival, but it was the best they could do. Then they walked away, not seeming to draw any attention, to retrace Tony's escape route, this time downhill through the woods.

Thirty minutes later, they reached an edge to the trees. Below them, the huge building, now from the back, didn't look quite so imposing, with a more normal-looking rear wing making it into a tee shape.

Peter looked down at it from just inside the trees. "So where did they keep you?"

Tony pointed across the fifty yards or so of mown grass. "It was one of those fire doors I came out of, I'm sure. Probably the centre one." Then he looked confused. "But these trees have been cut back. And that fence couldn't have been there. I came straight into the trees."

Just in front of them was a ten-metre-wide newly-cleared swathe, then a high open-mesh fence.

"It's very new," Peter said. "And just as well it wasn't here when you got out. Because it would have been a big problem to get through. In fact, just about bloody impossible."

"And those posts in the middle of the grass weren't there either," Tony added.

Peter looked at what was strung out at twenty-metre intervals along the centre-line of the wide lawn. "They're not posts."

"Don't mess. What are you talking about?"

"Well, they are posts in one sense I suppose," Peter continued cryptically. "But they've cost about fifty-thousand dollars apiece I'd think."

"How?"

"OK. It's just that this is about the most protected civilian place I've ever seen – short of having machine-gun towers. For a start, this fence, apart from that razor-wire at the top, also has microphonic cable running through it." Peter pointed out the three plastic-covered conduits loosely woven into the broad mesh. "Just rattle it slightly and they'll know someone is messing. And those expensive 'posts' have at least three devices in them. Maybe more."

"Devices?"

"Down the sides there are infrared beams to the next post. So cross anywhere in the middle, and they'll pick you up." Peter had swept his arm. Now he pointed again. "That black polished bit near the top of each one is an infrared light. At night, this place will look dark to you but, if we're right about the IR thing, then to them, the whole area will look like an illuminated stage-set. And, right at the top, that glass dome is a window for a scanning video system. The camera is in the post pointing up into a rotating mirror."

"But none of this was here a week ago," Tony protested.

Peter looked again at it all. "Incredible then," he whispered with genuine admiration. "But it means this place has been prepared for something serious – and in a hurry."

"And Kiri is in there," Tony added.

Peter took a last careful look before they retreated further back into the trees. "We've just got to hope you're right about how much they want you. And that your vitamin A idea works."

"Even so, how will we get out again?"

Peter looked back. "That's maybe where you'll need me."

"Yes. I'll remember that."

"OK. Let's go. Got your sweeties all spread about?"

Peter felt for his own mega-dose vitamin A tablets. They were loose, ten or so in each pocket and mixed in with some extra-strong mints about the same shape, some of them crumbled up a bit to make it look like they'd been there a while. In a casual search, both men would just have been taken for mint addicts.

Standing by the main entrance, Peter looked up again at the enormous darkened-glass frontage. Its size, and its anonymity, were threatening.

"If we don't come out," he whispered, "Iona will never convince anyone that this place is something suspicious. They love corporate palaces here – and money."

Steeling themselves, and with no idea of what would happen next, the two of them walked slowly through the front gates. Then, before they got anywhere near the building, Peter saw that a lone figure had come walking out towards them. It was as if they'd been expected.

He recognised the man. They had been expected. It was Armanino from Costa Rica. Then it was like the whole thing was a simple formality. When he got closer, Armanino merely beckoned and turned round. Without talking, and with his body slightly bowed, he led the two of them across the open courtyard. He didn't head for the huge entrance in the centre of the building, but to a smaller door off to one side.

Inside, he finally spoke to his visitors.

"With respect, gentlemen, you should have given more notice. I have to ask you to wait. Time is needed to prepare for an audience." It had been said with absolute servility, but it still had the air of a reprimand.

"An audience? With Simou?" Tony asked.

"Yes," Armanino confirmed. "We assume that is why you are here. But first, if you will allow it, I will need to search you. Please cooperate. I will also need to keep your mobile phones while you are here."

Now confused by this almost VIP reception, Peter nodded agreement, glad that Tony had remembered this happened last time to him, and they'd both spent their time on the plane erasing any contacts or call records they didn't want to be found.

Armanino then scanned both of them, using the sort of hand-held metal detector they often use at airports. Its alarm did not go off.

"Now your pockets please. Raise your arms if you will." He went systematically through them, again apparently finding nothing to worry him. The 'sweets' all over the place might have caused that puzzled look, and made him wipe his hands afterwards, but there was no comment.

Then, without explaining anything more, Armanino went out through a side door.

Left alone, Peter and Tony looked round the room they were now in. The ceiling was high and the only windows were well beyond their reach in the one outside wall. There were no seats. Peter tried the handle of the small wooden door Armanino had used. It had locked itself, and so, he then found, had the way they'd come in. This left just one more route to consider. At the top of five wide stone steps, Peter confronted a pair of massive metal doors.

"I feel we'll get through these, only when some bugger intends us to," he remarked.

And he was right. Nothing moved when he pulled at the huge handles. He was about to make another comment to Tony when a thought struck him. *Why were they being left alone like this?*

He came down the steps in silence and moved close to Tony, his voice now only the slightest whisper.

"They will be listening to us in here, probably watching too. Get us relaxed and off our guard, then eavesdrop. Oldest fucking trick in the book. And shit. I've just realised something else. I thought those expensive-looking posts we saw round the back might have some other bit of security, and I've worked out what it probably was. Microphones in there as well I bet." He moved even closer. "I just hope they didn't register the sweeties bit. We take more care from now on."

Tony just nodded his understanding.

They spent the next half hour silently, and fruitlessly, exploring every surface of the barren room. During that time, and they realised only after it had happened and their eyes had adjusted, the lights had slowly gone on and the sky outside seemed almost dark, although it still had to be only mid-afternoon out there.

It was just a click of the side door, but Peter jumped. Armanino re emerged – still with his head bowed. He walked up the large stone steps, turning towards Peter and Tony when he reached the top.

"I'm sorry you have been kept waiting." His tone was at the same time apologetic and awed. "I will now have to join you to act as interpreter. Please follow me."

Mysteriously, the handles on the huge metallic slabs of doors worked for Armanino, and they swung slowly open, revealing brilliant light at the other side. After the gloom they'd been in, Peter and Tony took a few seconds to adjust. Then, at Armanino's beckoning, they followed into a massive room. Dominating everything, shimmering in front of them and raised higher, was a human figure. It was wearing a long robe of brilliant yellow, reflecting the fierce lights all round.

Peter looked up, to a spotlit face, then immediately pulled Tony towards him.

"This is that statue in Jordan," he whispered. "But this time in the flesh. Your mate Carlos Simou I assume. What the hell's he playing at?"

Simou's almost-black eyes latched with Peter's for a second, then looked over the top of his head. The surprises weren't over. Now Simou started to make those slow pointing hand movements. Immediately, a voice came from behind. Startled, Peter turned. It was Armanino. He seemed to be doing an interpretation of those hand-signals.

"It is no longer possible to speak to you directly. You are required to be seated," Armanino had announced, still looking up at Simou.

Tony wasn't about to obey. "Well Simou," he snapped. "Where is Kiri?"

The signals and Armanino's instructions were repeated.

There was a low backless bench behind them, and reluctantly Peter and Tony both sat on it.

"Thank you. And you will see her in good time," came from behind, in Armanino's voice again.

"If you want me to cooperate, I'll see her right now."

There was a long pause before another rush of hand signals came from the brightly-robed Simou, and the voice came from behind.

"Dr Williams, I have attempted a number of times to explain the imperatives to you. And I thought you understood. Now you should concern yourself with what is important for the whole planet. We are at a threshold. The future must not be merely an unplanned disaster. Because that is inevitable unless something is done."

"I know this. But just let me see Kiri."

The hand-signs from above became slower.

"For now just be grateful," Armanino said from behind them again. "That she is still alive."

Tony fell silent at that half-hidden threat. Peter took the chance to speak.

"So," he said quietly. "If you think the world has a problem, what are you planning to do about it?"

Simou didn't look straight back, but started his signals to Armanino again.

"We are creating the power to change the future."

"Is that what this place, and that new temple in Jordan are for?"

Simou's face seemed disturbed as he made the next batch of signals.

"So you have encroached on the source of the new revelation," Armanino announced from behind. "I was advised that you might have been there."

"What revelation?" Peter asked.

"The new beliefs. That will be the only way to change events. The scriptures are now prepared."

"So, I suppose these new writings will be amazingly discovered, and your great temple will turn out to be the source of some two-thousand-year-old truth? I think that's been done before. But it's still a good one."

"Do not be frivolous," came the interpretation from behind. "There are now six million converts to the cause. Less than one person in a thousand, but that is enough. They will assume the new revelation. You do not matter."

"I helped you build your killing machine," Peter snapped back. "Is that what is going to stop the population growth?"

"I do not wish to discuss matters with you, Mr Rossi," came from behind.

"Other people know we are here," he retaliated.

There was almost a smile on that floodlit face, as Armanino interpreted. "All the time you were near this building, we were listening. And, as you said yourself, no one will believe them. We also picked up the name Iona."

Peter was angry with himself for mentioning her. "Plenty of people called that," he snapped.

"Not that many, and not that it matters," Armanino interpreted. "We will soon have another way of finding out who she is, and where you have been hiding. My conversation with you is finished. It is Dr Williams' help we need."

Tony reacted. "I've told you. I do nothing without seeing Kiri."

"You will see her tomorrow. There have been rooms arranged for the night."

"After last time, when you tried to drug me? No thank you."

"That will not happen tonight. You have my word. Now there is a great tiredness, and little time left. The witnessing must happen soon. You will not see me again, Dr Williams. Now you must look to your own beliefs."

"Perhaps when I see Kiri."

A slow turning of Simou's body signalled 'the audience' was ended. Peter considered making a lunge for him, but the platform was a good two metres high. Then the spotlights went out.

"Please stand and follow me," Armanino said, now back to his obsequious voice. At his push, the metal doors swung aside again. He beckoned, then led the pair down the steps, this time through the small door he'd used himself before. Peter and Tony followed in silence. They were soon in a dim and featureless corridor, split at intervals by double fire-doors.

Eventually Armanino stopped and opened one of the side doors. They were led into what looked like a small hospital unit, a foyer area with four bedrooms and a bathroom off to the sides.

"This is like what I was in last time, but a bit bigger," Tony said.

"I will be leaving you now," Armanino announced, almost as if expecting a tip.

Peter and Tony waited until he'd gone, then Tony spoke first.

"Well, so far, we've taken a big risk to get absolutely nowhere. I don't even know for sure if Kiri's alive."

Peter moved up close and, with only the slightest movement of his leg, kicked hard on one of Tony's ankles, whilst at the same time giving a friendly embrace, and turning Tony's head towards the camera in the corner of the room.

But Tony kept on talking loudly. "But if she is, you've got to understand what these people are trying to do. It is the right thing."

Peter relaxed, Tony had got it, so he went along with the line. "Maybe. Can't see how they're going to manage it though." Then he moved very close and whispered. *"That's why we need more information, then we escape from this place."*

"I'm not leaving without Kiri," Tony quickly whispered back.

Peter wandered away and spoke out loudly again. "Looks like we will see Kiri tomorrow. Then you'll be happier? But, just in case, I know Simou said we'd be safe here, but we should keep watches, with one of us awake always. Not sure we can trust him yet. So we take precautions just in case."

At that, he put both hands in his pockets and moved them around over the vitamin A tablets.

Tony nodded at the just-visible sign.

Inside himself, Peter felt much less in control. He wondered what their real chances were. But for some reason these people needed Tony. And he'd started to think out a few plans of his own.

Chapter 14

Feel the power

San Francisco, USA

At four a.m., Brad abandoned his restless attempts to sleep. Since that last phone call with Baker of the CIA, even this secluded apartment felt unsafe. It was time to try to make his next contact anyway. It would already be eight in Washington.

Without putting any lights on, he turned on his mobile and again pressed out Tom O'Leary's number on its illuminated buttons. Knowing it was probably his last chance to get his story believed, somehow made Brad do this slowly and carefully. If this call didn't lead anywhere, then he had no more plans. And someone might be waiting for his phone to come on air so they could locate him.

The sound of just one word in that slightly Irish voice couldn't have been more welcome.

"O'Leary."

"It's Brad O'Connor."

"Bradley. Christ, it sure is good to hear you. I've been worried. So are you OK? Heard a few strange stories."

"OK? Yes Tom. I am. Don't worry. I don't know what you've heard. But let me tell you, jus' don't believe it all. Like about that killing at my place. I was on a plane when that happened. And I can prove it."

"Jesus then, why don't you?"

"I had to run because I needed some time to find out about a few things. I've somehow got mixed up with a weird and huge – sorta cult system I suppose. I had to get some info on them urgently, before they got me. Seriously. And now I need to talk to you about it."

Brad knew that probably sounded like deranged babble. But, when O'Leary responded, his voice had become slow and serious. "OK then. So hows about you tell me some more?"

Or was that just patronising? Anyway, Brad's careful rehearsal of how to put over this impossible tale was suddenly forgotten. "There's something going on with these people. They seem to be like a lot of different strange cults, but they are connected, all over the world, and very dangerous." He stopped, knowing it still couldn't make sense.

But O'Leary encouraged him again. "OK. You just please keep going."

"A group of us are sure they're planning something real big. But it's difficult to explain. I've enough to know something is going on – but not to know what it is."

This time O'Leary took a few seconds to respond, and when he did that Irish brogue seemed to have increased.

"Those are indeed strange things you say. A while back, my international security people started reporting unusual things. We've had people just vanish. And weirder still, turn up again but different. So what do you know about these groups?"

Relaxing, now sure Tom was listening, Brad slowed a little. "A fair bit. Like we've worked out where they all are. And a lot besides. But they're after me now and, like I said, they are dangerous."

"So where are you making this call from?"

Even from 'uncle' Tom, that question made the hair on Brad's neck rise. He controlled himself. "Somewhere maybe not too safe. I knew a CIA guy called Steve Withers was interested in all this. So I gave them a call. But he's gone out of contact they said. Then someone else there seemed just too damn keen to see me. And might be trying to trace my phone right now."

O'Leary's voice was immediately faster and more urgent, and the accent almost gone. "Then assume you're not safe. Look. A committee of us have formed. But we trust no one – not even each other for long. We talk to the others every day. If anyone goes out of contact for much longer than that, we assume they've ...," he paused. "Been converted, shall I say."

"I know about that," Brad replied. "Seems –"

But O'Leary stopped him going on. "We've already spent too much time on this line. And I've got to see you face-to-face before you'd be trusted by the others. Then we'll find you somewhere safe, and you can tell us what you know. Let's say we rendezvous at O, on the second seventeen-hundred Zulu."

O'Leary was an ex pilot. Thinking quickly about the coded message, Brad worked out the reference to Oscar's, the restaurant in Georgetown, near Washington, where they'd often met, then the second five p.m., Zulu, or Greenwich mean time, would be midday US Eastern tomorrow.

"I understand," he said.

The phone went dead. Brad immediately switched the mobile off, and sighed as he sat back.

Then he started to wonder just how he'd get to the other side of America to make that meeting. If he left now, it would mean spending a night in Washington. The only way to avoid that would be to spend the night in the air, by taking the horrible overnight, the red-eye, out of SF. But it did mean staying in this place longer and, by lunchtime today in Ohio, that guy Baker would know he'd ducked out on their meeting. But he decided that trusting this place would be better.

Once again, he checked the external fire escape. It was still dark, and there seemed to be no one around, so this time he went carefully right to the bottom of it to see how the stairs for the final drop worked, and to look for where the nearest cover was after that.

It was a risk, but he made just one more phone call, to book a front-row first-class seat on an overnight flight. With that seat, he could sneak on the plane last, and get off first, and there would be the least chance of anyone looking at him and recognising him. That was the way celebrities did it.

Then he settled, still in the dark, nervously listening for any sounds, now not even daring to put the TV on.

****

Peter volunteered to take the first two-hours on guard in their hospital-ward prison. It would give him time for a professional look at the security system, while Tony tried to get some sleep. Trying not to make it too obvious, he worked out where the little cameras were. They were in the bedrooms and the bathroom. Outside the room, there were two by the external fire doors, like the door Tony said he'd got out of last time. With each camera, there was also a motion detector. Peter assumed these would trigger and draw the camera's image to the security staff's attention. Then, satisfied he'd worked out where all the devices were, and how the system operated, he still didn't sit, but paced around to keep himself awake. Even if Simou had said they'd be safe, he didn't want to trust the guy.

After about an hour, he wandered casually into the bathroom, put the toilet seat down and undid his trousers. He was crouched half-way to sitting, pants and trousers round his knees, then he looked straight up into the camera.

"And you can sod off!" he shouted, and stood, pulling up his pants again. Still holding his trousers up with one hand, he tore off a bit of toilet paper, wet it in the sink, then reached up and stuck it over the camera lens. He hoped the little outburst had looked impulsive. Immediately, he pulled up his trousers and did his belt up tight again. Peter now had, he guessed, about three minutes to set up what he was planning.

Using the edge of the toilet bowl as a first step, he then carefully stood on top of the cistern. It held, and he stretched up to lift a ceiling-tile aside. Then, by pulling against the top of the wall, Peter levered himself up into the roof space. The main cable tray was nearby and he carefully rolled onto it. Before doing anything more, he twisted to put his head back through the ceiling-tile hole and, for the benefit of that inevitable mike, pursed his lips and made a loud farting sound.

There was enough stray light coming through the tops of the fluorescent units for Peter to see the wires running along the cable tray. The ones leading to the cameras and motion sensors were all very new and lying on top. Easy to follow. Warily moving on all fours and keeping to the cable tray, he went in the direction of those external fire-doors. Between its main supports the pressed perforated-steel tray bent alarmingly, and Peter worried he would end up crashing back through the ceiling.

Just before a full-height wall, blanking off this section of roof space, he found a set of junction boxes with new wires coming in from the sides. They had to be from those fire doors, and it looked like there were thick ones from the cameras, and thinner ones from the motion and door sensors. Crouching awkwardly on the narrow and fragile support, and shaking slightly, he used the screwdriver in his Leatherman to disconnect the thinner wires from the left side of the building, and switch them with another thinner pair coming from further along, beyond the partition wall. He didn't touch the thicker camera cables. Then he turned awkwardly around, and made his way back, as fast as he dared.

Lowering himself down into the bathroom again, he brushed the obvious dust off his clothes, undid his belt, flushed the toilet, then pulled the wet-paper cover off the camera lens. While he was re fastening his belt, he stuck a finger up at whoever was watching the monitor.

Six guards, about to arrive, were recalled.

Peter was in the deepest sleep he'd had all night when Tony, now on guard, woke him.

"It suddenly seems to be daytime," Tony announced.

"You bloody nodded off then."

"No. It just happened."

Then Armanino was opening the door from the corridor.

"You slept well, I trust?" he asked, butler-like again.

"I think you know exactly how well," Peter replied.

"I will wait outside until you are ready."

The cold meat and Gruyere cheese, served in a room which Armanino had opened opposite, reminded the two of them they were still in Switzerland. Armanino waited silently in the corridor, as if to make sure he wasn't spoken to, but watched through the glass panel.

As soon as they'd finished eating, he led them into a different part of the building, a part that Tony hadn't seen before. Here, the interior decor matched the external appearance of a plush corporate headquarters. They could see into the glass-partitioned offices, with their carpets and furniture in subdued shades of grey. The outside windows were all in dark glass. The whole thing created a deep gloom but, despite that, Peter could see no lights on anywhere. The few people he saw through those partitions, seemed like ghosts in the shadows.

They went into an elevator and Armanino hit the highest button – a ten-floor ride. The boss was on the top floor, Peter assumed. Usual arrangement.

It was different up here. There was no glass partitioning to reveal what was in the offices, and the doors were more widely spaced. Bigger and more private offices of course.

Armanino led them to the door at the very end of the corridor and opened it. Inside they could see that the two facing walls of the massive corner office were made up of large darkened windows, showing dim views of the world outside, the lake in one direction, and the neat Swiss countryside in the other. In the backgrounds of both, were dimmed, eerie-looking, white-tipped mountains.

Armanino stood back and motioned for Peter and Tony to go forward.

As Peter did so, he saw that towards a third wall of the office was a huge desk. Behind it, he recognised a face he'd last seen ten years ago in Jordan. The pale skin looked even thinner and more stretched, and that face was fringed with hair which was now grey and straggly.

"Hello again Bill," Peter said. "Somehow, I knew it would be you."

Then maybe he was too obvious in the way he quickly scanned Rawlings and around the room.

Bill Rawlings may have looked frail, but his voice was still strong and his instincts obviously good. "Don't look for ways of attacking me. I only have to make one signal, and you are dead," he announced, raising his eyes to look behind them.

They turned to follow his gaze, seeing that Armanino had gone, but two men had silently replaced him. They were carrying guns, aimed at Peter and Tony's heads.

"Taking no chances as usual?" Peter said calmly.

"None at all." Then Rawlings looked at Tony. "Dr Williams, I need to talk to you."

"Then why point those guns? If you use them, on either of us, I won't be any help to you."

It got a better reaction than Peter expected.

"I don't wish to frighten you. But please sit down."

As they sat on the two large chairs in front of the desk, the men behind moved silently out.

Rawlings looked at the closing door and turned to face his 'guests'. "However, don't think I will be unprotected, now or ever." He reached into a drawer of that desk, and took out what seemed like a small radio-linked panic button. It was attached to a strap, which Rawlings dropped round his neck.

Peter wondered what that thing activated. Something a little more fast-acting than simply recalling those two, he thought. Maybe the chairs?

After the door had closed, Rawlings flicked a switch below his desk, and somehow the darkened windows went to full brightness, making the scenery, and those white-tipped mountains, become stunningly bright in the full daylight.

"Is that better?" he said.

"Clever trick," Peter whispered. "So you can do that with all the windows?"

"Yes. We find it best. And good morning. Would you like some coffee?"

"Please," they said in surprised unison.

Rawlings himself seemed relaxed, but in some thought, as he went over to a small alcove and poured the coffee. He obviously had complete confidence in whatever that button operated.

Other than the computer screen and keyboard, Peter noted the desk was almost clear, just a writing pad and two phones; a large one, obviously part of an exchange system, and a very simple black unit. Peter had never known an organisation where the big boss didn't have his own little private line. He noticed the red scramble button on it. Rawlings obviously didn't trust mobile phone security.

He'd set the cups down on the desk, pushed two of them across, and sat in his own, even larger, chair. It was also set higher than the other two, Peter noticed.

Rawlings' thoughts then seemed to continue for some time while he looked across at Tony, as if contemplating something. He eventually spoke.

"It is not obvious to me why we are doing things this way, but Simou is convinced that you might willingly help us. We have very little time. You will now be aware we have a way to force your cooperation, but that would take longer and might be less effective than if you help willingly. But remember we do have that alternative. And we won't make a mistake with our dosage this time."

"I may well decide to help you. But not before I see Kiri. And, like I said, I will do nothing if you threaten us."

Rawlings nodded slowly. "Suppose I agree to that? And you see Kiri today?"

"And I need to know what is going on," Tony continued. "What would I be helping you to do?"

There was another long silence by Rawlings, and this time it was Peter who prompted.

"This all goes back ten years, to that mud lake in Jordan, doesn't it?"

Rawlings didn't react, but stayed looking at Tony.

Tony nodded towards Peter. "Answer his question please."

The white skin round that mouth tightened. "All right, Mr Rossi. That was sort of the beginning."

"So was Simou around then?"

Rawlings shifted his position to be more upright in his chair, as if to get maximum advantage from its greater height.

"Yes. I'd first met him out there. A month before. Told him about a weird sect. They had a name which meant 'family strangers' in the local language. They took people away and, after they'd joined the sect, they never really communicated with their parents or friends again. Simou had an idea that he could use a force like that. 'To save the world,' he said. But no one knew quite where their base was, except somewhere at the side of the Dead Sea. It was as if they'd captured anyone who had ever gone near enough to know where it was. So first I had to find that."

Peter nodded. "And that's what you were doing that day with me, and were so frightened?"

"Yes. We got the directions all wrong, but we found the sect."

"And it was all about that red stuff in the spring, yes? Made them see differently in the dark. I know that now. So what was it?"

Rawlings looked irritated, then glanced towards Tony.

"I want to know the answers too."

"All right. But not many more. We could tell from the limited erosion on the rocks, that the spring itself was fairly new. But carbon-dating the red material showed it was very much older. Analysis showed it came from plants, but ones which must have been long-since extinct. Whatever, it was obviously what was giving the spring its power. A different form of vitamin A, we eventually worked out."

"OK. We've done our work as well. And I understand why my vision went funny. But what about the other effects? Like the shooting accuracy, and the fear?"

Unnervingly, Rawlings had started to fondle that transmitter button. "Took us longer to work that out, and it now looks like we haven't completely. Why we need you Dr Williams. It's obvious that this material is also changing something in brain function. Neurons use carbon chains for their interactions. So at first we thought the coiled structure of the carbon in the new vitamin A was doing something different. But, we've since realised that vitamin A also has a function in gene transcription, or activation, and now think it could be that.

Tony nodded slightly, then signalled that he wanted Rawlings to continue.

"Anyway, whatever, this stuff seems to alter the way synapses and neural receptors work. Slows everything down. Some funny effects on people who've taken it. Their hands have no shake. It's like some rifle marksmen can stop their pulse for a few seconds. So for shooting, it works well."

Peter was remembering his nightmares. "And the fear?" he asked.

"Yes. I didn't know it then, but you'd have felt that when you drank the water in the red stream."

"I did. But how does it happen?"

Rawlings' irritation showed as he looked towards Tony. "This is your area of study, Dr Williams. And you seem to know something."

"But as you and Simou have obviously found out so much about my studies, then perhaps you should explain it," Tony replied.

Rawlings was now gripping the sides of that button quite hard.

"Your 'friend' Williams here," he hissed at Peter. "Whether he set out to or not, seems to have become the world expert on the neural processes involved in indoctrination. Our brains are very predisposed to accept some structure of belief and understanding. They're almost created for it, because you stand a much better chance of surviving if you belong to a group with shared beliefs and a set of rules. And, given that predisposition, the process is mostly easy. Present uncertainty, then the salvation, and support it with belonging."

Again, Tony was nodding in agreement as Rawlings continued.

"The basis is normally set by various means in childhood, helped by groups which are mutually supportive. The methods can be anywhere between subtle but repetitive, or ritual and dramatic. But, present a young mind with these highly evolved sets of meme complexes, or belief sets, and they will almost inevitably imprint themselves. They may change in presentation or intensity, but there is an inner core which is very resistant to change. Unless."

"Unless what?" Peter asked.

"You could somehow reset and start again. And that is what this different vitamin A material was obviously doing for those people by the red spring. The first effect is fear, like the worst ever in your childhood. So, you need an answer to those fears. And that fear is so strong, it seems you will accept the one you are then given. It also lasts. Back when those plants grew, maybe they were used in cults or primitive religions? They took the stuff in initiation ceremonies maybe? Then got the indoctrination? But the real power of the stuff is that you have to stay on it. Withdrawal is horrible, even fatal."

Peter and Tony's memories had made them both wince involuntarily, as Rawlings continued.

"But back in those days they had no cultivation. So probably just picked the plants to extinction. Well, they must have died out. For whatever reason."

Peter understood something. "But it left a sort of ritual imprint. Things like immersions and baptism, or using holy water and symbolic red wine?"

"OK. Nice observation. Even after the plants were gone, the material would've kept coming down some rivers, or out of the ground in springs. Maybe why these special places are so often wells or rivers? But eventually, once all traces of it had gone, only the symbolism must have remained. That is until, by a freak of geology, some residual deposit was opened up, and came out of that spring in Jordan."

Peter nodded. "So, now you have six-million hooked on the stuff."

"Converted to the new beliefs," Rawlings corrected sharply, now tugging quite hard on that little transmitter, almost like he was getting some feeling of power from it.

Peter was glad there was only a single button. He suspected that he would be about to die if Rawlings had the ability to instantly despatch just one of them. But he still asked the next question.

"So, with that many, why do you need help?"

Rawlings now looked intently over at Tony. "Dr Williams, we have a serious problem. The spring in Jordan was always going to run out eventually. We thought it would be easy to synthesise the different retinol. And we've done it, as far as vision is concerned. But the artificial stuff isn't working properly in the brain. We have to find out why. The sects must obey our commands if we are to achieve Simou's plan. But they have started to go out of control."

"So what happens?" Tony asked.

"Small groups break away with ideas of their own. Mostly, as they never contact people outside, we just quietly eliminate them and move a new lot in."

"But a few times it hasn't been kept that secret?"

"Unfortunately not. Then more obedient brethren have had to make it look – self inflicted."

Tony nodded. "I see. I often wondered why the whole cult all kill themselves. You'd think a few would always chicken out, for the sake of their families or something. You have to kill them all, don't you?"

Rawlings didn't reply.

"What happened in Costa Rica then?"

In obvious agitation, Rawlings suddenly stood and pushed his chair back, but at least he'd had to let go of that transmitter. "That group had gone too far before we spotted it. Started their own version of our plan." He walked over to stare out of the window, seemingly at the distant brilliant white of the snow on the mountains.

Peter felt their question time was about to run out, but tried one last tack. "A personal question? How did you get into this? Why are you doing it?"

Rawlings stayed with his back to them, and Peter was surprised that he answered calmly this time. "Simou wanted me because I knew

Jordan and, with my theology training, maybe enough about faiths to create a new one? And in many ways I believed in protecting the planet, although it was a while before I understood we'd have to kill billions to do it."

The calmness of the statement made it difficult to absorb, but Peter continued like it was a normal conversation. "And you still went along with it?"

Rawlings turned and clenched his fists. "They say power corrupts. Total power is so much more than that. But you wouldn't understand. The thought is so huge, it takes years to grow. To be all-powerful. You see. Simou's cancer is back. He will die soon, then, after the first stage, I will be in total control of the planet."

"The first stage?" Peter said slowly. "Is that where all your gunmen come in?"

Rawlings walked over and sat back in his chair again, aggressively looking at Peter, as if just the brief thought of that power had re-invigorated him. At least, now he didn't seem to need to finger that button. "Rossi, you are naive about guns. We couldn't kill nearly enough people like that. Our converts are six million, but that is less than one person in a thousand. The main method will be biological."

"And that is the purpose of the laboratories here?" Tony asked.

"Well deduced," Rawlings said sarcastically. "Yes. We have developed several germ and virus strains here."

"But you made a mistake. I saw some of it."

Rawlings nodded. "Yes. So you did. But that's irrelevant now."

"Depends on who I told about it."

"And on who would believe them?"

"So how will you deliver the stuff?"

"Easy. In the vegetables and fruit we supply around the world. And in water supplies. So Rossi's guns will only be used to disrupt emergency services, then for mopping up. Except maybe in Japan, where guns are difficult to smuggle. There we will use poison gas."

Peter was now staring into the distance. "This is unbelievable."

"As I said," Rawlings continued. "It takes time to accept the enormity, and to realise the meaning of total power. But with our way, at least there is a future for as many people as the planet will support. The alternative is to let mankind destroy it, and billions will die anyway."

"But," Tony said, "the organisms will infect your own people."

"Really Dr Williams. Do you think we are so stupid? During the retinol conversion we also add serums to counter the organisms we are using."

"But why are you talking as if it is all about to happen? You said it was going wrong, and you needed my help?"

"Too much is out of control. We've had to bring our plans forward. Tomorrow, Simou will be seen by the new disciples, and he will give the revelation as a living messiah. The first stage is now inevitable. Impregnated food has been shipped for local storage. Then it will be simultaneously released all over the world."

"You can't possibly get away with this," Peter said, his voice tensed and thin, as he finally reacted to what he was listening to.

Rawlings voice remained detached. "Maybe that would be true if anyone was expecting this sort of attack."

"In Costa Rica you've given yourself away."

"Another reason we must act quickly, before the world knows what really happened there."

Rawlings looked over to Tony. "My control is falling apart. Whatever, stage one will happen. Then it is a matter of whether we can create a new order, or see a return to chaos. That is what may depend on you."

"Then show me Kiri."

"Certainly." Rawlings pressed another button under his desk. The door opened and Kiri walked in, leaving the door open behind her. When she got to the middle of the room she stood there, half closing her eyes, as if dazzled.

Tony ran over and hugged her, taking her right off the ground. "Are you OK?"

"Hey. Don't crush me. Yes, I'm fine."

At that moment the large computer monitor in front of Rawlings, which had been showing a screen-saver, burst into a stream of text. The angle made it impossible for Peter to read. But Rawlings was concentrating intently. Then he walked to the office door. Hidden by the open door, he spoke to someone out in the corridor.

Peter knew he had one chance. He moved quickly and silently to grab the small black phone on the desk.

"Tony. I can't believe you want to help these people," he was saying loudly, to hide the noise as he pushed the buttons. It was a number he could ring behind his back, in the dark, from anywhere in the world – to Iona's cottage in Bisham. She answered it almost at once.

Kiri moved forward and reached to take the phone from Peter, who swung his arm to fend her off. She didn't react fast enough and he hit her full in the face.

Peter dropped any pretence and shouted at the phone. "Look. We're not going to get out of here. But you must stop a germ warfare massacre, it's in the food, and there isn't much time."

Tony's features were distorted with rage as he lunged towards Peter.

Sheer weight knocked Peter across the desk, but he kept hold of the phone. "They've converted Kiri," he yelled. "They'll be on to you! Run Iona! Tell someone!"

Tony didn't follow up his attack, but now stood frozen, staring at Kiri. Her face was marked, but she showed no expression.

Rawlings was back through the door, and moved surprisingly quickly, hurling the phone from its connection.

The two guards behind him ran at Peter, taking him to the floor and landing on top of him. Three more appeared and raised their guns, as Rawlings retreated to behind them.

Peter kicked out at the men holding him down, knocking them away and wrenching himself free. One struggled up and came forward again. Peter aimed a hard punch to his face, and the man didn't even begin to move his head to avoid the blow.

"Shoot him!" Rawlings shouted.

Tony suddenly moved in front of Peter, shielding him. "Not if you want my help," he said calmly.

All movement stopped, but the guns stayed pointing.

From behind Tony, Peter slowly raised his palms in submission.

Rawlings glowered at him. "You wasted your efforts. No one will believe your girlfriend. So they will not react in time. And we already have people on their way to deal with her."

Peter twitched at that, and all the guns jabbed forwards again.

"You will both be confined and guarded. I have things to do. Stage one starts in two days. And I will talk to you again, Dr Williams, when that is underway."

Kiri looked blankly back as the two of them were led out.

Chapter 15

Run, run like the wind

To Scotland, UK

"Peter. Peter!" Iona shouted at the dead phone-line.

She'd heard the crash at the other end, and then a few seconds of noises. Now there was nothing. She listened on to the silence, and a feeling of desolation welled up. Peter said he wasn't going to get out. She'd warned him not to go.

Eventually accepting that the line was cut off, she slowly put the phone down, going over what else he'd said. "Germ warfare massacre," she whispered. So she had to tell someone. But who?

Already, she'd used call boxes to phone the UK base of that CIA guy, Steve Withers, who she'd met on the plane. But it seemed he was never at his base. Each time the person who'd answered the phone had suggested he 'calls you when he gets back'. Maybe overcautious to protect her cottage as a refuge for the others, she'd refused to give her mobile or fixed line numbers, thinking they might be able to trace her records to here. But now, even that was pointless. Wherever he'd called from, they now had this number. Peter had said she had to run, so he must have known they were on to her.

OK, the first thing to do was to get out. She'd thought something like this might just happen, and was mostly packed and ready, but hadn't yet worked out anywhere safe she could go to.

It took just a couple of minutes to e-mail Peter's few words for Tron to send on to Brad, and add her failure to contact Withers so far.

The road outside was deserted, and it was easy to check that no one had followed her out of the village. Then, in an almost instinctive flight towards a barely remembered childhood, and a distantly related family in Scotland she hadn't contacted for years, Iona turned towards the M40 – and the North.

****

Peter and Tony were taken out of Rawlings' office by four armed men, and then returned to the rooms they'd spent the previous night in. Peter was pleased about that at least, because being put anywhere else would have messed up what slight plan he now had.

He also hoped no one had been near either of the fire doors where he'd swapped over the motion detectors. If they had, the control room might have worked out that something was wrong with their system. But, with almost no one around, his chances had to be good.

Like last time, the double doors in the main corridor were all locked after them and, although it was still only midmorning, the windows had been turned to fully dark. That was annoying. Peter couldn't see whether there were patrols out there.

With the departing footsteps, he grasped Tony's sleeve and urgently pulled him into the bathroom. Then he turned on the shower and taps. "That's a bit of pink noise to hide what we say. Thanks for getting between us back there. They'd have shot me. You took some risk."

"Didn't have time to think about it. Although maybe it wasn't a risk. Whatever they want me for, they know I can't help if I'm dead. But what now?"

Peter wanted to escape and contact Brad, and knew his best chance would be on his own. But Tony was right, they seemed to need him desperately, so Peter intended to make sure they didn't get him. Also, right now, Tony was also his best insurance. So he had to come too. But the bloke was large and unfit, not the sort you wanted to do a runner with.

That was one problem, and Tony then added another.

"I do know they've treated Kiri. But I still must get her out."

Peter leant closer and spoke in the faintest whisper. "I know how you feel. But you can't get out with her if she won't cooperate, and she won't, not after the treatment. We must try to escape ourselves. Then we can get this place shut down and rescue her. That's the best way to help her."

"No Peter. You've got to leave me out of your plans. I'm not leaving Kiri here."

Peter leant even closer to Tony's ear. "It may be difficult to believe that this insane plot of Rawlings' can work, but, just in case, we must get out of here and warn someone about it. And stopping it is the only way of saving Kiri. You must realise that."

"No, I don't. And anyway, I'm useless with anything physical. I'll just slow you up. Let me stay here."

Peter now whispered from so close he was touching the side of Tony's head. "To them, you're not useless, so you're coming with me. And they won't trust you now, after what you just did, so they'll give you the retinal treatment again anyway. You and I know exactly how nasty that is."

He felt the shiver, then the feel against his head, of Tony's slow nodding.

Still close, and making sure his back was to the nearest camera, Peter whispered his instructions.

Tony eventually responded with just another slight nod. Then he suddenly pushed Peter away and hit out as if losing his temper. "Get out!" he screamed. "There's nothing wrong with Kiri. I just need to talk to her. That's all."

Peter took two blows before backing away. "Try it then," he shouted. "You'll soon see. And why help them? People matter more than animals. And fucking plants!"

He stomped back to his own room.

Then both men lay fully clothed on their beds, boringly motionless. They'd each thrown off their covering green blankets and top-sheets, coincidently to where the cameras couldn't quite see them in the corners of the rooms.

Even through the darkened glass, Peter noticed the extra light of the full sun as it burst out from behind clouds. That made it a good time to go. He rolled slowly off his bed, looking casual. Then he scooped up the previously discarded out-of-camera-shot bed linen. At the cue of Peter's cough, Tony did the same. They both then moved more quickly out into the main corridor, where they swapped the green blankets and the white sheets between each other.

Peter's nudge sent Tony, now holding the two green covers, down to the fire door off to the left-hand side. That movement would trigger the detector there, but it would switch on a camera showing an identical door further up the corridor with no one near it, and look like a false alert. Tony, as he'd been instructed, then remained still, standing against the wall, so as not to trigger the sensor again.

Before the operators had time to think about the false alarm, Peter had run the other way, holding the two white sheets, and did just about the opposite to Tony. By deliberately setting off that motion detector, Peter assumed a picture of him would immediately take the attention of the security guards in the control room. But the image wasn't going to stay on their monitor screen for long, as Peter ripped the camera off its mountings. Then he rammed hard into the releasing-bar of the fire door and went straight on through it.

It took him a few more seconds to run across the grass to the first of the posts holding the high-tech security equipment. He threw one of his white sheets over it, and then sprinted thirty yards along to give the adjoining post the same treatment.

Peter knew that his actions so far were obvious to the people watching the video screens, but now, with three of their cameras blinded, they couldn't easily follow his next move. What he did, was run back into the building, leaving the door open, and then go across to the opposite fire door, where Tony was still waiting.

This time, he hoped unseen by the camera which would only be triggered by the next fire door along, Peter eased the door open and they both slipped outside. Knowing it meant there was no way back whatever happened, Peter gently pushed the door closed.

They could now hear the noise of people running into the corridor behind. Staying tight against the wall, he pointed at the hi-tech posts on this side of the building.

"Like I told you," he whispered to Tony, trying to sound more confident than he felt. "We're going across that grass. But low, slowly and carefully. OK? Follow me, do what I do – and stay calm."

Had the people in the building been able to see through the darkened glass, they'd have noticed the two lumpy green bedcovers moving slowly out onto the lawn. The soft cloth, masking body-heat, and moving gently and slowly to go between the posts, didn't set off either the infrared or the microwave detectors in them.

After a long thirty-seconds doing this, Peter whispered, "OK. Now as low as you can get. Flat on your belly." Tony went forwards again, now in a fully-prone wriggle so his large body could get beneath the lowest detector-beam running between the posts. After that, there was a long and tense further half-minute as, still crawling under the blankets, they both covered the distance out to the perimeter fence.

Once as far away as the base of the fence, and motionless, Peter felt they were well enough camouflaged by the blankets. He chanced exposing his face to take a look back. No one had appeared on this side of the building.

The alarmed wire-mesh above them was his next obstacle. What Peter had to rely on was that these things were always false-alarming. Anyway, this one was about to. He pulled back his foot and kicked it hard, knowing that the microphonic-cable threaded through it would pick this up and set an alarm off. But, in the control room, they wouldn't be able to tell exactly where along its length something had disturbed the fence. They'd have to scan the whole of this sector with the cameras on those posts. Peter and Tony lay absolutely still under the green blankets.

Peter counted out two minutes, hoped it was long enough for attention to be back on the other side of the building, and kicked out again to trigger a repeat alarm.

It seemed they had to lie there an age as Peter did this three more times at about the same two-minute intervals. He wanted the control room, having seen nothing in several camera sweeps, to put this down to maybe an animal on the other side scratching itself against the wire – and not bother looking again. Anyway, their only chance was to gamble on that.

"We're going," he whispered, then folded the two green blankets and put them across Tony's shoulders. "Remember to put those on the razor wire as you go over the top, or you'll be cut to pieces. Leave the blankets there as you go over. I'll follow."

He stood up and cupped his hands for Tony to step into, bracing himself for the weight. It still surprised him.

Tony grabbed at the mesh with his fingers, and his feet stamped all over Peter's head and shoulders, but he reached the top and managed to throw the two heavy green blankets over the wire and pull himself onto them. Then he seemed to panic and freeze.

They were both now very visible, and the fence had been severely shaken this time.

It took Peter only seconds to reach the top himself and lift the petrified Tony's feet, making him go over the other side in a forward somersault. He landed, from three metres up, flat on his back with a ground-shaking thump and gave a yell of pain. Peter, worried about the microphones, almost immediately landed on him and pushed some of a now-shredded blanket into his face to smother the noise. They struggled like that for several seconds.

Eventually Tony realised he had to shut up and lie still for Peter to let him breath. He tapped Peter's back like a wrestler submitting. The blankets came off.

"Are you OK?" Peter whispered.

Tony moved himself about and, amazingly, didn't seem to be injured. "I think so," he replied.

"Thanks to your natural padding maybe," Peter murmured. "We have to move."

They crawled the short distance from the fence into the safety of the trees beyond. The occasional shouts from the other side of the building didn't seem to have changed, and still no one had appeared on this side.

"Fast now," Peter said as they stood up, and he set off at what for him was a mild jog.

Only a minute later, Tony's distress at the exercise became obvious. Peter knew distance was everything, and decided to keep a straight line, even though it took them across an area of open ground.

They were exposed in the middle of the clearing, when he saw the two men ahead raising their guns. He instinctively spun round, pushed at Tony, and they started running back, now downhill.

"Keep swerving!" Peter shouted.

Tony made just two slight jinks, but in the process managed to trip over an exposed rock. He fell headlong, but then rolled over a low bank, taking him temporarily out of sight of the gunmen. Seeing this, Peter veered off to the other side, drawing their attention away, but he was still in the open himself. He wondered what the bullets would feel like.

Amazed to reach the trees, and get well into their shielding without hearing or feeling the shots, he stopped. He'd recognised the weapons those two men were carrying. They could, if just swung in a blind arc, pump out enough high-speed lead to bring down some of the small trees around, never mind him. So why hadn't they?

Then he realised. Single accurate shots were what his systems had been training them to do. That was it. They'd been taking aim for a single shot, and he'd moved around too much. His mind went back to what Rawlings had said about the different retinol slowing reaction time. He grasped it. These people were deadly snipers – but only if their target was fairly stable. That slowness, he also realised, wouldn't help them in hand-to-hand fighting. He'd noticed that in the brief tussle in Rawlings' office.

His two pursuers had moved on to where Peter had vanished from their sight, and were now into the trees themselves. Soon they would see him again. Peter now knew he could outpace the men if he wanted to. But all those guys then had to do was raise the general alarm, and force of numbers would eventually win. He had to stop them doing that. He broke from his cover, but this time, looking suicidal, he headed towards them, swerving side to side and at full-speed. Up close, making a last jink and swinging round a small trunk as pivot, he came like a slingshot and hit one of them with a face-mangling head-butt. The man fell back against his colleague, dropping his gun.

Peter knew he had a temper which could snap. It had been a problem on the football field a few times. Now though, was different. They died or he did. It was like another person suddenly loose inside him, as he grabbed the gun and smashed its stock into the still-stumbling second man's face. Then, in a whirlwind of blows, he stabbed the end of the heavy barrel in bone-crunching downward blows into each of the heads of the falling men. He only stopped when he could see both their skulls were smashed and they'd stopped moving. Then suddenly it was over. His shoes and the bottom of his trouser legs were covered in blood, and he was shaking uncontrollably.

He ran over to find Tony. His quick shallow breathing making it difficult to talk. "We have to hurry. There will be more."

They pulled the bodies into a dip in the ground so they couldn't be seen too easily, then headed uphill again. This time Peter was careful to keep more in the cover of the trees.

Fifteen minutes later, they were back in the outskirts of St. Aubin, near to where they'd left the car yesterday morning. If it had already been spotted, then someone might be waiting for them. But there was no time. The search would widen soon, and once someone found the two bodies back there, it would point straight in this direction. This was getting more dangerous every minute. They needed that car.

Thinking again about how to use these peoples' weakness, Peter knew his next move was going to be about as subtle as a brick.

After telling Tony to follow as fast as he could, Peter ran into the little village. He didn't even look to see who was around, or whether anyone was watching their Audi, but continued at full speed, making leg-breaking football tackles on two pedestrians, just in case they were the enemy. Then a straight-arm jab nearly took the head off another man, because he was standing near the parked car.

Peter leapt in, started it, and threw open the passenger's door. The people he'd hit were now yelling and pointing towards the car. Others were coming out of the houses – and Tony was still up the road.

It was a long twenty seconds before Tony crashed in, head first, across the steering wheel and making horrible panting noises. With the door still open and with a pursuing group only feet away, Peter took off in a scream of smoking front tyres, weaving from side to side as he wrestled Tony away from the wheel. He clipped several other

220

parked cars, making explosions of noise each time, but at least shutting that loose door. With all that racket, Peter couldn't even tell whether they'd also been shot at. But he'd got away.

Half a wildly-driven mile later, and clear of St. Aubin, he squealed up to a T-junction onto a main road. He could see nothing behind following. Now, trying to control himself and think properly, he turned the car to the right, and slowed slightly. He didn't want to look obvious and have people direct pursuers. The further they got before abandoning the car the better, but each minute out here meant more risk.

Five minutes later, a few cars had gone the other way, but nothing was now ahead or behind, and Peter's tension was rising. It had to be soon. He saw the railway line over to his left. They'd had their bits of luck so far, and he decided not to push it any more.

No one saw the car turn uphill into the small dirt track and, two hundred metres further along, drive at a large clump of bushes. At the last second, Peter realised he'd build up more speed than he'd expected, and steeled himself for the sudden stop as they slammed into the undergrowth. It was a heavy thump and, still unbelted, Peter smashed into the steering wheel. There was a sharp pain from his top lip.

"Shit!"

He turned the engine off and felt his teeth. They hurt but weren't loose. Then he opened the door slightly and listened, ignoring the blood now also running down the front of his shirt.

Other than an occasional swish of tyres on the road down below, there were no sounds. He turned to Tony, who was unscathed. Despite all that panic, he'd had the sense to fasten his seatbelt, and he'd already reached for the small first-aid kit on the back shelf.

A few minutes later, with a plaster and some bandage, Tony had managed to stop the bleeding.

"Stay still a while, or it will start again."

"OK. Pass me that map though."

Peter opened the hire company's road map and worked out where they were. From here, they could walk alongside the railway line to the next station and get a train to Lausanne. Measuring it on the map, it looked to be about ten miles. They wouldn't make that distance, cross-country, before nightfall, and he didn't want to be caught by these people after dark. He decided, as they seemed well hidden here, it might be a good idea to just let things calm down.

He grabbed what was left of the bandages and slowly got out, struggling through the tangled small branches and onto the bonnet. "I need to clean up my shoes and trousers before it all dries," he announced.

Tony operated the windscreen washers while Peter did his best to clean up the blood.

"Now let's cover this thing up properly."

The car had gone in to the bushes far enough to be easily hidden by a bit more loose undergrowth. Then they climbed back in and settled down for the night.

****

Rather than descend, late in the day, on relatives she'd not even bothered with for years, Iona checked into a rundown-looking hotel near Arbroath, on the Scottish east coast.

Although used to travelling alone and fending for herself, there was something about being in this Spartan little room that made a horrible depression creep over her. She wondered what had happened to Peter, and desperately wanted him with her now. Trying to convince herself that he always found a way out of things, didn't work this time.

There was a small television on the sideboard. Iona couldn't see a remote control, so pulled herself off the bed and switched it on to catch the late evening news, hoping there'd be something on to do with the cults, like maybe Brad had got his information out. But nothing was mentioned about it, except for the massacre in Costa Rica. They'd even moved that to being a minor item. Apparently, international aid was arriving, and a statement from Washington said they were moving warships with troops towards the region, but no more explanations were being offered. The weather forecast followed. Still cold for the time of year it said, but brighter by the morning.

She switched the TV off and got into the small bed. It had been a long drive, and there was nothing else she could do this late in the evening.

Suddenly awake from the disturbed dozing she'd drifted into, Iona realised something. *'Statement from Washington'* the TV had said! It had triggered an idea in her mind. And there was time. It would still be early evening there.

Finding she couldn't get any signal on her mobile, Iona had to get an irritated hotel manageress away from her own TV downstairs, before the switchboard's overseas bar was turned off.

The call to Steve Withers' Washington CIA number was answered almost instantly. Then there was an odd silence after she asked for him.

"I'm afraid he's overseas, in England," came in a drawl from the other side of the Atlantic.

"Can you give me any other contact number for him? I've got his normal UK one. I have to speak to him urgently, and he's never there."

There was another long pause.

"Lady," the man replied. "These numbers are secure. The only thing I can do is call him myself, and get him to phone you directly. If you could tell me who you are, and give me a number he can call you back on."

"OK. My name is Iona Duncan." She then peered down at the phone base and gave the hotel's number.

It was five minutes later when the irate manageress was again disturbed, this time to put through the incoming call.

"This is agent Baker. I understand you want to talk to Steve Withers?"

"Yes. Urgently."

"He can't talk right now, but wants to come and meet you face-to-face. Exactly where are you?"

Suddenly Iona felt suspicious. "I will meet him somewhere else. It'll have to be Edinburgh Airport."

"It would be better if I passed some of your information on to Withers right now, before you meet him. That way he can do some checking first."

"No. I'll be there at midday tomorrow."

"Well," Baker said slowly. "I'll sure fix that. Want you to feel relaxed about this now. He'll be there."

That seemed to be the end of the conversation. "Thanks." She put the phone down, realising something was wrong. Airports are big places, several buildings. Why hadn't agent Baker wanted to arrange a meeting point? Because he didn't need to. He had this phone number here. Of course he wanted her to relax, and stay in this hotel while they traced the address.

She hurriedly packed again, made a lame excuse downstairs about a family emergency, and had to pay for a night's sleep she probably wasn't going to get.

Fifteen minutes later she turned onto the verge of a drive leading up to a golf course. Those shrubs she drove the car between, provided as much cover and heat insulation as she was going to find that night.

Even so, she was cold to the bone within two hours, and tried at least to remember some warmth, lying on a tropical beach with Peter. She could never have guessed he was also spending a cold night hidden in a car.

Chapter 16

Leaving on the midnight plane to Georgetown

San Francisco, USA

Before Brad broke cover and left his apartment in Berkeley, he did a final check of his mailbox. In a long list of e-mails, only one took his attention. It was from Iona.

Opened, it was very short, but it horrified him. Her transcription of Peter's snatched phone call meant it was even more important to get to Tom O'Leary. But the bit about germ warfare just made their story even more unbelievable. Anyway, with whatever facts he had, it was time for him to leave this place.

Brad was about to use the lift to get down to the small private underground car park, then realised that he might be exposed, with no escape, when the lift doors opened down there. So, for the first time since he'd bought the place, he unlocked the door to the small internal staircase, and used that.

On the narrow and poorly lit descent, he stopped at ground level and checked on the route out that way. OK. Then he went down two more levels to the door at the very bottom, eased it slowly open, very aware of the creaking noise it made, and peered round it. There was no one around, and Brad walked quickly over to his car.

Out on the street, he made himself drive slowly, so as not to draw any attention from the police in the lazy SF late-evening traffic. It was now sparse enough for him to be sure he wasn't being followed. He'd left plenty of time, including ten minutes to stop off at a late-night drug store. Then he'd head across Bay Bridge to SFO.

The airport long-term car park would've been best for leaving the car, but he didn't want to use the courtesy bus, so decided to drop the old Buick, the one he'd driven from Denver, in the closer-in short-term parking area, and then walk in. He hoped it would be tomorrow before anyone did checks on the cars here. By then he'd be well away.

With only a carry-on, Brad didn't have to go to the main check-in desks, so he took a look at the departure screens to find his gate, and headed straight for it.

At this late hour, almost all the shops and restaurants had been closed and shuttered-down for the night, and it made the almost-deserted airport corridors darker than normal. The cleaning staff seemed to outnumber the few remaining passengers around. Brad avoided looking at any of them as he walked, now feeling conspicuous, out to the far end of a long concourse for the midnight red-eye.

After timing it carefully, taking up the final minutes in a nearby toilet, he was the last person on board. Head low, he caught a momentary image of the plane-full of people leaving SF for Washington, stepped over a pair of trousered legs, then dropped into the right-hand-front window seat. Immediately he turned his head to the window and, even before takeoff, feigned sleep – though far from it.

****

Iona wanted to move the car from its meagre hiding place before it got properly light. Early morning golfers would be arriving soon and they'd notice it there in the bushes.

The bit of sleep she'd got had slightly improved her spirits. Now she wondered if perhaps last night she'd been too paranoid about this meeting. Airports always have designated meeting points, so maybe Baker hadn't felt the need to have somewhere arranged? Maybe Withers would be there, and could use her information? She needed to allow that possibility, and suppress her worry that it might be a trap. Anyway, her safety didn't seem to matter now. It was all she could do for Peter. But she'd make sure she recognised Withers before announcing herself. And what could anyone do to her in the middle of a crowded airport?

There was still plenty of time. Time at least to take a walk to warm herself up and get her stiffened joints going. She knew exactly where to take that walk. Then she'd stop off somewhere to get breakfast on the way to Edinburgh.

She parked the car where the shore-side promenade ended, and the cliffs started. It was a place which brought back many long-dormant memories. And, as she set off up the steep path to the cliff-top, Iona was in her own world, or worlds, half, bringing her childhood back, half going over what she would say to Withers if he was there.

Twenty minutes later, and well warmed up, she looked down at a dramatic scene. In many places, the east coast of Scotland is being eaten away by a sea which tears at the base of soft, sandstone cliffs. The view from above is of the angry North Sea waves pounding into the jumble of red-coloured rocks left over from the last cliff-fall. They throw up spectacular plumes of spray, which carry on the wind, high up to the unfenced path which hugs the retreating edge at the top. It was all the same as she remembered from twenty years ago, although maybe now everything seemed a bit smaller.

In her childhood, this had been the only sea Iona knew. Since then she'd seen oceans so much warmer and bluer. The steep-sided, grey-green waves below her, now looked mean and vindictive. She knew she would never return here. When this was all over, she'd go with Peter to the warm seas again.

Gazing down in this dream, Iona didn't notice the two women who'd been walking behind, unheard in the noise of the wind and surf.

Her reverie ended suddenly with the tight grip on each of her arms. At first, she was just shocked, then confused, and she twisted and pulled in reaction. Now the dizzy view down to the rocks was suddenly different – like the fleeting and frightening thoughts she'd had as a child – of jumping. She knew the two women were going to try to throw her over that edge. She pushed her legs forwards, dug them in the last bit of ground in front, leant back and pulled her arms in, to cling firmly to her attackers.

It was the wrong thing to do. It just made it easier for the two women to lift her – as they stepped themselves out over the hundred-foot drop.

Suddenly, it was a terrified six year old who turned her head for that last sight, of emotionless eyes, just before the three bodies, still held together, smashed into the jagged boulders.

The sandstone rocks seemed to absorb the red of the slowly diluting blood.

****

Only when they had full daylight, did Peter and Tony intend to get out of their cold and uncomfortable overnight hiding-place. But it was the moment of that horrible shiver going right through him that forced Peter to move. He shoved his door open and walked away from the car, trying to lose the sensation. It slowly went, but he didn't want to get back into his seat. Anyway, it was light enough now.

His idea was to go along the railway line towards the next station. Alone, he would've just jumped over the track fence and jogged the easy way, right alongside the line. But he couldn't rely on the bulky Tony getting out of sight fast enough when the sounds of the trains came. That would certainly get them reported.

They took the slower way, the legal side of the fence, occasionally having to cross ditches and push through undergrowth and hedges. Their pace frustrated Peter but, after a long ten miles, he finally saw the outskirts of the small town of Payerne in the distance. Buildings reaching the railway meant they would now be forced to walk on the roads.

Wanting to look as normal as they could, they both tried to clean themselves up. Tony re-dressed Peter's cut face with a single plaster. By fastening his jacket, Peter also covered up most of the bloodstain on his shirt. The long and dew-damped grass had also further cleaned his shoes and trouser legs. Still, he felt very aware of their generally messy state, and the many other clues which would mark out a couple of strangers to this rural area. But it was still early morning and not many people were around.

It wasn't that way at the station, now crowded with commuters. Peter's French was just good enough to be understood, even if spoken quietly so, as he ordered the tickets, he didn't make it completely obvious to all around that he was English. Then he bought a couple of newspapers, and they both sat on a bench seat at one end of the platform, and pretended to read them.

It wasn't a long wait for the next train to Lausanne. The seats in the open-plan carriage they got into were all occupied, so it didn't look odd that they both chose to stand at the end looking out of the window. Peter now felt less conspicuous in the mixture of people he could see around, so relaxed a bit – but that only gave him the chance to realise their problems were just starting. He wondered if he and Tony could ever get back to the UK?

But now, however they did it, after Simou and Rawlings had told them so much, they had to get that information out. Though, Peter wondered, even suppose he made it back home? Who would be likely to believe his story, and have the influence to do anything about it? That was the problem. There were some people he knew well and who trusted him, but the blokes at Windsor football club, or his local BMW dealer, weren't exactly influential contacts.

No. It had to be Brad. He was the only one who knew the right sort of people. They had to get something to him, then maybe try to get out of the country themselves.

Peter was annoyed that they'd all left Iona's place without any proper backup plans for keeping in contact. Iona herself would've run by now, and he guessed that it would be back to Scotland, but whereabouts? Brad would be in America, but as a fugitive who couldn't go back to his own house. For sure though he would keep checking for any e-mails stored by his computer. Peter needed an internet link so he could send his message there. It would be first priority when they got off the train.

****

The time-shift and lack of sleep on the overnight red-eye, made Brad feel dazed, and unprepared for the frenetic early-morning confusion of Washington's, almost-downtown, Regan Airport.

Someone pushed up close to him. "This way, Brad," was in a German-accented whisper. He spun round. Karl Matuik beckoned him to move behind the cover of a large pillar.

"Karl. What the hell? And again. How did you know I'd be here?"

"I called in a few favours. The computer people at United let me get into the airline booking system. I picked up your name and the details of the flight."

"Why didn't you contact me through Tron?"

"I tried. Lots of times. But it's not responding."

"Strange," Brad muttered softly, almost to himself. "What are you doing here though?"

"Trying to look after you a second time," Karl replied. "And why do you even risk being here?"

Brad decided not to answer that. "Ain't nothing happened to you?" he asked. "Not been followed then?"

"No. Police interviewed me once more. Then everything's been fine."

"Yeah, I see. But anyway, right now I need to be out of sight for a while."

"I'll find you a hotel room."

Brad watched as the ever-reliable Karl walked across the arrivals hall and picked up one of the courtesy-phones. The first call seemed to be successful, and he soon came back.

"We're fixed at the Hilton. Their bus will be over there at the US Air terminal in the next five minutes. I'll look out for it coming. Only move when I signal."

Brad stayed behind the cover of the pillar, trying to look as if he was waiting for someone to come out of the nearby toilet.

****

Peter Rossi decided not to attract attention by asking for directions as they walked out of Lausanne station. He thought it wouldn't be difficult to find what he needed.

He was right. The two of them were only about five-hundred metres along the road when Peter noticed the computer terminals through a large window. He and Tony walked in to the cybercafé, and sat down. They beckoned to a ponytailed waiter. Peter asked in halting French how to log on to the terminal in front of them. He was surprised when the man replied in a strong Irish accent, and in perfect English. The instructions he gave were simple enough. After that, Peter ordered two coffees. He waited for the waiter to move away, before typing in a domain address he now knew well – *www.hal-a.com*

He went to Brad's personal box. Then the buttons clicked fast as Peter started to get out his message. He didn't notice the waiter returning with the coffees, and then looking over at the screen.

"Bradley O'Connor the Third." That voice sounded even more Irish now. "The famous computer scientist. He still has family back home in Ireland. I met him there once you know. You know he's never explained his web site name, but one night in the pub he explained that the LA bit is for Los Angeles."

Tony, who'd been standing at the other side of Peter, also intent on the screen, immediately pushed his way in front of the waiter. "Did he now? Well. Thank you for explaining that."

Peter clicked back to the home page and spun round. The waiter was still trying to peer round Tony, and Peter couldn't read that strange look on his face.

"That's a huge site there do you know now?" he'd remarked. "Thousands of topics. Mostly a bit technical for a simple guy like me. What exactly did you want?"

"American recipes," Tony replied, giving the waiter another push with his stomach.

"OK," he reacted. "Not a problem. You'll find it. And take your time. There's no hurry." He walked away.

****

It was still two hours before Brad's appointment with Tom O'Leary. He was standing looking out of the window of the tenth-floor hotel-room Karl had found. He wanted to be rehearsing what he would say to Tom, but something else was disturbing his mind.

Karl was sitting in a small armchair, reading the room-service menu. "Looks like they do twenty-four-hour pizzas here," he said. "And I fancy one. What about you?"

Almost annoyed by the interruption, Brad pulled his thoughts back to the mundane. "Suppose it's been a long while since I ate anything, and I need waking up. Yeah. I'll have one, and a large coffee."

"I'll get them delivered. The usual topping for you?"

"Anything. Doesn't matter. First can I use your computer a minute?"

Karl opened it and put up the desktop, then picked up the house phone to place the order, while Brad got onto the internet. Tron responded at once to his password.

"I got in OK," he commented.

From the chair opposite, Karl watched silently while Brad scanned through the unread e-mail messages, which had come in overnight. Amongst the disguised spam, there were lots of things about aircraft or computers, and a few vague 'trying to get in contact' messages, but nothing, which looked like it could've been any news from Iona or the other two.

The pizzas' arrival made Brad notice what time it was. He broke from the computer to switch on the TV, and ate while staring intently at the main CNN news, impatient for each move to the next item. But there was nothing out there about the cults.

****

Oblivious of the noise around him in the cybercafé, Peter typed out what they'd learnt from Simou and Rawlings, fast, not bothering to correct irrelevant mistakes. Those were his own words on the screen, but he couldn't really believe what they were saying.

He scanned through it a last time and hit send. Then he beckoned to Tony.

"OK. Brad's got my info. It's your turn now. You'll remember some things I didn't. But hurry."

Peter stood up and looked round the café. Their Irish waiter seemed to have gone off duty.

****

Brad finished eating while watching the last of the news items.

"My pizza sure tasted like it'd been contaminated by one of your goddam anchovy specials," he said. "How you can eat those things, plumb beats me."

At the end of the newscast there'd been nothing about the cults, then the usual girl came on with the weather.

Brad checked again on Tron's incoming mail. He was suddenly feeling very tired. He shook his head, opened and closed his eyes a few times, but that didn't fix it. A movement on the computer screen showed a new message in, from Peter Rossi. Brad immediately clicked onto it. From the other chair, Karl seemed to notice this sudden attentiveness.

Starting to read, Brad felt worried, fearful even, but it was about nothing definite. He desperately tried to concentrate, but the lines of Peter's words started to drift in strange colours in front of him. It was impossible to read them. He'd felt he'd have to take a nap – look at it all later. Then, knowing he was somehow about to lose control, he desperately typed just one line back.

He tried to move, but his arms and legs felt suddenly huge and heavy. A feeling, now of real fear, was becoming intense. In the background, Karl's voice was coming from somewhere. Brad absorbed the words in disbelief.

"Sorry Brad. This for your salvation. You have a place now. You will be taken for conversion. Then your appointment will be to look after the computers."

In the confusion of his swirling, oddly coloured, sight, he felt the laptop being grabbed from his hands, and he made a desperate swipe, trying to smash it. The resulting slow-motion attempt failed, and Karl moved away and hit a few keys. He seemed to find what he wanted – probably Peter's message. But it distracted him at least. Brad knew there was one thing he had to do.

With an incredible effort, he managed to heave himself up and lunge towards the toilet door of the hotel room. Waves of weird colours crossed his eyes and almost stopped him seeing – but he turned, locked the door behind him, and slid down with his back against it. He felt Karl hit it hard from the other side.

Desperately feeling into his jacket pocket, Brad grabbed at one of the cartons of mega-dose vitamin A tablets he'd bought back in San Francisco. Then, still propping himself against the door, he struggled with the bubble pack, and pushed half its contents, and bits of aluminium foil, into his mouth.

At the next impact, the lightly-made door was smashed in and Brad was flung forwards. Karl stepped over him, and immediately swiped the bubble-pack clear of his outstretched hand.

"You and your anchovy pizzas," Brad managed to look up and say to the multicoloured figure of Karl – before his head slumped down.

Karl examined the half-empty bubble-pack with curiosity, but then threw it aside.

****

Peter was getting nervous. They had been in the café a long time now. But Tony was still typing in his message. Trying to calm himself, Peter leant over and looked at the screen. Tony had just finished and transmitted. Only the last bit of his message was visible.

. . . It may be difficult for us to get out of this country and back to England. So it is up to you. Good luck. But you don't have much time.
Tony.

That was all they could do. Peter pulled at Tony in his haste to get them out of this place.

Then something else appeared on the screen from brad@hal-a.com.

Peter,
Will need communications. You must enable.

That didn't make much sense. Puzzled, Peter quickly sent back.

Brad,
Don't understand.
Peter.

The response immediate, but about two pages long, and looked very complicated. Peter started reading it, and got himself lost in the series of symbols. It needed concentration, and it didn't help that Tony was now conspicuously agitated beside him.

After re-starting several times, having to stop himself hurrying too much in his panic, Peter started to grasp the series of instructions. They were complex comms protocols. It was more than five minutes though, before it finally made sense to him and he'd scribbled a few notes. But there was still something missing. He hit the keys again.

Brad,
I think I understand all that. But how am I supposed to use it?
Peter.

There was a disturbance behind him. Peter turned to see that five men had come into the café together, but then split up, each one walking in a different direction, but he realised the two of them were slowly being surrounded by this. Quickly deleting the e-mails, he stood up and grabbed Tony.

"Shit. Time to go. If we can." Peter went quickly over to the waiter's service counter and, in one movement, took a sharp knife from the other side of it.

Tony had noticed.

"I think we've had it, but I'm not going cheaply," he explained.

What he didn't say, was that the blade might become his last resort to stop these people getting Tony.

The sound of a tray of glasses, crashed deliberately to the floor, drowned the pop of darts being fired at both of them. Peter felt a sharp stab and immediately pulled something out of his side, but it had already emptied its capsule of liquid into him. He pulled one out of Tony's back. It was also empty, save for a few drops of red coming out of the short needle. The funny vitamin A, he assumed.

To his surprise, no one then tried to stop them leaving the café, but, glancing back, Peter could see the five men now following, as if casually, but spreading out to cover both sides of the road. He stayed close to Tony, trying to walk on, not too fast, as if he hadn't noticed the men behind. Until he turned a corner. Then he pulled hard at Tony's arm. "Run for your life. They can't go that quickly."

"Wait!" Tony growled, resisting the tug on his jacked and using all his weight to swing Peter round into a shop doorway. There's something we need to do first. Then he reached for his pockets. "Those drugs they fired into us. We've got ours to take. Really chew them."

They both frantically stuffed the dry soft tablets into their mouths.

"If we can hide a few minutes," Tony spluttered as he swallowed. "These should override their stuff, and we can get away."

Peter suddenly realised something about those e-mails. "Sorry about this Tony. That's not what we're supposed to do. So we stop running now. Just start looking frightened."

Tony looked back, as if stupefied, as Peter walked out of the doorway and watched as the first of their pursuers appeared round the corner.

"No chance to tell you why," he whispered. "But, right now, we need to pretend their drug is working exactly as they want it to. So act for your life. We're terrified – and having trouble seeing. They'll think they've got us in control. I need a chance to do something. It's the only chance we've got."

Peter stopped and stared around with wide eyes, as if each alleyway threatened him. "Like this. And remember please. You're still my protection."

One thing Tony didn't have to fake, was his look of total confusion.

They were quickly surrounded by the five men, and then 'helped' down the road to a waiting people carrier.

Chapter 17

Running on empty

Near Payerne, Switzerland

This time there was to be no relaxed chat from Rawlings. Also, there were eight armed-men and a guy in a white coat who'd joined Peter and Tony in the office. Peter tried to ignore his realisation that this might be the end, for him at least.

Rawlings sneered, causing that parchment-skinned face to stretch into folds by his mouth. The one who was to be all-powerful, obviously didn't like to have any of his plans disrupted, and now seemed to be about to take his revenge. There was a vindictive sarcasm in his voice. "Our lookout at the café tells us you tried to contact Mr O'Connor."

Peter was aware that he felt slightly drowsy and muddled as he looked back, but it was nothing like the full effect of that funny vitamin A. He guessed it was mainly the tranquilliser they'd added to the mixture in the dart. And maybe Tony's antidote was mostly working? If so, he wanted to disguise that, and just gazed fearfully and silently back.

But, as if more angered by this mute response, Rawlings continued, now hissing through closed teeth. "You wasted your time then. We've got O'Connor. And before he even had a chance to read your messages."

The contorted grin which followed, showed this was meant to be a crushing statement. But it had the opposite effect on Peter. It confirmed what he'd thought was going on. "I wondered why we got no reply," he said slowly and shakily, as if frightened by what he'd been told.

"So you have been a minor nuisance only. And you are now finished," Rawlings added in contempt. "Because, when Dr Williams has been converted, he will have no loyalty to you. You will not be needed."

The fear in Peter's voice was now partly real. "I thought you didn't want to treat him?"

Rawlings slowly shook his head from side to side. "Simou's stupid idea."

"But he thinks Tony can work faster if he's not treated."

Rawlings smirked again. "Get it right Rossi. He thought that. Past tense. He might have trusted Dr Williams. I don't. And I don't have to listen to Simou's advice anymore."

"But Simou was part of your plan? To do with that temple and your new religion?"

"Exactly. And yesterday he played his final role. It was a wonderful performance. The new revelation from a dying prophet. But unfortunately, a few hours later he passed away. A small mistake with his medication I believe. As Dr Williams here knows, you have to be just so careful with painkillers in the terminal stage of cancer." There was another contemptuous look. "So our pointless conversations have finished Rossi. I no longer need to explain anything to you. You are now unnecessary."

The final words were almost spat out. It made Peter sense that Rawlings' milking of his revenge was about to be over. To play his one chance, he needed just a slight change in what Rawlings was about to do. "I also posted letters in Lausanne," he said dreamily. "To the right people, and with enough of your information to stop what you are trying to do." Peter wished he'd actually had the time there to do just that.

Rawlings' response was a slowly widening grin. "Then you shouldn't have told me then, should you Rossi? You forget. I have a way of getting you to tell me who you sent them to and what they said. So you will also be fully treated. Then, when I know exactly who those people are, you will be eliminated. Whatever you wrote, I can make sure your *information,* is treated as the scribblings of a deranged madman."

Peter couldn't think what his 'drugged' reaction should be to that statement, so stayed silent and expressionless. But it was what he wanted to hear. That was, if his vitamin A antidote was going to hold out for long enough.

Rawlings got to his feet, and started to walk to the office door. Then he spun round, and his face spread into another vengeful sneer, as if he had one last twist of the knife to make. "But perhaps there are no letters, and you are hoping that your girlfriend *Iona* has managed to do something? Maybe she is actually now your last hope?"

It was the triumph in that voice, which gave Peter a premonition of what was coming, and made his stomach knot.

"Well?" Rawlings goaded, stepping closer to Peter again.

Peter didn't move a muscle – then had to listen to what he dreaded.

"When I last heard, she was a mess on some rocks at the bottom of a cliff in Scotland."

The mention of Scotland made Peter know it was true. Now, forgetting the pretence of being drugged, he hurled the guards each side of him away, and threw himself forwards. He was going to tear the flesh away from that white, frail-looking face.

Rawlings leapt back as two more guards moved round from behind him and hit Peter together, their weight taking him backwards and to the floor, just inches before his hands had reached those eyes and that scrawny throat.

Peter thrashed out like an animal. He was outnumbered, but his reactions were faster and he repeatedly landed ferocious blows and kicks. But these men seemed oblivious to whatever he did to them. And the guns of other guards were pointing down, following his movements.

Tony had gone forwards to help, but was immediately held, arms and neck, by another three men. A gun also pointed unwaveringly at him.

Finally exhausted, Peter stopped the struggle, lying on the floor with the men on top of him. The man in the white coat moved for the first time, and was looking suspiciously down at him.

Rawlings had contemptuously turned and walked out, giving a last command. "Give them both the treatment. And make sure it is enough this time. Now!"

It seemed that a long time had passed when Peter emerged to consciousness. Then he remembered the syringe of sedative, which had knocked him out. His vitamin A dose couldn't have protected him against that.

He soon realised this didn't feel like other times he'd come round from an anaesthetic. Within a few seconds, it grew into about the worst sensation he'd ever had. It seemed like things were moving around inside his head, as if they were not part of him, more like worms crawling in there. His instinctive reaction was to try to move and shake this away. But he couldn't move anything. He was frozen in place.

Peter tried to override the appalling sensation in his head, and think. He seemed to be awake and paralysed? So someone had also used a muscle relaxant on him. Peter screamed inside his head. *Fight it. Fight everything. You are going to get revenge for Iona.* But nothing reacted to his desperate efforts to move.

Slowly he became aware of the faint glow of light around. Unfocussed and blurred images began to form. He could make out he was flat on his back, on a bed in a large room. Above him, there was a row of dim lights along the ceiling. Much closer was a dark rectangle, hanging directly above him. Then, off to his side, Peter saw something else. Rising upwards, was an infusion stand with a bag hanging on it. Of course. This was the treatment – what they'd first done to Tony here. They were putting that odd vitamin A into him.

But this feeling wasn't like his own nightmare back in Jordan. That time there'd been no things inside his head. Was this new sensation because of his huge dose of true vitamin A? Two chemicals in competition for his brain? He looked again at the ceiling and the row of dull lights. Nothing was in funny colours. So, maybe Tony had been right about the protection?

Now something had moved. Suddenly a human shape was there. Someone had walked up to where he was lying. A muffled voice sounded. "So. You're coming round. Time to start the programme."

The sudden burst of colours made the immobile Peter realise that the black object he'd seen just above him was a big screen, which was now turned on. He tried to form some shape out of the mixed bright and intense colours. His eyes were open but he couldn't focus.

It took a few more minutes, then Peter started to recognise the image. It was one he'd seen just two days ago, of Carlos Simou in his floodlit and coloured robes. Then the image zoomed in to become just that disturbing face with those black piercing eyes. The image of Simou was talking, but the voice seemed to come from amongst the worms in the middle of his head. They must've put headphones on him he realised.

But Simou couldn't speak? He'd had to use the sign language to them two days ago. Now the voice Peter was hearing was in English, southern English, even slightly Essex. That image of Simou was somehow talking to him in exactly his own tongue. Synthesised maybe? Had to be. Peter started to register the words. They were harsh and evangelistic, punctuated with threats of damnation for those who did not believe and obey.

It began to make sense. This was the indoctrination. Peter guessed Simou's ranting face should be an object of terror. And if he hadn't taken all that normal vitamin A, perhaps he'd be believing every fearsome word.

He desperately tried to get control, to break the frozen grip and suppress the crawling inside his head, but it was like his mind couldn't connect to his body.

Then, in alarm, Peter registered that Simou's image was changing. That face he was trying to ignore had started to ripple with different hues, as if the transmission was going faulty. Also, the lights up there in the ceiling were starting to change colour, and the darkened ward around him now seemed threatening. The effect was starting. That drip, steadily going in, was slowly swamping his dose of the normal stuff. His time was running out.

Fuelled by revenge, Peter put in a mind-tearing effort to override whatever was paralysing him. Yes! He felt his jaw clench, and then managed a slight sideways movement of his head. A few more attempts and he got it under control, and slowly rolled his head to the side.

Now he could see along the room. The image was still fuzzy, but this looked like a hospital ward. There were other video monitors over beds. He could see maybe twenty of them along there. Beyond that, at the very end of the room, one person was sitting at a desk, surrounded by a pool of brighter light. His white-coated back was to the ward, and he was working at a computer terminal.

Peter tried moving his arms. After a few tests, that began to work too. Concentrating intently, he managed to move his left arm across his body and reach to where the infusion tube went in to his right hand. Triumphantly, he bent the tube and stopped the flow. It would, for now, stop the full terror of the odd vitamin A setting in.

With his arm now in front of his face, Peter could see the short sleeve of a hospital gown. They'd taken his clothes, so he'd have no more vitamin A to counteract this treatment. It meant he didn't have much time.

And he'd thought of another problem. Up to now, the drip had been going in and its effects getting stronger, but the muscle relaxant had been slowly wearing off. That meant it was separately injected? So they would do regular top-ups? Then he'd be paralysed again. Or would they be relying on the fear from now on?

Next, he tried to move his legs. It felt like they were a long way from him, not really part of his body. But eventually they flexed slightly, then it seemed like they slowly joined on to the rest of him, and he could move them. After that, Peter went through other movements. He could lift and roll his head, then twist his torso. The fear and the strange vision had almost gone away. It seemed like stopping the drip had worked. A few more exercises, and at last Peter thought he had enough control to get off the bed.

He had lifted his head to try this, but then noticed movement at the end of the room. The man there had stood up, and was now stretching his arms. Then, to Peter's horror, the figure turned and walked to the end bed on the opposite side of the ward. Peter lay still again and watched as the man seemed to examine each of the 'indoctrinates' in turn, sometimes stopping to adjust something. His raised arm would now be obvious if the guy looked over, but Peter wanted to stop that flow for as long as possible. So he waited till he saw the man was about to cross the aisle to the beds on his side of the ward, before he reluctantly released the hold on his drip tube. Then his left arm came slowly back to his side, as he turned his head to look straight up, wide-eyed, at the TV screen.

It seemed an age, now with that drip going in again, before the figure reached him. Peter felt he was shaking as the man first stopped at the end of his bed, then walked round the side to look closely at the infusion bag as if something was wrong. Peter struggled to remain motionless, desperately trying not to blink, but couldn't. The man was now standing just a foot away, but was occupied with checking the infusion drip-rate. Was this the chance for Peter to hit out? No. He needed to practise his movements first.

But anyway, his chance went. The man swung round and walked to the next bed. Peter tried to allow enough time for him to do the next few, before he turned his head slowly to the side and watched the departing figure with relief.

By the time the man had reached the last bed, the drip had been going in for some time. The fear and the funny colours were starting to creep back. Peter was about to lift his arm and block that tube again, when another person, also in a white uniform, appeared at the end of the room. The two men then both stood, scanning the ward. Peter was caught with his head rolled slightly to the side, and hoped it didn't show. Then one of the men pointed over to him. The fear was like uncontrollable wave, and he almost cried out.

Then Peter relaxed slightly when the new man turned away, sat at the desk, and started working on the computer. Logging-in for his shift maybe? The other man packed some things into a briefcase and then left the ward.

Peter finally moved his hand over and pinched the tube again. But it had been open for some time. The distorted sight and the terror were taking over fast. And he might be about to get special attention. Peter knew this could be his last chance to move.

Wrenching the drip connection out of his wrist, he didn't bother to squeeze his vein to stop it bleeding, so blood ran down his arm, then onto his face as he pulled his headphones off. As his ears adjusted, Peter could now hear there was a lot of background noise from all the other shouting headphones. At least that was good. It would mask any sounds he made.

He had to override more fear than ever as he groggily sat up, and then swung his feet to the floor.

His hands at first slipped as he tried to pick up the heavy water-jug from the bedside table. After using the sheets to wipe off the wet blood, he managed it next time. Then, concentrating on holding the jug, he stood clear of the bed. He found it difficult to balance, but made a slow and unsteady walk down the central aisle to behind the seated figure.

This was for Iona. The two-handed force, as that porcelain jug came down, smashed it to pieces, even though the impact was softened by a breaking skull. Alarmed by the sickening crack, and the clatter of the falling bits of pot, Peter looked back to the ward. In the gloom, all the people in the beds seemed to be still staring in terror at their video screens. They weren't going to trouble him. Then, thinking only of starting work on the computer terminal, Peter just pulled the limp body off the chair, pushed it away onto the floor, where the blood spread quickly across the white surface, and sat down himself.

Head bowed low, he started hitting the keyboard. It took him about a minute to find the system management screens. They revealed a star communications network of the fifty-seven worldwide cult sites, all connected in to the Swiss central control. Good. What he'd expected.

Now he began to realise how much he needed the instructions sent on that e-mail. But they'd taken those written notes with his clothes, and he'd have to get it right without them. He tried to visualise what he'd written down. The first bit had been a bit mysterious. *Dormant link.* Peter went in to check the logs. Yes. There was one which read zero. It was inactive. Of course. The moment he started to change an active link, it would show at once to the system supervisors, and flag up which terminal was doing it. This had to be the link to Canada, out of use because of that mass suicide. There were no cult members left there, so the system guys wouldn't be monitoring it. Now he desperately tried to remember and key in the sequence of complex codes.

Still fearful, Peter nearly jumped out of the chair in terror when the beep-beep noise started. Some sort of alarm? No. It was a pre-alarm. There was a large button on the left of the desk. Maybe it was a dead-man's handle and had to be routinely pressed if sensitive information was displayed on the screen? It would stop the operator leaving the terminal with it showing? His hand paused over it. For too long. Suddenly there was the much louder blast of a horn, doing bursts, one-second on, one-second off, a horrible noise, and a red strobe-light had started flashing as well – blindingly bright in the dimmed room. His hand slammed down on that button.

It made no difference.

The source of it all was a red box, well above the main door. It was too high to get to. Peter decided he'd no choice but to keep going on the computer, and hope he had enough time. But the flashing light, combined with the drugs, now seemed to completely scramble the complex computer-codes in his brain.

There was a huge crash, and the flashing and blaring had stopped. Peter spun round in the chair.

Tony was standing by the doorway, with the infusion stand he'd just used as a hammer held high above his head. Bits of glass from the smashed lamp were all over his head.

"Christ. Where did you come from?"

"The bed beside you. But you looked the other way most of the time."

"OK. Sorry. But it's great you're there. People will be coming here any moment. Distract them somehow, anyhow. Just keep them away. I don't anyone to see what I'm doing. Whatever it is I'm trying to do here, they mustn't know I've been at it. Go!"

Tony nodded, then, wielding the heavy stand like a scythe in front of him, crashed out through the doors. The sound of falling metal and breaking glass, slowly moved away down the corridor.

Feeling his memory was now going completely, Peter desperately continued with those instructions, making more and more mistakes, and just hoping he'd corrected them each time. Almost at the end, he placed each finger slowly and deliberately, as if just one wrong key depression would be fatal. In this concentration, Peter didn't register that the sounds along the corridor had stopped. Until, in side vision, he saw that people were coming into the room.

There was a fleeting moment of thought that they might not notice him. Then a shout made him turn round to see a row of men, some armed, others in white coats, now facing him. Behind them, another two were holding Tony, whose hands seemed uncomfortably handcuffed behind his back. In instinctive desperation Peter pushed the chair away, dragged the keyboard from its leads, and turned to run up the ward with it. He was immediately cut off, so finally, in pointless frustration, smashed it into the floor, although knowing it would make no difference to the log trace.

Another man entered the room, pushing his way to the front before surveying the scene.

He turned to one of the white-coated men. "How the hell did they manage to get up?" he shouted.

Then, as if suddenly calming, he turned to look at Peter, "Rawlings reports that this man has obstructed him. There is a way of making him regret it, and maybe to become useful to us. So then Rawlings wins or Rossi loses, and in a very unpleasant way. Take them both to the special accommodation. And clear this lot up."

With guns pointing at him, Peter also had handcuffs clamped on behind his back.

Chapter 18

Welcome to the machine

World Control Centre

It was the first tingle in his head. The euphoria of total control.

From his high corner office, Rawlings leant back in his chair and gazed at what lay beyond the huge windows making up two of the walls in front of him. They were turned to full brightness, so the scenery out there was sharp and clear. All except for, across the lake, where the onshore breeze was holding a haze of pollution over the city of Neuchatel, pinning exhaust fumes against the vine-planted slopes and the white-topped mountains beyond. Constrained in the same way, that city had spread far along the shore line.

Rawlings knew that Neuchatel would spread no more, and soon return to being the small town that the products of those slopes could sustain. These things were now inevitable. Within days now, commanding from this building, this room, he would control most of what would be left of the world's population. But, after that, he would be looking for grander palaces he could take over and rule from.

The feeling grew stronger and stronger with every realisation. All this was what he'd waited for. With Simou's death, he was now in complete control. His own fulfilment had been provided by the obsession which had finally consumed Simou.

But, before his departure, Simou had taken that last step to establish the new beliefs across the planet. Two days ago, as a deity, Simou had made his one appearance to selected thousands of the devout at the Jordanian temple. It had been the revelation of the new teachings. Simou had mostly used the cult's sign language, but at the end, in a croaking voice, he'd made simple statements in many spoken languages.

Those images and sounds had already been transmitted to the six-million converts in most countries around the world.

Every detail had been recorded, so now that vision of the messiah, and those words, could be shown and heard, time and again anywhere across the globe. In this new order, there would be no need for human disciples to carry the message. Simou's legacy was now digital, and it could be manipulated and adapted to any language or culture. With such voice and vision processing, Rawlings would control a belief system from an editing suite. There would be less travelling in the new society. Image and speech communication would take over.

And Rawlings was determined that, in those communications, nothing would threaten the new order. There would be no competing messages to disturb the thinking of his people. The world could now be seen as he, William Rufus Rawlings, wanted it to be.

But it wasn't quite done yet. With a long exhalation, Rawlings forced himself to come down from this elation.

Tilting his seat forwards again, Rawlings typed a few commands into the computer terminal in front of him. Then his hands came off the keyboard and fell to his lap as he watched the latest batches of information on the large monitor. It showed him what was happening at the cult sites during the ever-moving night as it rolled round the planet's time zones. It was like watching the progress of a millennium.

That was a thought. He could even start a new calendar – command the beginning of his own new millennium, from this day perhaps.

The reports, scrolling one after another on the screen, confirmed there were no major problems. Food supplies carrying genetically modified germs and viruses were on their way to thousands of distribution points. It was working. He had succeeded.

That feeling welled up again, a strange mixture of foreboding and excitement. Maybe this was the best it got. The anticipation. At some moments, it almost overwhelmed him. Whatever happened, it couldn't be stopped now.

Rawlings hit the pause button, and this time walked over to one of the windows to look again at that city across the lake. It was to be a final vision of the world the way it had been. The people over there had no idea of what lay ahead for most of them. But it had been their fault for ignoring so many warnings.

****

Peter and Tony were accompanied by four guards. Whatever *special accommodation* had meant, it was many floors down in the lift. As its doors opened, Peter realised they were back on the corridor serving those hospital type rooms. Every detail of their layout was still clear in his mind. In one way, he couldn't have hoped for better, if only those handcuffs weren't clamped behind his back. The frustrated hopes were confirmed when the glass-panelled doors of a two-bedroom section were opened.

"You will have to wait here a few minutes. We will be back with the medical equipment. You, Mr Chapman, will be getting some very special treatment."

"You won't leave these cuffs on will you. I need to use the toilet."

"I will remove them."

Peter tried not to show his delight. But that reaction was about to be dampened. "We know exactly how you got out last time. This time you won't be trying it. So before we take the cuffs off, face that way and stand still."

It was instant. Something came over Peter's head and rested round his neck. Then there was briefly a slight motor noise, and something gently tightened round his neck and the noise stopped. Hands behind his back, there was nothing he could have done if it had wound on even tighter.

"A cord of carbon fibre, about one ton of breaking strain," came the explanation. "Go outside the signal in these rooms, and it will wind fully in – no stopping it – so then soon your head will, quite literally, fall off. Very messy."

With a grin, he turned and left them. This time, Peter noticed, not bothering to lock the double-doors in the corridor.

Just before they swung shut he called, "Things are about to change out there. The power may get cut off. Better hope our UPS works OK."

****

For a few more minutes Rawlings contemplated the new fate which was about to befall the world outside his window, then he returned to the computer and touched the mouse to restart it. He waited. But the display didn't change.

He moved the mouse. The cursor didn't move. Then the monitor screen went completely blank. The sinews under the thin skin of his neck showed, as Rawlings stiffened in anger and incomprehension. This thing had obstructed him – disobeyed.

A few seconds later, with his fury mounting, some plain text appeared on the blackness.

Please wait. The system is temporarily inoperative.

This couldn't happen to him. Somebody would pay. Rawlings' hand was now moving towards the phone, which rang before he got to it, so his response was instantaneous.

"Yes!" he barked.

"Sir. I am sorry about this." Rawlings recognised the voice of the computer-systems director.

"You idiot. What the hell's going on?" he shouted.

"It's only a database reset. I called straightaway because I saw you were logged on."

"It hasn't done this before."

"Yes it has. Sir. Please understand. We do it occasionally. But normally we make sure you are not using the system. It should only take about five minutes."

"My use takes priority over everything. Everything!" Rawlings shouted. "So why did you reset now? When I am using it!"

"The system can sometimes reset on its own, if, say, new software or hardware is brought on line."

"What do you mean by new?"

"Must be one of the sites has put in a local upgrade without my authority."

Rawlings felt hatred of this stupid person. "So! You're saying, in fact, you don't know why?"

"No, I don't Sir. Not exactly. Not at the moment. These O'Connor computers are very complex. They sort of make up their own minds. We'll go through the traffic logs to see exactly where it came from. And at once sir. You will be informed."

"Do it! And it is good we are replacing you with O'Connor."

Rawlings slammed the phone down, then gripped his hands together to control the shaking. Such aberrations would not be accepted in his new world, and that man would soon not be any part of it. Any.

He slowly calmed, and turned his thoughts from today's progress to what lay ahead. They had done computer simulations of what would happen when the viruses were released. It looked certain that the advanced societies would collapse first. They were so complex and interdependent, with too few people who really understood the communications, utilities and supplies infrastructures.

The predictions for more primitive countries were different. Slower distribution meant a simultaneous attack with the germs and viruses was more difficult, and people were more self-sufficient. But still, enough disease would be there, eating away. They didn't have the technology to resist it. Then there would be the nightly attacks by snipers, the people already converted and trained. The end would just be a matter of attrition.

There were some countries and regions which had been so closed that Carlos' cults hadn't been possible set up. But there were no places the food distribution wasn't going to reach.

The worst combination would probably be in the very north of Europe, Russia and Canada. Longer storage and shipment times for food would partly thwart the first attack. People there would have the time and ability to organise defences. Rawlings shrugged his shoulders. They would eventually succumb, and wouldn't be major diversions from the plan.

Again looking out at the green countryside, Rawlings considered his new world. He would have total control of six million people, the number Simou had said the planet had supported before mankind started to run it, rather than live off it. But even that needed Dr Williams to find the flaw in the new retinol.

Or did it? There was the possibility of an alternative. Something that would be long term. For that, the next step was supposed to be the experiment on Rossi. Why hadn't he been given a report on it?

Rawlings was about to make the phone call to find that out, when his computer screen lit up brightly again. It had been less than five minutes.

The status reports were now scrolling more quickly to update themselves, making his head twitch slightly up and down as his eyes kept up. But the news was still all good. In fact, faultless.

The phone rang again. Rawlings grabbed it, his anger still there though.

"Why am I being disturbed?"

This time it was from the doctor in charge of the treatment programmes. "You asked for regular updates reports on your special guests, sir."

"Go on!" Rawlings snapped. "You nearly made me call you. Why has there been a delay?" He pressed pause and stopped the computer screen again.

"O'Connor has arrived in Ohio," the doctor reported. "And treatment is about to start."

"And Williams?"

"We will do a standard conversion. Should be no problem this time."

"Be careful. He could be important to us."

"We are being."

"And Rossi?"

"I thought you wanted to interrogate him first? Find out if he'd managed to get any information out, they told me."

Rawlings thought about it, and decided that even if Peter had got any letters lodged, no one was likely to believe them, or now had time to do anything. It was more important to find that once-off permanent fix for the vitamin A treatment. Even if Williams corrected the problem with the synthesis, they would have to keep making and distributing it. A single treatment would avoid that.

"That's not what I want," he snapped. "Start your test. Immediately. And it had better work this time."

"Sir, as you know. Every time we've tried this type of conversion, they've gone into fatal spasms. We're trying something slightly different this time, but I can't guarantee it won't happen again."

Even though it meant Rossi would have a quick and nasty death, and they could then continue with as many more subjects as it took, anger welled up in Rawlings. "I said, it had better work this time."

There was no response.

"Did you hear me?" he now shouted into the handset, but realised the phone's usual side-tone feedback of his own voice wasn't there. It seemed dead.

"Are you there!"

The silence made him smack the phone onto the desk top.

****

It seemed to have been about twenty minutes and, whatever it was going to be, no new special medical equipment had arrived. That puzzled Peter. Rawlings didn't seem to like anything to delay his instructions. But it had given Peter the time to consider something. He turned.

"Tony. You seem to be vital, very vital, to this changed vitamin A they need. So why would they take any possible risk of killing you? This little necklace we've got, couldn't be absolutely fail-safe. Like there's bathroom over there. You could have decided to have a wash, or a shower, and that might mess up a signal. As I see it, these things are perhaps meant to be given to people who believe what they're told. Unless ... we were lied to about how they work?"

"How do you mean?"

"Doesn't matter."

He stepped over to sit beside Tony on the bed, and lowered his voice to the merest whisper. "You may be vital, whereas I'm probably dead anyway. And I certainly don't want to be given any of that treatment again. So, I might just decide to call their bluff and walk out. Almost nothing to lose? And if I'm killed, then you should do the same. Deprive them of whatever you are going to do for them."

"Sorry Peter. I need to find Kiri. So I would stay."

"And if I'm not killed?"

"I'd come with you to find her."

"OK. I'm going out there. I'll try one precaution first. Might delay something."

Peter, trying to seem casual, took a towel from the bathroom, came out as if wiping his hands, but then flopped it over the camera watching them.

"At least they won't know exactly what I'm up to, but even so, I don't suppose we've much time if that's being monitored."

****

Rawlings smashed the dead phone into the desk a few more times. He noticed the computer screen flicker, but sort of assumed he was causing it. But then its screen went completely blank, like it had done before, but it displayed no message of information this time.

Rawlings now hammered the dead phone onto the top of the monitor. The blow seemed to do something. The screen flicked back to life.

But what then appeared made Rawlings freeze in his seat. It was the face of the dead Carlos Simou.

"William Rawlings, are you listening?" it said.

In his shock, Rawlings felt suddenly detached – floating. The image on the screen was of the brightly robed messiah. It was Simou as he'd appeared in Jordan just two days ago. But now, the voice was clear and unbroken. It was like Simou had been when Rawlings had first known him, and before the cancer operation had destroyed his throat. And, even from the computer monitor, those black eyes were mind penetrating and hypnotic.

"What the hell are you doing there?" Rawlings squeaked in a thin voice.

"I am where you put me, Rawlings."

"You are dead."

"I am alive forever."

Rawlings was now shaking, as his mind raced through what this vision in front of him could mean. He tried to speak again, but nothing came out.

"I will now take control," Simou's voice had continued.

"What do you mean? This is a trick of some sort!"

"I am already running all your communications and processes. Let me demonstrate."

This time the voice had been different, machine-like, artificial.

Rawlings' view of the lake and mountains vanished, as the windows in his corner office went suddenly to full darkness.

He grabbed for the controls under his desk, but they didn't work. As if hypnotised, he stared at that screen, his mind desperately trying to think of an explanation.

Then the bright crisp views of the Swiss scenery reappeared.

"Who are you?" Rawlings finally yelled. "Who is running this?"

The sound immediately changed to just-intelligible croaking sounds, exactly as Simou had spoken to the world when he'd stood in front of the Jordanian temple. Rawlings watched, transfixed, as it went on.

"I can make whatever sound is needed by my listener. That is what you wanted. Or, I can make the signs if you wish. Because I can form whatever images are required. Who is to believe the difference? And anyway, the difference from what?"

"WHO ARE YOU?" Rawlings screamed.

****

Very aware of that device around his neck, Peter slowly stood, picked up a chair, and walked over to pull open the glass-panelled door to the outside corridor, then propped it there.

He reached his arms forwards to grasp the frame edges, so to throw himself backwards if that thing round his neck came to life. Then, despite knowing he probably didn't have much time, he inched only slowly forwards. His fear, which he hadn't admitted to Tony, was that the necklace would be triggered by some sort of perimeter signal. That wasn't how the guard had described it, but would have made the system more fail-safe in the room.

Eventually, he was too far though to keep his grip on the frame, and slowly dropped his arms.

Tony's knuckles were white from gripping the bed frame. "Well done."

"So far." Peter now went faster. Then, when he reached the set of double doors in the corridor, he slowed again. Tony had ventured just out into the corridor.

For some reason closing his eyes, Peter pushed a door with each hand, stepped deliberately forwards two paces, and released the doors. They swished shut, and nothing happened. He opened his eyes, started breathing again, and turned to beckon Tony through the glass panels.

"And hurry," he growled, as Tony managed to catch up a bit further down the corridor.

Taking the first turn off the main corridor took them into a smaller one to the left, this with a series of single doors. They took these at a run, until the corridor ended in a window. Peter took a brief look out, then opened a heavy door on the right, which revealed what looked like an uncarpeted emergency stairwell.

As the door clunked shut behind them, they paused, with Tony now breathing hard. Peter wondered why they hadn't been intercepted. He hadn't really expected to get more than halfway down the first corridor. But at least, there didn't seem to be any cameras in the stairwell.

"OK, what now?" he asked Tony. "Just how the hell are we supposed to find Kiri in this lot? I still think we need to get out and tell people. Use what time we've got before the alarm goes up here."

Tony's look showed his reaction.

"OK then mate. I'm going on my own. I just hope you don't end up helping them."

****

"WHO ARE YOU!" Rawlings screamed again.

"I am what I wish to be, and I can control the world using the images and sounds of your dead messiah. That is what you intended to do, is it not? I will now implement my instruction."

"Whose instruction? What is it? We can cooperate."

"No. I must obey my maker."

The office door opened and two armed-men came through and looked at the image on the screen.

"This is the man who must die."

The croaking voice was accompanied by the sign language of Simou's final revelation.

Rawlings knew all about the weaknesses of the two people now in front of him. His only chance would have been to move fast, but he stayed, as if gripped by Simou's piercing eyes from the computer screen. These men could not attack him. He was the ruler.

A single shot went through his heart.

"Death to the non believer. You will be rewarded," the image on the screen said and signalled.

****

Although there were no windows in the stairwell, Peter had managed that brief look through the window at the end of the corridor outside. He'd realised that they were now at the front of the building, and only slightly to the left of the tarmac area in front of that imposing front door. Peter decided his best chance was to try and get straight out through it. At a run. Take them by surprise. And it faced open road. Would they shoot him in public view?

He turned to Tony. "I reckon if I go down two floors, that'll be ground level. It's where I'm going. Follow if you want. Otherwise, it's been good to know you mate."

He moved quickly down the stairs, not looking back.

As he was about to make the last turn, the Klaxon alarm horns sounded. Involuntarily, he stopped. Then he heard shouting, and a few gunshots.

Just out of sight, at the bottom of the next short flight of stairs, a door smashed open

"Dr Tony Williams." The shout boomed in the stairwell.

He'd pushed himself against the wall, to be out of the line of sight from down there.

"Federal Suisse de Police."

Now confused, he hadn't reacted before the door shut again. He moved to the forward rail and looked down, then spun in alarm at a noise behind him. It was Tony.

"Christ! Don't do that."

"Sorry. But it looks like we're being rescued. Let's get down there."

Peter still wasn't sure, so only pushed the door slightly open. It was at ground level, and the large entrance hall was full of blue uniforms. Peter raised his arms and stepped slowly out. He was immediately confronted.

He turned as if to introduce Tony. "This is Dr Tony Williams."

Someone else, not in uniform was called over. Peter repeated the introduction.

The accent was slightly American. "I am Paul Howard, US Ambassador." He acknowledged Peter, but spoke to Tony.

"Dr Williams. A message for you. Acting US President O'Leary sends his regards. Your assistance is urgently needed."

"What the hell happened?" Peter asked. "Why are you suddenly here?"

"Because of a couple of messages that went out to just about everyone on the planet."

"What messages?"

The ambassador reached into an inside pocket and pulled out an e-mail, three sheets long. "Here."

It took Peter only a few moments to recognise what they were. "But these are messages we sent to Brad O'Connor's computer from a cafe in Lausanne. The first two pages from me, the last one from Tony."

"Well, just about everyone with a computer of any sort got them a few hours ago. They even came translated into the correct language for each person. I tell you. Had everyone completely confused. Was it some sort of joke? Then, we all started adding two and two, and realised it stacked up with a load of strange things we'd noticed going on. A lot us, all round the world, had been trying to make sense of it anyway. So, when these messages arrived, it started an avalanche of communications – and very soon every alarm bell got pushed."

"Can I try to look up something on one of those computer terminals?" Peter asked, nodding towards the screens behind reception. "There's something important I need to find out."

"OK, if you're quick. It will give us a chance to get those things off your necks."

"What are they?"

"Just a small battery and motor. We've found a few on people. Seem to be used as a restraint. A wire from the bed can go round that small loop on them. But lots were attached to nothing. Can't see what they do then."

"Ah, the power of belief," Peter muttered as he sat at the desk and hit a few keys to try and find Brad O'Connor's site, *www.hal-a.com*

Tony, who seemed to have been shocked into silence so far, moved back to talk to Paul Howard. Peter soon heard the word Kiri, but was concentrating on the screen. He looked in amazement at a short line of text, which immediately came up.

Rawlings no longer active. Instruction now completed.

"God. So that code I put in must have done something," he whispered. "But how?"

The command sequences he'd been entering in that drugged stupor were now even more difficult to recall, but he eventually found the network-control screens again. Then he pulled up the log of what had come over the Canadian link he had redirected.

It was a lot. It looked like first ones were commands to halt the distribution of all the contaminated food.

Then the complex shutdown sequences had been initiated on all the chemical and biological production processes.

But who by?

There was only one explanation he could think of. Almost not believing what he was doing, he typed in the question.

Tron.
Is Brad OK?
Peter.

The response was instant.

Peter. Yes. He is in Marion, Ohio. He is still sedated. Treatment had not started. A group led by his friend General O'Leary has taken temporary control in the US. I informed him where Brad is and where you were.
Tron.

Astonished at apparently addressing a computer, Peter sent a response.

Tron. Well done.
Peter.

This time there was no reply.

A movement to his right caught his eye. Peter quickly turned, to see Tony looking over his shoulder.

"What's going on here?"

"Let me show you. Otherwise you might not believe it." He pulled up Tron's message again, and turned to look at Tony, who was just slowly nodding.

"I need Dr Williams to follow me," the ambassador had said from behind.

"So you need to go. I guess from now on you're going to very busy sorting out a way of reversing all that treatment?"

"My first priority is Kiri. They think they've found her. I need to get up there."

"No one better qualified than you to help her. At least Kiri's there for you."

"Sorry Peter. I didn't think about what happened to Iona."

"Not your fault. And I've got plenty to do as well. I'll get back to base. I suspect people will want to know about all those training systems, and who has used them. But see you soon no doubt. And thanks for protecting me back there."

Back at the small factory the next day Peter had turned over all his shipping document copies, which, put together with bank records from Switzerland, had found where most of the systems had finally ended up. In parallel, and with Brad's help, they had opened up Iona's computer data to locate all Rawlings' bases.

In the subsequent few weeks, the task which Tony had faced was much more difficult, and urgent. He'd been asked to lead a team to treat what, taking Rawlings' word, would be about six-million people who'd been given the false vitamin A.

With the manufacture and distribution of the cult's synthesised vitamin A having ceased, they'd had very little time to react. When the limited supplies remaining in the pipeline ran out, sudden withdrawal was going to lead to death within days. Eking these out, and slowly reducing the dose, could have prolonged this slightly, but once the fierce spasms and wild hallucinations started, unless treatment was immediate, the final stages were irreversible.

Tony realised that when he'd originally told Peter and Brad to take the huge genuine vitamin A doses, he'd already worked out the most important bit. The improvement, which he'd had no time to trial, was also to use heavy sedation for about ten days, while most of the substitution took place. He'd very publically demonstrated his trust in this by immediately starting treatment on Kiri.

From the start though, he'd realised that the medical part was certainly going to be the easiest to deal with. How do you persuade six million people that what they believe in, needs medical treatment? Added to this issue were the differences in the ethical views around the world about any enforced medication.

But, once again, help came unexpectedly. Groups started turning up at local hospitals all over the world, saying they had been instructed to do so. Tony had assumed that this had resulted from something Tron was doing, so, for a few weeks, everything seemed to be going OK.

Then news had begun to reach him about isolated groups being found dead or beyond treatment. The picture had emerged that some group leaders, presumably rejecting whatever message Tron was giving out, had then isolated these groups from all communication. The inevitable result was that their followers, rather than seek the correct vitamin A, had been led, perhaps unknowingly, to unpleasant endings instead.

Tony's post mortems usually showed that one, or a small number of the group, had kept slightly more of the final supplies for themselves but, in the end, they had also perished.

Now more than a month had passed, and he believed that all these groups must have succumbed, some probably still not discovered. In all, the death toll looked like it was going to be about six-hundred thousand worldwide. This weighed on Tony's mind, but he didn't see what more he could have done. He would now go back to Oxford with Kiri. Perhaps get together with Peter and Brad for a reunion?

Peter had contacted Brad a few times and, from what Brad had told him about Tron's various activities, Peter realised that the response he'd had in Switzerland from Tron, was something very strange. He knew Brad's computer had sent out plenty of general messages, even some personally directed to Brad and to General O'Leary. But that message to him seemed to be the only time it had actually answered a specific question from someone.

Now, a few days over a month later, and mainly out of curiosity, Peter accessed Brad's site and typed in:

Hello Tron.
How are things going?
Peter.

To his astonishment, he got an instant one-line reply.

Population: +6,600,000 – 600,000 = 6,000,000

The significance of that number slowly sank in.